The "Kinda" Secret Pineapple Island Swingers' Resort

Jade Dollston

Cover Design by KB Barrett Designs

Editing and proofreading by **Chrisandra's Corrections**

⚠TW: parental abandonment, domestic violence (not between the main characters)

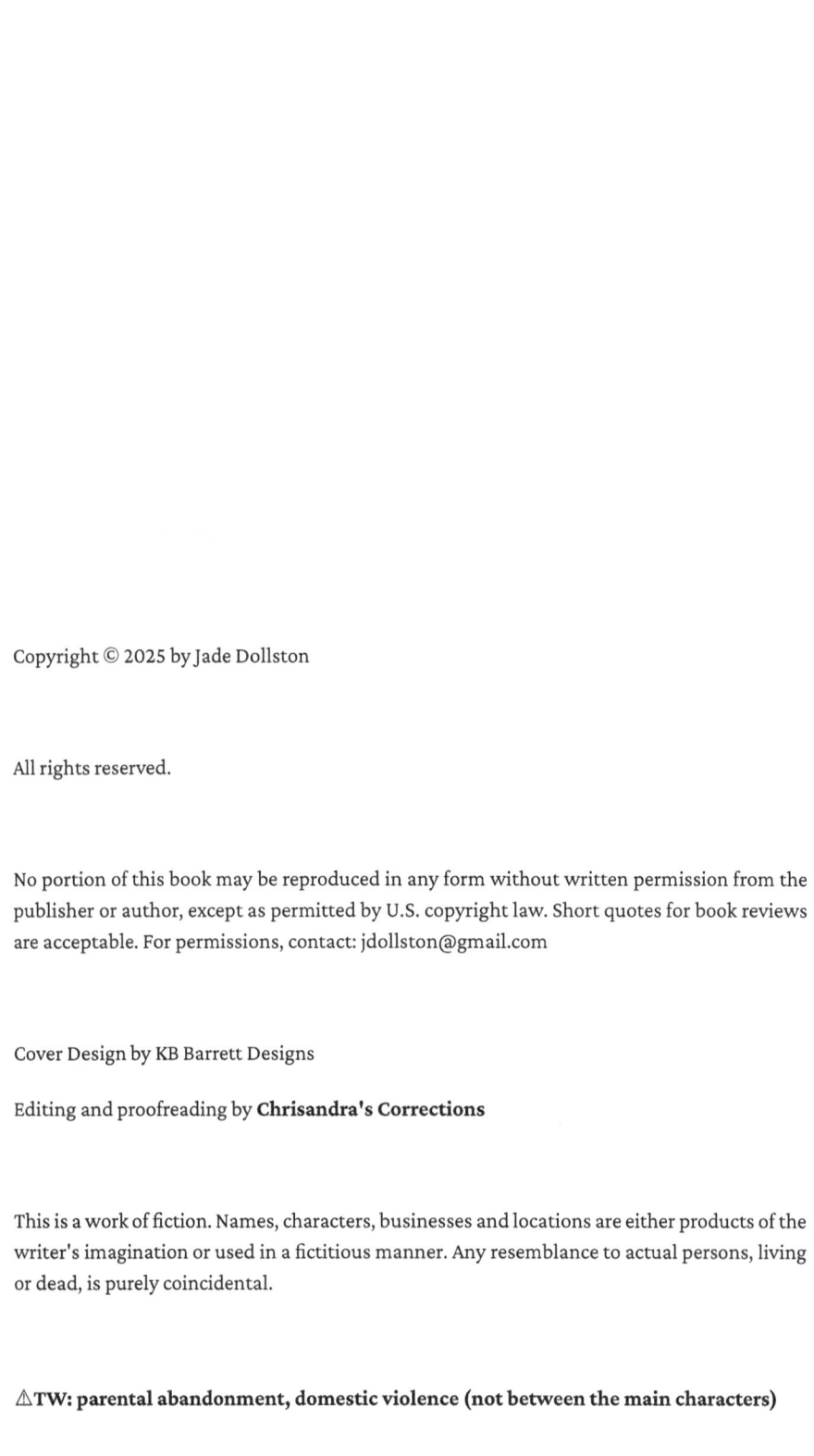

Contents

This one goes out to my amazing Street Team.

I named all the swingers in this book after you... may you have as much fun as they do.

Chapter 1

Reno

I didn't fuck the owner's daughter. It was a blow job.

"Swain, get in my office."

That phrase ranks near the bottom of things any man wants to hear, barely squeaking in above "We got your STD test results back. Please put on this gown and try not to touch anything."

But this directive came from my hockey coach rather than my doctor, so my summoning today seems to be of the career variety rather than a medical one.

Ah, you'll live to ride another day, I silently tell my cock as I run the soapy washcloth over him.

"Now, Swain!" Coach Belford bellows from the other side of the door, so I drop the cloth onto the black-and-white tiled floor with a wet plop. And like the smartass I am, I stroll from the shower room as naked as the day I was born, dripping water in my six foot, four inch wake.

"Fuck's sake, Swain," Coach groans, averting his gaze when I walk into the locker room. "Put some goddamn clothes on. *Then* come to my office."

"Just doing as I was told, Coach," I say amicably, earning me some much deserved grumbles as he stalks out the door and into the green-and-white bedecked hallway. Pretty sure I hear the word cocky being bandied about, but I wisely refrain from making a cock joke. I've done enough to amuse myself for today.

After returning to the shower and rinsing the soap from my body, I dry off and dress in a long-sleeved Raptors shirt and sweats, since this May is unseasonably cool, even for Denver.

"I'm here, Coach," I say, settling onto one of the tiny wooden chairs across from his desk. I'm pretty sure he bought the damn things at an elementary school fire sale. It's probably a power move on his part since he's sitting in his very roomy leather chair with an indiscernible look on his face.

"Reno," he sighs, and I'm instantly on high-alert at the use of my first name. He always calls me *Swain*. Or sometimes *asshole*, depending on the situation.

"What's going on?" I ask, and he leans forward with his forearms on his beat up wooden desk, his eyes downcast for a long moment before lifting to mine. I see something there. Regret, maybe?

"Son, you're being traded."

A bomb explodes inside my head. At least, that's what it feels like. I hear the boom and feel the painful shatter. My lips move, but I don't speak.

"I'm sorry, Reno."

At least I can still hear.

Noise finally makes its way up my throat and out of my mouth, a strained sound that I quickly wrangle into a question. A word, really.

"Why?"

"The official party line is that the new owner wants fresh blood."

"B-but I've been the best goddamn defenseman in the league for six years running."

"Actually, last season, you were second." *And that still chaps my ass.*

"Barely, and only because I missed two weeks after having my knee scoped. But I rehabbed my ass off in physical therapy and returned four weeks ahead of schedule." *And played through the pain with a fucking smile on my face.*

"I know that, Reno."

Something he said clicks in my head like a light bulb. "Wait, you said the *official* party line is that the new owners want new blood. Is there an *unofficial* party line?"

Belford's lips close into a tight slash before he emits a long sigh. "Word got back to Mr. Priestner that you fucked his daughter in a broom closet at the welcome party last week."

Oh. That.

"I didn't fuck the owner's daughter," I insist. "It was a blow job."

Coach closes his eyes and shakes his head. "Swain..."

"And I didn't know that was his daughter. She just told me her name was Tiffy and she wanted to have a little fun. I assumed she was a puck bunny. You know, one of the many that are always invited to our parties?" I say with more than a little indignation.

"Her name is Tiffy Priestner, and she is Roland Priestner's daughter."

"Well, I didn't know that at the time," I argue. "She grabbed my junk and literally led me down the hallway by the dick. I was..."

I pause, and Coach Belford arches an extremely bushy eyebrow. "You were what?"

My eyes drop to the floor, and I suddenly feel vulnerable. "I was trying to move on for the first time in months. Since the... *thing* last year."

Coach's mouth turns down, and I see the pity in his eyes at my mention of the *thing*. He sighs and runs a hand over his crew cut.

"It's been a helluva year for you, Reno, so that makes this situation that much harder. I wish there was something I could do, but this came from the top."

I feel a sudden stinging on the insides of my eyelids, like someone squirted pepper juice in my eyes. "I've been with the Raptors my entire career. This is my team." My molars clamp down on the inside of my cheek before I ask the next question. "Where are they sending me?"

Detroit would be okay. They're big hockey fans up there. Or maybe somewhere in the Northeast. Or Canada. Hockey is huge in Canada, so that wouldn't be bad.

His answer was none of those.

"Dallas."

"Fuuuck," I groan, throwing my head back and immediately having to right myself when the chair attempts to tip over backward. "I don't want to go to Dallas, Coach."

Would I be required to wear cowboy boots? Learn to ride a horse?

"I know," he sighed, "and I really hate to lose you, even though you can be a pain in my ass. You're a damn good player, Reno Swain."

He sounds so sincere, and my entire face compresses. Eyes closed. Lips clamped shut. Cheeks sucked in to control my emotions.

Finally, I open my eyes. "Who is the *fresh blood* I'm being traded for?" Even I can hear the bitterness dripping from each syllable.

"You're being traded for a first round draft pick."

My eyes bulge out so far I'm concerned I may go blind from the pressure. "I'm being traded for a goddamn rookie?"

Belford nods. "Mr. Priestner wants to get Fredrickson Mitchell. He was the best college defenseman in the country this past year." My coach—er, *former* coach, I guess—didn't look thrilled to be trading someone with over a decade of experience on the ice for a newbie in the pros.

I refrain from saying that Mitchell is an overrated, cocky little son of a bitch. I have to admit he is a good player. A good *college* player, though there's a huge difference between that level and the NHL. Mitchell has been playing against good players, but every time he steps on the ice from now on, he'll be playing against the best of the best. Men who are bigger, stronger, faster, and infinitely more determined to earn their exorbitant paychecks.

Placing my elbows on my knees, I cram my fingers into my curly, dark hair and stare at my size fifteen tennis shoes. My life was already a shit cake, and Coach just topped it with a drizzle of more poop.

My chest hurts, but I force myself back upright after a minute of silence, resting my palms on my knees. "Is this final? Is there anything I can do?"

The apologetic look on Belford's face gives me the answer, but he speaks it aloud anyway. "I'm sorry, but it's final."

The realization sinks in with a harsh thud.

The Raptors don't want me. *She* doesn't want me.

No one wants me.

Chapter 2

Juliette

"I love his penis" and other brilliant prose I've written.

I GLANCE OVER THE surface of my desk, assuring I have everything so I won't have to get up for a while. Laptop, check. Glass of Dr Pepper with the little pellet ice, check. Bowl of Starburst candies... the cherry ones only, check. Notebook and pen, checkity check.

Yep, that oughta do it.

Wiggling my butt in my desk chair, I link my fingers and stretch them out in front of me. *I'm ready. I'm ready.*

"Okay," I say to myself, blowing out a whistling breath through my pursed lips. "I've got this."

Twiddling my fingers like a concert pianist, I place them on the keyboard and stare at the empty screen. The cursor blinks mockingly at me, as if to say, *loser... loser... loser.*

I fucking hate that cursor. She's a shady bitch.

For Pete's sake, Juli. Just type some words. Any words. You can go back and refine them later. Gnawing on my bottom lip, I begin to work on the spicy scene that's had me stumped for a week.

His cock is thick and big, and I look down at it. I love his penis so much.

I pause and stare at the words on my screen. "Fuck, that's horrible," I say aloud, deleting the stupidest sentence I'd ever written. "Penis... penis... what can I say about this character's penis?"

Hell, it's been so long since I've seen one in person, I'm not even sure if I could accurately describe a dick if one smacked me in the face.

Pulling up a folder labeled *Inspirational Cocks* on my computer, I'm suddenly concerned that when I die, my father will find a folder full of penis pictures. Then he'll keel over from cardiac arrest. *Sorry, Dad.*

I slide my phone toward me and tap out a text to my author friend, AK Landow.

Juliette: Hey, if I die, I'm designating you to erase all the sketchy shit from my computer.

I receive an immediate response.

AK: Gotcha, babe. Any particular documents?

Juliette: The folder titled Inspirational Cocks.

AK: Will do.

AK: Also, forward me the entire cock folder. Please and thank you.

I click over to my email tab and attach the folder before hitting send. Then I flip through a couple photos and make some notes of things I could describe about the male member.

Length, girth, color, veins. Okay, this is good. The veins are always a nice touch. Every woman loves a nice, veiny cock with all that yummy friction, right? I click through the next few pics and let out a shriek when I get to photo number seven.

"Holy hell, what is that?" I rear my neck back to put some distance between me and the monstrosity on the screen. This particular peen bends to the left at a sharp angle. And the hair. Dear god, the hair. I tilt my head to try and get some perspective.

"Oh, honey, who broke your dick?" I ask the owner of the virtual penis on my screen. "Bless your heart."

My phone pings, distracting me from the mutant wiener.

AK: What the actual fuck is number seven?

Juliette: I was just trying to figure that out. It's quite unfortunate looking.

AK: Maybe this is from the seventies before man-scaping was a thing.

Juliette: Probably. Why does it flop to the left like that?

AK: No clue. My husband always tells me I'm going to break his cock, but I think whoever was with this poor fucker actually accomplished it. I feel inadequate.

Juliette: LOL. Keep trying. *Sends GIF of Rob Scheider saying "You can do it!"

AK: Doing Kegels now. Rob better prepare himself tonight.

Juliette: Just thought of something else on my computer that definitely needs to be erased so my family doesn't find it. It's a spreadsheet called Sex Toys.

Juliette: Oh, and the entire BDSM folder.

AK: Why don't I just delete your entire hard drive?

Juliette: That would probably be best.

Setting my phone aside, I take a fortifying sip of my soda before starting again, determined to get some words on paper, metaphorically speaking.

For the next fifteen minutes, I write. And it's... not bad. Not good either, but at least it's something. I reward myself with a cherry Starburst, sucking on the sweet and tart candy as an idea comes to me. *Oooh, he could—*

KNOCK, KNOCK, KNOCK.

With closed eyes, I do my best to ignore the door and concentrate. It's right there on the tip of my brain. Something to do with the way he uses his tongue to—

KNOCK, KNOCK, KNOCK.

"Ugggh, fiiiiine," I whine, stomping my feet in a mini hissy fit before answering my front door to find my elderly neighbor standing there.

"Ms. Mijares, how are you?" I ask, suddenly remembering what I was going to write before I'd been interrupted. *Please hurry, Ms. Mijares, before I forget again.*

"Juliette dear, do you think you could run me to the market? I need to pick up a few things. I haven't gotten my new glasses since my cataract surgery, and I'm not supposed to drive yet."

I hesitate for only a second. Ms. Mijares is an absolute sweetheart, and none of her grown children live nearby, so I really can't say no, right?

"Of course. Just let me grab my shoes and purse." After seating her on my couch, I jog to my writing nook, which is really just a spare bedroom, but writing nook sounds so much fancier. I quickly jot down a few words in my notebook so I'll remember the idea I had, and then we're off to the market.

When Ms. Mijares said she needed to get a few things, what she meant was, *I need to buy half the store.* We spend an hour and a half in the Mexican market while she lingers over cheeses, chiles, tortilla masa, and vegetables.

I smile and do my best to be helpful, even though I'm as antsy as a chihuahua on crack. My deadline is a dark cloud over my head, raining down huge drops of anxiety.

"Thank you for the help. You're such a good girl," my neighbor says when I help her carry the bags of groceries into her house. "You want to help me make tortillas?"

I love making torts with my sweet neighbor, but if I don't do some work on my book, I'm never going to get it done on time. I'm already way behind.

"I would love to, but I have a lot of work to catch up on. You know, for the summer reading program," I kind of fib. We do have a reading program for the kids at the library where I work, but I've had that planned for months.

I've only shared my side career as a romance author with a few people in town, and my seventy-year-old neighbor isn't one of them. Not that mature women can't read romance, but Ms. Mijares definitely isn't the type. She once told me she couldn't finish a John Grisham novel because the language was, and I quote, "just way too foul for me."

If she read one of my books, she wouldn't make it ten pages before she'd feel compelled to set it on fire and pray for my eternal soul while sprinkling me with holy water.

"That's okay," she says with a kind smile. Her big, brown puppy-dog eyes look up at me as she pats my arm. "I just thought it would be nice to have some company. I'll bring a fresh batch over to you when I'm done."

Gahhhh! Why is she so darn nice? And why am I? Because the next thing I know, I hear myself saying, "You know what? I can stay for a few minutes."

Two hours later, I enter my house with warm tortillas separated by foil, a bowl of freshly made salsa, and a container of Ms. Mijares's orgasmic queso blanco.

"At least I don't have to waste time cooking dinner," I tell myself, slathering some butter on a tort and dipping it into the salsa. I finish two of them and am contemplating a third when my phone rings. I smile at my little sister's name on the screen.

"Jordie! What's up?"

"Hey, Juli. I was wondering if you could swing by and pick me up tonight. I don't have a lot of gas in my car."

"Pick you up for—" I start to ask when it hits me. *Dad's birthday.* I quickly cover with, "Of course I can. Um, what time did we decide?"

"You forgot, didn't you?" She sounds amused, and I check my reflection in the mirrored surface of the toaster. I have a chunk of strained tomato in my hair.

"Hush your mouth, or I'll write you as the villain in my next book," I warn, swiping at the red stain, which only serves to smear it. *If I can ever get to work on the damn book.*

"That's cool with me. And we're supposed to be at the restaurant in an hour, dingbat."

Her nickname doesn't bother me because it's true. I'm the quintessential dingy blonde. Not stupid, mind you. I've got a brain; it just tends to go in a million different directions at once, leaving me with stretched deadlines and salsa in my hair.

"Does Xander want to ride with us too?" I ask, referring to our brother who goes to the same college as Jordie.

"Nope, he's at his girlfriend's apartment, and it's only a block from the restaurant."

"Alrighty, I'll be there in a bit," I tell Jordie, dashing to the bathroom. *As soon as I take a shower.*

****

Driving time combined with the family dinner took another three hours away from the time I'd planned to write, but it was totally worth it. Spending time with them is one of my favorite things to do.

"How's football going?" I ask my sister as I drive through the streets of Dallas, Texas to drop her off at her dorm.

She scrunches up her shoulders in excitement. "So good. Spring training went well, and I think I'll be able to keep my starting position for my sophomore year."

"Of course you will," I assure, patting her hand. "You were one of the only freshmen to start last season, and you killed it."

Jordie bounces up and down, and I stifle a laugh. My little sister adores football. Women's collegiate football is kind of a new thing, full contact, not flag or touch. And don't even dare to call it powderpuff, or you'll get an earful from these amazing athletes. Or they might tackle you to prove their point.

A couple years ago, the women banded together and demanded the respect and attention they deserved as elite athletes. All they wanted was a chance, and they'd fought until they got it. Most major colleges now had a female football team, and lots of high schools did too.

Jordie's voice rises in glee. "I got a call today saying there's a new professional league in the works for us. I mean, we've all heard the rumors, but now it's official. By the time I graduate, it should be up and running."

I feel her thrill running through me. She and the other players deserve this... getting to do what they love and getting paid for it. But my heart also squeezes in worry.

Keeping my voice as casual as I can manage, I ask, "Will there be a team in Texas?" *Please say yes.*

"Are you kidding? The greatest football state in America? Heck yes there will be a team here. It's going to be in Houston though." Her eyes go dreamy. "I hope I get drafted there so I can be close to all of you."

Even in the thinning light of evening, I can see her dreams flashing through her aqua-blue eyes. Eyes that match my own.

"I hope so too," I say, meaning that with every beat of my heart. Jordie is the baby of the family, and I'm very protective of her.

"Tell me about your new book," she says, switching the subject. "You didn't say much about it at dinner."

I groan. "Because there's not much to tell. I'm only on chapter two."

"When is it due to your editor?"

"A month," I admit, feeling the pressure sink down onto my shoulders.

"Shit, Juli."

"I knowwww. I've tried to write all day, but I haven't gotten much done. I keep getting distracted." I pull into a space in the parking lot outside her dorm and put my vintage Volkswagen van in gear.

Jordie purses her lips and makes a little humming sound. "Didn't you tell me the library is closed for renovations over the next few weeks?"

"Yes, we got some damage during that tornado. Luckily, none of my book babies were damaged. The board voted to get us a new roof and windows, and we're closing down to get ready for summer."

"You should go off the grid. Get out of town and ignore the rest of the world for a while. No phone, just your computer."

"That would be nice, but I can't just go without my phone. What if one of you needs something?"

"Then we'll deal with it like the grown-ups we are." At my skeptical look, Jordie rolls her eyes. "Fine. You can take your phone so we can get in touch with you in case of an emergency."

"I'll think about it," I told her, reaching across the console of my van to hug my sister. "I just want you to know how proud I am of you."

"I'm proud of you too, sis. But I'd be even prouder if you'd get your damn book finished on time. I need something to read this summer."

"Get out of here," I say, kissing the side of her head before giving her a playful shove. I stay parked and watch as Jordie reaches the dormitory door and turns to give me a wave before scooting safely inside.

Then I drive to my home in Pine Tree Falls on the outskirts of Dallas. Not sure where the name came from. While there are pine trees aplenty, there are absolutely no falls. Unless you count that time Mrs. Walman slipped in the produce aisle at the local Piggly Wiggly grocery store. It was the talk of the town for weeks.

Pine Tree Falls is a cute little community, close enough to Dallas that I can easily get into the city but far enough away that I still get that small-town feel I love so much. Bubba lives here too.

I'm the oldest in my family at age thirty-six, then my brother Bubba, who's thirty-three. Xander and Jordie were later-in-life babies for my parents, and they're twenty-two and twenty, respectively.

Finally reaching my house, I fix myself a glass of Dr Pepper and then make a beeline for my writing nook. "Okay, time to get some shit done," I tell myself.

I flip open my pretty pink sparkly notebook to find the note I'd made before going to the store with Ms. Mijares. My eyes narrow at the words.

Globe, apple the cock.

My eyebrows creep together. What the hell does that mean? Cock makes sense, *but apple the cock*? And globe? That could refer to the globes of my female character's butt. She does have a great ass. As I attempt to decipher my messy handwriting, my phone vibrates with an incoming text.

AK: How's the writing going?

Juliette: So so bad! I can't get inspired.

AK: You should write a female character whose superpower is breaking cocks. Call her The Mangler. Featuring cock number seven in your folder.

Juliette: I'll keep that in mind.

AK: I can feel the sarcasm even through text. Why are you having trouble with inspiration?

Juliette: I guess it's more that I can't just sit down and write. I keep getting distracted by life.

AK: Ahh, you're in need of a writing retreat.

Juliette: That's what my sister said.

AK: Genius supporters - 2, Distracted author - 0. Just fucking do it.

Juliette: You're right.

AK: That's what I like to hear. Find a beach somewhere. Hot dudes running around half naked? That's what you need for "inspiration."

Juliette: Do the words "globe" and "apple the cock" mean anything to you?

There was a long pause before her next response.

AK: You've been scribbling in your notebook again, haven't you?

Juliette: Yes, how do you know me so well?

AK: Because you always do this. And you have the handwriting of a drunken kindergartener.

Juliette: I would be offended if it wasn't true.

AK: Stop texting and go book a trip.

"Bossy ass," I mutter, switching out of the text app and opening the travel one I use. My finger taps on the "Late Bird" button. This particular app finds hotels and resorts that haven't filled all their rooms for the upcoming time period and offers significant discounts. Kind of the opposite of "Early Bird."

Using the filters, I search for beach locations and begin scrolling my options. A bunch of family resorts pop up, and I shake my head. *Nope, that won't do.*

I adore kids, which is the problem. If there are children there, I'll spend my time making sandcastles on the beach and playing Marco Polo in the pool with them. Further refining my search to "adults only," I survey the results.

I veto the first four for various reasons. *Too expensive. Rumors of bed bugs. Low customer ratings. Caters to the elderly.*

And then... my eyes land on result number five.

Hmmm, Pineapple Island Resort and Spa.

I tap on it and scroll through the reviews first.

Beautiful tropical location.

Cool, relaxed vibe.

Most fun I've had in years.

Great for relaxation or playtime.

This sounds right up my alley, so I click over to the photos and attempt to not drool. It's beachside, the sand white and the water a clear blue. There's an enormous Roman pool, which seems to be the centerpiece of the resort. It's surrounded by palm trees and a cute bar that boasts high-end liquors.

The lobby appears well-appointed, and the rooms look clean and inviting. I notice all of them have two queen beds. Some of them even have three beds, which seems weird since it's not a family resort.

But what really grabs my attention are the hammocks dotted throughout the grounds. I picture myself reclined back on one of them with my laptop resting on my stomach, typing away as the sea breeze gently sways me from side to side.

And the best thing is that it's all-inclusive, so I won't be wasting money on overpriced resort food and drinks. Actually, that's the second-best thing. The best is the price.

Could this be right? According to this, a seven-day trip is totally in my price range, but I'd have to leave in two days. I save it under my favorites and return to the main menu to search for airfare. My nose wrinkles. Booking this late is going to cost a lot, but I think I can swing it with my book income and my salary as the head librarian at Pine Tree Falls Library.

Taking a deep breath, I go back to the Pineapple Island Resort page and click “Book It!”

A pop-up appears and catches my attention.

Flash sale! Book an additional week and save 50% on your entire vacation. Book TWO additional weeks, and you’ll also receive FREE airfare from most major airports.

“What?” I shriek at my screen, navigating to the airport page to see if DFW is listed. It is indeed.

Excitement makes the tips of my fingers tingle. Three weeks away is exactly what I need to finish my book, and this deal is too good to be true.

Before I can talk myself out of it, I accept the offer and sit back in my chair with a satisfied grin.

Pineapple Island, here I come!

Chapter 3

Reno

I'm done with women.

"This is total horseshit," my friend and now-ex-teammate, Lane Rivera, says. "I don't want to have to work with some fucking rookie when we could have you." The brown skin of his forehead wrinkles into a frown.

The other member of our group, Marcus Rhodes, shares a similar expression of disgust. "They're really trying to get Fredrickson Mitchell? His name sounds like a goddamn law firm."

My two buddies share a look before Lane's dark eyes fix on me. "We'll make him feel *real* welcome."

"Don't you two go getting in trouble, or else Priestner might trade you too," I grumble, staring down into my beer.

"That Mitchell prick deserves it after that interview he did on ESPN," Marcus says with a sneer before quoting Fredrickson Mitchell in a mocking voice. "I'm the best defenseman in the country, including the pros."

The buzz of the bar swirls around us, but we ignore it, including the frequent looks cast in our direction. But that's what happens when three giant, famous hockey players enter a bar, even though we claimed the most inconspicuous table in the back corner. One of the bouncers hovers a few feet away to ward off unwanted attention.

I sigh. "Maybe I'll just retire from hockey and become a commentator or something."

Both my friends look horrified. "Fuck no," Lane says. "You're at the height of your career, Reno, and you're not letting those assholes take what you love from you." He jabs a finger into my chest. "You're going to fuck Priestner up the ass by having your best year ever."

God, my friends are good for my soul.

"Agreed. Fuck them. And I'll bet Princess Tiffy didn't even get in trouble," Marcus adds as he clicks on his phone. "Yep, look at this."

He turns his phone and shows us the screen, where Tiffy Priestner is posing with both arms up in front of the Louvre. The Instagram caption reads, "Daddy sent me to Italy this week!" along with a million hashtags.

"Christ almighty, she doesn't even know which country she's in," I groan.

"And who the hell names their kid Tiffy and expects her not to grow up to suck cock in closets?" Lane asks, making me snort out a laugh.

Marcus scratches the back of his blond head. "Was the blowy even worth it?"

"It was barely a two-spurter," I admit.

"I feel like I'm partly responsible. For the situation, not your abysmal lack of jizz," he clarifies. "I'm the one who goaded you to get off your ass and get back into the game when the princess was eye-fucking you from across the room."

I empty my glass and smack the mug down onto the wooden table with force. "Not your fault, bro. You know I don't do anything I don't want to do."

"True. You are a stubborn fuck." Lane motions for the waiter to bring us another round. "You're going to be fine. Dallas has some good players. Baylor Ward is amazing, and from what I understand, he's a damn good guy too."

"He is," Marcus agrees. "I played with him in college, and he's a stand-up guy. I'll message him later and tell him you're my boy and to take care of you."

My phone dings with an email notification, and I pull it from my hip and swipe to check it. My eyes freeze on the screen.

"What's wrong, Reno?" Rivera asks, obviously reading my face.

I blow out a breath. "It's an email from the travel agent with the plane tickets for my trip."

"What trip?" he asks, and I raise my gaze to his.

My lips twist to the side. "I was supposed to leave for my honeymoon in two days."

"Oh. Fuck," he says with a wince. "You forgot to cancel it?"

"I guess so. Leia planned and booked it, using my credit card, obviously."

"Obviously."

"I'll just email the agent and tell her the situation. I'm sure it's non-refundable, but whatever."

I begin to type out a response when Marcus lifts a hand the size of a tire. "Wait. Where were you supposed to go?"

Lowering my phone to the table, I shrug. "Some island in the Caribbean. Like I said, I let Leia plan her dream trip."

He drums his fingers on his lips. "Hmmm."

"Hmmm what?"

He points his index finger at me. "You should go."

I give him a dubious arch of one dark eyebrow. "I should go on my honeymoon by myself?"

"Nah, dude. You should go on a *vacation* by yourself." He makes a rainbow with his hand. "Just think. Sun. Sea. Chicks galore... in swimsuits." He literally sings that last word.

"I don't know, man. Doesn't that seem kind of lame?"

Lane shakes his head, obviously warming to Marcus's dumbass idea. "I dunno, Reno. I think you should go too. You need to get away from here for a while. How long is the trip for?"

I had no clue. Checking the return date on the plane tickets, I say, "Two weeks."

"That will be perfect. Two weeks of having someone wait on you hand and foot. Island vibes. Plenty of scantily clad women."

The images roll over in my mind, and I actually begin to consider it. I wouldn't have to cook or any other mundane daily tasks. I could just veg by the pool or on the beach and drink myself into oblivion while feeling sorry for myself.

Best of all, I could put off making plans to move to another state because I honestly couldn't bring myself to think about that for a while.

"Maybe..." I allow, and they both pounce, rattling off all the reasons I should go.

It took thirty minutes and two more beers before I finally relented. "All right, all right. I'll go. But only so you two will shut the fuck up about jet skiing and fresh fish."

Lane smacks me on the shoulder. "That's the spirit!"

"But absolutely no women. They're nothing but trouble," I inform them with a final slash of my hand. "I'm done with women."

Chapter 4

Juliette

Why are those pineapples upside down?

A warm salty wind slinks through the slightly open window at the front of the shuttle van and teases the ends of my blonde ponytail. I close my eyes and inhale the peace, only opening them when the tinny voice of the driver comes over the speaker.

"If you'll look to your right, you'll see a field of pineapple plants. Fun fact about pineapples: each plant produces only one fruit and then dies. But don't you worry. Small plantlets called suckers grow at the base of the plant, and they are planted to grow even more pineapples."

I dip my head to look out the window, seeing hundreds of shrubby plants growing low to the ground. I had no idea they couldn't produce more than one pineapple. My mind begins churning. I could probably work that fact into a story. I pull out my notebook and jot down a few ideas. Maybe an analogy related to love where a dying relationship spawns new growth. Perhaps a sucker joke in there as well.

The male voice continues. "And to your left, there's a grove of coconut trees. Beyond that is a vegetable garden. Pineapple Island Resort prides itself on growing most of the fruits and vegetables that are prepared in our gourmet kitchens." Then the man chuckles. "But pineapples are definitely our favorites here at this resort. Am I right?"

Everyone cheers, and I join in. The shuttle is a large flamingo-pink passenger van and, besides me, there are two couples and four women onboard who all seem to know each other.

Seated in the second row on the left side, I watch as the couple in front of me share a sweet kiss before the woman glances back at me. I quickly look away, embarrassed that I'd been staring. They're a lovely couple, him with golden hair that sweeps over his forehead and her with porcelain skin and a mass of auburn curls.

They whisper for a moment—no doubt talking about the creeper behind them. Then the woman turns in her seat to give me a bright smile.

"Hi, I'm Jane Ford, and this is my partner, Gaston Chevalier."

"So nice to meet you," I say. "Sorry I was gawking earlier. You two just seem really sweet together."

She laughs a throaty chuckle as Gaston swivels around and rests his forearm on the seat. "We don't mind," he assures me. "Are you here by yourself?"

Stranger danger!

But I can't really deny it since I'm sitting alone, so I do the next best thing, letting them know that, while I don't have anyone physically here with me, I'm not totally out of touch with the outside world.

"Yes. My father was worried about me coming alone, so I have to call him every night when I'm safely locked in my cottage. Otherwise, he'll send in the troops." *There. That should do it.*

I don't mention that after my best friend went missing on our Spring Break trip in Mexico seventeen years ago, I haven't been outside the United States. Mostly to appease my fathers... both of them.

My dads aren't a couple or anything. Emmett McNamara is my biological father, and Isaac is my stepdad—who I call Pops—and I adore them both.

"Fantastique," Gaston says. Judging by his name and accent, he's a Frenchman.

Jane gives me a kind smile. "You're welcome to eat dinner at our table tonight. We'd love to get to know you better."

"That's really sweet, but I was planning to turn in early and order room service. I have a lot of writing to do tonight."

Gaston perks up. "Writing, you say? I'm an author as well."

"He's a professor of psychology at Georgetown," Jane tells me, her chin lifting in pride. "Gaston has written three textbooks and has another in the works."

I feel my cheeks blush. "I don't write anything as cerebral as textbooks, I'm afraid. I'm a romance author."

One of the women behind me leans forward, her brown eyes sparkling. "Oooh, are they spicy romances? I looooove the spice." She has a bit of a southern accent like me but sounds more Louisiana than Texas.

"They are," I assure her with a smile. "I write under the pen name Juli Mack."

The woman lets out a shriek that causes the van driver to jolt and almost swerve off the road. "You are! I recognize you now!" She turns to her other three friends but keeps a finger pointed at my face, very nearly poking out my left eye. "Y'all, this is Juli Mack, the author I'm always talking about."

The four women surround me, Louisiana-girl sliding into the seat beside me, her blonde friend still behind me, and the other two hopping to the dual seats across the aisle from me. I learn their names are Ann, Wendy, Donna, and Stephanie.

They each wear a brightly colored tee with *The Unicorn Unit* printed on the front, as well as a twisty unicorn headband on their heads. I can tell they're a lot of fun.

The women let me know they've all read at least five of my books thanks to the recommendations of Wendy, the one beside me, which is an awesome feeling. I'm not super famous, but I do get recognized by hardcore romance readers from time to time.

Wendy pulls out a worn paperback of my very first book, *Slow and Low*. "I've read this nine times, and I brought it with me to read at the beach to make it an even ten." She scrunches her nose apologetically. "I hate to be *that* person, but would it bug you if I asked you to sign it for me? I know you're just here to have fun, but I'd kick myself in the ass if

I met you and didn't get you to sign it. I've read all of your books, but this is my favorite one ever."

"I don't mind at all," I laugh, digging through my ballerina-pink backpack for a pen. "I'm actually here to work on my next book. I've been having trouble concentrating at home." I sign her paperback *To my friend, Wendy. Much love, Juli Mack,* and hand it back to her.

She clutches it to her chest, looking pleased. "Thank you."

One of the ladies across from me, Donna, I think, lowers her voice and asks, "What's your next book about? Or is it a secret?"

"It's called *The Playbook.* The main characters are a librarian and a football player."

Ann, the blonde behind me, bounces in her seat. "Oh, I love sports romance. You haven't written one of those in a while."

Yeah, there's a reason for that, I think but don't say out loud.

Stephanie, a woman with dark skin and soft black curls, waves her hand in the air. "Oooh, while you're in your sports era, I vote for a hockey romance next."

Not a chance in hell, sister.

"I'll keep that in mind," I say aloud.

The vehicle turns onto a driveway, and I get my first glimpse of the resort. Excitement fills my chest. It's been so long since I've been on any kind of tropical vacation.

Two enormous white-stone pillars flank the guardhouse, and shiny gold pineapples gleam from each. A golden metal arch connects the two pillars and reads *Pineapple Island Resort and Spa.*

Why are those pineapples upside down? I wonder for a second before I'm distracted by the gorgeous scenery... lush green lawns and lines of palm trees that curve perfectly with the turns in the white and pink shell drive.

The main lodge comes into view, all reddish timber with a high peaked roof. The van pulls beneath the wide portico, and everyone stands.

A couple that had been at the back of the van inches forward to introduce themselves to everyone as Erin and Jason Alvin. "This is our first time here," Jason says.

"Oh, you're gonna love it!" Stephanie gushes. "We all met here five years ago and come back every year."

Return customers... that's a good sign.

Inside, I'm handed a slushy drink with a wedge of pineapple on the lip and am guided to a long teakwood reception desk. A tall, lean woman with mahogany skin and box braids greets me with a Jamaican accent.

"Ms. McNamara, welcome to Pineapple Island. My name is Kat. Do you have any specific requirements as far as cottages are concerned?"

I hitch my backpack higher onto my shoulder. "Something quiet, please. I'm going to be doing some writing while I'm here."

She taps magenta fingernails—which perfectly match her lipstick—against a silver keyboard with soft clicky-clack noises and nods. "Excellent. I'll put you in cottage four. It's one of the farthest from the lodge. The closest neighbor is cottage five, and that one is currently unoccupied. It should be nice and peaceful for you there."

"That sounds perfect. Thank you."

Her pretty bottle-green eyes twinkle with mischief. "I do hope you're not planning to be all work and no play, Ms. McNamara. We like to have a good time here, and I'm sure everyone will be dying to spend time with you."

Letting out a self-conscious chuckle, I tell her, "That's very sweet of you. I definitely plan to enjoy the sunshine during the day. The photos of the beach and pool I saw online were amazing." I place a hand on my chest and feign a swoon. "But the hammocks! That's what sold me."

"The hammocks are my favorites too. In fact, there's one directly behind your cottage." Kat hands something to a brown-haired porter lingering at her shoulder before returning her attention to me. "This is Malcolm. He'll take your bags to your cottage, and they'll be waiting for you when you arrive."

Her voice is like warm silk, and I could seriously listen to her reading the phone book and be enamored. “I love your accent,” I tell her. “Could you pretty please come to my room and talk me to sleep later?”

She laughs. “That could be arranged. Or I could send my husband, Jevaun. He’s a massage therapist here at the resort. His hands, combined with his voice, will turn you into a pile of pudding. You’ll sleep like a baby when he’s done.”

“That sounds amazing. I’ll think about it.”

“We also offer couple and group massages if you find someone you’d like to spend time with while you’re here.”

Group massages? Who would want a bunch of other people there during relaxation time? I inwardly chuckle. Probably those crazy unicorn ladies. They seem like they could turn anything into a party.

Kat slides a yellow folder across the teakwood, pulls out a map, and points with a red pen. “This is where we are now, and this is your cottage. You’ll just follow the path to the left when you leave the lodge. Would you like someone to escort you?”

I take a sip of my drink. It’s fruity without being overly sweet, and I’m pretty sure I taste a hint of prosecco on my tongue. “I think I can find it.”

“Wonderful. Our grounds are large, so if you get lost during your stay, or if you feel uncomfortable walking alone at any time, call the front desk. There are signs along all pathways with a location code. You just give that to them, and security will come and escort you within a couple minutes.”

My shoulders sink in relaxation, probably both from the drink and the sense of security I feel at her words. After what happened with my friend Evie all those years ago, I can’t deny I had a hint of trepidation about coming to a tropical location.

“That sounds great. Thank you, Kat.”

“My pleasure. I’m the manager here, so please let me know if there’s anything you need.” She points with her pen toward the back door of the lodge. "You mentioned the pool earlier. We actually have two. The main pool is just through that door, and swimwear is required there."

"Okay," I say because *duh*. Swimsuits are required at the swimming pool. I'm not going to wear a ballgown, lady.

Then Kat circles something on the map. "The other pool is located here and is clothing optional. As is this section of the beach." She draws a square on the paper near what is obviously the ocean.

Clothing. Optional. As in, you don't have to wear clothes?

A giggle escapes me, and I try my damnedest to make it sound cool and nonchalant, but I fail miserably. I sound like Woody Woodpecker.

"Great. Heh heh heh heh. Super. I'll just... you know... run over there without... clothes." I wave a hand. "No biggie."

Amusement tips Kat's lips up on one side. "Robes are provided in each cottage for your modesty while walking to the pool and beach."

"Right, right, of course." I do that weird-ass laugh again. "Heh heh heh heh. I'll wear the robe and then just..." I mime flapping open the edges of an imaginary robe. "Patow! Naked Juli is here!" That came out way louder than I meant for it to.

Oh god, help me to shut up now.

But alas, I don't. I continue, leaning forward with wide eyes. "I'm assuming there's sand at the, um, *clothing-optional* beach?"

She clears her throat, and I'm pretty sure she's trying not to burst into laughter. Or slap me upside my crazy head. "Indeed. Our beaches are full of beautiful white sand."

"Wow. Okay. Sand with all those... crevices... and sensitive regions." This doesn't sound pleasant at all, and my mind fills with all the complications. "Is there some kind of special ointment one could use for coochie chafing and ass rashes? And I imagine the men would need SPF one-thousand on their penises. Oh! And what if you're just lying on the beach relaxing, and a sand crab tries to crawl inside your..."

Kat, the dear, dear woman, handles my bizarre rant with the utmost professionalism when she interrupts. "Perhaps it would be best to stick to these areas at first," she says, putting giant stars on the map to highlight the non-nudey swimming areas of the resort.

I slam back the rest of my slushy drink, giving myself a brain freeze in the process. With a wince, I bob my head up and down. "Right. Definitely. I'm just gonna..." I pick up the map, stuff it into the folder, and twirl it wildly around the room. "Gonna head to my room and unpack. Because I brought clothes. To wear."

I take off at a rapid clip, halting when Kat calls, "Ms. McNamara, you're going the wrong way."

"Right. Yep." I pop the P and do an about face, shooting finger guns at the double front doors. "This way. Bingo-bango."

Well. That wasn't awkward in the slightest.

By the time the sun is settling into the horizon, so is my mortification. But only slightly.

Bingo-bango? Coochie chafing? Really, Juliette? I shake my head at the memory as I tuck the rest of my clothing into the drawers of the ash dresser. I'll just have to take measures to avoid that Kat woman at all costs while I'm here. I imagine myself rolling across the lobby floor and hiding behind furniture and plants with the *Mission: Impossible* theme song in the background.

Dun dun dun-dun, dun dun dun-dun. Doo doo dooooo.

Grinning, I pull my phone from the pocket of my floral maxi-dress when it rings.

"Hi, Daddy."

"Hey, baby. I got your text that you arrived safely, but I wanted to hear your voice."

"Miss me already?" I tease, and he lets out a self-deprecating chuckle.

"I know you're thirty-six, but you'll always be my baby girl. Is everything okay there?" I hear the worry in his voice and know he's picturing himself in the place of Paul Bouvier's after his daughter disappeared and was never heard from again.

"Great. It's very nice. They have location markers on all the paths, so if I feel unsafe, I can just call security from my phone and tell them I'm at marker 2-A or whatever. Then they'll be there in a jiffy. So you don't need to worry about me."

"Okay," he sighs. "Sorry if I'm being overbearing."

"You're not," I assure him before pivoting the conversation. "This place is so beautiful and relaxing. I think I'll get a lot of writing done here."

"Good, sweetie. I loved your last book, by the way. Chapter eight was hot."

Yes, my dad reads my books. And yes, it was awkward at first but I'm used to it now.

"Thanks, Dad. You should put that technique into practice sometime. Have you had any dates lately?"

He chuckles. "Naw. Maybe you could write a book about a woman who falls for a fifty-something mechanic who always has grease stains on his shirt. You know, to inspire me."

I laugh. "I'll do it. I think Ms. Mijares's daughter is single now. She's really pretty... a little younger than you, but if she can cook like her mother, you'd be in for a treat."

"I'll think about it." It's his standard answer and means no.

"If we're still both single by the time I turn forty, I think we should move in together and rescue a horde of cats."

I can hear the smile in his voice. "Sounds good to me. Oh, and can you send Isaac a message? I talked to him earlier, and he was worried about you too."

"Will do," I assure him. My dad and stepdad get along swimmingly for two men who both married the same woman.

"Do me a favor and pay attention to your surroundings while you're there. You tend to walk around with your head in the clouds."

He's not wrong, and I smile into the phone. "I promise. And I'll check in with you tomorrow, okay?"

"All right, baby. Love you so much."

"Love you too, Dad."

As soon as I hang up, a knock sounds at my door. I open it to a squatty man in the Pineapple Island Resort uniform of a short-sleeved khaki shirt and matching shorts.

"I have your room service order, Ms. McNamara." He holds up a covered tray.

"Thank you. Just let me grab my purse—"

"No tips, ma'am. Everything is included here at Pineapple Island Resort."

"Oh, right. Thank you."

He hands over the food and nods politely before offering me a departing wave. I take the tray to the small kitchenette and remove the top. I'm greeted by the sight of plush strawberries, fat purple and green grapes, a variety of cheeses, and of course, loads of juicy pineapple slices. A small container of gourmet crackers rests on the side.

After eating my fill, I notice a basket of goodies on the coffee table in the small sitting room. The furniture is made up of brightly colored cushions and soft-gray wood, and I take a seat on the couch.

A small card reading *Welcome to Pineapple Island Resort and Spa* is propped against the wicker basket, and I slide it into my purse. I always keep something from every trip I go on. Whether it's a small notepad from a hotel I'm staying in or the name tag from a book signing, I like to have a small memento to remember where I've been. I plan to add this pretty card with the embossed pineapple logo to my collection.

Sorting through the contents of the basket, I find snacks, bottled water, wine, and a small box. I open the box to find a pretty bracelet with a pineapple charm on it. "How cute!" I say aloud, sliding the jewelry onto my left wrist and admiring the way it glints in the overhead light.

Digging deeper in the basket, I come across a handful of condoms in various colors and flavors as well as a bottle of lube and... a lemon? I pick up the last item and turn it over in my hand. It's velvety soft and has a button on the side. When I press it and the device vibrates to life, I realize it's one of those clit sucking toys.

Okay, Pineapple Island Resort. I see your kinky ass.

While I have a variety of sex toys for—*ahem*—book research, I've never used this particular one, though I've seen ads for them. Maybe I'll try it out tomorrow. Again, purely for research purposes. It's definitely something my female main character would use.

See? This trip is a good thing. It's already giving me ideas for my book.

Taking the lemon to the bathroom, I thoroughly clean it before retrieving the condoms and lube and stowing them all in the nightstand drawer between the beds. *Not that I'll be needing the condoms while I'm here.*

The beds are gorgeous, with soft yellow covers and white gauze draping down from the four carved posts of each. After I get some writing done tonight, I'm going to sleep like a baby beneath those plush covers.

Returning to the living area, I take the food items to the kitchen, stowing the water and wine in the refrigerator and the snacks in the small pantry closet. Then I feel the pull of the ocean guiding my bare feet across the floor and to my bedroom.

This side of the cottage faces the ocean, and I pull aside the vertical blinds to find a sliding glass door. There's a button beside it, and when I press it, the back door slides smoothly open. Stepping onto the wood-plank back porch, I press my palms against the white railing and lean forward.

The sun is completely gone, and the moon is rising above the water, casting its feathery glow over the gentle waves. Closing my eyes, I flare my nostrils and drag in the myriad of scents.

The saltiness of the water. The hint of sweet pineapple from the fields. The lush aroma of the bougainvillea I saw planted around the cottage.

And I relax, letting my toes curl against the smooth wood beneath my feet. Without a care in the world except for my writing, every ounce of stress blows away on the supple island breeze.

This is exactly where I need to be. No worries.

And absolutely no distractions.

CHAPTER 5

Reno

I'm a stellar pervert

MY FLIGHT FROM DENVER was delayed by three hours, so I missed my connecting flight in Miami. Now it's nearing dark as the van slides between the columns of the resort entrance.

That's when I get the first inclination that something is off. *Are those pineapples upside down?* I squint in the dim light, but we're already past them, creeping up the shell drive and beneath a tall portico.

"We're here, Mr. Swain."

"Thanks for coming back for me, Frank," I tell the driver as I stand, and he twists around and gives me a toothy grin.

"Of course, sir. I hope you have a nice stay. The porters will handle your bags, so just head right through those doors, and you'll see the front desk."

I offer him a tip—which he refuses—and step down from the van. Music plays in the distance, and the scents of food and sea air fill my nostrils. I realize the only things I've eaten today were airplane snacks, and I'm suddenly hungry. Grasping the pineapple handle on the door, I pull it open and step inside onto a terracotta tiled floor.

"Ah, you must be Mr. Swain," a tall Black woman greets from behind a wooden counter.

Despite my weariness from the long trip, I force a smile when I approach. "I am. Sorry about the late check-in."

"It's no problem at all. Frank informed me when he left the airport with you, so I took the liberty of putting in an order with the kitchen for a sandwich. I assumed you'd be tired and hungry after your journey and might not feel like going to one of the restaurants."

Wow. Talk about service.

"Very kind of you. Thank you."

"Of course. I'm Kat, the manager here. Let me just go over a couple things with you, and by the time you get to your cottage, your food and luggage will be waiting for you."

The woman points out various things on the map, including clothing-optional areas, and my suspicions are piqued. When she notes the nightclub, which is called "The Upside Down Club," I broach the subject on my mind.

"Pardon me, Kat, but may I ask you a question?"

She smiles graciously. "Certainly."

I lower my voice. "Um, is this a swingers' resort?"

Her head tilts to the side as her eyebrows lower. "It is. Were you not aware when you booked?"

I grit my teeth. "I didn't personally book the trip. My former fiancée did. It was supposed to be our honeymoon."

Kat presses her fingertips over her lips. "Oh my. And she didn't tell you?"

My head shakes back and forth in the negative. "No."

"Am I to assume that you're not into the lifestyle?"

Rubbing a hand down my face, I utter a simple, "No."

The woman purses her lips, looking displeased. "If I may be so bold, perhaps it's best that she's your *former* fiancée."

"Yeah, no shit," I grumble, anger at Leia bubbling in my gut. *How the fuck could she think this was okay?*

Kat pats my arm. "The most important thing about this lifestyle is communication. It's something that needs to be discussed in depth and most definitely not something one would spring on their partner without their permission. Especially not as a honeymoon trip."

"It's not that I find anything wrong with it. I think people should do whatever the hell they want in the bedroom, and it's no one else's business. It's just not something I'm interested in."

"Totally understandable. It's not for everyone."

A long sigh escapes me. "I know my stay is probably not refundable, but I guess I should cancel. Is there another hotel on the island where I can stay until I figure out what to do?" *Just go home, Swain. This entire trip has been a bust so far.*

Kat presses her lips together and shakes her head in apology. "I'm sorry, no. The island is privately owned, and we're the only resort here."

"Shit. Okay, so is it all right if I stay here for the night? I'll just book a flight home as soon as I can get one."

She props her elbows on the glossy countertop, folds her hands together, and rests her chin on the backs of her knuckles. Her shrewd green eyes regard me.

"I have another suggestion. Since you came all this way, why don't you just stay here and enjoy yourself?" When I open my mouth to protest, she lifts a single pinky to quiet me. "Hear me out. Pineapple Island is a stellar resort, if I do say so myself. Yes, we do accommodate those who like to indulge in adult activities of their choosing, but we also offer many other amenities. Our restaurants alone are worth the stay. The beaches are the absolute best in the Caribbean, and I dare you to find scenery more beautiful anywhere in the world."

I give her a polite smile. "Everything I've seen so far has been top-notch."

"First and foremost, we're a vacation destination. People come here to relax and unwind, and by the tense set of your shoulders, I can tell you need that." She's not wrong there, and I make a conscious effort to lower my shoulders. "Our guests usually don't indulge in much more than some overt flirting in the public areas. They save the rest for their private cottages or the playrooms we have available. Things do get a little more playful in the clothing-optional areas, so if you stay away from those, I'm sure you won't find anything offensive to you."

I pull at the back of my neck, which seems to have developed a bit of a crick. "I'm not offended. At all. It's just that..." a long breath heaves from my lungs, "I had a not-so-great experience with a... group activity once."

The tilt of her head is sympathetic. "Well, it's not like anyone is going to tie you up and force you into a polyamorous situation." One of her brown shoulders lifts and falls in a casual shrug. "Unless you're into that."

The twinkle in her amused eyes is so cheeky, I bark out a laugh, feeling myself loosen up. "Good to know."

Kat's smile widens. "We've left a welcome basket in your cottage along with a card that explains all the rules, which can basically be summed up with the three Cs." She straightens and ticks them off on her fingers. "Consent. Communication. And consideration."

Cracking a smile, I say, "Those are big ones for me too, but a couple of them were missing in my last relationship."

Kat tucks the map back into the yellow folder. "Seems so. Now, a few things you need to know. Breakfast and lunch are casual here at Pineapple Island, but dinner is a bit nicer. We try to spread it out so everyone doesn't show up at once, so we ask that you sign up for your dinner time on the sign-up sheet." She points a manicured finger toward the end of the reception desk. "We put it out down there first thing in the morning, and the times are first come, first serve."

"Got it. Anything else?" I'm suddenly very hungry and extremely tired.

"One more thing. You'll find a bracelet in your basket. Like this one." She taps the pineapple charm on her wrist. "If you wear the bracelet, it signals to the other guests that you're open to play. If you're not wearing the bracelet, they shouldn't bother you with offers to join them."

I nod, feeling a little better. "Makes sense."

"We've found it works well to keep everyone comfortable. Sometimes a couple finds that they need some time just for themselves, and the bracelet system helps avoid any unwanted invitations."

"Thank you for being so welcoming, and I hope you don't think I was being judgmental at all. I'm not. I was just caught off guard."

"I totally understand. We welcome everyone here as long as they are respectful, which it seems like you are, Mr. Swain. You were just put in an awkward position." She hands over the folder and nods toward the front doors. "If you'll head out those doors, you can follow the signs on the path to the left. I've put you in cottage five. I think you'll enjoy the... *scenery* there."

She gives me a wink and a sly smile that I can't quite decipher.

As I walk along the limestone pathway, winding myself through the immaculate landscaping, a sense of calm comes over me. The farther I walk, the quieter the music becomes, giving way to the crooning melodies of tree frogs and nocturnal birds.

A wooden arrow sign directs me toward cottages four and five, and I follow the curved path through the trees to find two cozy white cottages with light-blue shutters. Jogging up the steps to number five, I use the key card from the folder to open the door.

The inside is casual yet nicely decorated, and my eyes light directly on a platter placed on a small dining table. Removing the lid, I'm a little shocked. I expected maybe a grilled cheese or even a peanut butter and jelly sandwich, but when I lift the top layer of toasted Focaccia bread, I find what looks like brie and prosciutto with crisp arugula and some kind of balsamic dressing.

My stomach instantly makes its needs known, and I sit, picking up the sandwich and taking a huge bite. "Damn, that's good," I mumble around a mouthful. Kat wasn't lying about the food here. The sandwich is accompanied by hand cut truffle fries, and I quickly scarf down every bite, licking my fingers when I'm done.

With my belly satisfied, I dig out a bottle of water from the welcome basket and down it in three gulps.

I wander into the bedroom, where my suitcase is sitting neatly on a luggage rack. Ignoring it, I open the vertical blinds and then the back door.

The gravitational pull of the soft blue moon drags me onto the back porch, and I shove my hands into my pockets and stare out at the water.

I'm not directly beachside, but it appears to be less than a five minute walk.

My hand falls on my phone, and I pull it out, snapping a pic of the ocean lit by the moon with palm trees framing the scene.

My entire being sags with a calmness I didn't realize I'd feel. The weight of the world seems lifted from my shoulders in this beautiful place. I'd been concerned I would think of Leia the entire time, but this is honestly the first time she's even crossed my mind.

I'd been filled with anger and hurt the first few months after the *thing*, but I'd thought of my ex less and less recently. And now I couldn't even picture her here with me.

Pocketing my phone, I lean against one of the posts with my arms crossed over my chest and glance around in the dim glow. It's peaceful here, tranquil and beautiful. I'd planned on booking a flight home tomorrow, but perhaps I could stay a couple days. This place might do me some good.

My eyes fall on the back porch of cottage four... and I freeze.

Now, I don't believe in spirits or fairies, but if I did, I would have been convinced I'd stumbled upon my very own moon nymph. Her feet are bare, and floral fabric flutters around legs that seem to go on for days, ending in the curve of a perfectly popped ass.

Her hips lean forward onto the railing, and I've never wanted to be a two-by-four piece of wood more in my entire life. Speaking of wood...

I palm my rapidly stiffening cock behind the zipper of my travel-wrinkled black shorts. It's been a while since my body has responded so fervently to a woman. Even during the ill-fated closet incident with Tiffy—she'd had to kiss my neck and rub her tits all over me for a few minutes before I had even the hint of an erection. But now... just looking at this goddess that doesn't even know I exist... I'm in full-blown boner mode.

Her body is lithe, with two swells on her chest that are covered by a pretty blue-and-white fabric. I venture a guess that they'd be even prettier bare and in my mouth.

Drawing my eyes up her slim neck, I find her face upturned to the moon, lids closed and lips open, as if she's soaking in the night, absorbing it into her skin and lungs. Though I can only see her in profile, I can tell her face is stunning, with smooth cheeks and a cute, upturned nose.

She's so still she could almost be a statue, so I startle at the sudden movement of her hand. My gaze follows it as she reaches up to tug the band holding her ponytail in place. She shakes her head and silk surrounds her, blowing around in a turbulent maelstrom of blonde hair that appears almost silver in the cool blue light of the moon.

Fuck, I want to bury my hands in all that silk—pulling, tugging, massaging—while I sink into her from behind.

My cock jerks, approving of that idea. The greedy motherfucker is currently attempting to perform a jailbreak from my pants. It's borderline painful.

Stepping back closer to the cottage, I drape myself in the shadows of the outdoor shower and quietly unfasten my button and zipper.

What the fuck are you doing, Swain? Hell if I know, but I'm aching for this woman I've never even seen in full light. She looks so beautiful, the vision of her almost ethereal.

Like she was made to be taken in the moonlight.

Lowering the waistband of my boxer briefs, I release my dick and take it in my hand. The heat of it sears my palm, the heaviness thick and throbbing. Shifting my hand up to my tip, I find it leaking my desire, and I use the wetness to lubricate the first stroke.

God. Yes.

My hips begin to pump against my fist as the goddess ruffles her fingers through her hair and then drifts her hand down that pretty throat of hers. I have to grit my teeth when she continues downward and pauses long enough to give her left tit a squeeze.

What a temptress.

As my hand continues to stroke my weeping cock, she leans forward toward the ocean. That serves to jut her ass out, and I imagine myself gripping the rounded contours of her hips and plunging into her. Over and over. Drawing out her wetness with my rough handling. Then I'd slide one hand up her spine, beneath those gorgeous locks that hang almost to her waist, and grip a handful at the base of her skull.

My breathing grows ragged and then halts in my throat when she reaches down to gather the skirt of her dress in one fist and bunch it up around her thighs. I'm greeted with the delicious sight of toned, tanned legs that I'd like to wear as a scarf.

She fans the material, probably to ward off the humidity of the night, and my mind conjures up beads of sweat on those sexy legs. And wetness of another kind. If I were behind her, I'd pause long enough to drop to my knees and take a long taste of what I'm sure would be heaven. My mouth waters at the thought of making her come on my tongue.

What kinds of noises would she make? Soft, pretty ones? Or is she a screamer?

The thought of my name on her lips shoves me straight into an orgasm.

I smash my lips together and internalize my groans of pure pleasure as jets of my release jerk from the head of my cock and land on the floorboards. It's a lot, definitely more than a weak two-spurt climax, and I sink my shoulders back against the house for support as my knees weaken.

My brain is fuzzy with the sense of euphoria that can only be achieved after a very satisfying orgasm. But it quickly clears when the woman straightens and looks around, her eyes pausing on the shadows that shroud me for a few seconds before moving on.

Did one of my groans accidentally slip past my lips? Was my ragged breathing too loud?

I look down at my softening dick in my hand and immediately feel pathetic. This lady was trying to enjoy a quiet moment alone, and here I am, jacking off in the corner like a common pervert.

No, I'm a stellar pervert. That one spurt went at least two feet.

Shaking my head at my own lame joke, I watch as the woman opens her back door and disappears from view, but not before the breeze carries a whiff of something fruity and sweet toward me. It mixes flawlessly with the musk of my sex, and I inhale it with the greed of a starving man, knowing instinctively that the scent came from her.

What the fuck is wrong with me? This isn't me. Hiding and jerking off and sniffing random women. Next thing I know, I'll be peeping through windows and stealing panties.

You're just hard up, my man. You saw a stunning woman and took matters into your own hand—literally.

That rings true. Maybe I need to get back out there and have a mindless sexual encounter. But this is definitely not the place to do it. And if the temptress is into sharing or swapping or whatever, then she's a million percent not the one I need to do it with.

I close my eyes and tilt my head back against the wall, knowing my vacation is over. I'll book a flight out tomorrow.

Chapter 6

Reno

My eyes are up here, sweetheart

THEY SAY THE ROAD to hell is paved with good intentions. If so, I'm headed straight to purgatory.

When I wake up Monday morning, I fully intend to get an immediate flight off Pineapple Island. The only problem? Planes only fly into the small airport on Wednesdays and Sundays. So barring a medical emergency, I'm stuck here for two more days.

Come to think of it, the way I acted last night could possibly be an indication of some kind of brain condition. Perhaps a medical transport off the island wouldn't be out of the question.

Though for some reason, I still hadn't changed my flight.

To take my mind off my little back porch indiscretion, I dress in running clothes and leave through the back door of my cottage. I don't even look at the house next door.

Okay, *maybe* I peeked over there once or twenty times, but only to make sure the occupant wasn't glaring at the freak next door who had come all over his porch at the mere sight of her. She'd probably be speaking into the phone.

Yes, officer, I can see the wanker. He's six-foot-four with dark hair and green eyes. Of course, I'd be happy to identify his penis in a lineup.

The thought of her eyes on me makes said penis perk up a bit behind my black Nike Pros. What color would her eyes be? She's blonde, so they're probably blue.

I banish the weird, obsessive images from my mind when I reach the beach, pop my earbuds in, and begin to run. As my feet pound the sand, I contemplate what I want to do about my career.

I could retire from hockey and go into broadcasting. That would completely fuck over Roland Priestner, because without me to trade, he'd lose the high draft pick he'd negotiated. That option appealed to me on a very petty level.

But am I done playing? Am I ready to give up the sport I love so much?

The idea makes my stomach clench, and I know the answer. No.

I'm going to have to suck it up and go to Dallas. It's my only choice. *Trades happen all the time, Swain. Stop being a fucking drama queen.*

Though I never thought it would happen to me. At the beginning of my career, I convinced myself that if I worked hard and became the best, I could stay with the Denver Raptors until I decided to retire. That was the game plan. That was the dream.

And now that dream is over.

The heavy metal music in my ears is only background noise to my thoughts, the beat thumping to the same rhythm as my heart. I lift a hand in greeting to a couple taking a leisurely stroll down the beach. They smile and wave back.

When I reach a bluff, I stop, jogging in place while I check my black smartwatch. I've run almost two miles, and my heart is pumping at a slightly lower rate than my trainer suggests for high-intensity cardio.

Turning around, I head back up the beach, pushing myself harder to get my heart rate up a smidge. My form is as perfect as it can be running on sand, arms churning and long legs eating up the distance to my cottage. By the time I arrive, I'm a sweaty mess. As soon as I get inside, I remove my shirt and drop down to knock out my daily allotment of pushups and situps.

Then I text my numbers to Otto, which reminds me of someone else I'll be leaving behind in Denver. Otto has been my trainer since I started in the NHL. I'll miss that big, hairy bastard.

I'd neglected to unpack last night, so after showering, I take out a few things from my suitcase and place them in the dresser drawers. Checking my watch, I decide it's time to try out one of the restaurants for lunch.

Swing On In is a buffet-style restaurant that offers a wide variety of dishes, and after getting my food, I sit at a table by myself. I've just cut into my Moroccan apricot chicken when the air around me changes. With a thousand tiny bolts of electricity sparking against my skin, I jerk my gaze up from my plate.

And there she is. My moon nymph walks through the wide arched opening to the restaurant in a cute little yellow sundress. I recognize her immediately even though her blonde hair is fashioned into a loose braid that hangs over one tanned shoulder. A pretty smile kisses her lips, and her eyes sparkle in the light from the elegant chrome and glass fixtures hanging overhead.

I realize I was wrong last night. This woman doesn't need to be taken in the moonlight. She should be fucked in broad daylight, maybe even with additional lamps and spotlights so I wouldn't miss a single perfect inch of her. She's the picture of brightness and sunshine all balled up into a tall, lean frame.

She. Is. Magnificent.

My eyes are riveted to her as she crosses the room to the long stretch of food laid out along one wall. And I'm pretty sure I'm not the only one staring. It would be impossible not to. The woman walks with confidence and grace.

And then she trips.

I'm halfway out of my seat on reflex, but she rights herself with a laugh. And not a tittering, girly laugh. No, this gorgeous creature lets out a belly laugh that flies across the room and strikes me in the gut.

Then, in the ultimate act of self-deprecation, she performs a little curtsy and waves with a royal air, a brilliant smile still on her face as chuckles bubble around the room. In that moment, self-deprecation becomes my favorite personality trait in the whole world.

My chair is facing the buffet line, so I'm able to watch the temptress choose her food, laughing with a couple beside her. When she turns, our eyes meet, and all the damn cheesy clichés take effect.

The entire world stops turning on its axis. Time stands still. My mouth goes dry.

One tiny cell in my brain seems to have some common sense and yells out a reminder. *No more women, Swain. Remember?*

But my chin ignores the warning and gives a welcoming *come here* jerk. Her cheeks inch upward, and straight white teeth are revealed in a sweet, engaging smile.

Her white-sandaled feet bring her toward the dining area—toward me—and I smell that sweet aroma again, the one I'd smelled last night.

"Can I sit here?" She indicates the turquoise padded chair across from me, and I nod.

"Of course," I say, forgetting all about my stalwart vow to avoid women.

"Thank you," she replies in an alluring southern drawl. Her voice is a slow melody with a softness around the consonants. "I'm Juliette."

She holds out a hand, and I realize I'm still holding my fork with a chunk of chicken on it. Setting it down, I reach for her hand and shake it. Juliette has a firm grip, but her skin is soft.

"Nice to meet you. I'm Reno. You smell really good."

Fuck's sake. Where's your game, Swain?

But she doesn't seem to mind, holding up her arm to give me a sniff. "It's pomegranate. Isn't it yummy?"

I hold her wrist gently and run my nose up and down her skin—just a couple inches—and I love the small hitch of her chest at my touch.

So, so yummy.

"Best thing I've ever smelled," I tell her.

A flush rises on her cheeks, the same color as one of the flowers I saw outside my cottage this morning. The pink highlights a few freckles that dot her cheeks and nose, which only makes her more appealing. She manages to be adorably cute and a vixen at the same time, the perfect combination of charming and sexy.

In the light of day, I see that her eyes are actually aqua, framed by thick lashes that don't seem to have even a swipe of mascara on them.

In fact, I don't think she's wearing makeup at all. Juliette is a natural beauty, something I'm not used to from the puck bunnies that usually chase me.

I release her arm, and she reaches for her glass of water, taking a long drink. "Did you see my grand entrance today?" she asks, surprising me by not shying away from her stumble.

"Maybe," I hedged, taking a sip of my own water.

She laughs. "I blame it on my big ole feet. My dad calls me grace. Well, when he's not calling me dreamer."

"Dreamer?" I ask.

"Yep, I tend to have my head in the clouds. I love clouds, don't you?"

"I, uh, guess I've never thought about it. They're just... there." I swirl a finger in the air.

"There's a hill behind the resort. I'm thinking of going up there to do some cloud gazing. You want to come with me?"

I'm taken aback. And tempted. But I shake my head and lie. "I have plans today."

"Oh, I wasn't going today. I have a lot of writing to do. I was thinking tomorrow." Her aqua eyes flash up and down my body in a quick assessment. "Unless you don't think you're physically able to climb a hill. You look kinda out of shape."

I bark out a laugh at her blatant goading. And is she flirting with me? Yeah, the flash of humor in her eyes and the bite onto her bottom lip tells me she is. So I fucking flirt back.

"I can promise you, *all* my physical abilities are superb, Juliette."

She lifts one sardonic eyebrow. "I guess we'll see. If you're brave enough to go with me."

I glance down at her arm and see the pineapple bracelet there. The bracelet that tells me she's into the swinging lifestyle. I've learned that after you've been burned, you don't stick your hand back into the fire. But in that moment, with this gorgeous woman staring expectantly at me, I jam my entire hand directly into the flames.

"You're on. What time?"

"Afternoon? I'll probably sleep in because I'm a night owl and get my best writing done at night."

I finally remember I have an entire meal in front of me and pick up the fork I'd hastily dropped earlier. I take a bite, savoring the sweet and spicy combination of the chicken dish.

"What kind of writing do you do?"

Juliette takes a bite of her own food, a grilled fillet of fish with some kind of creamy sauce over rice. "I'm a romance author."

Leaning forward, I lower my voice. "Do you write those spicy novels I've seen on TikTok?"

She wiggles her eyebrows. "I do. The spicier the better. Nothing like a dirty-talking man."

Fuuuuck.

"How many books have you written?"

"I'm working on my twenty-fifth right now. That's actually why I came here, to get away from the distractions of home." She makes little circles in the air with her fork as she ticks them off. "You know, neighbors, family, job."

I'm a bit flabbergasted. "You've written twenty-four books, and you work too?"

Juliette nods and takes a bite of her broccolini. "Yep. I'm a librarian in a small town."

Visions of a cardigan sweater, pearls, and a tight skirt pop into my mind, and I have to shift in my seat. "Do you wear glasses?"

Her grin widens. "Do you have a sexy librarian kink, Reno?" she asks sweetly, and I chuckle.

"Maybe."

She darts her tongue out to wet her lower lip and drops her voice to a conspiratorial whisper. "I do wear glasses sometimes when I'm writing for a long time."

"Dear god," I sigh dramatically, enjoying this flirting game we've got going on. "Tell me more."

"I also make notes in my notebook, so I usually have a pencil behind my ear." She leans closer, and her voice turns even more sultry. "And sometimes I chew on the eraser when I'm deep in thought."

Fuck, that sounds hot. "Mmm. With your hair in a bun?"

Juliette scoffs. "What kind of librarian would I be if I didn't wear a bun?"

I brush a little bit of sauce from the corner of her bare lips. They're the perfect shade of rose even without lipstick, and I can imagine them wrapped around the end of a pencil. Or other things. *Thicker* things.

Our eyes are locked, green ones to aqua. "I'm going to get a library card as soon as I get home."

"That's good. There's nothing hotter than a man with a book," she purrs. "Make sure to check out some of my books when you get there."

I'm fully hard behind the zipper of my black cargo shorts. "You bet your ass I will."

We're both leaning over the table, so close we're sharing air, but our flirty little moment is interrupted when someone bumps into our table.

"Shit, sorry," a woman says. "Oh, hey, Juli."

"Victoria, hi!" Juliette says brightly, sitting back in her chair and smiling up at the woman and her partner. I'm pleased to see her cheeks have that pretty blush on them again, and I subtly adjust my cock in my pants.

Victoria's got a cute dark hairdo, and the guy with her is a Latino man who is looking at Juliette in a way that makes me want to punch him in the fucking face.

Victoria glances down at Juliette's bracelet. "Elvis and I were wondering if you wanted to come over to our cottage and play tonight." She looks at me. "Your friend can come too." Then her gaze falls to my bare wrist. "I mean, if he wants to. You're welcome to come by yourself."

Juliette reaches out and grasps Victoria's hand. "That's so sweet of you, but I'm going to have to buckle down and get some writing done tonight. Maybe another time?"

"Of course. Just let us know when you're available." The woman pivots and stretches out a hand to me. "Sorry, didn't mean to be rude. I'm Victoria Martinez, and this is my husband, Elvis."

"Reno," I reply, not giving my last name as I shake both their hands. "Nice to meet you." It's not. Because they want the same woman I want, but I'm trying to be polite.

"Everyone is so friendly here," Juliette says after they move on. "This morning at breakfast, two other couples asked me to hang out with them tonight."

I'm sure they did. She seems blissfully unaware of her own appeal, which only makes her more appealing.

"What's your writing goal for today?" I ask, resuming my meal, but it doesn't taste quite as good as it did a few minutes ago. I don't want Juliette to "play" with any of these other people. I selfishly want to tuck her into my bed and keep her there for the next two weeks.

You're leaving in two days, Reno.

"I want to get two chapters done today and then four tonight. It's ambitious, but I promised myself a cloud-watching excursion tomorrow if I finish," she says, taking another bite of her fish.

I resume eating as well, though I have no idea what I'm even putting in my mouth at this point. I'm too busy looking at Juliette. Watching her push food into her mouth. She's not sloppy at all, but she eats heartily, not like a prissy little food-poker who never actually takes a bite. I like that.

"What time did you sign up for dinner tonight?" I ask.

She pauses with her fork halfway to her mouth. "Sign up?"

"Yeah, you have to sign up for a time. Apparently it keeps everyone from showing up at the same time and overcrowding the restaurant."

"Shit, I didn't know that. Where do you sign up?"

"In the lobby. There's a sheet on the reception desk. Most of the early spots were full when I signed up earlier, so you might get stuck in the nine o'clock time slot."

Her face drops. "Oh. Well, I'll just eat in my room tonight."

"We can add you to my table," I say hopefully, but she shakes her head.

"No, it's fine. I'll probably be working anyway. And the room service was good when I ordered in last night."

"What about tomorrow night? Since you're sleeping in, I can sign us both up in the morning before my run."

She smiles that brilliant smile again. "That would be great. My last name is McNamara, and I'm in cottage four, if you need to put that down."

"Cottage four? I think we're neighbors then. I'm in five," I say, like I'm not fully damn aware she's staying in the house next to me.

Her eyes narrow playfully. "Are you going to be one of those pesky neighbors who drops by unannounced to ask to borrow a cup of sugar?"

"Would you give me some sugar if I came by?" I flirt.

"I might, if you ask me nicely," she shoots back, and *fuck,* I like this woman. Her eyes dart down to my forearm, which is resting on the table, and she scrapes her teeth along her bottom lip. I'm not ashamed to admit that I flex. Just a little bit.

Juliette continues staring, and I make a huffy noise in my throat. "My eyes are up here, sweetheart," I say sternly, and those aqua orbs lift and widen into saucers before she picks up my teasing tone.

"Shut up," she scolds with a giggle, throwing her napkin at me. "You shouldn't just leave those things lying around where anyone could see."

"So you're into forearm porn?" I ask, catching a whiff of pomegranate on her napkin.

Her lips tip up into a smirk. "I've been known to appreciate a nice set."

I hold one out for her inspection. "And are mine nice?"

Juliette drags a hand from my elbow to my wrist, and my blood ignites. "Hmmm, very muscular, and you have nice soft hair. Not too much like a Sasquatch but enough to be manly." Then she traces a thick vein with a single fingertip. "Your veins are nice and bulging. I'd say you definitely have porn-worthy arms."

My veins aren't the only things that are bulging right now, I almost say, but instead, I nod to her empty plate. "If you're done, I'll walk you to your cabin and let you hold one of my veiny, muscular, hairy-but-not-Sasquatchy arms on the way."

"That's an offer I can't refuse. You sure it's not too far out of your way?" she asks with a sweet, teasing tone.

I rise and walk around behind her chair to pull it out. "I think I can manage." Doing my best not to strut like a goddamn peacock when she wraps a cool hand around my forearm, I lead her out into the tiled corridor.

"There's a side door that leads to our path over here," she says, tugging me lightly toward a side hall on our left.

I resist, guiding her in the direction of the lobby. "Let's just check the dining sign-up sheet. I hate to think of you eating in your room by yourself tonight." *And I want to spend more time with you before I leave on Wednesday.*

"N-no, that's okay," she stammers nervously. "We can—" Juliette cuts herself off and makes a little squeaking noise before diving behind a large potted plant.

What the...

I spot one aqua eye peering between the wide leaves of whatever tree is planted in the green pot and think, *fuck it.* Ducking behind the tree, I squat down beside her, pretty sure the huge planter is not effectively hiding my large frame. I don't exactly have the kind of body that can go incognito.

"What are we hiding from?"

"Shh," she cautions, pressing a finger to my lips. I valiantly refrain from biting the pad of it, though I desperately want to.

"What are we hiding from?" I ask again, this time in a whisper. My eyes follow her finger as she points at a familiar figure tapping past in a

Pineapple Island uniform and high heels. "We're hiding from Kat, the manager?"

Juliette nods vigorously, her gaze staying on Kat until she disappears behind a wooden door marked *Employees Only*. Then she stands and lets out a sigh of relief that's so heavy, it rustles the leaves on our hiding place.

"Come on," she says, grasping my hand and dragging me toward the side exit. I have no idea what the fuck is going on, but I'm damn well about to find out.

Once we've made the turn to the narrow path leading to our cottages, I haul Juliette to stop and step in front of her. "What is going on? Did that woman hurt you or something?" My blood boils at the thought. They both wore the pineapple bracelets. What if they'd hooked up or something and...

"Nooo," Juliette wails, covering her eyes with one palm. "I just embarrassed myself to death in front of her yesterday, and I've vowed to avoid her until I leave."

I pull her hand away from her face and lift her chin with my knuckle. "Tell me what happened."

She blows out a raspberry and rolls her eyes. "It was stupid. She mentioned the clothing-optional parts of the resort and pointed them out on the map." Juli shakes her head. "It's not like I'm offended by nudity or anything, but it caught me off guard. A bunch of naked people all walking around and just being all nakedly casual struck me as funny, so I let out this weird-ass fake laugh."

She demonstrates, and I press my lips together to keep from busting a gut. It was a bizarre laugh. "Is that all?" I manage, and Juli winces and shakes her head.

"No. Then I started rambling on about sand in personal crevices and coochie chafing and ass rashes. Then I flashed her."

I choke on my own spit. "You flashed her?" *Lucky Kat.*

"Well, it was more like pretend flashing. She mentioned that there were robes you could wear to the nudey parts of the resort, and I envisioned myself showing up and having to take off my robe in front of a lot of people." Juliette pulls open the lapels of an imaginary robe and loudly says, "*Patow! Naked Juli is here.* I literally said that, Reno. Out loud. To a perfect stranger."

By this point in the story, I'm about to bite a hole in my cheek to keep from laughing. "I'm sure Kat has heard much worse," I say in what I hope is a soothing tone.

"She thankfully cut me off when I started going on about the orifices that sand crabs could wander into."

I can't hold it back another second, and a loud laugh escapes from deep in my chest. Juliette plants her hands on her hips and glares at me for a long moment while I guffaw like a hyena, until the hilarity gets the best of her and her lips curve into a reluctant smile. Then we're both laughing our asses off.

My sides ache when I'm finally able to catch my breath. "I can't decide if coochie chafing or the whole patow thing was my favorite."

Juli drops her forehead to my chest and lets out a residual giggle. "Why am I so ridiculous?"

I rest a gentle hand on the back of her head. "You, Juliette, are the most delightful person I've ever met." We stand like that for a long while, both of us content. Every inch of my skin feels warm, and I don't think it has anything to do with the tropical heat.

She finally steps back and takes my arm again. "I'd better get to work if I'm going to meet my goal for the day."

When the path forks, we take the one toward her cabin. "So our date tomorrow is contingent on you finishing six chapters?" I ask as we reach her door. *Did I just call it a date?*

Juliette nods. "Yep, I can do it. I already have one partially written." She turns toward me with her back against the front door.

I take the opportunity to prop an arm against the doorframe. Gotta show off my porny forearms after all. Grasping her chin between my thumb and forefinger, I tilt her head up and put on my sternest look.

Leaning into her space to put my mouth against her ear, I whisper, "I want you to get inside and finish all your chapters. Do you understand me, Juliette?" I deepen my voice into a growl. "Can you be a good girl for me?"

My words have the desired effect, and her fingers clench against the microfiber of my charcoal-gray shirt at the same time she lets out a sensual whimper.

"Answer me," I command, loving the slight shudder that runs down her luscious body.

Juliette's hands flatten against my chest, and she draws back her head to look up at me. Her eyes are slightly glazed for a moment, and I internally high-five myself for my dazzling ability to induce that lust-fueled daze.

But then a sexy smirk plays with the corners of her mouth, and something flutters in my belly and shoots down to my groin. Juliette McNamara has taken charge of the situation, and I'm her rapt audience.

Taking a step closer, she pats my cheek and, with her sweet southern drawl, purrs, "Baby doll, I'm always a good girl."

Fuck me. Now I'm the one in a daze.

CHAPTER 7

Juliette

He's totally not my type

I LEAN BACK AGAINST the inside of the door and press a hand to my heaving chest. If I were wearing pearls, I'd be clutching them like a motherfucker.

Sweet baby bunnies in a basket. I just had lunch and engaged in the flirting Olympics with Reno Swain.

Yes, I recognized the hockey defenseman for the Denver Raptors the instant he gave that cocky little chin jerk in the dining room. The chin jerk I should have ignored but didn't.

I'd been drawn to him like a moth to a flame... like bees to honey... like a horny author to a hot hockey player. Choose your simile.

You don't date hockey players, Juliette McNamara, I remind myself.

But you can use your little flirtation incident to write a steamin' hot scene for your book, my stupid self reminds my smarter self.

Dashing to the bedroom, I dive onto my bed and flip open my laptop with thoughts of Reno flashing through my head. His cockiness and swagger. His million-watt smile. His forearms.

Dear. God. The forearms. Braced on either side of my head while he's on top of me. His hips working like pistons. His strong back putting in some damn fine work.

And let's not forget that very obvious bulge that was barely contained behind those black shorts.

I begin typing, my brain a rabid organ coming up with the words I'd been seeking for what seemed like forever. Any hint of writer's block went up in smoke—as did my panties—as my fingers flew over the backlit keyboard.

Though Reno hadn't blatantly talked dirty to me today, the velvety timbre of his deep voice is my inspiration, and I write like a demon. Word after word. Steamy sentence after steamy sentence. Page after page.

An hour later, I sit back against the headboard and re-read everything, blushing when I realize I had accidentally typed Reno's name three times in place of my male main character's name, Reid. I quickly make the changes before I jot a handwritten note in my notebook to change Reid's eyes from blue to green in the previous chapters.

The reasoning for that is embarrassingly obvious. Reno Swain, also known as Reno Swoon to puck bunnies everywhere, has the most gorgeous green eyes, a shade darker than sea glass. I also decide to change Reid's hair from a dark-brown crew cut to an inky black that spills over his head and swirls into loopy, soft curls. That change was also inspired by my lunch partner.

Going back to the beginning of the chapter, I add in a few more details. Like the way Reno's—*I mean, Reid's*—intense green eyes never leave Anna the entire time he's inside her. There's just something so hot about all the eye contact while fucking missionary.

I also add in a description of the mess Anna makes of those silky curls of Reid's.

Hmmm, maybe some scratches down his back? Yes, definitely. Deep ones that draw blood to the surface of his otherwise perfect skin.

That inspires a new idea for a sweet post-coital shower scene where Anna lovingly cleans the wounds she'd left on him. I open up a new chapter and begin typing, my mind feeling clearer than it has in months. The sweet scene eventually turns into a dirty one where Reno—*no, Reid, dammit*—bends her over and fucks her from behind.

Water sluicing over bare skin. The slapping of wet flesh as things get rough. *Fuck. This is goddamn hot.*

I read the newest chapter again, proud that I hadn't gotten the name wrong this time. It's good. Damn good. And my panties are a drenched mess beneath my sundress.

My thighs are clenched so tightly together you couldn't slip a hair between them, so after uploading the new chapters to two of my beta readers, I set my laptop aside and strip off my dress and panties.

Thinking of the toy in the nightstand, I reach for it, praying it holds enough charge to get the job done. It sure as hell isn't going to take long. The welcoming buzz is music to my ears, and I slide the lemon-shaped device through the lips of my sex. *Shit, I'm not even going to need lube. I'm wet enough to fill up a kiddie pool.*

It takes a few seconds to find the right spot and play around with the settings, but once everything is settled, I press my head back into the pillow with a loud groan. Of *his* name.

"Reno. Fuck. Right there."

Closing my eyes, I feel full, soft lips around my clit. A wet tongue lapping up everything I have to give. Deep-throated curses that tell me he's enjoying this every bit as much as I am.

My free hand slides into his hair, tugging those inky locks and grinding my pussy against his face.

"Yes, don't stop. Please don't stop."

"Not. Stopping. Ever," he says between licks. "Say my goddamn name while you come all over my face."

"Reno. Reno. Reno," I chant, arching my hips up as his big hands cup my ass and he goes feral on me, lapping, sucking, even applying some well-placed nibbles.

And that does it. An orgasm slashes through me, traveling up my spine and darkening my vision at the edges. "So good," I pant, wringing out every ounce of bliss from my climax.

My body is loose as an overcooked noodle when I collapse back onto the bed, my breathing fast and heavy. When I finally open my eyes, I'm surprised to find I'm alone. There's no hair twisted between my fingers. No wet mouth smiling up at me from between my legs. No Reno Swain. Just a yellow sex toy held in my trembling fingers.

"Wow, you give good head, lemon," I tell it before dropping it onto the mattress beside me. I'm suddenly exhausted and pull the cushy duvet over my naked body.

My nap is short—only thirty minutes—but I wake up invigorated, ready to tackle another chapter. This one isn't spicy, but it's filled with flirting and banter between the two main characters. The words rush from my fingers like a waterfall, and I laugh out loud several times.

Plot twists and sex scenes are fun, but the stuff in between is what I love most about writing. Building a story from the ground up... giving my characters personalities and watching them grow and develop... yeah, that's my jam.

I knock out that chapter by five in the afternoon and stand from the bed. My shoulders and neck are tight, and since I'm ahead of schedule, I decide to reward myself with a Dr Pepper and a walk.

Throwing on fresh panties, shorts, a T-shirt, and sandals, I stick my key card in one pocket and my phone in the other. As I leave through the front door, my eyes drift over to cottage five, and I grin to myself. *If he only knew the fantasies I had about him earlier.*

Inside the gift shop, I pay for my drink and then run into Ann and Stephanie, two of the Unicorn Unit ladies, as they're perusing the magnets and shot glasses.

"Juli, so good to see you," Ann says, giving me a hug. "When are you going to come play with us?"

"Yeah," Stephanie adds, "Chris and Inge Ricci—remember, we introduced you to them at breakfast?—they want to have playtime at their cottage. Victoria and Elvis are coming too."

I think about it. One night of socializing wouldn't kill me. I'll be here for three full weeks.

"That sounds fun," I reply, "as long as we're not playing Monopoly. Most boring game ever." I make a face.

Stephanie and Ann burst into laughter, and Ann smacks my arm. "You are so funny, girl." She wiggles her eyebrows. "We were thinking more along the lines of Twister."

"Now you're talking my language," I say. I used to love playing Twister as a kid. "How about, ummmm, Wednesday night? I'm in the groove with my writing right now, so I'm rewarding myself." I hold up my Dr Pepper in a salute. "I'm going to stretch my legs for a few minutes and then get back to it. And I need to write a few chapters tomorrow too."

"Sounds great," Stephanie gushes. "We'll see you about nine at cottage twenty. It's one of the deluxe ones."

"I'll be there," I promise.

Deciding to do my leg stretching at the beach, I meander down one of the sandy paths leading to the water. Slipping out of my sandals, I walk in the surf, loving the feel of the cool, blue water against my feet.

My phone buzzes in my pocket, and I pull it out and check the display. It's from Eden Osbourne, one of my beta readers.

Eden and Holly are what I like to call my first line of beta readers. I send them chapters as I finish them, and they critique them, letting me know of any problems or potential plot holes. Then, once the book is finished, I send it to the rest of my beta team. After everyone has read it and given their opinions, I'm ready to send the manuscript to my editor.

I smile at the email from Eden on my phone.

From: Eden Osbourne

To: Juli Mack

Re: What the hell did I just read?

Seriously, woman. Those were the hottest chapters I've ever read. I had to call my husband and tell him to come home early from work. He said to thank you profusely from him, BTW.

You know I adore everything you've ever written, but you have leveled up with this book, and I can't wait to read more. Whatever you're doing, keep doing it! Hopefully, it's firsthand experience giving you all this inspiration. *wink wink*

I'm so proud of you.

Hugs,

Eden

Her last sentence makes my heart happy. I've never met Eden—never even seen her face—and yet I feel like she's a close friend. She's been an ARC reader for me since my very first book over a decade ago, and a few years back, I asked her to start beta reading for me. *Best decision ever.*

Eden is incisive and sharp as tack, and she's become a voice I can count on to tell me if something isn't working. She's also got a wicked sense of humor, just like me.

While I'm reading the email again, a notification for a FaceTime call from Holly appears. Besides being my other first-line beta reader, Holly is also married to the older of my two brothers. Plopping down onto the sand with the Caribbean ocean at my back, I answer.

"Hey, sis!"

"You're a dirty, dirty bitch," she says immediately, and I burst into laughter.

"Why, thank you, madam."

"Who's the guy?"

"What guy?" I ask, feigning innocence, though I know exactly what she's getting at.

"Who did you bang to bring out beast-mode Juli? And is he as foiiiine as you describe him in those chapters?"

"I didn't bang anyone," I hedge, but the skeptical look on her pretty brown face tells me she's not buying it. "Okay, I had a *flirtation* with a guy at lunch."

She squeals in utter delight, wiggling like a hyperactive puppy as she stirs something in a saucepan on their spaceship of a stovetop. "I knew it!" Holly turns her head and calls, "Babe! Juliette's getting laid!"

"I'm not getting—"

I stop talking when my brother's handsome face appears, fighting for screen position with his wife. "Who is he? Is he being nice or do I need to kill someone?"

Sigh.

"Hey, Bubba. It's... a guy I met at the resort. And we're *not* sleeping together. We just had lunch."

I can't tell them his name. They'll recognize it, and Bubba will go thermonuclear. Reno Swain is one of the biggest playboys in the NHL.

But wait... didn't I hear he had a girlfriend or fiancée at some point? Maybe last year? I do my best to avoid any hockey news, so I'm not even sure if that's correct.

"I don't like it," Bubba proclaims.

"You don't like lunch?" I ask with faux sweetness, and his dark eyebrows smash together.

"You know that's not what I mean. You're on some island by yourself, and—"

"And she's a grown-ass woman who knows how to take care of herself," Holly interrupts, handing him the wooden spoon in her hand. "Here, stir the sauce and don't let it burn. I'm going in the other room to have some girl talk with your sister."

Bubba purses his lips and blows me a kiss. "Love you, sis. Make good choices."

The scene on the phone blurs as Holly pulls it away. "What you mean is make *boring* choices," she retorts. I hear a smack and know she's just swatted my brother on his ass.

"Watch yourself, woman," he calls as she walks away. "I'd think you would have learned your lesson by now."

"Bring it, big sexy," she says over her shoulder.

"Can you *not* call my brother that in front of me?" I whine.

Holly's curly black hair bounces as she flops onto their pristine tan couch. She ignores my complaint, as usual. "I read those chapters and then dragged that man upstairs and had my way with him earlier. It definitely made the top ten list. My vagina may never recover."

"See? This is the problem when your friend marries your sibling. I know entirely too much about my brother's sex life."

"Write a book about it. Everyone loves a friend/sibling trope." She settles back against the cushions. "Now tell me about the guy."

"It's really nothing. He's totally not my type," I lie.

"Soooo he's not tall with light eyes, dark hair, and an athletic build? He doesn't have forearms that... wait... how did you phrase it?" Holly rolls her eyes upward and taps the corner of her lips before quoting part of my book in a breathy voice. "*Tan, strong forearms that are worthy of their own highlight reel. Thick veins meander from his big hands until they disappear beneath the sleeve of his polo. His dark arm hair is soft beneath my fingertips, and powerful muscles flex as he lifts me and slams my back against the wall, knocking the breath from my lungs.*"

One of her eyebrows quirks up almost to her hairline.

I blow out a resigned raspberry. "Okay fine, maybe he does look like that, but he's definitely not someone I need to be dating."

"Who said anything about dating?" she asks, popping a chocolate truffle into her mouth. "If simply having lunch inspired *that*..." She twirls her hand vaguely. "Just imagine what some full-on, between the sheets, against the wall, on the floor, filthy-talking sex could do for your writing."

"You have chocolate in your teeth," I say, deflecting.

Holly runs her tongue over her front teeth but doesn't let the subject drop. "Seriously, Jules. I think that first chapter you sent got me pregnant. You should totally hook up with this mystery guy."

"So just a vacation fling?" The idea appeals to me. It's been a while since anyone has turned me on as much as Reno Swain.

"Yep. Let him worship you for a couple hours, kick him out, and then write like the sexy beast-woman you are. Then I'll read it and defile your brother some more." She bobs her eyebrows up and down. "And the next day, just rinse and repeat until the book is done."

Could I do that? Just use a guy sexually for inspiration for my book? Not that I think he'll complain. I know how to make it worth his while in the bedroom. And against the wall. And on the floor.

Fuck.

Eden's email flashes through my head. She said something similar. *Whatever you're doing, keep doing it!*

Mind made up, I smile at my friend. "Okay, I'll turn on the charm when I see him tomorrow and see what happens."

Holly lifts a fist in solidarity. "Get it, girl! Astonish him with your pussy prowess."

She is ridiculous, but I love the hell out of her.

CHAPTER 8

Juliette

That's all I have to say about that.

I AWAKEN WITH A smile on my face late Tuesday morning. I'd written four more chapters last night, had another go with Mr. Lemon, and fallen into a deep, sated sleep at about two in the morning.

Sitting up in my bed, I pull my laptop from the nightstand and open it up. After reading through the comments from Holly and Eden in the document, I make the necessary corrections and start on the next chapter.

This one is filled with funny friend-group banter, and I bang it out before lunch. I think a lot of the writer's block I'd been experiencing came from indifference about this book, but now I'm thrumming with excitement. My characters are really taking shape, and the chemistry between them is off the damn charts.

Kind of like your chemistry with Reno Swain.

After my shower and morning routine, I dress in denim cutoffs with fringed hems and a lime-green tank top. The hill I'm hiking up today isn't steep enough to require hiking boots—thank goodness because I don't own any—so I slip on my black Adidas with bright-green stripes and then slide the adorable pineapple bracelet onto my wrist.

With nimble fingers, I fashion my long blonde hair into a pretty fishtail braid, thinking of Dad and Pops while I do so. When I was a little girl, Dad's rough mechanic hands couldn't manage more than a slightly lumpy ponytail, but Pops's fingers were a bit more handy when it came to girly hairdos.

There was a braid craze in my elementary school in the nineties, and when I came home from school crying about my tragic, braidless existence one day, Pops picked up a couple of books on braiding hair from the library. Together we learned to do a simple braid and then a French braid before moving on to more complicated styles.

I send both of my fathers a *hey, I'm still alive, hope you have a great day* text before heading down to the lunch buffet. While I'm in line, I meet and chat with Brittany and Melissa Richardson, a same sex couple who I learn live in Chicago. They're adorable, walking down the line with their pinkies linked while they push their trays with their free hands.

Deciding not to eat anything too heavy since I'll be doing some exercise—which I hate—I settle on a refreshing pasta salad with small chunks of veggies, Italian meats, and mozzarella. I try—and fail—not to search for a certain spicy-book-scene-inspiring hockey player when I stroll into the seating area.

I take a seat at a small teal table near the windows overlooking the main pool area. Not the nudey one, thank goodness, because if there were *things* flopping and bobbing on the other side of the glass, I would probably begin craving hot dogs, and I didn't see those on the buffet.

Then, as if there's an environmental shift of some sort, the air around me condenses and warms my skin, and I raise my gaze to the entrance of the restaurant.

He's here.

If I'd said that out loud, it would have been breathy in that wanton hussy kind of way. Luckily, I'm playing it cool. Except for the goofy grin I can feel my traitorous lips performing.

His eyes scan the dining room, and I can't help but wonder if he's looking for me too. My question is answered when his scanning drags to a halt on me. I'm giddy. Especially when he smacks me in the gut with that panty-dropping smile of his.

He gives me a little head bob that says, *I'm coming for you, baby.* At least that's what my lusty brain is imagining in his deep voice. In reality, it's probably something much more benign like, *I'm going to grab some lunch. Save me a seat.*

Still.

In a valiant effort, I don't watch Reno move through the line, instead concentrating on my food. Three bites of pasta and two sips of tea later, he appears tableside. He's looking damn delicious in charcoal cargo shorts and a forest-green V-neck tee that molds to his torso like a second skin. His dark, curly hair is stylishly messy, with one piece that swoops down almost to his left eyebrow.

"Can I sit here, or were you saving it for someone else?"

I pretend to glance around the room before arching my neck back to look up at him. "Well, I was saving it for someone tall, dark, and handsome, but I guess you'll do."

Commencing Operation Flirty Pants.

He chuffs out a laugh and sits across from me, setting down his tray that holds a plate of grilled fish over cauliflower rice. "Are we still on for cloud gazing today?"

"If you want. It's a good day for it." I glance down at his dark-green shirt. "But only because you got the memo to wear green today. Otherwise, I'd have to leave you here."

"Ah, are we going to be one of those couples who have to color-coordinate their outfits?" he asks, forking up a bite of his food. "I mean, not that we're a couple or anything." He blushes. Literally *blushes*, and it's cuter than a bucket of kittens.

"Oh, we definitely have to coordinate. Tomorrow the designated color is pink."

"Because on Wednesdays we wear pink?" he retorts, and I laugh.

"A guy who gets *Mean Girls* references. I'm impressed."

Reno brushes imaginary lint from his shoulder. "I'm a man of many talents." He leans forward, his voice dropping to a marvelously indecent rasp. "Were you a good girl yesterday, Juliette?"

Have freaking mercy.

The number of times I imagined those words from his perfect lips while I was masturbating with Mr. Lemon last night should be illegal. But I maintain my cool and give him a slow eyebrow.

"I was *the best* girl. Seven chapters."

"Wow, I do appreciate an overachiever."

"I'm ready to show you the wonders of cloud gazing. Did you bring the equipment?" I ask him with a straight face.

His green eyes widen. "I didn't know I was supposed to. Is it something we can... rent?" He looks completely confused.

Unable to hold back my laughter, I let it loose and shake my head. "I'm teasing."

Reno visibly relaxes, his mouth curving into a wry grin. "All right, funny girl. Are you ready?"

After stopping by one of the side patios of the main lodge to pick up a beach blanket and a small cooler of water, we head to the back of the property.

"We probably should have brought some breadcrumbs to drop," I say with concern as we reach the bottom of the hill. "I can be... directionally challenged."

Reno leads me with confidence toward the head of a dirt trail. "It's okay. I'm good with that kind of stuff."

"Glad you are. I got lost in the grocery store one time."

He laughs as we start heading up the path that meanders through the lush greenery. "You're joking, right?"

"Nope. Just to clarify, I was only seven, and it was back in the storeroom, which is where the restrooms were. I found the ladies room okay, but when I came back out, I couldn't remember which way to go. There were just stacks of boxes everywhere, and it all looked the same."

"I can imagine that would have been scary for a kid," he says, walking beside me on the wide trail.

"I was only gone for about five minutes before my dad came looking for me. He found me eating an apple I'd dug out of a box."

Reno snorts. "Why were you eating an apple?"

I shrug. "I was convinced I was lost forever in the back of the Piggly Wiggly, and I guess my survival instincts kicked in." Giggling at the memory, I say, "Dad picked me up and took me to the front to pay for my pilfered apple. After that, he always walked me all the way to the restroom and waited by the door."

"And your mom?"

"She wasn't around much during that time in my life."

Reno reaches for my hand and folds it inside his much larger one. I like it way more than I should.

"I'm sorry, Juliette."

"It's okay. She wasn't a bad mom; she just wasn't a good mom. She sent cards and gifts on holidays and birthdays, but she wasn't a nurturer by nature." I squeeze his hand. "But I had two great dads."

"Two?" he questions as we veer to the right.

"Dad is my biological father, and Pops is my stepdad, though I don't think of him that way. They actually shared custody of me and my three siblings, which sounds bizarre, but it worked."

"Wow. It's amazing that they got along that well."

I release a soft chuckle. "They called themselves the Delphine Caldwell Support Group. That was my mom's maiden name."

The trail grows a bit steeper and narrower, and Reno keeps a firm grip on my hand, glancing over his shoulder at me as he takes the lead. "How old were you when your parents divorced?"

"I was almost two. Shortly after the divorce was final, she married Pops and almost instantly got pregnant with my brother Bubba."

"So she had Bubba when you were about three?"

"Yep. Delphine stayed until Bubba was a year old and then took off." I watch the bunch of Reno's thick calf muscles as he climbs. "I became instantly attached to my brother when he was born. That's why our dads decided to go for the unusual arrangement. They didn't want to separate us. Luckily they found a judge willing to go along with it, and they were granted fifty-fifty custody, so Bubba and I spent half our time with Dad and half with Pops."

"That's really cool. Where did Delphine go?"

"Oh, let's see... We got postcards from Oregon, Arizona, D.C., a small town in Michigan, and Virginia. She had a bit of a wandering soul. After three more marriages and divorces, she came back home when I was a teenager."

We crest the top of the hill and find a flat spot in the emerald-green grass. Reno sets down the cooler before taking the blanket from me, shaking it out, and spreading it on the ground. "Did she have more kids?"

I sink down onto the blanket, and Reno sits beside me with his legs bent, elbows on his knees. My fingers itch to touch that swirl of hair over his forehead, but I manage to control my urge.

"Not with any of the other husbands, but apparently, she and my dad hooked up and she ended up pregnant. Again. So he married her. Again."

"This is like a damn soap opera," he says with a chuckle.

"No shit. So shortly after I turned fourteen, Xander was born and two years after that, they had Jordan."

"And did Delphine stick around?"

My lips roll in between my teeth, and I shake my head before lying back on the multicolored blanket. "Why don't we look at the clouds now?"

Because in the words of Forrest Gump...

That's all I have to say about that.

Chapter 9

Juliette

Hump me like a ladybug

Reno's eyes stay on my face for a long moment, but he doesn't ask me any more questions. Instead, he stretches out on his back beside me and sweetly links his fingers with mine.

"Enthrall me with your cloud acumen, Juliette McNamara," he says.

With the vastness of the sky above me and a hulking hockey player beside me, I relax. "The fluffiest clouds are called cumulus, and they're the best for finding shapes. Like those over there," I say, pointing up at a collection of bright white clouds against the brilliant blue of the sky.

"What kinds of shapes?"

"Anything." I swivel my head toward him, and he does the same. "You've really never found shapes in the clouds before?"

"No, and now I feel wholly inadequate," he says wryly.

"It's okay. I've got you," I tell him, and his eyes soften on mine, glistening like pale emeralds, and *is he closer than he was a few seconds ago?* Dragging my gaze away, I point to a long cloud on the right side of the grouping. "What do you think that one looks like?"

"Ummm, a white blob?"

I laugh. "No, use your imagination, silly."

"Why don't you help me out with the first one since I'm a newbie?"

I study the pale fluff. "Hmm, I think that one looks like a sexy bunny."

A laugh bursts from Reno's mouth, and it's deep and seductive. "A sexy bunny?"

"Yeah. You can see the ears there." I trace them with my index finger in the air. "And he's lying on his side like this."

Releasing his hand, I turn on my side and strike a pose, resting my jaw on my fist. "It's like he's saying, 'Hey, ladies.'" I wiggle my eyebrows for effect.

Reno mirrors my position and, in his best Joey Tribbiani voice, says, "I'm Sexy Bunny. How you doin'?"

That makes me giggle. "Exactly. It's like a whole new world opens up in the sky when you set your mind free to imagine."

His lips crook up into a devastating smile. "You really are a dreamer, aren't you?"

"Does that bother you?" I ask in a feathery voice that I've never heard come from my mouth before.

"Not a bit. I like it." He brushes the backs of his knuckles down my upper arm, and my entire limb feels like it's been doused in lava... in a good way, not in an *I'll be spending the foreseeable future in the burn center* way.

"Good because other than me undergoing a complete personality transplant, I don't envision it going away anytime soon." And since he seems to be okay with touching, I reach up and smooth that glossy curl between my forefinger and thumb. It's as soft as it looks, like rich silk against my skin.

"You should never change for anyone, Juliette." Reno's voice goes a bit raspy, and my name on his lips is a soothing melody. "You make me want to dream with you."

Flipping hell. He is seduction personified in a six-foot-something frame of muscle and sexuality.

"Anyone can dream," I tell him. "Why don't you go solo on the next cloud analysis?"

He makes a little hum of agreement and rolls onto his back but not before sliding his arm beneath my head. It's a smooth-as-hell move, but I allow it, resting the back of my head against his biceps. His big, muscular, strong, hard, delicious biceps. I'd wager a month's salary that Reno Swain's upper arms could give those veiny forearms a run for their money.

"What are you doing?" he asks when I pull out my phone and snap a quick picture.

"Getting a pic of Sexy Bunny. I want to remember him forever," I say dramatically.

Reno laughs. "Send it to me too." He rattles off his number, and I program it into my phone before sending the photo.

For the next few minutes, we stare silently up at the sky until he points to a misshapen oval cloud. "That one looks like the Grinch's head," he proclaims. "See that little tuft on the top that looks like his hair?"

"That's a good one," I praise, and for a long while, we lose ourselves in the clouds, the left side of my body pressed against his right side. We manage to find Tony Soprano, a Big Mac, a bird smoking a cigar, and two very cheeky ladybugs having sex.

"Who knew ladybugs liked it doggy style? I would have taken them as missionary fans," Reno muses as we regard the rounded shape that appears to be mounting a similar one.

"Oh, the wonders of the animal kingdom," I laugh. "Cloud gazing isn't usually so... erotic."

"Maybe it's the company," he ventures, pivoting his head to look at me. All softness is gone from his eyes, replaced with flinty green fire. As if our movements have been choreographed, we both roll until we're facing each other.

"Perhaps it is. I've never cloud gazed with a man before."

Reno lets out a low growl and grasps my hip, hauling me closer with the ease of moving a stuffed animal. "Come here, dream girl."

And *ohhhhh.* That's a really good nickname.

Our bodies are pancaked together, and he's all hard muscle and warm skin when I rest one hand on his broad shoulder. His forehead tilts forward to touch mine.

"Can I kiss you, Juliette?"

I enter my Marilyn Monroe era when my breathless reply leaves my mouth. "I'd be disappointed if you didn't."

His lips curve into the hint of a smile before they brush across mine like a whisper. Then he pulls back, his eyes exploring every inch of my face like he's trying to memorize me. I do my best to hold back my frown. That is *not* what I expected when he asked to kiss me. I was hoping for some tongue action with a side of groping. Or maybe I was wishing he'd hump me like a ladybug, which is honestly the most bizarre statement I've ever thought.

"Reno..." I start, and his eyes drop to my lips. *That's right, buddy. Focus on the target zone.*

"Shhh, dream girl. Just let me look at you for a second," he murmurs.

Oh. Well. Alrighty then.

His hand trails from my hip and up my arm, leaving a path of hot goosebumps on my bare skin. Then he cups the side of my neck, his thumb drawing ovals against my jaw. I'm mesmerized by his eyes moving over every inch of my face. I've written about characters being eaten up by someone's gaze, but I'd never experienced it in real life. Until now.

Until Reno.

He's so intense, his irises darkening as he takes me in. His voice is a rumble that I can feel as much as I can hear it. "You are... so beautiful, baby."

If not for his big hand spanning my neck and lower face, holding me in place, I think I could melt through the blanket and be swallowed up by the earth.

Then his mouth is on me, lips pulling against mine with tender sucks as his fingers close around the back of my neck. It's a show of possession and dominance, and I'm not complaining about it a bit.

When his tongue slips out and seeks entrance against the seam of my mouth, I open for him, welcoming the glide of his tongue over mine. We let out simultaneous groans, and I feel my nipples pebble through the thin fabric of my top.

My hand slips around his waist, and I anchor our bodies together with my palm against his back. When I feel him harden against my stomach, my brain short circuits with little sizzles and pops that seem to override any rational thoughts. But who the hell needs pesky-ass thoughts when you're kissing Reno Swain?

I arch my back to press my belly against his length, and *oh*... What a length it is. Even beneath our layers of clothes, I can feel that he's... substantial. The noise he makes from the back of his throat vibrates into my mouth, a feral hum wrapped in lust and need.

Gliding his hand down my spine, Reno brushes briefly over my ass on his way to my knee, which he grasps and pulls over his hip. His thick cock nestles between my legs, directly against my heated center, and my hips move of their own accord in small, pulsing thrusts.

I've never been so attracted to a man in my entire life. I've never met a guy and instantly wanted to take him to bed. It usually takes a few dates so I can get to know him better, but what I do know of Reno Swain, I'm drawn to. On top of being hotter than a Hemsworth, he's also sweet and funny, a man I can laugh and joke with.

Our chemistry bursts around us in lively bubbles, and my hand ends up in his soft curls as he deepens the kiss. Reno is a stellar kisser, not too wet, not too eager, only a strong confidence that turns me right the hell on. But I want more. *Need* more.

With a little moan, I tug at him and roll to my back. He follows without complaint, wedging his hips between my thighs as he covers me with his big body.

Our tongues twist and dance as our lower bodies segue into a slow rocking motion that positions the head of his dick directly against my clit. I draw my knees up and lock my ankles around his waist as he sets a rhythm. Forward. Back. Circle.

Reno pulls back with a long, delicious suck before pressing soft kisses to each corner of my mouth.

"Is this okay?" he asks, those stunning green eyes glued to mine.

Answering his question without words, I rub against his hardness in a dirty grind that draws a low groan from his chest.

"Fuck, baby. I've never needed someone like this," he says, mirroring my thoughts from a couple minutes ago. Thankfully he doesn't stop that forward, back, circle motion that's driving me wild. "You're making me lose my mind."

"You're not the only one," I pant. Damn, I'm seriously close to coming already. "This is even better than in my fantasies."

Realizing what I'd just said, I start to backtrack when the biggest grin covers Reno's face. "You fantasize about me, dream girl?"

My eyes roll away so I don't have to look at his damn handsome face. "Yes, okay? Are you happy? I thought about you as inspiration while I was writing yesterday."

I didn't think it was possible, but his cock seems to thicken between my legs, as if my admission turns him on. "Please tell me it was a sex scene."

Hearing the word sex from his lips is an aphrodisiac for me, and I lift my hips from the blanket. "Can we stop talking about this and get back to what we were doing before?"

He rests on one arm and uses his other hand to gently grip my jaw until I can't help but meet his eyes. "Tell me."

"They were spicy scenes," I admit.

"Do you need more... inspiration?" That question is accompanied by a firm thrust against my sex that almost pushes me over the edge.

"Yes. Please," I breathe.

Reno tilts my head to the side and kisses his way across to my ear. "What's your next sex scene about?" The scrape of his teeth across a particularly tender spot on the side of my neck has my eyes rolling back in my head.

"He's going to hump her like a ladybug," I pant.

"Aha, got it. I think ladybug is the new doggy," he murmurs with a chuckle against my flesh. "I'm confident I can help you with that."

Oh, I'll just bet you can, I think. Reno's hip action is nothing short of elite, and I'm sure he could fuck a woman until she went cross-eyed.

Speaking of hips, he rolls his and drags his length up and down my denim-covered slit, and a shudder passes through my entire body. I'm so wet, I'm probably leaving a damp spot on the front of his charcoal cargo shorts, but I find it hard to care because...

"Reno, I'm almost there," I whimper, desperate to tip over the edge of my orgasm and—

Suddenly he's gone, and my confused body aches for his weight on top of me again. Prying open my heavy eyelids, I find him stretched out beside me, breathing heavily through gritted teeth.

"Someone's coming," he tells me.

"And it was almost me," I snipe a second before I hear voices coming up the trail. Then I giggle. "Oh, you mean coming, not *coming*."

He gives me a sardonic grin and sits up, tugging at the hem of my top, which has ridden up from all the activity. Then he reaches for two bottles of water from the cooler, twisting off one lid and handing it to me before rolling the other cool bottle across his forehead.

I sit up and take a long swig as Inge and Chris appear, followed by Victoria and Elvis. "Hey!" I say a little too chirpily—because they came within seconds of seeing my O-face—but they don't seem to notice.

"Oh, hey, Juliette. We didn't know anyone was up here," Victoria says, glancing at her husband. "We can go somewhere else."

"No, that's okay," Reno says quickly, standing and picking up the cooler to hold in front of his dick, which appears to be trying to Hulk-smash its way out of his pants.

He holds out a hand to help me stand. "Yep, we were about to leave anyway, but I'll see you guys tomorrow night." I bend to pick up the blanket, and when I stand, I catch Chris's eyes on me. More specifically, on my backside.

"Looking forward to it," he says, very obviously checking me out. *In front of his wife.*

Forcing a tight smile, I roll the blanket into a ball and hold it in front of my body as we wave goodbye and Reno leads me toward the trail.

We walk for a few minutes, both of us silent, which is weird for me. I tend to talk a lot.

I don't want to mention the ogling. I mean, what if I imagined it? That would make me sound conceited. But did Reno notice too? Is that why he's being so quiet? I relax my face, push the thoughts out of my mind, and think of a different subject.

"Which movie do you think has the best music soundtrack?"

Reno seems startled from whatever headspace he was in, and as the trail widens, he pauses to let me catch up to him. His hand captures mine, and his warmth calms my frayed nerves a bit.

"*Top Gun*," he says without much thought, and I laugh.

"That's such a dude answer, but I can't argue. I actually hated the song 'Take My Breath Away' when I first heard it, but then I saw it in the movie, and it changed my whole perspective."

"What's your favorite soundtrack?"

"I don't have a favorite. It really depends on my mood, but *Footloose* and *Forrest Gump* are high on my list."

"Both solid choices," he says with a sage nod. "Would you make me hand in my man card if I said I love the music from *Dirty Dancing*?"

I laugh. "Trust me. Your man card is secure." There's no denying that Reno Swain is innately masculine, and not the toxic kind of masculinity. He gives off a protective vibe without being overbearing, and he's gentlemanly without coming across as patronizing.

And he's sexy as hell. I picture our naked bodies tangled up in the sheets while we go at it ladybug-style.

If that's even what Reno still wants. I glance down at his shorts. He's softened a bit, but there's still a pretty firm semi happening down there, and he occasionally hitches his step as if he's trying to subtly readjust.

"You want to come to my cottage?" I ask when we reach our cozy little area of the island, and his answer comes quickly.

"Hell yes." His lips twist to the side. "I mean, if you want me to."

"I do," I tell him, and he takes the blanket from me while I unlock the door. As soon as we're inside, he tosses the cooler and blanket aside and backs me against the door.

"I signed you up at my table for dinner," he tells me, bracketing my head with his forearms. "We have three hours until we have to leave. How many orgasms do you want your female character to have?"

He says it with all the confidence in the world, like whatever number I spout, he can achieve it. I lift one brow and shoot back with another *Mean Girls* quote.

"The limit does not exist."

The warmth of his chuckle gusts across my lips. "I look forward to finding out what your limits are, dream girl." He steps into me, his body hard and hot against mine. "I liked spending time with you today."

I tilt my head back against the door and look up into his pretty green eyes. "I liked it too."

Reno cradles the side of my face in his big palm and strokes his thumb over my bottom lip. "I just want to make sure we're on the same page. I'm not looking for anything serious."

"I'm not either," I assure him, nipping at the pad of his thumb. "Just a fun island fling."

And it wouldn't work out anyway because he lives in Denver, and I live in Texas. He still hasn't mentioned his last name, and I haven't let on that I recognize him. If he values a bit of anonymity, I don't mind giving that to him. I'm sure he deals with enough craziness in his career.

He leans forward and kisses my lips softly. "Good. I don't want you to think it's about you. I think you're funny and beautiful, and if it weren't for your lifestyle, I would definitely want to pursue something with you outside of a vacation fling."

My heart sings and then stutters over one word. "What do you mean my *lifestyle*?"

Reno frowns a little. "You know, all this," he says, circling his hand in the air to take in the cottage. The cottage I'd booked as a writing retreat. Is he talking about my books?

"Are you judging me for the spicy sex stuff?" I ask, a bit of a bite to my tone. I detest people who put down others for what they read. Or write.

His eyes widen a little. "No, not judging at all. People are free to do what they want. I just don't want to be involved... personally."

I. Am. Fur-i-ous.

Placing my hand on his chest, I take two giant steps forward, pushing him back. "You know what? I think I want you to leave."

He jerks his head back in surprise and reaches for me, but I swivel away and yank open the door. "Juliette, I swear, I'm not trying to be an asshole here. Surely you understand that not everyone is into that."

"Yep, totally understand. But I don't want to be involved with those kinds of people... *personally*." I throw his sentiment right back in his face with a sour smile on my lips and a sweeping gesture of my hand toward the door.

He looks crestfallen, but what did he expect? That he could insult my *lifestyle* and I'd be okay with it? I certainly wasn't looking for any kind of relationship either—especially not with a hockey player—but he didn't have to get all self-righteous on me.

Reno walks out onto the small porch and turns to face me, something akin to remorse on his face. "I'm really sorry, Juliette. I didn't mean to hurt your feelings. I thought we could just have, you know, a bit of fun doing the inspirational thing for your book." He lifts his hands and lets them fall in a gesture of confusion.

Keeping my hand on the doorknob, I step into the doorframe until we're almost chest to chest. "Oh, I'm feeling really inspired to write right now. In fact, I'm going to write a chapter where the woman kicks out the closed-minded jerk who went all judgmental on her."

I start to close the door, but on second thought, I pull it back open and leave him with one final parting shot. “You probably couldn’t handle what I like in the bedroom anyway.”

Then I slam the door in his stupid, stunned face.

The handsome asshole.

CHAPTER 10

Reno

Homey don't play that.

I STAND IN BEWILDERED silence for minutes. What the actual fuck just happened?

Through the door, I can hear Juliette's footsteps stomp across the floorboards so hard the cottage rattles. Raising my hand to knock on the door, I lower it, raise it again, and finally let it fall to my side.

Maybe she needs some time to cool down. No, she *definitely* needs time to cool down.

An angry Juliette McNamara was a force. A beautiful, captivating force with aqua-blue eyes that seemed to flash with a life of their own. My cock grows an inch in my pants, and I glare down at my crotch.

"What the fuck is wrong with you?" I ask him, but he's unashamed. "Read the room, man. It's not going to happen."

But why? That was the question that came from both my big and little heads. I was just trying to be honest with Juliette before we started so there weren't any unreasonable expectations afterward. But I'd inadvertently gone and insulted her.

I stare at the door for another minute, willing it to open. Of course it doesn't, so I turn and head next door to cottage five. Once inside, I go straight to my bedroom and flop onto the comfortable bed.

Goddamn, she was sexy when she got riled up... the pink in her cheeks... the fire in her gorgeous eyes. I like a woman with a backbone, and Juliette definitely has that. But she's also sweet and thoughtful, and I like that side of her too. She's easy to be with. It's almost effortless.

The woman next door is on my mind when I fall into a restless sleep. Two hours later, I wake up feeling like shit, but I pull my carcass from the bed and take a shower. My stomach makes its needs known, so I dress and head for the dinner restaurant with a renewed sense of purpose.

Maybe she'll show up for dinner. It's a completely delusional thought, given her anger earlier, but I can't help but wish. My breath catches each time a blonde enters the dining room, and then it puffs out in disappointment when it's not her.

I have no idea what I even eat. By the time the waiter brings my dessert, my thoughts are still on Juliette. Is she okay? Has she eaten anything?

Plastering a smile I don't feel onto my face, I say, "My dinner partner was unable to make it. Would it be possible to get her food delivered to her cottage?"

"Of course, sir. What would she like?" He whips out a slim menu on a small black board and passes it to me. I read over the selection of steak, chicken, vegetarian pasta, and a variety of seafood dishes. Fuck. I don't know.

Glancing down at my own plate, I assume I had the shrimp since there are discarded tails there, though I don't remember eating them. I have the impression it was good though.

"Let's do the shrimp and cheese grits. Italian dressing on the salad."

"Excellent. And for dessert?"

My gaze drops to the bottom of the menu. "The seven-layer chocolate cake." Sweet and decadent, just like the woman I can't stop thinking about.

"And will you be taking it with you, or would you like us to deliver it?"

More than anything, I want to take it to her, but she might very well dump it over my head if I arrive on her doorstep.

"You can deliver it to cottage four. And ask whoever delivers it not to mention that I ordered it. Just tell them to say they're bringing it as a courtesy since she didn't show up for her reservation."

Juliette will see right through that flimsy excuse, but maybe she'll still eat it if she doesn't know for sure. She needs to eat something.

Once I'm back at my cabin, I sit on the couch and pull up the airline's number on my phone. I stare at it. And stare at it some more, my finger hovering over the call button.

Tomorrow is Wednesday, the day I should be flying off this island. I should just hit that button and ask the airline to change my flight. The ringing of my phone startles me, and I bobble the damn thing before catching it. Turning it over, I see that it's my mother calling.

"Hey, Ma."

"What's wrong, honey?"

My mother, ladies and gentlemen. Two words from my mouth, and she knows something's up.

I can't exactly tell her about Juliette because what is there to tell?

Hey, Ma. I'm at a swingers' resort, and I saw this gorgeous woman who made me jack off on my porch, and then we had two meals together before going cloud gazing. We saw a sexy bunny, and by the way, have you ever seen two ladybug clouds going at it in the sky? Completely fascinating. Anyhoo, I kissed her, and for the first time in a long while, I thought about more. But she's a swinger, and you know homey don't play that. When I tried to be honest with her, she got pissed off and kicked me out of her cottage, and I'm not even sure what I did wrong. But I can't get her off my mind, so I sent food to her room. Because I'm worried about this woman I've known for two days. What's up with you?

I scratch that well-formed response and go with my other truth. "I'm being traded, Ma. To Dallas."

There wasn't even the hint of hesitation. "Okay, so we'll move to Dallas. I'm tired of all this cold weather anyway."

Let me just say for the record: I. Love. My. Mother.

"What about your job?" I ask.

"I'm sure there are abusive assholes in Texas too. I'll find a shelter or facility there that's in need of a good counselor."

I can't help the burst of laughter from my lips. "I love it when you cuss, Ma."

"I can curse," she insisted in her sweet voice. "Just last week, I said the s-word when I stubbed my toe."

"Oh nooo! Not the dreaded s-word!"

"Not everyone can be a potty mouth like you," she responds with a sniff. "And if I can't find another job, I'll just be a couch potato and live off my rich son."

That makes me laugh again because she would *never*. "Nothing would make me happier than that. I'd love for you to retire and relax a bit."

"I don't want to retire. What I do makes me happy. You know," she adds thoughtfully, "I just assumed you'd want me to move with you. If that's not what—"

"Ma, of course I want you to move with me. We're the Dream Team, remember?"

"In it together," she replies like she always does, and I suddenly feel better about the move. If my mother can take this change in stride, then I need to suck it up and do the same.

"I'll start looking for a place for Gramps."

"Reno," she says hesitantly, "I mean, it's totally up to you but... well..."

I try not to sigh in exasperation. "Spit it out, Ma. What do you need?"

"Dallas is a bit bigger than Denver, so it might be nice to live in the suburbs instead of in the city. You know, a bit less hustle and bustle?"

"I'll see what I can do. Would you like a house or another apartment?"

"Ooh, a house would be lovely. It would be nice not to have people only a wall away."

"Wouldn't you miss smelling Mrs. Garvey's cooking?" I ask teasingly. My mom's next door neighbor tends to use a lot of pungent ingredients in her recipes. Of course Ma never complains, but the amount of air freshener she uses daily could fumigate a small city.

"Getting away from that would be a plus," she says with a laugh.

"Good. I'll try to find us houses close to each other."

"You know my budget, right?" she asks anxiously.

"I do."

I'm already making plans to find her a nice fucking house and put a giant down payment on it so she'll have a very minimal monthly payment. Somehow I'll work it out with the realtor so my mom won't know.

I know better than to offer to buy her a house outright, even though doing so wouldn't even put a dent in my wallet. Ma asserted her independence over two decades ago, and I'd never want to take that sense of accomplishment from her.

"Well, I'm getting excited now," she says, her voice almost a squeal. "It will be a new adventure."

"I hope so, Ma."

"It will be," she insists, strengthening into mom-mode. "You're going to grab life by the horns and make it your own. If I can do it, you can too."

Something relaxes inside my chest, and I nod even though she can't see me. Switching hockey teams seems like nothing compared to what she went through when I was ten years old, and I need to stop feeling sorry for myself and do exactly what she said.

Grab life by the horns and make it my own. And I'm going to start by not leaving this island until I talk to Juliette McNamara and figure out where I went wrong.

"I love you," I say as my heart fills with emotion.

"I love you too, son. Oh, and I saw Gramps earlier. He was having a good day and said, and I quote, 'Tell Reno I hope he's getting some vacation nookie while he's there.'"

"That sounds like him," I chuckle. "Give him my love."

"I will." She pauses before saying, "Anything else you need to talk about?"

"No, Ma. That's all," I fib. "I was worried about the trade, but you made me feel better."

"That's my job," she chirps happily. Nothing pleases her more than helping other people, especially her family. "We've got this, Reno."

"Because we're in it together."

"We damn sure are, son."

I hang up with a smile on my face. Hearing a noise from outside, I peek out the front blinds to find a uniformed woman walking up the path toward the cottage next door. She knocks, Juliette answers, and the employee hands her the tray.

After a brief conversation, the blonde beauty glances over to my cottage, and I let go of the blinds and dip into a crouch beneath the wooden sill. *Shit. Did she see me?* When I hear footsteps again, I risk another glance to see the employee walking back up the path... without the tray.

She accepted the food. A sense of victory passes over me, and like a fucking psycho stalker, I stare out the blinds for thirty minutes until I see Juliette's door open again. She places the food tray on the porch table, and my heart turns into a bass drum when I see that the plates are empty.

Satisfied, I carry my phone into the bedroom, undress, and turn off all the lights except for the lamp beside the bed. Since I can't stop thinking of the woman next door, I pull up the reading app on my phone and look up Juli Mack. As I settle against the headboard, I scroll through her books and finally select one that looks good to me.

Then I begin reading.

Chapter 11

Reno

Groveling is best done on your knees.

I SLEEP IN THE next day since I'd stayed up reading till two in the morning. Juli Mack, a.k.a. Juliette McNamara, is a damn talented writer. The plot had blown my mind with its twists and turns. I'd even downloaded the next book in the series because I'm dying to know what happens with the next couple.

After eating a protein bar and doing my morning workout, I head down to *Swing On In* for lunch. When Juliette doesn't make an appearance, I have another tray of food delivered to her cottage.

Then I change into my navy swim trunks with a white tropical leaf pattern and head to the beach. Finding an open lounge chair, I settle in to read the next book in Juliette's series.

Two hours later, I reach a particularly spicy scene, and her words from yesterday pop into my head. *You probably couldn't handle what I like in the bedroom anyway.*

Fuck me, that was so goddamn hot. After reading her stuff, I think I know exactly what she likes in the bedroom, and I think I'm exactly the man to inspire her. My cock rages inside my trunks, and I set my phone down and close my eyes.

I've heard the term *one-handed read* before, and I completely understand the phrase now. More than once I'd had to take care of business while reading last night.

Not exactly something I can do out here on the beach, so I make my way into the ocean, hoping the cool water will help with my erection situation. I dive beneath the surface, and the water is so clear, I can see schools of brightly colored fish darting away from my intrusion into their world.

I should see if Juliette wants to go snorkeling. *Which would be a fine idea if she were actually speaking to me,* I think sardonically. After a long swim, I walk out of the water and shake my head to sling some of the wetness from my hair.

As I pass two men with their lounge chairs pushed close together, one of them says, "Um, excuse me?"

"Yeah, what's up?" I ask, and he pulls down his aviator sunglasses to reveal hazel eyes.

"This may sound weird, but... are you Reno Swain? The hockey player?"

I give the man a smile. "I am." He turns to his partner with an *I told you so* look, and I chuckle. I had seen a few people staring at me and figured they probably recognized me, but no one at this resort had mentioned it until now. "I'd appreciate it if you'd keep that on the down low though."

He mimed locking his lips and tossing away the key. "Your secret is safe with me. I'm a huge fan, by the way."

"Thanks, man. I appreciate it." We talk hockey for a couple minutes, shake hands, and then I go back to my spot.

Reclining the chair all the way, I lie on my stomach and read another eight chapters before calling it a day. On my way back up the sandy path to the resort, I remember that it's Wednesday, and Juliette had said we should wear pink. After mentally scrolling through the clothes I'd packed, I realize I hadn't brought anything pink, so I veer toward the main lodge.

In the gift shop, I purchase a pink polo with the *Pineapple Island Resort and Spa* logo on the chest and head to my cottage. I don't even know why I did that. I probably won't even see Juliette tonight.

That thought bothered me more than it should. I barely knew this woman and yet... I wanted to.

While rinsing off beneath the outdoor shower on my back porch, my eyes stayed glued next door looking for any sign of movement. Her light's on in what I assume is her bedroom, but otherwise, I see nothing.

Sighing, I close my eyes and lean my head back to rinse the salt water from my hair. Then I strip off my shorts and turn beneath the spray, washing off thoroughly before grabbing a towel from the rack and wrapping it around my waist. I'll take a better shower inside, but I hate the dry feeling on my skin after getting out of the ocean and wanted to at least clean the salt and sand off me.

Once I've dried a bit, I toss my shorts over the railing before going inside and hanging up my new shirt. When my phone pings with a text, I almost trip over my own feet to get to where I'd tossed it on the bed. My head gets tangled in that drapey shit that's hanging from the posts of the bed, and I curse until I manage to free myself.

It's not from her. I try not to feel disappointed that it's my friend and teammate, Marcus.

Marcus: Hey, I'm with Lane. Got a minute to FaceTime?

Me: Yeah, hit me up.

A few seconds later, we're connected, and I smile at my buddies.

"Whoa, dude. You are tan," Lane drawls. "You're almost as dark as me."

I glance down and see the sharp demarcation of my tan line around my waist as I lean back against the dresser. "Yeah, I got some sun today."

"You're not naked are you?" Marcus asks, and I slowly lower my phone down my bare abdomen, singing a little burlesque tune as I do. He covers his eyes and groans in misery. "God, please make it stop."

I laugh and raise the phone back to my face. "Kidding. I have a towel on. I just got back from the beach."

"How is the resort?" Lane asks. "Is it nice?"

"Oh, it's very nice," I say, lifting an eyebrow as I lead up to the bombshell I'm about to drop on them. "It's also a swingers' resort."

Eyes widen and mouths gape on my phone screen. "You've gotta be fucking kidding me," Marcus breathes. "Your ex booked your *honeymoon* at a *swingers' resort?*"

"Yup. Sure did," I assure him.

Lane shakes his head, lips turning up into a sneer. "That's some next level fuckery right there." He chuckles. "Not that I wouldn't trade places with you in a heartbeat. Unlike you, I'm not opposed to group activities."

Marcus strokes his stubble thoughtfully. "Has anyone recognized you? Because I'm not sure how this would play out in the press."

"I think a few people have, but only one guy has come right out and asked me. I don't think it will be a problem because everyone here seems pretty chill." I shrug. "It's like they respect other people's privacy like they want theirs respected."

"I can see that," Lane muses. "If they blab that you're there, they have to admit that they went to an adult resort as well."

"So I'm assuming you're not... participating?" Marcus asks.

"I'm not."

My friends eye each other. "He hesitated," Lane points out.

"I did not hesitate," I insist.

They ignore me. "I definitely sensed some hesitation there," Marcus notes.

"Uh-huh. It was like *pause - I'm not.*"

Their gazes return to me, and I roll my eyes. "Fine. There's a woman here that's caught my interest."

They lean forward, faces as eager as junior high girls at a sleepover. "Tell us."

Rubbing a hand over my still damp hair, I say, "Her name is Juliette, and she looks like a fucking Barbie doll." Lane rolls his hand to indicate that I should continue. "She's pretty amazing. She has this personality that's so sweet and funny."

"And what are you going to do about it?" Marcus asks with a smirk.

"We hung out yesterday and made out for a while. I thought things were going great—headed in a certain direction, you know—but we had a... disagreement or something when we got back to her cottage." I scrub at my temple with my fingertips. "Fuck, I don't even know what went wrong, and now I can't get her off my mind."

Lane's forehead creases. "What kind of disagreement?"

I walk them through our conversation, and the furrows in Lane's face grow deeper. "Let me get this right. You actually told this Juliette chick if it wasn't for her lifestyle, you'd be interested in having something with her after your vacation?"

"Well, yeah. I was trying to be up front with her so she didn't have any expectations, and she said she didn't want anything serious either. She seemed to want me as much as I wanted her. And then..." I shrug because I'm still a bit perplexed by her reaction.

My buddies share another look before turning back to me. Marcus smirks. "Dude, you know you're not supposed to chew all the gummies at once, right?"

Lane smacks him in the chest with the back of his hand. "You idiot, he's on an island. He's obviously smoking the wacky weed, not eating it."

"I'm not on any mind-altering substances," I grind out. "What the fuck are you two talking about?"

Marcus nods at Lane to take over, and he does. "You went too far, see? You should have made it clear that you wanted a vacation fling and not a relationship. *Then you shut your mouth.* Where you fucked up was bringing her lifestyle into the mix."

"Agreed," my other friend says. "It comes across as judgy, which we all know you're not. People get insulted when you criticize their choices."

"I wasn't criticizing," I protest.

"We know," Marcus soothes, "but it probably came across as *I would totally like you enough to pursue something if it wasn't for this flaw.*"

My frustrated grumble vibrates my chest. "That's not what the fuck I was trying to do. I was trying to explain why we had to be temporary without hurting her feelings. I wanted her to understand she's, you know, beautiful and sweet and worthy, but I guess I ended up doing the opposite." I tug at the back of my neck.

"You were doing the right thing," Lane says quietly. "You just went about it wrong."

I clench my molars until the grinding becomes audible. I hate myself for hurting Juliette's feelings.

My friends share another of those looks that are starting to get on my damn nerves, and Marcus's lips twitch. "Why do you even care what her lifestyle choices are? It's not like you're going to marry her or something. People have vacation flings all the time, and as long as both of you are on the same page, you should be fine. Whatever she does on her own time is her business."

"You're right," I agree as hope fills my chest. "I need to go talk to her and try to explain."

"Maybe she would understand if you explained... *everything*?" Lane suggests pointedly, and I try not to grimace.

"I'll see how it goes." I give them a grateful smile. "Thanks, guys. I think I just needed a fresh pair of eyes and ears. I appreciate you both, but I really need to run. I've got some groveling to do."

"One last thing," Marcus says before I disconnect.

"What's that?" I ask, a little impatient as a plan begins to take shape.

A sly smile creeps across his face. "Remember that groveling is best done on your knees."

I bust into the gift shop as the clerk is counting the money in her register.

"Oh, Mr. Swain," she says in surprise, her eyes dropping to my torso. "Is there something wrong with your shirt? It seems to fit well."

I glance down at the hot-pink shirt I'd thrown on after the quickest shower in history.

"No, it's fine. I just need some flowers." Gesturing to the cooler in the back, I ask, "Is it too late?"

The woman, whose name tag reads Karissa, smiles. "Not at all. Are these for Juliette?"

My eyebrows lift in surprise. "Oh, uh, yeah."

"I thought they might be. I saw you two having lunch together. She is such a sweetheart. Always a smile for everyone she meets."

Except for me right now.

We head to the glass case at the back and cool air hits my face when she opens the door. My eyes scan over the floral arrangements. They're all nice but not what I'm looking for.

"Do you have anything... bigger?" I gesture with my hands.

Karissa's lips twist to the side. "Hmmm, no, but what if we combine a couple of these into a bigger vase?"

"Yes!" I practically shout in agreement.

She giggles. "I just got some new ones today. Hold on."

I inspect the arrangements and choose two multicolored ones I really like before the clerk returns from the storeroom with two glass vases.

"We have this red one, which is super elegant, and then this aqua one with a pearlescent finish." She holds them both up for my perusal, and I point at the aqua one.

"That one. It matches her eyes."

Karissa flashes a knowing smile. "Fantastic. And which flowers would you like?" I point them out, and she beams at me. "Those match her personality perfectly. Just all bright and full of sunshine."

I help her carry everything into the storeroom and watch in fascination as she goes to work, rearranging the flowers and making a new bow with shiny purple ribbon.

"How's that?" she asks, stepping back and tilting her head in appraisal.

"It's a masterpiece," I assure her. "Thank you so much for staying late and doing this. Can you charge it to my room? Cottage five."

"Certainly, and I'm happy to help. I love seeing new love blossom."

Her brown eyes go all dreamy, and I don't have the heart to tell her these aren't *love* flowers. They're more like *I'm in the doghouse* flowers.

I pick up the vase and give the sweet clerk a side-hug. "Thanks again, Karissa. This is even better than I imagined."

As I walk out, I hear her say, "Go get her, tiger!"

Chapter 12

Juliette

No other cocks need apply.

Popping another cherry Starburst into my mouth, I read over the romantic scene I'm working on. I've eaten at least a pound of my favorite candies over the past day. I really should get on some kind of workout program, but I don't want to.

The result of me holing up in my cottage for the past twenty-something hours produced eleven chapters. Damn good ones too. My argument with Reno sparked something in my brain, and I've been a writing machine since I booted him out.

Drawing on the anger and disappointment, I pounded out some of the best emotional scenes I'd ever written. I'm still polishing this one, but I sent the others to Holly and Eden a few hours ago.

A twinge jabs my lower back, and I decide I'm done for a little while. Standing from the desk chair in the corner of my bedroom, I stretch my hands above my head, lengthening my spine. It feels amazing after sitting for so long.

I'm supposed to go over to Chris and Inge's cabin at nine for game night or whatever they have planned, but it's only five now. I have plenty of time to take a walk down to the beach and then maybe grab a bite to eat.

A frisson of guilt pokes me in the gut. Someone's been sending food to my room, and I'm pretty sure it's Reno, even though I ditched him for dinner last night.

Stop it, Juliette. You have no reason to feel guilty. Reno Swain is a judgmental asshole who doesn't deserve your time. That little fact hasn't stopped me from replaying his lips on mine in an unending loop. I practically made a damn mental movie trailer out of our time on top of the hill.

After using the restroom, I search for my sandals. The right one is beside the back door, but the left one seems to have grown legs and walked away. Mumbling curses, I drop to my knees and search the floor, finally locating it beneath the bed.

With both feet now shod, I go to the back door and pause with my hand on the button when I hear water running. *Is that the toilet?* I traipse back to the bathroom and find that the toilet is fine and the noise seems to be coming from outside.

Peeping through the blinds, I have a perfect view of cottage five's back porch. More specifically, the outdoor shower. And even more specifically, *Reno Swain* in said shower.

He's wearing nothing but navy and white swim trunks, and his eyes are closed, head tilted back as he scrubs at his hair. While I watch like a stalkery little stalker, he rubs his hands over his ripped torso. The man is pure beefcake, with broad shoulders and a chest a woman could curl up on and take a catnap.

His chest has a bit of hair, which tapers down into the happiest little happy trail ever. I like hair on a man. Not like a bear on Rogaine, but I find a nice smattering quite masculine.

My eyes drop to those abs that look like they've been carved of tan granite. Sharp lines demarcate each muscle so clearly you can count them. So I do. There are eight of them. Eight!

I'm like the Count on Sesame Street. *Vun muscle I'd like to lick syrup from. Twooo muscles I'd like to lick syrup from. Threeee—*

Before I can get any farther, he drops his swim trunks.

And there's his penis. Yep. Right there. And the damn thing deserves its own zip code. It's not erect, but I can still see that his length and girth are impressive.

Forget all the dicks in my *Inspirational Cocks* folder. Reno Swain *is* my folder now. The whole damn thing. No other cocks need apply.

He rotates slowly, giving me a view of a muscular, creamy ass. *And it's not the only thing getting creamy*, my very filthy mind thinks as I squeeze my thighs together.

The show is over way too quickly, and I only get one more brief glance of his, *ahem,* frontal assets before he's wrapping a towel around his waist, covering what's hidden between those tan lines on his abdomen and upper thighs.

And can we just talk about the thighs for a second? I remove my fingers and let the gap close in the blinds, but I can still picture those thick quads and hammies that bunched beneath that golden skin as he turned in the spray of the shower. The man could crack my skull with his brawny upper legs, and I was surprisingly okay with that. I mean, who needs a skull when my brain is already mush?

No, Juli. You are mad at him, remember?

Yes, but maybe we could duct tape his mouth to shut him the hell up while we...

Absolutely not. He's a jerk.

Sighing, I exit cottage four without a backward glance at cottage five—and the penis and thighs that currently reside there.

When I return from my walk, I get a text notification from Holly.

Holly: Just read the latest. Who hurt you, babe?

I burst into laughter as I unlock my back door and enter my bedroom. Another message comes in before I can reply.

Holly: Never mind. FaceTiming you.

As I slip off my shoes and flop onto the bed, my phone rings, and I answer it, smiling at her beautiful face. "Hey, woman."

"Someone wanted to see his Aunt Juli," she sings, bending and picking up something... or more accurately, *someone*.

The most adorable child ever created pops onto my screen with a scream. "Chewyyyy!"

"Aidennnnn!" I yell back.

All his tiny teeth are visible when he laughs. He seriously has the best laugh, mouth open and emitting nothing but pure, childlike joy.

"My Chewy!" he insists, pointing at me. My nephew is thirteen months old and can't quite pronounce Aunt Juli, so I'm Chewy.

"I am your Chewy," I assure him. "And you're my Aiden."

He blows me about ten enthusiastic kisses in a row, which I return with equal fervor. Holly watches our interaction with a smile, her nose buried in his black curls that are streaked with umber.

Then, as if showing me so much love has completely tired him out, he leans back into his mother and yawns. "Night nights, Chewy," he tells me before closing his sweet brown eyes.

"Night nights, baby boy," I say quietly, but he's already snoozing.

"I swear, I've never seen another kid who can go to sleep at the drop of a hat," Holly says, readjusting her son onto her shoulder.

"Tell me what he smells like," I request, missing all the senses my little nephew brings to the table.

Holly presses her button nose into the light brown cheek of the toddler. "He smells soft, like baby lotion and..." She gives him a deeper sniff and scrunches her face. "And a little bit like wet dog. He helped me bathe Chester earlier."

I laugh. "Go lay him down. I'll wait."

The view on the screen switches to the ceiling of their home for a few minutes before she returns and picks up her phone. "I swear, I'm the luckiest mom in the world. Aiden is such a good sleeper."

"His eating is excellent too. He pretty much eats anything you give him."

Holly snuggles back against the couch. "He does. They always say if your first kid is easy, your second one will be a hellion. I'm sure this next one is going to refuse to eat anything and will want to party like a rock star all night long."

I freeze at the same she does, both of us realizing what she'd just said aloud. "*This next one?*" I repeat, excitement bubbling in my belly. "Holly, are you pregnant?"

"Shit." My sister-in-law face palms herself and groans, "Didn't mean to say that. Bubba and I wanted to surprise you when you got back. He's already picked out a T-shirt to give you and everything."

"I won't say a word, and I'll act surprised," I assure her, bouncing in place on the bed. "Eeeee, I'm so excited, Holly. Tell me everything."

"Well, I went to the doctor this morning for a regular checkup, and bam! He walked in and told me my urinalysis showed that I'm expecting. I almost fell off the table."

"How far along are you?"

"Haven't seen my OB yet, but Dr. Fergus estimated that I'm only about six weeks."

"Soooo, around January?" I ask, doing a quick calculation in my head. She nods. "Is Bubba excited?"

Her laughter is a bubble of happiness. "What do you think? He's about to freaking burst at the seams. He immediately called my OB's office and made an appointment for tomorrow, even though I'm a grown-ass woman who is capable of making her own doctor's appointments."

"He loves taking care of you," I say softly, loving the shit out of my brother right then.

Holly nods. "He does. He's such a nurturer. I'm a lucky woman."

"You are indeed. I hope I can find someone half as good as him one day." A bitter edge cuts through my next words. "But I'm sure I won't. I've been spoiled with awesome male figures in my life, and it will be hard for anyone to live up to them."

"There are still good men out there, Jules. You'll find someone," she says before turning the subject around. "So, I ask again, who hurt you? Because that was some angsty shit you wrote."

"You liked it?"

"Loved it. Very dramatic, but you managed to make it funny too. Anna's ranting monologue was epically hilarious."

"Thanks." Holly stares at me, waiting with arched brows until I blow out a long exhale. She's not going to let this go. "You know that guy I was telling you about?"

"Ah, the mystery man that you actually told me very little about? Sir Forearms?"

"That would be the one. We spent some time together on Monday, and then we went back to my cottage."

Holly lifts and lowers her shoulders one at a time in an anticipatory kind of dance. "Ooh, give me all the juicy details."

"Jesus, the man can kiss," I whine. "And he's so freaking gorgeous it almost hurts my eyeballs to look at him."

"And?" she asks with a hint of impatience.

"And he's an asshole. He insulted my *lifestyle.*"

My sister-in-law goes into indignant mode, her hazel eyes flashing. "What the hell does that mean? You're a librarian, for fuck's sake."

"Right? He was telling me he didn't want anything serious, and I'm totally fine with that," I say, tapping the center of my chest with my fingertips. "I'm not in the market for a relationship, and I let him know we were on the same page. Then he said he just wanted to make sure because outside of a vacation fling, he couldn't be with anyone in my *lifestyle*."

Holly shakes her head. "What's with all the lifestyle bullshit?"

"The only other thing he really knows about me is the writing gig, so I asked him if it was the spicy sex stuff that he didn't like." I lean forward and narrow my eyes. It still angered me to think about. "He said yes."

"Oh. My. God. What a prickface," Holly rants. "He probably couldn't handle a real woman anyway."

I giggle. "That's what I told him right before I slammed the door in his face."

"Good for you, girl. You don't need that kind of negativity." My friend cranes her neck forward, her eyes narrowing into squinty slits on the screen. "Uh, Jules. What is that?"

"What?" I swipe at my mouth and chin. "Do I have something on my face?"

"No, *that*. On the wall behind you." She jabs her finger vehemently.

I look up to see the metal decoration mounted above the headboard. "Oh that's a pineapple. The place I'm staying at is called Pineapple Island Resort and Spa, so there are pineapples everywhere. I have no idea why they're all upside down though."

Looking back at my phone, I see Holly sitting there with her mouth agape for a long moment. I'm about to ask her what's wrong when she throws back her head and lets out a laugh that's so loud, I'm surprised it doesn't wake up my nephew.

"What's so funny?" I ask, but she continues her hyena routine for another full minute. Tears stream down her face, which has turned an alarming mahogany color. "Holly!"

"Ju-li-ette," she gasps, my name coming out in three distinct syllables as she wipes at her face with her palms. "You are truly my most favorite person in the entire world."

"What about your husband and child?" I ask flatly, still not sure what the hell's going on with her.

She waves a hand absently. "Okay, fine. It's a rotating list, and since I don't have to change your diaper or share a bathroom with you after you've had a burrito-eating contest with the guys, you're currently in the lead."

"Gee, thanks," I deadpan. "Why do you find the pineapples so entertaining?"

"Jules, I hate to tell you this, but..." She takes a dramatic pause before announcing, "You, my dear, are at a swingers' resort."

My head jerks back in shock. "No I'm not."

Holly rolls her eyes. "Google what upside down pineapples mean."

Skeptical, I pull my laptop from the charger and rest it on my thighs. Thirty seconds later, I let out a gasp.

"Oh my god. Oh my... Holly! Oh my god! I'm at a swingers' resort!" The words come out at warp speed.

My eyes are glued to the computer screen, but I can hear her snicker from my phone's speaker. "I know, Jules."

I turn my gaze back to her, and she's not even trying to hide her amusement. "How did you know that stuff about the pineapples?"

"It used to be a kind of secret symbol for couples who swing to identify each other. Like an upside down pineapple welcome mat or door knocker. But I think it's pretty much common knowledge now."

"Common knowledge?" I shriek, swirling my finger toward my laptop. "I'm common, and I did *not* have this knowledge!"

Holly chuckles. "Juliette McNamara, you are anything but common."

"Great. I'm an uncommon dingbat," I mutter, turning my attention back to the article on my computer.

"You are an absolute sweetheart, Jules. Perhaps a tad dingy." She holds her fingers a half inch apart. "But in the most delightful of ways."

Reno had called me delightful too. I pull my thoughts from him and read about unicorns in the swinging community. "Ah, there are a group of women here who call themselves the Unicorn Unit. I'm guessing you know what a unicorn is?"

"It's usually a woman who enjoys playing with a couple. She's typically bisexual."

"I'm amazed that you know all this," I muse, bringing my eyes back to my sister-in-law, who is smirking again.

"Bubba and I may have dabbled in the lifestyle a bit."

"Dabbled?" I shout, feeling my brain attempting to explode into confetti. "You *dabbled*?"

Holly shrugs. "For about a year. We had a lot of fun but ultimately decided it wasn't for us."

"I feel like I really shouldn't know this information about my brother," I say, pretending to cover my ears.

She tilts her head to the side and gnaws the inside of her cheek. "You know, Jules, I'm thinking that Sir Forearms probably wasn't talking about your books." Making a little circle toward me with her index finger, she says, "I think he thinks you're... *a swinger.*"

My eyes practically pop from my head. "Oh shit, Holly. I think you're right. I thought it was weird that he used the word *lifestyle*, but now it makes sense." I squish my lids shut and massage my temples for a long moment. "But he's at this resort too, so why would he be concerned about swinging?"

Holly crinkles her nose in thought. "Dunno. Maybe he's just there to get his jollies for a few days but doesn't want that in his life on a permanent basis."

"I need to talk to him," I decide. Then another thought invades my brain, and I gasp. "Holy shit."

"What?"

"Holly, I got invited to one of the cottages for playtime tonight. I thought they were talking about board games or maybe a dart tournament or something."

My friend falls over onto the couch, absolutely losing her shit. "This is... absolutely... the best story... I've ever heard... in my fucking life," she gasps through her laughter. "Dart tournament. You would have gotten a bullseye for sure."

Her hilarity continues, and I can't help but join in because seriously, this is some funny shit. *How the hell did I get myself into this crazy mess?* When my sides begin to ache from laughing so hard, I blow out a long breath and compose myself, fanning my face with one hand.

"Okay, okay," I say as another giggle escapes. "What the hell do I do now?"

"First of all, you need to talk to Sir Forearms. Then you need to find whoever invited you to the party and explain the misunderstanding."

"They're going to think I'm a complete idiot," I groan.

Holly puts on a stoic face that I'm pretty sure is forced. "You're not an idiot. You were just unaware of something you've never been exposed to."

"Thanks, Holly," I say, appreciating her loyalty in the face of my humiliation. "Listen, I need to go fix all these... issues."

"Okay, babe. Keep me updated."

I narrow my eyes in warning. "Do not, under any circumstances, tell my brother about this."

"Oh, come on, Jules," she whines. "Just let me—"

"No!" I insist. "If you tell him, I will sneak into your house and paint the soles of all your Louboutins black."

Her face contorts in horror. "You wouldn't!"

"Oh, I would. You know how Bubba likes to tease me, and I don't need to give him any more ammunition. I'd never live this down."

"Okay, fine," she huffs, pursing her lips in a pout. "You don't let me have any fun."

"You'll live," I deadpan.

"And so will my Louboutins."

"As long as you don't tell. Otherwise..." I draw a slash across my throat in warning.

"Evil bitch," she mutters before blowing me a kiss. "Love you, crazy."

"Love you too."

After we disconnect, I spring from the bed with urgency, slipping my sandals on and heading for the front door. I need to find Reno immediately and explain this whole situation. And to find out exactly what he was talking about yesterday. If he wasn't judging my author career...

Slinging open the door, I rush out and run face first into... flowers? I stumble backward and almost fall on my ass when I feel a strong hand grip my upper arm to steady me.

"Whoa, Juliette. Are you okay?"

Rubbing my nose, I try to hide my surprise. "Reno?" He's on my front porch with a gigantic floral arrangement in a pretty aqua vase.

His face is as solemn as a judge's. "Yeah, I, um, I'm sorry about yesterday."

"I'm not a swinger," I blurt, and his eyebrows shoot upward as I go into full babble mode. "I booked this place online, and I had no idea about pineapples. I mean, of course I know about pineapples, but not the upside down ones and the symbolism behind that. My friend just told me, and I was shocked, and I'm totally not into that lifestyle. In case that's what you were thinking. Not that there's anything wrong with it."

"So you're not into swapping and sharing sexual partners?" he asks suspiciously, and I shake my head vehemently.

"Not at all."

Reno's lips curl into a slow smile. "Somehow, coming from you, that explanation makes perfect sense."

"I thought you were judging me because of the kind of books I write, and that really pissed me off."

His face falls. "No, I would never. In fact, I started reading your books last night." He gives me a shy smile. "I finished one and started on another. You're such a talented writer, Juliette."

I'm grinning so big, I feel like my face may crack in two. "Thanks. You really like them?"

"I really do. I'm reading your cowboy series and couldn't put them down. Spent the whole afternoon reading at the beach."

I know. I saw your tan lines.

My cheeks heat at the memory of naked Reno as he continues. "I hate Martin, by the way. What a douche."

A laugh escapes me at the scowl on his gorgeous face. "Everyone hates Martin, but he redeems himself in book four."

"Then I'll have to keep reading." Reno scrapes his teeth over his bottom lip as he holds out the vase filled with roses, dahlias, orchids, and a lot of other blooms I can't identify in a multitude of colors. "I wasn't sure exactly what I did wrong, but I got you flowers because I'd obviously hurt your feelings."

Melting. That was the only word to describe my insides because that's about the sweetest thing I've ever heard. He didn't even know what I was upset about, and he brought me apology flowers.

"Thank you," I tell him, taking the flowers and leaning forward to kiss his cheek. "These are my favorite color."

A little furrow appears between his eyebrows. "Which color is your favorite? There are, like, ten different ones."

I tilt my head. "All of them. It changes depending on my mood."

Reno laughs and shakes his head. "I'm always surprised by your answers. I never know what the hell you're going to say."

"I like to keep you on your toes," I tell him, backing up and allowing him into my cottage. He closes the door behind him. After taking a sniff of the flowers, I set them on the small dining table and turn, leaning my butt against the surface. "So, it was the swinging lifestyle you were talking about yesterday?"

He rubs a hand over the top of his messy dark hair. "Yeah. It's just not something I'm into."

"Then can I ask what you're doing here at this resort?"

A low chuckle rumbles from his mouth. "I guess I'm like you and ended up here accidentally. It's kind of a long story, but I'll tell you if you'll have dinner with me." His green eyes shine with something that looks like hope.

To my credit, I wait an entire five seconds before saying, "Yes. I'd like that."

Reno steps closer, trapping me against the table. Not that I'm complaining. He smells fantastic, a mixture of the ocean, flowers, and man.

Taking my face in both hands, he lays a soft, slow kiss on my lips, his tongue toying with mine briefly before pulling back. It's a seductive promise, his eyes blazing with hunger. And not for dinner.

"One hour. Wear something pink."

Then he brushes his thumb along my lower lip before turning and walking out the door. I stare dumbly, my entire face tingling like someone dumped a bottle of champagne over my head.

A smile pulls the corners of my lips up as I realize... It's Wednesday, and he was wearing a pink shirt.

Chapter 13

Reno

Life is too short to eat lemon Starbursts.

Once back in my cottage, I shower again and shave before changing into black pants and actually adding some product to my hair, which I normally don't do. Then I brush my teeth and make a call to the dining room to arrange for sommelier service. It's not included in the resort fee, but I give zero fucks about how much it costs.

Fifty-nine minutes after I'd left, I knock on the door of cottage four. I'm fully expecting Juliette to call out that she's not ready and to give her five more minutes. Which would mean thirty. At least that was always my experience with Leia.

All the air seizes in my lungs when Juliette opens the door dressed in a bright pink... thing. I'm ninety-nine percent sure it's called a romper, a one-piece outfit with shorts that show off legs that seem to go all the way up to her ears. The short ruffled sleeves cling to her upper arms, leaving her tanned shoulders bare and supremely lickable. A sheer pink skirt drapes from the back, and she's paired it with silver jewelry and heels, giving the ensemble a slightly fancier look.

Struggling to get my mouth to actually form intelligible words, I finally say, "You look absolutely gorgeous, Juliette." Okay, not the most poetic statement ever, but it's the truth, and she seems pleased with the compliment. She dips her chin and gazes up at me through her lashes.

"Thank you. You look really handsome." She fingers the collar of my shirt, the backs of her knuckles brushing against my throat. "I like you in pink."

I like you in everything. Though I'd like to see you in nothing.

Instead of voicing my dirty thoughts, I ask, "Are you ready to go?"

She grabs a small silver clutch from the table and turns back to me. "Ready."

I step back and let her exit onto the porch before I close her door and check to make sure it's securely locked. Her hand is warm and soft when she takes my elbow, and I guide us down the path to the lodge.

When we arrive, I give my name to the hostess, and she smiles. "Right this way, sir." As we follow her, I place my hand on the small of Juliette's back, gently stroking the long, blonde hair that feels like silk beneath my fingers.

"Your hair looks really pretty like this," I tell her, my mouth close to her ear as I hold out her chair for her. I don't miss the slight hitch of her breath.

"Thank you," she says as I round the ivory quartz table and take my seat across from her. It's a quiet, intimate spot near a window with a stunning ocean view. "I always wanted curls when I was growing up, but my hair has always been straight as a board."

"I was the opposite. I hated my curly hair as a kid and made my mom keep it short." Running a hand over the top of my head, I say, "Until high school when I realized girls like curls."

Juliette laughs. "Gave you a whole new outlook, huh?"

"Guess it did."

She looks around at the room with its hardwood floors and muted chandelier lighting. Candles and small pastel floral arrangements dot each table. "This is so nice. It's the first time I've eaten here."

"The food is good too. Are you hungry?"

"Starving. I've been focusing so hard on writing, I haven't made time to get dressed up and come down here." She lifts an eyebrow. "Though someone has been sending food to my room the past two days."

I flash her a chagrined smile. "I wanted to make sure you weren't hungry."

A woman in a dove-gray suit stops by the table and introduces herself as Liza, the sommelier. After chatting with her for a few minutes,

Juliette and I decide on a glass of Sicilian Bianco to start, a bottle of the Gaja Barbaresco nebbiolo for dinner, and a Riesling for dessert.

Once Liza departs, my dinner partner leans across the table, her aqua eyes wide as she whispers, "I have no idea what she was talking about. We could end up drinking vinegar for all I know."

I chuckle. "I'm not an expert, but I know a little about wines, and they'll be good."

She relaxes and wipes faux sweat from her forehead. "Whew!" Her eyes dart over my shoulder and then widen. "Oh crap."

Glancing behind me, I see a group of women being seated at a table. I'd noticed them around the resort, usually wearing unicorn headbands, though tonight they're dressed nicely for dinner, sans horns. I'm aware of what unicorns are in this community but wonder why Juliette has a problem with them.

"What's wrong?" I ask, turning with concern to my date, who seems to have shrunk down in her chair.

"A couple of those ladies invited me to a party tonight for *playtime*." She raises her eyebrows in significance. "Before I knew what kind of *playtime* they were talking about."

Hiding my smile behind my hand, I ask, "And I'm assuming you're no longer interested in going to the party?"

She shakes her head. "No, and I know I need to tell them, but I don't want to hurt anyone's feelings. I'm not exactly knowledgeable on the whole *etiquette of canceling on a group sex party* thing. How exactly do you say, 'Hey, I think you're really sweet, but I don't want to have sex with you?'"

I can't help my chuckle at that. She is so damn cute.

"I can see where that would be awkward, but I'm sure if you're just honest with them, they'll understand."

"You're right," she sighs, picking up her menu and staring down at it. "I'll be honest later. Right now I just want to blissfully stare at this menu and pretend like I haven't gotten myself into this pickle."

Smirking, I pick up my menu and read over it. "Would you like to split an appetizer?"

"Sounds good. I'm thinking of getting the prime rib for dinner with horseradish on the side. So maybe a seafood app?"

"Hmmm, the seared scallops?"

She peeps at me over the menu. "I love scallops. That sounds great." Then her eyes shoot over my shoulder and she quickly raises the menu to cover her face again.

Taking it from her, I put on my stern voice. "Juliette, I want you to enjoy our dinner, and you're going to be fidgeting the entire time if you don't get this over with. Just go talk to them."

She rolls her lips in and scrunches her nose. "You're right. I'll go. It'll be fine." Straightening her spine, she stands and brushes her hands over her hips. "Perfectly fine."

About a minute after she goes, someone drops off our wine and takes our orders. When I glance behind me, I see Juliette returning with a huge smile on her face.

"Everything good?" I ask, rising to hold her chair for her again.

Her blonde hair sways as she sits. "Better than I expected. We had a laugh about it, but it was like they were laughing *with* me, not *at* me, you know? They were so kind and understanding."

"Good," I say, taking my seat. "I ordered the food while you were gone."

"What did you decide on?"

"I'm getting prime rib as well."

Juli folded her hands beneath her chin. "You seem to eat pretty healthy when we've had lunch together. What's your guilty pleasure food?"

I pop an eyebrow. "My guilty pleasure food?"

"Yeah, you know... something you love that you really shouldn't."

"Cheetos," I say immediately, and she lets out that full-bodied laugh I like so much. It's not loud or annoying, just genuine.

"Oh my god. You're such a bad boy," she teases. "Regular or Flamin' Hot?"

"Either. I'm an equal opportunity Cheeto eater. What's your guilty pleasure?"

"Cherry Starbursts."

"Why just the cherry ones?"

Juliette shrugs. "Because they're my favorite. I found a place online where you can order an entire bag of one flavor. Life is too short to eat lemon Starbursts."

"Words to live by," I say, lifting my glass of wine, and she does the same. We clink and each take a sip.

"Mmm, that's good." She sets down her glass and tilts her head. "So tell me how you ended up here accidentally."

I take another fortifying drink of my wine before starting. "This was supposed to be my honeymoon trip."

Juliette's lips part, and she reaches for my hand, stroking her thumb across my knuckles. "I'm so sorry, Reno. What happened?"

Turning my hand over, I link our fingers together. It feels comforting, this simple act of hand holding.

"I'd been a happy bachelor for my entire adult life. I wasn't looking for anything serious, but a few years ago, my grandfather started showing signs of dementia. One day, a couple policemen showed up on my doorstep, letting me know he'd been found at a park wearing only his underwear. It was almost freezing outside, but luckily a nice man saw him and gave him his coat before calling the authorities."

"That's so sad," Juliette says, her mouth turning down at the corners. "But I'm glad someone found him."

"It could have been so much worse. Gramps had been married to my grandmother for around fifty years when she died. He seemed to go downhill quickly after that, or maybe it had been going on for a while before she passed, but no one noticed because Grandma kept an eye on him." I blink out at the ocean for a long moment before returning my gaze to my date. "I guess it made me rethink my life. They were so in love, and I realized I wanted a partner and not just meaningless hookups."

She nods. "That makes sense. Something like that can really change your perspective."

I give her a small smile. "It's not like I set out on a frantic wife search or anything, but my goals slowly began to shift. I actually began dating instead of just being..."

"A playboy?" she fills in with a smile.

"I was going to say man whore, but that sounds nicer," I admit with a chuckle. "I dated a few women, but no one really clicked. And then I met Leia at a party, and she was really nice and flirty. I asked her out, and our first date was good, so I asked her out again."

Juliette watches me in silence, but her thumb rubs a soothing line between my thumb and forefinger. She is so fucking beautiful, her makeup applied with a light hand. There's something pink and shimmery on her eyelids, and her lips are a glossy rose color.

I have to force myself from my Juliette-induced haze so I can continue. "I decided to date her exclusively, and she was all in. Things went really well, and after a year, I proposed."

We both take another drink of wine with our free hands, and I swirl my glass before setting it down. "That's when Leia started to change. All kinds of red flags began popping up, but I ignored them."

"What kinds of red flags?" the woman across from me asks in a soft voice.

"The wedding planning process became a nightmare. Despite coming from money, Leia had always seemed down to earth, but she became a bit of a Bridezilla. I convinced myself that after the wedding, things would go back to normal." I shake my head at my own stupidity. "Then she quit her job at the marketing firm where she worked, and she couldn't afford her apartment anymore."

Juliette's eyebrows pressed together. "Why did she quit?"

"She said she wanted to focus on making her special day the best it could be, and work was taking up too much time."

"*Her* special day?"

One corner of my mouth creeps up into a humorless smile. "Red flags, remember?" A sigh escapes me. "So I told her she could move in with me. That's when those flags started waving like crazy."

"But you still ignored them," Juliette says. There's no judgment in her tone. It's simply a statement.

"Yup. She became very critical of my work schedule."

"Well, you can't help that," my beautiful date says a bit indignantly.

"Exactly." *The NHL doesn't cancel games just because my fiancée wants to go to Aspen for the weekend,* I think bitterly. "My busiest time of the year is October through April, but Leia insisted she just had to have a fall wedding for the aesthetics—something about the colors and leaves and stuff—so she planned it for last September. I reminded her of how busy I'd be, but she said it was fine, and we could just put off our honeymoon until May."

I pick up my wine glass and stare into it before setting it back down without drinking.

"Then about six months before the wedding, she told me she wanted to try something before she got tied down."

Juliette's lips part on her sharp intake of air. "Tied down? She literally said *tied down*?"

"Her exact words," I confirm. "She told me she'd always wanted to try a threesome, and this would be her last chance to do it, and would I please be willing to give that to her?"

The aqua eyes across from me go round as saucers. "Wow. Okay."

"Yeah, I wasn't exactly comfortable with it. I'm not a prude by any means. I'd done that a couple times in the past but with casual hookups. The thought of sharing my future wife with another man didn't sit well with me." I scrape my bottom lip with my teeth. "But after a few weeks, I finally said yes. I wanted to make her happy."

"Oh god, Reno. That's..." Juliette takes a long drink of her wine. "I don't even have words."

A suited waiter appears beside us and sets down a sleek, rectangular turquoise plate between us. "Your seared scallops," he says. "I'll have your dinner out shortly."

"Thank you," I say, releasing Juliette's hand and instantly missing her soft warmth. We each put two scallops on our plate and take a bite. The meat is flaky and salty on my tongue, with a hint of sweetness.

"This is really good," Juliette says, meeting my gaze across the table. Her eyes are bright but soft at the same time. "You don't have to keep going if it's too painful."

Heaving out a long breath, I shake my head. "No, it's okay. I realize now that Leia and I weren't meant to be. It took me a while, but... I'm good."

Shockingly, I realize it's true. I'd harbored the resentment and hurt for so long, it practically became part of my skin, but somehow I'd barely thought of my former fiancée since I'd been here on this island. Like the pain had been scraped away by the Caribbean air.

And maybe by a certain sweet blonde with big blue-green eyes.

"Okay, so you went through with the threesome?" Juliette asks, and I nod. "How did you choose the other person?"

"I let Leia give me suggestions since it was her idea. She said she would feel better if it was someone we knew instead of finding a stranger online."

"I guess that makes sense, though I could see where that would have its own set of problems."

"Yeah, no shit," I scoff, thinking of the *problems* that had ensued. "She said she'd feel comfortable with Jeffrey, who was a friend of mine from high school. He'd been to our house numerous times, so she knew him pretty well."

Juliette took another bite without looking, her attention focused on me. "And was this Jeffrey willing?"

I glug back the remainder of my wine and place my empty glass on the table. "He was. Before that night, I sat down with Leia and told her this was only a one-time thing, just so she could have the experience she wanted. She completely agreed, so we set it up."

Reading the unspoken questions on Juliette's face, I went on. "We went through with it, and everything was going fine, you know... during."

"Was it difficult for you?" Juli asks.

"I mean, it was enjoyable to a point, but yes. It was difficult. I kept telling myself it was only one night, and then Leia and I could go back to how we were before. We were in the middle of *things* when she said she thought it would be totally hot if Jeffrey and I kissed."

Juliette's eyebrows practically shoot off the top of her head. "Are you..."

"No, I'm not bisexual, but Jeffrey is. I've never been attracted to men."

My date presses her lips together and shakes her head. "Reno, I'm all for pushing boundaries, but no one should ask you to touch or kiss someone you're not attracted to."

"Agreed. Jeffrey looked at me, like he was trying to determine if I was into it, but I just kind of nervously laughed it off and suggested that we concentrate on Leia since this was her fantasy."

"Good for you," Juliette says indignantly, the color rising in her cheeks. "I can't believe she had the nerve to ask that in the middle of everything. She never brought it up with you when you talked about it beforehand?"

"No, and it never even crossed my mind to set that boundary." Movement catches my eye, and I see our waiter headed our way. "I think our food is here."

He presents our food with a fancy flourish of his hand and then opens the wine, pouring a taste into a fresh glass for me. The bold flavor is warm and delicious, and I nod my approval before he serves Juliette and I each a glass.

Once he's gone, we dig into our food, garnering soft noises of satisfaction from both of us. I love watching Juliette eat. She fully enjoys her food, and it makes me enjoy mine even more.

After a few bites, she asks, "What happened after that night was over?"

"Afterward, I could still picture it in my mind, and I didn't like it at all, but I pushed it away and tried to move forward." I take a sip of wine. "Leia went into full-fledged wedding planning mode. We barely saw each other because she was always going to some tasting or a meeting with the planner."

As I add some horseradish to my au jus, I think about that time a little over a year ago. I was so confused.

"Leia started pulling away. We were no longer... intimate at all. I still stupidly thought things would get better once she had her perfect wedding. That she would be happy with just me." The bitterness in my voice was unmistakable.

Juliette winces. "Sounds like she's one of those women who cares more about the wedding than the marriage."

"You're not wrong. She started going nuts with the spending. Her parents are wealthy and have always given her pretty much anything she wanted, but even her father put a lid on it after she insisted on a pair of fifteen-thousand dollar shoes for the wedding."

Juliette chokes on a bite of asparagus and pulls her napkin to her mouth while she coughs. "Did you say fifteen thousand for a pair of shoes? That she would wear *once*?" she croaks. "You could buy a damn car for that."

That makes me laugh. "Exactly, but I bought them for her anyway." I bite into my bottom lip and shake my head at my stupidity. "I'm not sure what I was trying to prove by doing that."

Juliette reaches across the table and drifts her fingers across the back of my hand. "You loved her and were trying to make her happy."

I wince. "That's the thing. I'm not sure I was in love with her anymore. And it wasn't just the sex stuff," I say quickly. "We barely even talked, and when we did, it was only for her to ask me for more money. I started to realize Leia wasn't the person I thought I knew. For some reason, I still thought I should do my best to make it work. I mean, the damn wedding was only a few months away at that point, and then all the craziness would settle, right?"

"But it didn't?"

"Not really. Her dad had put a stop to all the frivolous spending, so I started footing the bill for whatever crazy thing she wanted. She commissioned ten ice sculptures for the reception." I shake my head and give Juliette a wan smile. "You don't even want to know how much those cost. It's fucking frozen water, for Pete's sake, but the artist apparently thought he was Michelangelo working with the finest Italian marble."

My date swallows a bite of her meat and shakes her head, blonde hair swaying around her shoulders. "Don't tell me. It will only spoil my appetite, and this prime rib is too good to waste."

"No doubt. The chef here is amazing," I say, taking another bite before continuing. "Anyway, I was looking forward to the big day finally arriving, and I'm a little ashamed to say I was more excited about it being over than actually being married to Leia."

"That's totally valid, Reno. Weddings can be stressful."

I nod my agreement. "I'd finally managed to get past the whole threesome thing. Did my best to make it just a distant memory of a wild night. But about a month before the wedding, she brought up doing it again since she didn't get the *full experience* the first time."

Juliette pauses with her fork halfway to her mouth. "But it was only supposed to be once. That's what you had discussed beforehand."

"I'm aware," I say flatly. "But Leia wouldn't let it go. She said she was really hoping there would be some sword crossing." I let out a humorless chuckle. "I'll be honest, I had to look that term up."

My date waves her hand beside her shoulder like she's answering a question in class. "Oh, I know that one. I may have been blissfully unaware of what upside down pineapples represent, but I know about crossed swords. It's a thing in the book community." Then her smile fades as the realization hits her. "She wanted you and Jeffrey to..."

"Yep," I confirm.

"But you're not bisexual. It's not like you can just change your sexuality on a whim because someone else wants you to."

"That's exactly what I told her. The next week, she changed her tune a bit and asked if we could do the threesome thing again, just one more time. No crossing of the swords involved."

"And you said no?"

I nod. "I said no. Actually, I said fuck no and stormed out of the apartment."

"I don't blame you," Juliette says, crossing her arms over her chest and scowling, the picture of indignation. *On my behalf.* I find it incredibly endearing. "Is that when you broke up?"

Heaving out a sigh, I shake my head. "It probably should have been, but no. I called my two best friends, Lane and Marcus, and they met me for drinks. They both agreed with me that this was a fucked up situation and said I should call off the wedding."

"But you didn't?"

Pushing away my empty plate, I lean back in my leather chair and rub a hand over the top of my head. "I thought about it. But when I was on my way back home, my mom called."

Juliette's face is gentle with sympathy. "Let me guess. She was excited about the wedding?"

I blow out a breath through my nose and bob my head up and down a few times. "Yes, but she also said something else that made me pause." Glancing out at the sun setting over the water, I focus on the beautiful scene for what I was about to say. "I didn't have the best dad growing up. But my mom told me that night that she was proud of me and said she'd always worried that growing up like that had damaged me. She blamed herself because she thought I'd never get married."

My eyes pull back to Juliette when I feel her take my hand. Then she lifts it and presses her pretty lips to my knuckles. "You're a big softy, Reno."

The corners of my lips pull up. "Don't tell anyone."

She entwines her fingers with mine. “Your secret is safe with me,” she says, and the tension in my shoulders dissolves like sugar in water. Juliette McNamara is by far the easiest woman I’ve ever been with. I feel like I could talk to her about anything.

“Anyway, the discussion with Ma calmed me, and when I got home, I sat Leia down and had a heart-to-heart. I asked her how she would feel if I asked her to have a threesome with her female best friend, and she got pissed at me.”

“What a hypocrite,” Juliette mutters. “I don’t think I like this Leia character.” Her eyes brighten. “Ooh, would you mind if I named the villain in my next book Leia?”

I let out a laugh from the bottom of my gut. “I wouldn’t mind a bit. Go for it.”

“Done,” she affirms. “What happened next?”

“I told Leia to put herself in my shoes, to think about how it makes me feel like I’m not enough.” I nibble the corner of my bottom lip. “I let her know I wanted a monogamous marriage and that I wasn’t going to discuss bringing someone else into our relationship again. Full stop. Then I asked her if she was in or out.”

“What were you hoping the answer would be?”

I close my eyes for a long moment. “To be honest, I was torn. Half of me wanted the validation that my fiancée was choosing me, but I think part of me would have been relieved if it had gone the other way.”

I refill our wine glasses with my free hand and take a long glug. “She finally apologized and told me she was in. She cried and we hugged, and then I suggested we go to bed and make up.” My jaw clenches. “Leia said since the wedding was just a few weeks away, she wanted to wait until our honeymoon. It had been months since we’d been together, and yet I went to bed alone. Again.”

“Can I ask you a personal question?” Juli asks.

“Well, since I’ve just told you about one of the shittiest times in my life, I’d say yes,” I say with a chagrined smile.

She leans forward and whispers, “Is Leia blind?”

"Um, no," I reply in confusion. "She has good eyesight."

My date's lips purse. "Then how the hell did she go so long without climbing you like a tree? Because damn. You're not exactly hard to look at, Reno."

My pants suddenly feel too tight at the thought of Juliette climbing me. Riding me. Scraping my back with those pastel pink nails while I take one of her pretty nipples between my teeth and...

Fuck.

"I guess she has good willpower," I reply gruffly, shifting in my seat to get my growing dick into a more comfortable position.

"Hmmph. Or she's stupid." Juliette cocks her head. "So wait. How did you end up here? At a swingers' resort?"

"Leia booked the honeymoon," I say flatly, and Juliette's eyes widen again.

"You went through with the wedding? Oh my god, are you married now?" She tries to pull her hand away, but I hold onto it.

"We never got married," I assure her, and she visibly relaxes. "It was close though. We made it all the way to the day of the wedding. I was at the altar."

"Oh no," Juliette whispers, tears beginning to rim her eyelids.

"I was standing there with my groomsmen and the preacher. All the bridesmaids came down first and then the six flower girls, sprinkling autumn leaves along the aisle. The music changed and everyone turned and waited for the bride. And waited. And waited. Finally the wedding planner fast-walked up the aisle and whispered to me that Leia needed to talk to me." I shrug. "And that's when I knew."

"Shit, Reno. I'm so sorry."

"The thing is, I felt more annoyed than hurt. Well, I guess I was embarrassed too. I'd specifically asked her if she was ready to marry me during our heart-to-heart talk, and she said yes." I shake my head and swipe away the tear that had broken free down Juliette's soft cheek.

"And she still strung you along and waited until there was a room full of people," she says, her anger not concealed by the tears. "Classic narcissistic move."

"You nailed Leia with that," I say before wryly adding, "Unfortunately, that wasn't the only time she'd been nailed."

Juliette gasps. "Nooooo!"

"Yep. I got to the bridal room, and she was taking off her dress. She slung it over a chair and kicked off her shoes and then proceeded to burst into tears." Juliette rolls her eyes. "Then she admitted she and Jeffrey had been having an affair for months. It started even before we had the threesome."

Juliette raps a knuckle on the table. "You know what? I feel like flipping this table over right now. How fucking dare she!"

I can't help but chuckle at the vision of this woman wreaking havoc in this fancy dining room.

"Trust me, I thought about flipping some shit over too."

"What did you do instead?"

"I grabbed the dress and the ridiculously priced shoes and told her I was going to burn them. She freaked the fuck out, but I marched from the room, knowing she couldn't follow because she was in her underwear." I massage my jaw with one hand. "Then I went into the main room where everyone was seated, handed the clothes to my buddy Lane, and punched Jeffrey in the face."

Juliette's lips pop into an O, but before she can say anything, the waiter comes by with a dessert menu. We order, and then she leans forward. "What happened next? Did you really burn the dress and shoes?"

"After I punched Jeffrey, I turned to the crowd and asked if anyone else there had been fucking my former fiancée. You could have heard a pin drop. Then Lane and Marcus dragged me out the back door and stuffed me into the limo, where we proceeded to get shit-faced drunk while the driver cruised us around town."

"Please tell me you changed the locks on your apartment."

I nod. "Marcus handled that before we got too far into the booze. And no, I didn't actually burn the wedding clothes. The next day I took them to a women's shelter and donated them. They put them up for auction and raised a shit-ton of money."

Juliette's fingers tighten around mine. "That was a really thoughtful thing for you to do."

"Yeah, I guess. I also gathered up Leia's clothes and took them to the shelter. They have a program where they provide work clothing to the women who are trying to start their new lives."

"I completely approve," Juli says. "You got some revenge while also doing something really good."

"I still felt the need to set something on fire, so the next night, Marcus, Lane, and I had a bonfire at Lane's house and burned all the pictures of Leia and me."

Juliette giggles. "Have you always had pyromania tendencies?"

"No," I tell her with a grin, "but it felt damn good."

The waiter serves the Riesling and our desserts, turtle cheesecake for me and some kind of fruit tart for Juliette.

"I'm sorry things didn't work out with Leia," she says sweetly.

Taking a bite of the delicious cheesecake, I tilt my head to the side and swallow. "I was miserable and angry for months after we broke up, but..." I twiddle my fork as I think about the right words. "I have more clarity now, and I realize she wasn't the right one for me. So I guess it turned out for the best."

Juliette's lips turn up at the corners. "Sometimes things work out in unexpected ways."

I return her smile. "Yeah, I guess they do."

She finishes almost all her dessert and pushes her dish away before resting her chin in her palm.

"It makes more sense now, the reason you said you couldn't pursue someone who was into the swinging lifestyle." Her head tilts to the side, and her pretty blonde hair falls over one bare shoulder. "I mean, I know there's a difference between full-fledged swinging and your situation, but the mechanics are similar. So it's completely understandable that you wouldn't want to be involved in that. I'm sorry I jumped to the wrong conclusion and kicked you out."

"It's okay. Water under the bridge." I eat one more mouthful of cheesecake and set my fork down. "I'm honestly okay with other people doing whatever they want. I know swinging is very fulfilling for some couples, and I think that's awesome."

"From what I've read, it's not something you just jump into on a whim. A couple needs to have complete trust and a whole lot of communication about it." Juliette takes a sip of her wine and arches one brow. "It's certainly not something you surprise your new husband with for your honeymoon."

A half smile slides across my lips. "I still can't believe she booked this place without talking to me about it."

Juliette's aqua eyes laser into mine. "I can't say I'm sad you're here though."

Reaching across the table, I take her hand and kiss the back of it. "I'm not sad I'm here either."

In fact, I'm really fucking glad.

Maybe I should send Leia a thank you card.

Chapter 14

Juliette

Absolutely no relationships with a hockey player. Period.

We take the scenic route back to our cottages to walk off some of the huge meal we just ate. I take off my shoes since we're walking along the beach, and Reno keeps my free hand firmly in his.

"How's the book coming?" he asks.

"Really good. I've been a writing machine, and I'm actually ahead of schedule."

The moon is full above us, casting enough of a glow for us to see without turning on our phones' flashlights. Reno stops and tugs me around to face him, his eyes searching my face.

"Are you still interested in being... inspired?" He cups the side of my neck, his thumb wrapping lightly around the front of my throat, and I know he can feel my moan vibrating against his hand. Because he smiles. Smugly.

I wet my lips with the tip of my tongue, and those green eyes drop to watch before making a slow trail back up to my aqua ones.

"I could always use more hands-on experience to enhance my writing," I say, and I mentally pat myself on the back for achieving master level in the coyness department. Okay, maybe not master level, but at least I didn't grab his crotch and tell him to rock my world. I'm calling it a win.

"Hands-on?" he asks with a quirk of his brow.

I tilt my head and run a hand up his chest. His wide, very firm chest. "Oh, would hands-on activity be too much for you to handle?" I ask in my sweetest voice. "Or were you wanting to just talk about it?"

Reno chuckles, knowing I'm baiting him and not caring. "How about if I talk about it *while* my hands are on you?"

"Will it be dirty talk?"

"Is there another kind?" he scoffs with a shake of his head like I'm the most ridiculous person ever.

"Okay, I'll allow you to inspire me," I say with faux imperiousness.

"Good," he murmurs, pulling me forward by my damn neck and dipping his head to take my lips. As soon as his mouth covers mine, my toes curl—freaking *curl*—into the sand. No one has ever made my toes do that from a kiss before.

But Reno's tongue is stroking against mine in a velvety twist of sensuality, and it's not just his mouth contributing to my knees feeling like jelly. One of his hands has migrated to my lower back and is holding me tightly against his body. I taste the sweetness of the Riesling mingling with the richness of chocolate as we kiss, and I drop my shoes and bag before ringing both arms around his neck.

What feels like an hour later, but also like no time at all, he pulls back with a final soft peck. "There. It's settled now."

I lick his taste from my lips. "What was that? A kiss contract?"

He grins, and *fuck, he is a pretty, pretty man when he smiles.* All white teeth and full lips and model-like cheekbones. And those freaking green eyes that shine in the moonlight. Then his smile fades, and his expression turns serious.

"Just us, right? While we're here?"

"Of course," I assure him, dragging my fingers through the soft curls at the nape of his neck. "How long are you staying on the island?"

Reno hesitates for a brief second, as if he's not sure, before replying. "My trip is supposed to be for two weeks, so I have eleven more days here." I'm still amazed and offended on his behalf that his ex had the gall to book this resort for their frigging honeymoon.

"I booked for three weeks, so I have a week more than you."

The wind coming off the sea blows a strand of hair across my face, and Reno releases my neck to brush it away and twine it around his index finger. "Will eleven days give you enough time to get through all the spicy scenes you need me for?"

Oof. I feel like a bit of a... pimp-ette when he puts it like that. "It's not just those scenes. I can also get inspiration from simply spending time with you." My tone brightens when I remember something. "Like maybe you could go with me to the waterfall on the other side of the island. That's on my list of places to visit, and if I'm there, I can better describe how everything looks and smells and feels. I promise I'm not just using you for your body."

His smile is positively feral when he presses his hips forward so I can feel... *dear heavens to Betsy, there's a big ol' erection against my stomach.*

"Does it feel like I'm complaining?" he asks, gravel rasping his voice. "You can use me any way you want, dream girl."

My kitty cave decides this would be a fine time to clench around nothingness, letting me know she's ready and willing to indulge in every fantasy this man is promising.

"So that's a yes to the waterfall?" I squeak, fully aware there's a waterfall of a more carnal variety currently gushing between my legs.

"That's a yes to everything," he replies before kissing my forehead, and *good grief*! I do love me some forehead kisses. "What's your next scene in your book about?"

My brain currently resembles a pan of scrambled eggs, but I manage to remember where things are headed next in the story. "Reid is starting to have feelings for Anna, but he's trying to deny it."

"Of course he is," Reno replies with a tsk. "Men are so fucking stubborn."

I laugh as he caresses my lower back with his big hand. "He decides if he can reduce their encounters to just a sexual level without emotion, all those pesky feelings will go away. So he's going to completely defile her. You up for that?" I give him a flirty eyebrow.

"Oh, I'm an excellent defile-er, dream girl. What did you have in mind?"

"I was thinking a nice, hard fuck against the door."

The flesh of my stomach is suddenly being poked by a very insistent penis that seems to be growing by the second.

"Hmmm," Reno hums, biting into the corner of his bottom lip. "I'm not sure how *nice* it's going to be. Can I interest you in a *not-so-nice* fuck?"

Images flood my brain and saturate it in lust. Reno pounding into me without mercy. His strong hands holding my ass. "I think I can grant you some leeway in the execution." The thought of him holding me up makes my eyebrows inch together. "Look, I'm not exactly petite, so if it's too much..."

His eyebrows mirror my own in a look of severe consternation. "Are you doubting my strength, Juliette?"

I rest my hand on the base of my throat in my best impression of a Southern belle clutching her pearls. "Oh, heavens no," I drawl. "I was simply saying that I'm tall so not exactly—eeeep!" My words turn into a squeal as I'm suddenly upside down over Reno's shoulder.

Then he squats and picks up my bag and shoes like he doesn't have a fully grown woman on his shoulder. *No wonder the man has the ass and thighs of a machine. He could probably squat my Volkswagen.*

"Reno! Put me down!" I insist.

"No," he insists right back as he begins to jog—freaking *jog*—up the beach.

"I feel like I'm having a conversation with your ass," I say, admiring the flex of his posterior while I brace my hands on his waist to minimize the bouncing.

"He's a very good listener," Reno shoots back as he cuts up the path toward our cottages. At least I think this is the correct path. Hell, I'm not sure because of my previously mentioned navigational shortcomings. Not to mention that I'm currently upside-freaking-down.

"You're a brute," I declare with absolutely no heat behind the words.

"Thought that's what you wanted." He gives me a light swat on the butt, and I grit my teeth around a moan. "I've read some of your books, Miss Juli Mack, and I know your secret."

"Oh, please enlighten me," I say.

He steps up onto the back porch of what I realize is his cottage and gently sets me on my feet. Despite carrying me while jogging, Reno isn't even breathing hard.

"You like a man who takes charge," he announces, setting down my purse and shoes before stepping closer and herding me until my back is against the door. "You want a man to tell you exactly what he's going to do to you and then follow through with every dirty thought."

"Y-you think?" I stammer because his body is crowding mine as his mouth drops to my ear.

"I know," he whispers, taking a quick lick of my earlobe. "I also know you like a man to bite you here." His teeth sink into the fleshy part of my ear, and this time, there's no holding back the groan. Because I do like that. It's my go-to spot. I guess it comes through in my writing.

"I don't like smug men," I proclaim, earning me a chuckle from Reno.

"Liar," he murmurs before sucking on my goddamn earlobe like it's his very own cherry Starburst. "Would Reid go down on Anna before he fucks her against the door?"

"I, uh..." Yes. Fuck yes, he would. But what if Reno doesn't like doing that? "It would be diner's choice," I answer breathlessly.

He gives me a lopsided grin, and one of his hands skims up my back. Two seconds later, he has my romper unzipped, and I'm naked from the waist up, except for my strapless bra. The man is smoothness personified. I didn't even hear the zipper.

"This is pretty," he says, eyes dropping to my cream bra as his fingers move over the delicate embroidered pink flowers adorning the cups. Then he uses the tips of two fingers to trace the mounds of my breasts, skimming just along the perimeter of the lacy fabric.

"You should see the matching panties," I tell him.

Reno wiggles his eyebrows at me. "Oh, I plan to, dream girl."

Fuck, I really like it when he calls me that.

My eyes flit around, and I let out a nervous laugh. "When I said against the door, I was thinking more, you know, *inside* the cottage."

Those two fingers slide up my chest, over my throat, and wedge beneath my chin, lifting until our eyes meet. “We can go inside if you want. Or I can fuck you here on the porch where anyone could walk up that path and see us.” My breath hitches, and he notices. “Does that turn you on, Juliette?”

Despite some of the wild things I’ve written about, I have never had sex in public. The closest I’ve come was having a mini-orgasm on the dance floor against a boyfriend’s leg back in college while we were dirty dancing. But the thought of being totally exposed while this big man rails me is making something flame up inside my gut. And I’m pretty sure it’s not indigestion. Nope, it’s desire.

I cast one more glance around. We’re on the far end of the island, and our cottages are relatively secluded in this location. That doesn’t lessen the thrill of public sex, and I find myself nodding. “It turns me on a lot.”

A smile creeps across Reno's full lips, and the next thing I know, he’s on his knees and my romper is tossed to the side.

How the hell does he do that without me noticing? Is he some kind of undressing wizard? Does he have a Harry Potter-esque get-the-girl-naked spell that makes clothing disappear? Like corpus revelio! And poof... you’re naked.

“Fuck. You are exquisite.” Those words pull me from my weird wizard thoughts, and I look down at the man who is eyeing me up and down. His hands trail down my sides. Not hesitantly, but the touch is soft. Almost reverent. Those green eyes have fire in them when he looks up at my face. “You are a goddess, dream girl.”

I can’t even reply because Reno is pressing worshipful kisses against my stomach, and my skin feels tingly with each caress of his lips. Big hands cup my breasts over my bra as he rubs his face against my belly. Even though he was clean-shaven at dinner, I can feel the hint of whiskers roughing my flesh and setting my skin afire.

There’s nothing I can do but bury my hands in that soft hair while he continues worshipping my body. Again, he does that magical thing where my bra disappears, and my nipples pucker at the exposure to the cool sea breeze that swirls around us. He warms them with his palms, but the tips only grow tighter—needier—and I groan into the dark night.

"Your tits are fucking amazing, dream girl." He thumbs both tips. "Such pretty pink nipples. So responsive."

"Take your shirt off," I demand. "I deserve some eye candy too."

With a soft laugh, he undoes the single button he had fastened on his shirt. He's apparently not using his undressing spell on himself because he pulls it off slowly, teasingly, exposing his tanned skin inch by inch to my wanton gaze. He drops the pink polo haphazardly onto the pile of my clothes and raises an eyebrow at me.

"Better?"

I drift a hand over his bare shoulder, feeling the muscles ripple at my touch. "Oh yeah. Mama likey," I drawl.

His big hands grip my waist, and he leans forward, taking my left nipple into his mouth. It's hot and wet, his tongue swirling slowly around and around the peak. Then he sucks hard, and my lungs seize as the sensation travels down my body and directly to my pussy.

Driving my hands into his hair, I let the silky strands slide between my fingers as he moans around me. "Fuck, baby. This pretty little nipple is getting so hard for me." He laps at it, closing his eyes as the rigid peak rubs against his tongue.

I slide my foot between his legs and nudge the top of it against his crotch. His eyes pop open, and I bite my bottom lip. "Seems like you're just as hard for me, big guy." And I do mean *big*.

"Yeah, no shit," he mutters, kissing his way to my other breast. "I think I could poke a hole through this porch right now." While he blesses the right nipple with the same attention as he did the left, I press the top of my foot firmly against him. He grinds, and I can feel the rock-like length of him.

Trailing my fingers down his neck and over his shoulders, I smile when goosebumps follow the path. Okay, maybe I'm also smiling because my tit is in Reno Swain's mouth, and he's gone all vacuum cleaner on me, sucking so hard my nipple will be sore tomorrow. With a graze of his teeth, I shudder, and his gaze rises to mine to gauge my reaction.

"Feels so good," I assure him, cupping his face so I can feel the hollowing of his cheeks.

Reno finally pulls back with one last flick of his tongue over the diamond my nipple has become, and he surveys his handiwork. "I think I've cleared the north forty. Time to get started down south," he tells me with a cocky grin.

"Definitely... needs some attention... down there," I pant, almost feral to feel his hot mouth between my legs.

He takes his damn time getting there, exploring my torso with lips and tongue, sucking and licking and kissing my damp flesh until I want to scream at him to get to work on the south forty. Now.

When he finally reaches the apex of my thighs, he drags his nose over the ivory lace of my panties and hums. "Fuck, dream girl. You smell exactly how a woman should smell. Sweet and soft." He inhales deeply and meets my eyes in the sliver of moonlight that reaches us on the porch. "And so goddamn aroused."

Seriously.

Almost came.

Reno hooks his fingers into the hips of my panties and works them down, steadying me as I step out of them, one foot at a time. Then he holds the flimsy fabric against his nose and breathes me in, his eyes closing in reverence.

"Mmm, can I keep these?"

I'm a little stunned. No one has ever asked me that before. Sure, guys have winked cheekily and stuffed my panties into their pockets before, but no one has ever *asked*. I don't know why, but I find that incredibly hot and endearing at the same time.

"Y-you can keep them," I stammer, and I'm surprised once again when he folds them neatly and tucks them into his pants pocket.

"Good. I want to have something to hold when I get back home and jack off to thoughts of the first time I ever tasted you."

Sweet Jesus on a pogo stick. This man...

All thoughts of panties and jacking off are brushed away when he grabs my right leg and slings it over his shoulder. I press my palms against the door for balance as he lowers his face. The first swipe of his tongue is against my inner thigh, and he makes a small noise of approval in his throat before licking the other side.

And then he turns his attention to where I need him. He hits the money spot on the first try, and my fingers curve against the glass. Smiling wickedly up at me, he does it again.

"Tell me how you would write this scene, dream girl," he commands.

"I, oh, um." He licks me up my center again, and I shudder. "You expect me to know actual words when you're doing that?"

Reno's chuckle is steamy against my pussy. "Just do your best." Then he plunges his tongue inside me, face pressed into me like he's attempting to fuse himself to me.

My brain works to find the words as he begins moving his tongue in and out. I focus on his mouth, his hands, his noises.

"I'm spread wide, one leg over Reno's broad shoulder as he dips his head to my sex." I inhale and let out a heaving breath. "His tongue is firm and hot when he slides it into me and grips my ass with one hand. Then he tongue-fucks me. Slowly."

I reach my hand down and continue narrating what he's doing to me. "My hand slides into his hair as he takes his time, tasting me like I'm his last meal. I know what he's doing... why he's not rushing. He's drawing my orgasm to the surface with each thrust of his tongue inside my pussy. Then he's going to make me explode all over his sexy mouth."

He growls against me, and the vibrations only push me higher. "I'm so close already, and all I want to do is grind my pussy against Reno's face until I come." My voice is softer, a little strained. "I wish I knew what he was thinking right now. If he likes how I taste. If his cock is as talented as his tongue."

He slowly slides his tongue from me and looks up. I can already see my wetness slicking his lips. Then he takes over the narration in his deep rasp.

"Reno's new favorite meal is Juliette's pussy. She tastes even sweeter than the wine they had at dinner." He takes a long lick from my hole to my clit. "He could savor her for hours, but he also wants to bury his *very* talented cock inside her until she screams herself hoarse."

His grin is cheeky as he drifts a hand up and down my thigh resting on his shoulder. "She has the longest, sexiest legs he's ever seen, and he plans to wear them as a belt while he fucks into her tight little pussy. But first, he needs to give some serious attention to that throbbing little clit that's just begging for his mouth."

"Yes," I agree instantly, and he flashes me a knowing smile before diving back in. This time he's not fucking around. His tongue alternates between long laps and tiny flicks against my most sensitive area, and I grip his hair tighter. My hips jerk back and forth as his slight scruff provides the most delicious friction against the lips of my sex.

"Come on, dream girl. Give it up for me," he growls between licks, and my back arches off the glass door behind me.

"Fuck. About to come," I push out as his lips wrap around my clit. He sucks, and I'm suddenly attached to a bungee cord, being pulled down, down, down until the rubber is stretched to its limit.

Then the tension releases, and I'm flying, soaring up into the clouds at warp speed. Higher than I've ever flown before. I'm not usually a screamer, but his name rips from my throat as I grind shamelessly against his face. "Reno. Oh god, yes."

The man is a master of oral sex, knowing exactly when to lick harder and when to soften his strokes against my sensitive flesh. His tongue is a gentle caress as I come down from the high of my orgasm.

Helping me to lower my leg to the ground, Reno supports my weight until my knees remember how to be knees. I don't normally come from oral alone. I usually need some accompanying finger action to get me there.

"Wow. That was definitely not your first rodeo," I pant, and he laughs before giving me a final soft kiss between my legs.

"Must be beginner's luck or something," he teases. "Maybe you'll let me practice on you some more."

"I suppose I could make that sacrifice," I tease back.

Pushing to his feet, he swipes a hand over his chin and steps closer to me. He really is the perfect specimen, and I'm not just talking about physically. A man who can make you laugh *and* make you come? *Yes, please.*

My heart thuds as I loop my arms over his shoulders. It's too bad we can't pursue anything outside of a vacation fling, but it would never work.

Because it would break my cardinal rule: *Absolutely no relationships with a hockey player. Period.*

CHAPTER 15

Juliette

Rule one is an asshole.

RENO'S HANDS DROP TO my naked ass, and he hauls me against him. His bare chest is warm, and his smattering of chest hair abrades my nipples in the best of ways.

"I can't wait to be inside you," he murmurs before scorching my lips with his own. His cock strains forward against the fabric of his pants, and I slip one hand between us to cup his length.

He moans into the kiss before pulling back. "Jesus, that feels good."

Sliding my other hand down, I unbuckle his belt and undo his black pants. "Please tell me you have a condom."

"Fuck yes, I do." Reaching into his back pocket, he extracts his wallet and produces a foil-wrapped packet, tossing it onto the small glass table beside the door.

"You're wearing way too many clothes," I inform him, using both hands to push his pants over his hips and down his legs. Reno kicks off his shoes and takes over, stripping down to nothing before standing to his full height in front of me.

Good grief, this man is gorgeous. He looks even more massive without clothes, and I should be intimidated by his sheer mass and raw strength, but I'm not. My lust has overridden every rational thought in my head. Much like men do, I'm now thinking with my genitals.

That damn dick though. It's bobbing out in front of him, the head glossy with his desire and the engorged veins visible even in the dim light. His length is nothing short of spectacular, totally spank bank material.

Well, that's going to be a challenge. One I'm anxious to tackle.

I reach for him, wrapping my hand around his girth. He's thicker at the base, my fingers not quite reaching all the way around when I stroke down.

"Fuuuck," Reno grits out, resting his hands on the door frame above me and closing his eyes. His big body is hovering over me, trapping me against the door. Not that I'm trying to get away. He allows me to explore him as his breath grows more and more ragged with every stroke of my hand.

His cock is rock hard, hot and heavy in my hand. I lean forward, nipping lightly at his shoulder before kissing my way to the base of his thick neck. "Does that feel good?" I purr. "Do you like me fucking this big cock with my fist?"

I can hear the smile in his voice. "I should have known you'd have a dirty mouth, dream girl."

Standing on tiptoe, I run my tongue up the side of his neck until I find a spot that makes his hips jerk. "I've been wondering what your dick would feel like. If you would be as big here..." I give him a tight stroke "...as you are everywhere else. Do you think you can make it fit?"

Reno grasps a handful of my hair and tugs until I look up at him. His eyes have darkened to the most intense shade of green, and his mouth takes the form of a wicked grin.

"I don't know, baby. Maybe I should check out how tight you are."

My vagina, which was completely sated a couple minutes ago, perks up. She's a fan of this idea.

"Maybe you should," I breathe.

His hand releases my hair and slides slowly down my body, taking a nipple-tweaking detour on the way. Then his middle finger trails through my center, and he lifts an eyebrow.

"I think we have wetness covered," Reno muses with more than a little smugness. "But let's see..." He inserts that digit inside me, and I clench around it. "Mmmmm... Houston, we have a problem."

I giggle and squeeze his cock on the next stroke, noticing how the muscles of his jaw clench when I add a twist at the head. "If you don't think it will fit, we can just go inside and talk about our feelings," I suggest sweetly.

Reno narrows his eyes, but I see the twitch of his lips, like he's fighting a smile.

"Let's not be too hasty," he replies, adding a second finger. "This tight little pussy is going to take every inch of me tonight. And you *will* like it. Understood?"

That last word is accompanied by the expert curl of his fingers against my G-spot, and *dear lord, I love a bossy man.*

"Yes, sir," I tease, earning me a groan from the back of his throat.

His voice seems to drop an entire octave. "I'm going to stretch you out with my cock until I can fuck you how we both need it. Hard. Fast. And so fucking deep you'll still be feeling me tomorrow."

Yep. I volunteer as motherfucking tribute.

Reno's tip leaks onto my fingers, and I increase my pace, using his pre-ejaculate to lubricate the glide up and down that solid length. In response, he adds a third finger to my pussy and presses his large thumb against my clit. We both pump our hips while we work each other over.

"Kiss me," I beg, and before the words have stopped vibrating my lips, his tongue is in my mouth, the kiss positively salacious. While his free hand cups the back of my neck, I take the opportunity to run my hand over his chest and around to his strong back. The man is freaking decadent, just muscles upon muscles.

Reno breaks the kiss and trails his lips across my cheek to my ear. "Come for me, Juliette," he grunts, rolling his thumb over my clit, and I shudder. I'm so close to exploding. Again.

"No," I whimper when he nibbles on my earlobe. "I want to come with you inside me."

His cock jerks at my words, and he grasps my wrist to halt my movement. "Stop or this is going to be over before we get started." Strain coats his voice as he slowly pulls his fingers from inside me and sticks them in his mouth. "Fuck, you're sweet."

Unable to wait another second, I reach for the condom and rip open the package with my teeth. Reno's hand brushes my messy hair back from my face while I place the rubber at his tip and roll it down his length. He watches like he's never seen a woman do that before.

A second later, I'm being lifted by strong arms, and I sling my legs around his waist. "Put me inside you," he demands before kissing me softly on the lips. "And let me know if it's too much."

Nodding, I grip his dick and run the head of it through my slit before notching it at my entrance. I flex my hips and take an inch of him, and we both moan at the hot, wet sensation.

My heels press into his back like he's my own personal horse, and I'm trying to coax him to giddyup. Reno fills me in one, hard thrust, knocking all the breath from my lungs and most of the sense from my brain.

Perhaps my earlier bravado was misplaced because Reno's cock is a damn monster. I'm stretched to my limits, but the burn is exquisite.

"You... are so... fucking tight," he heaves out between harsh breaths. "Are you okay?"

"Yes," I whimper. "Please move."

He circles his hips around and around, the base of his dick grinding against my clit. My pussy grows infinitely wetter, and I begin to soften around him, allowing him in more fully.

"More?" he asks on a harsh exhale, and I squeeze my legs around him and nod.

"Yes... everything."

Reno pulls back, the ridge of his crown dragging against my sensitive inner walls, before driving back in to the hilt. I cry out with the sensation, which is more pleasure than pain now, and his hands on my ass dig into my flesh as he readjusts me to another angle. *And ohhh, that's the spot.*

Then he lets me have it. At full force. It's like I'm a nail and he's trying to pound me into a wall.

"You are the sexiest fucking woman alive," he growls, finding my lips with his. This kiss is completely uninhibited, wild and sloppy as we each feast on the other's mouth. Long licks give way to sucking lips and nipping teeth as Reno rides my body like he owns it.

I've never felt so out of control with a man before, the primal urge to fuck taking over as he bites my bottom lip before soothing the sting with his tongue. But at the same time, I feel like a sexual superhero, powerful and strong, because Reno Swain wants *me*.

"God, I'm close," I cry out. Loudly. And I don't even care. At this point, the entire resort could pull up chairs and sip cocktails while commentating, and I wouldn't give a damn. As long as Reno doesn't stop fucking me.

His hot mouth is suddenly on my earlobe, his tongue laving it as he continues to nail me to the door with his giant cock. When he sinks his teeth into the cushy flesh, I lose my damn mind. Matching him with the perfect counter-rhythm, I churn my hips, finding that incredible dual friction against my G-spot and my clit.

"That's it, dream girl," he grinds out, talking me through it while I unravel. "You can do it. Squeeze my cock, baby. It's all yours."

That does it. There are no thoughts in my head except for reaching that ultimate peak of bliss. And I do. I'm somehow numb while feeling every beautiful sensation at the same time. Reno swells inside me, and my inner walls clamp down on his invading cock.

"Come with me," I implore. "Fuck, Reno. Come now."

He fucks me like an animal, complete with erotic grunts in my ear as I call his name to the heavens. It's rough and fast, every single thing a nasty fuck against the door should be.

Reno lifts his head and locks his eyes with mine while we come together. It's fucking intense, watching this man watch me during my most vulnerable moment... that moment nothing else matters but the pleasure.

Holding himself deep, he pulses out his release inside me, and for a brief moment, I wish he was going bareback.

Incomplete words escape me as I tumble down from the high of pure ecstasy. "Re—tha—so goo—I ca—Shit," I finally utter, and he grins the sated smile of a very happy man.

"Couldn't have said it better myself," he replies, pressing his body closer so I can feel the racing beat of his heart against my chest. He's gentle now, his hands still holding me up but not digging into the flesh of my ass. Soft lips caress mine, and he pumps in and out of me with unhurried precision. "You blew my mind, Juliette. And my balls."

I laugh against his sexy mouth. "It's only fair. I think you made my ovaries malfunction. Is there a factory reset button somewhere?"

His grin is pure cheek. "I'll search for it later when my lungs reinflate. It will have to be a very thorough investigation, but I promise to find all your buttons."

I have no doubt he can do exactly that.

Five minutes later, I'm on Reno's soft bed. His cottage mirrors mine, living area and kitchen at the front and bedroom with en suite at the back.

After carefully cleaning me up with a warm cloth and making me drink some cool water, he nestles in beside me and rolls my body to face his beneath the covers. "How are you feeling, Juliette?"

I love hearing my name in his deep voice almost as much as I enjoy him calling me *dream girl.*

"Tired and very satisfied," I report.

His big hand is gentle, brushing my hair away from my face before cupping my cheek. "You are always beautiful, but you took my breath away when you came."

I seem to be losing my own breath right now. "Thank you," I murmur, turning my face to kiss his palm.

"I'm serious. You are absolute perfection. Such a good girl for me." He presses kisses all over my cheeks, nose, and forehead before he continues. "I like everything about you, but especially your pretty smile. You could brighten up a rainy day when you smile." I am flabbergasted, utterly overwhelmed at his sweetness.

Of course I've had aftercare from partners before, but this is different. More than just making sure I'm okay physically. This is... *after-praise*? Yeah, that's a good term for it, and I'm a fan.

Ignoring that niggling feeling at the base of my brain that tells me this is dangerously intimate, I snuggle closer to his naked body and wrap an arm around his waist. Reno runs his fingers through my long hair as he continues to whisper his pretty words against the top of my head.

After a while, he leans back and lays a kiss between my eyebrows. "I better go get our stuff from the porch. My wallet, your bag, our clothes. Before I fall asleep from exhaustion," he adds with a self-deprecating chuckle. "Be right back."

He rolls from the bed, and I'm in a tailspin. As soon as his warmth leaves me, I miss him. And that's... *whew*. I don't know what it is, but it's not great. While my heart is warning me not to sleep in this man's bed, my body is screaming the opposite.

Falling asleep in Reno's arms is a horrible, wonderful idea, and I practically drool on myself as I watch his fine ass stroll to the sliding door. He is the perfect man, physically and... *No, Juliette. You have to protect yourself.*

Because I can already feel myself getting addicted to Reno Swain, and that could be perilous to my heart. This—whatever it is—will end in eleven days, and then I'll probably never see him again. It's best to lay out some ground rules.

Yes, rules. That's exactly what we need.

My resolve dissipates when he returns with our things, giving me a full frontal view. And let me tell you, his frontal bits are just as amazing as his behind.

Is he hard again? Already?

That's some serious book-boyfriend-level shit. Of course, I've written about almost instantaneous rebound times for men in my romance stories, but in real life? Yeah, that's usually not a thing. Even in college when the guys were young and raring to go, there was at least an hour turnaround between sexy times.

As Reno sets our clothes and my clutch on the dresser, I sit up and hold the sheet over my chest. *Like he hasn't seen everything already*, the smartass part of my brain drawls. But I feel like I need that extra layer of protection to work up my courage.

Also, my nipples could cut glass right now. So there's that.

"What's wrong, dream girl? You need to use the bathroom?"

"No, I—Yes, actually," I say, scrambling from the bed and dashing into the bathroom. *Chickenshit.*

After using the toilet, I wash my hands and regard myself in the mirror. My hair looks like a family of squirrels has made their forever home on top of my head, and scruff burn reddens almost every inch of me. There's something to be said about a man who's thorough.

I find a hickey on the side of my right boob, and when I turn, I notice finger-shaped bruises dotting my ass. I've been thoroughly used, and I have absolutely no complaints about it. Because Reno made sure I was satisfied before letting himself come.

After finger-combing my hair, I find a bathrobe on the back of the door, sling it on, and sigh. It smells like him. Black currant and bergamot are underlined with a hint of something sweet and rich. Maybe vanilla?

Trying not to inhale too much to avoid the temptation of his man smell, I tie the sash around my middle and march out into the bedroom.

Reno is reclined back on the bed looking tastier than a whole bag of cherry Starbursts, one hand propped behind his head. His biceps bulge, and he grins at me.

"You look adorable in my robe, Juliette."

"I look like Dopey," I retort, holding up my arms to reveal the sleeves that hang over my hands.

"Dopey is my favorite dwarf." His eyebrows pinch together. "Why are you standing at the end of the bed like that?"

"I, uh, I think we need to set some ground rules for our… arrangement."

He nods, sits up, and holds out a hand for me. "Of course. Come sit by me."

Ohh, this is not good. Being within touching distance of this man is a temptation I don't need when I'm trying to be all strong and poised and shit. But I do it anyway, sitting on the edge of the bed beside him.

While Reno rolls my sleeves up, I start. "I think we can both agree this is temporary, right?"

His eyes flick up to mine as he continues adjusting the sleeves. "Yeah," he says warily.

"Because neither of us are looking for anything serious." He nods his agreement, and I continue. "So I was thinking that spending the whole night together might send… mixed signals?" It came out as more of a question than a statement.

He frowns for a second before bobbing his head once. "I understand. For me, sleeping in the same bed is something I've only done with a girlfriend."

I'm struck with an odd sense of jealousy, and I inwardly scold myself. *Don't think of him in bed with Leia, Juli. Just don't.*

"Right," I say, forcing cheer into my voice. "And that's not what this is about. We're just… casual." I flip my hand over, palm up, to demonstrate exactly how *not-serious* our fling is. And how I absolutely *do not* want to climb on top of Reno and use him as my own personal body pillow all night.

"Riiiight," he echoes. "So rule one is no sleepovers. What else?"

My sex-sated brain can't think of anything else, so I deflect. "Do you have any rules you want to make?"

Reno fingers a strand of my hair almost absently. "Maybe we should limit talking about our personal lives. I mean, besides what we've already shared."

I feel slightly guilty that I haven't told him I recognize him, but I brush that away. The life of a professional athlete is rigorous and stressful, and if he doesn't want to talk about it while he's on vacation, that's fine with me.

"Agreed. That will be rule two," I say, and *how did my hand end up on his chest?* I rub the hard muscle of his pec. "What about when you leave here in eleven days? Should we stay in contact with each other once we're both back home?"

Reno's forehead furrows, his dark brows inching together. "I'd like to know you made it home safely."

Dammit to hell, why does he have to be so sweet?

"I can text you to let you know when I get home."

"And after that?" he pushes, those green eyes glued to my face.

I think about the distance between where we live. There are probably a thousand miles between Denver and my hometown in Texas. The last thing I want is another long-distance relationship—especially not with a hockey player.

"I think things could get confusing and complicated if we stay in touch," I tell him honestly.

His lips twist to the side. *Is that disappointment I'm reading there?* I think it is because I'm feeling a twinge of it myself. And that's why continuing to talk to him would be a very bad idea. Reno Swain would be too easy to fall for. Because despite what I try to tell myself, he's exactly my type.

"You're saying you don't want the random guy you met on vacation to keep calling and stringing you along?"

I give his shoulder a playful push. "Maybe I'd be the one stringing you along," I tease with a flip of my hair. "I'd leave you completely heartbroken, mister."

Reno laughs and hauls me onto his lap so I'm straddling him. "I have no doubt you would, dream girl." He toys with the belt holding my robe closed. "So I know we won't be spending the night together, per rule one, but are there any rules against me giving you a two-fer in one night?"

He looks expectantly at me as he unties the robe and slides his warm hands inside, around my waist. He's fully hard beneath me, and my body responds in full force with perky nipples and an even perkier vagina.

"I have no problem with that."

His grin widens and lights up his face before he flips me onto my back and pounces.

Yes, this man could easily become an addiction.

"I'll see you tomorrow at lunch," Reno says at my back door. He insisted on walking me "home" after round two, even though my cottage is only a few steps from his.

"Sounds good," I say, rising up onto my toes to kiss his cheek. "Let me throw on some pajamas right quick so I can give you your robe back."

"Nah, it's okay. There's another one in my closet if I need it." His hand cradles my face, and he leans in for a long, slow kiss that makes my knees weak.

"Beach tomorrow afternoon?" I ask.

"You in a swimsuit? Yes, please." He pats me on the butt. "Now get inside before you make me want to break rule one."

Reno waits for me to unlock my door and then hands me my clothes, shoes, and bag. I give him one more peck on the lips before going inside and sliding the door closed. He stands there with his hands in the pockets of his low-slung shorts, which he threw on to walk me to my cottage. He's commando, giving me a primo view of his imprint.

His head bobs toward the safety bar, reminding me to engage it, and I do, but my eyes don't leave his. I want to say screw rule one and invite him inside, but I know that's only asking for trouble.

So I close the vertical blinds, ignoring the ache in my gut when I can no longer see him.

Rule one is an asshole.

Chapter 16

Reno

How Reno Swain ended up in a nail salon

Here's how my Thursday went. I got up, ran, and did my daily workout before meeting Juliette for lunch. Then we hit the beach, got horny after a couple hours, and went back to her room for some afternoon delight.

When we were both fully satisfied, she wrote a couple chapters until it was time to go to the dining room, and afterward, we had more sex, which was just as phenomenal as Wednesday night's romp against the door.

And now… I'm back in my cottage alone. It's been the only dark spot on an otherwise fantastic day. And that sends my mind into a tailspin. I've never really enjoyed sharing a bed with a woman. Well, not for sleep anyway. I'm a big guy, and when it's time to snooze, I like to sprawl out and get comfortable. But as I lay on my back on the empty bed, watching the shadow of the rotating ceiling fan, I feel the phantom presence of Juliette along my side, like she's supposed to be here but isn't.

Which is probably why rule one is a good idea. I don't need to be having those kinds of thoughts.

Unable to sleep, I get up and pull out my laptop, which I haven't used a single time since I arrived on Sunday evening. At dinner tonight, Juliette had asked if I wanted to see her WIP. I told her hell yes; if she wanted to get kinky, I was down with it. She'd laughed and explained that W-I-P stood for *work in progress*. In other words, the book she was currently working on.

Tucking my laptop beneath my arm, I detour to the window facing cottage four and peek out. I can see the light around the edges of the blinds in Juliette's bedroom. "Pretty little night owl," I mumble, knowing she's probably writing away. *I wish...*

Shaking my head, I settle back onto the bed, find the document she emailed, and open it.

Then for the next few hours, I get lost in her words. The characters, the humor, the storyline. Every bit of it makes me want to devour more of it. I never thought I'd be a guy who reads romance novels, but here we are.

The ocean laps softly against the shore on Friday afternoon, and I open my eyes and stare up at the blue sky above. A group of clouds lined up in thin rows catches my attention.

"Those clouds look like an air filter," I say, and Juliette lowers her sunglasses and follows my gaze.

With a giggle, she says, "I always think that too. Those are cirrocumulus clouds."

I roll onto my side on the bright beach blanket we're sharing and prop myself on my elbow. She is so goddamn gorgeous.

"I love how smart you are," I tell her, and she scoffs.

"Need I remind you I've been wearing that playtime pineapple bracelet the entire time I've been here until you told me what it means?" She pulls her sunglasses back up to cover her eyes and announces, "I'm an idiot."

I scowl at her. I hate when she says she's not smart.

"You are not an idiot. Just because you're not well-versed in a lifestyle you haven't been exposed to before, it doesn't mean you're not intelligent. It's obvious by reading your books that your verbal skills are off the charts. Hell, I had to look up at least ten words when I was reading your WIP last night." I kiss her temple. "You are brilliant."

Her face flushes, and I don't think it's from the sun. "Thanks, Reno. I know I can be a bit ditzy sometimes, but..." She pauses. "I was diagnosed with Attention Deficit Disorder when I was eight." Her teeth fidget with her bottom lip before she continues. "It made me feel dumb because it took me so much longer to get my work done at school than the other kids. I tried medication, but both my dads agreed it dulled me."

My lips quirk up on one side. "Juliette, I couldn't even imagine you being dull."

"Oh, I was like a zombie when I was medicated," she informs me. "Pops did a lot of research and found a psychologist that specialized in kids with ADD and taught them coping mechanisms to get by without medication. She said a lot of kids do need the medicine to get by, but some are able to use other techniques. I wasn't a hyperactive kid, but my mind always seemed to be in overdrive."

"And she helped you?"

Juliette smiles affectionately. "Dr. Hough was fantastic. She wasn't covered by our insurance, but she worked at the university where Pops taught, so she treated me as a personal favor to him. She also used me as a case study, so I'm written up in a journal somewhere."

"Ooh, that sounds fancy," I say, pulling off her tortoise Wayfarer Ray-Bans and placing them in the bag beside her so I can see those pretty eyes of hers.

"I read it once when I was a teenager. It was pretty dry reading, but it was fascinating at the same time. It was kinda cool to see the story of J, which was how I was identified in the article."

"What kinds of things did she teach you?"

Juliette's lips twist in thought. "Well, if I was doing my math homework, I'd sit down and get out my papers. Then I'd realize I didn't have a pencil, so I'd get up to get one. After working a couple problems, I'd decide I was thirsty, so I'd get up again to get some water. And so on and so forth." The wind catches a strand of hair that escaped her braid, and she tucks it behind her ear. "So basically, she taught me to make lists. Lots and lots of lists. Dr. Hough gave me a sparkly little pink notebook and a matching pen, and I had to write down every single thing I might need when doing a particular task. Then, before I sat down to get started, I had to make sure I had everything on the list within arm's reach. There were a lot of other things too, but that's what sticks out the most in my memory. I still use a similar notebook."

My heart flips over at the wistful tone in her voice, and I imagine an adorable little girl with blonde pigtails who didn't understand how her mind worked. I grip Juliette's hip and roll her toward me, cradling her cheek in my palm.

"I've said it before, and I'll say it again. I think you are absolutely brilliant, Juliette. You are such a talented writer, and I think a lot of it is because your brain works differently than other people's."

Her smile lights me up inside. "Maybe you're right. Sometimes, I just close my eyes and let my mind take off in all different directions like a herd of wild horses. Then it's like I can see ideas in the air and lasso the ones I want. It helps when I want to come up with a trait that makes one of my characters unique. Or a plot twist that no one sees coming."

I laugh. "Your plot twists are fucking diabolical." My finger follows a droplet of sweat that makes its way down her temple. "Want to get in the water and cool off?"

Juliette nods. "Sounds good. It's hot as Hades out here."

Standing, I reach out a hand to pull her to her feet. She's in a red-and-white striped bikini that makes me have some very wicked thoughts. I'm already sporting a chub from rubbing suntan oil on her luscious body earlier.

As soon as Juliette steps onto the sand, she winces and does a little tippy toe dance. "Damn sand is hot."

"Hop on," I say, presenting her with my back. A second later, I feel her weight on my back and cradle her thighs with my hands. Then I take off running, jostling her as much as possible.

"You're a maniac," she shrieks with laughter. "Doesn't that hurt your feet?"

"Nah, the bottoms of my feet are tough as shoe leather."

A few of the other beachgoers catcall, and I get a wink and a thumbs up from a huge dude sitting on a low lounge chair near the water.

I've noticed this quite a bit the past couple of days when people have seen Juliette and I on the beach or at dinner. Lots of smiles and nods of approval. It seems the entire resort likes us being together.

Juliette echoes my thoughts when I slow down and walk us into the water. "You ever feel like the people here are pulling for us? They're like our own personal cheering squad."

"I was just thinking that," I tell her, taking us farther out into the crystal water until I'm in chest-deep. I pull her around to my front, and she koala bears me, legs around my waist and arms over my shoulders.

"This place has a very positive vibe. Everyone is simply here to have fun, and I love that." The bottom of her blonde braid swirls in the gentle current. "Even though I'm not into this lifestyle, I think I'd come back here."

"I would too," I tell her, surprising myself. Just a few short days ago, I'd been ready to abandon this vacation and go back home. But then I met Juliette, and my entire outlook changed.

She unwinds her arms and leans back, floating in the cool water with her legs still looped around me. Stretching her arms out to her sides to float, she closes her eyes, a serene smile coasting across her pretty lips. My cock instantly morphs from a chub to a hard-on as I support her lower back with my hands.

When she wiggles her center against my crotch, she notices my obvious change in dick status, and her eyes pop open. Arching her eyebrows, she pulls herself back up and presses those perfect tits to my chest.

"I don't know how you're getting hard right now," she muses. "Aren't guys supposed to get shrinkage in cool water?"

"You're here," is my simple explanation, my eyes counting the cute freckles scattered across her nose. "My dick defies the laws of shrinkage when he sees you."

I lean forward to trace my tongue along the tan line over one breast. The swimsuit top she wore yesterday was slightly larger than this one, so she has a sliver of white peeking out, and it's begging to be licked.

"Don't get me all excited," she pants as her nipple pebbles against my chin. "Remember I have a pedicure appointment later."

"You sure you wouldn't rather stay with me?" I cajole, trying not to sound like a needy little bitch. I drop my hands to cup her ass. The striped bottoms she's wearing are also smaller than yesterday's suit. Not a thong, but definitely cheeky enough to grab my attention.

Oh, who the fuck am I kidding? Juliette could get my attention wearing a potato sack.

She arches into me and lays her tender lips on mine. "You could come with me," she suggests. "Turn those shoe leather feet as soft as a baby's butt."

A nervous laugh escapes me. "Sparkly toenails aren't exactly my thing, dream girl."

"Oh, you don't have to get sparkly ones. You don't even have to get them polished at all. Lots of men get it done." She bites into her bottom lip and her nose scrunches adorably as a blush seeps up her neck and to her cheeks. "And I don't know... I was actually thinking about canceling because I'd rather hang out with you some more, but if you went with me..."

My heartbeat intensifies so much, I'm concerned I may attract hungry sharks. Because I want to spend every minute of my last nine days with her too. Her eyes stay locked with mine, the hue of her irises set off by the sea. Not the water directly surrounding us. That's too light. And not the deep blue near the horizon. No, Juliette's eyes perfectly match the aqua a few feet away from us.

"And you promise there will be no glitter polish?" I verify.

"Nope, not a trace," she replies, leaning forward to whisper in my ear. "And I can promise that I'll suck your dick when we're done."

And *that*, my friends, is how Reno Swain ended up in a nail salon.

"Swear to Christ, I'm going to buy one of these chairs for my house," I groan as some kind of mystical balls roll up and down my lower back.

"Right?" Juliette asks from the chair beside me, her eyes closed in relaxation.

I watch as the nail lady, Audra, squirts some gloopy, lumpy stuff on my right calf. "What is this stuff?" I whisper, and Juliette peeps one eye open before closing it again.

"It's a sugar scrub, and it's divine." Her hand reaches blindly for mine, and I link our fingers together.

Audra begins scrubbing the gooey, sandy stuff up and down my leg. It's abrasive but feels good as fuck. She repeats it with the other leg and then does some kind of hot stone massage that has me stifling multiple groans.

When she pulls out a device that resembles a cheese grater, I squeeze Juliette's hand. She looks over at me questioningly, and I dart my eyes downward in a *what the fuck is happening here* gesture.

She giggles and explains, "It's to remove the dead skin."

Audra turns into a filing beast, sawing at the bottoms of my feet with quick, practiced motions. I'm appalled at the amount of shit being produced.

"I think I'm going to have to forgo the parmesan cheese on my salad tonight," I murmur to Juliette, and she covers her mouth with one hand. But her indelicate snort of laughter makes me smile.

While Juliette is getting hot-pink sparkly polish applied to her toes, Audra proceeds to nip and file and buff at my toenails with all kinds of things that I'm pretty sure she purchased from some instruments of torture shop that's only frequented by terrorists and Sicilian Mafia members.

"Shit," I hear from my right, and I look over to see Juliette pulling her red *Librarians Do It Quietly* ball cap down over her eyes. "Kat just came in," she hisses, scrunching down in her seat like she's attempting to melt into it.

The resort manager's green eyes rove around the room but stop when they land on Juliette. Then she heads our way, her heels clacking across the terracotta tile floor.

"She's coming over here," I warn under my breath, and Juliette winces.

"Ms. McNamara," Kat greets, stopping beside my date's chair. Juliette lifts her face and plasters on a smile.

"Oh, hi, Ms., um, Kat." Her voice is an adorable squeak of awkwardness. So far, she'd been able to avoid the manager after her rambling diatribe on her arrival day.

"I'm so sorry about this, but when housekeeping was cleaning your room, there was a small accident."

Juliette's eyes widen, and she sits up straight, concern instantly replacing her embarrassment. "Oh no. Is everyone okay?"

"Yes, yes. Everyone is fine," Kat reassures. "But she accidentally broke your phone charger when she moved it to make your bed." She holds up a black cord with the USB end hanging on by a thread.

"That's okay," Juliette says, visibly relaxing. "I can pick up another one in the gift shop."

"Already done," Kat tells her, holding up her other hand, which is holding a box. "The only problem is that you had a six-foot cable, and all we had available was a three-footer. But," she adds quickly, "I have a longer one on order, and it will be here on Sunday when the first plane arrives."

"That's really not neces—" Juliette starts, but Kat stops her with a sharp shake of her head and a stern look.

"I insist on replacing it, and to apologize, we would like to gift you a free massage." Her eyes shift toward me and turn shrewd before returning to Juliette. "A *couples* massage. In-room. And dinner for two on the beach with the guest of your choice." She looks quite pleased with herself, and I get the feeling she put me in the cottage next to Juliette's on purpose.

"That's really kind of you, but seriously, I don't expect any kind of special treatment. It was just a charging cord."

"Here on Pineapple Island, we pride ourselves on taking care of our guests and minimizing mistakes. If we do make a mistake, we fix it," the manager says with an upward tilt of her chin, as if begging someone to defy her.

"Then I accept. Thank you so much, Kat," Juliette says graciously before cutting her gaze toward me. "And I'll see if I can find someone to enjoy the dinner and massage with me."

Kat laughs and hands her the charger. "I'm sure you'll find someone. I'll go arrange for the dinner, and by the time you're done eating, our massage therapists will have everything set up in your cottage."

"That was totally over the top," Juliette says a few minutes later as we're leaving the salon with our pampered feet. "Maybe we should walk around the resort so I can find someone to be my date tonight."

I give her a firm swat on the ass, and she yelps out a giggle. "If you're getting naked in your cottage, I'm calling dibs on being there."

She pulls me to a stop beneath a palm tree and swivels to face me, pressing her long body against mine. "If I tell you something, will you promise not to get mad?"

"Depends," I say cautiously, hoping I hadn't read the situation wrong. What if she didn't want me to be her date tonight?

Juliette nuzzles her nose against the side of my neck and whispers, "Even if you didn't agree to get a pedicure with me, I was going to blow you tonight anyway."

I tilt her chin up so I can see her eyes beneath the cap she'd put on before our appointment. "I have a confession too. I was going to go with you even if you didn't offer a blow job."

Her smile is brilliant and teasing. "In that case..."

I silence her with my fingers over her mouth. "Uh-uh. No take backs," I insist before removing my hand and kissing those perfectly plump lips.

The ones that would be wrapped around my cock later tonight.

I couldn't wait.

Chapter 17

Reno

Ride my cock like you're mad at it.

DINNER ON THE BEACH was absolutely phenomenal. The food, the gorgeous sunset... and especially the company.

We sat side by side in front of a linen-draped table facing the sea as a bevy of workers waited on us hand and foot, while also maintaining a respectful distance when they weren't serving or clearing. We started with a wine flight accompanied by a selection of delicious appetizers before moving on to the soup course, the entrée, and then a shared dessert. And more wine, of course.

I was unable to keep my eyes off Juliette as we ate, missing my mouth more than once because she was just too goddamn beautiful to look away from. And the thing was, she seemed just as enamored of me, leaning her body toward mine like the few inches separating us was a mile-wide valley.

Many soft kisses were shared between courses, and we fed each other sumptuous bites of chocolate soufflé with a blood orange drizzle that was the second-best thing I'd ever had in my mouth. Juliette held the top spot.

It was hands down the most romantic night of my life, and I don't know if it was the elegant setting, the flickering candles, or the soft rush of the water against the shore, but I began to fall for Juliette McNamara.

And that was a very bad idea. Because this was *just a vacation fling.*

Yeah. Right.

And now I'm lying facedown on a wide massage table in the living area of Juliette's cottage. As promised, the therapists had moved the furniture aside and had everything prepared when we arrived. Candles softly lit the room, and the smell of lavender and something else herb-y that I couldn't identify permeated the air around us.

Juliette lets out a quiet groan, and I pull my head from the circular pillow and look over at her. She's also facedown while Jevaun—who is Kat's husband—massages her shoulders. I, on the other hand, have a savage woman named Birgitta, who has the ability to find muscles I didn't even know I possessed. No fucking lie, the woman's biceps are bigger than mine, but she's a damn master at working out even the deepest of knots.

If I wasn't already falling for Juliette, I might ask Birgitta for her hand in marriage. And I'm only ninety-nine percent kidding.

"Turn over," my future betrothed orders in her thick accent, holding up the sheet covering my naked body like a tent. As I do, I notice Juliette doing the same, and we share a heated glance. *Yeah, sorry, Birgitta. I think I'm taken.*

I grow more and more relaxed as Birgitta works on my legs and feet, and by the time she moves up to my head, I'm practically in a stupor. The scent of warm peppermint oil blends with the other aromas, and I feel a tingling sensation on my scalp. It's heaven, and some time during the scalp massage, I drift fully off to sleep.

Hands, gentle ones this time, ease the sheet down my body, and I peel my eyes open to find Juliette on my table, kneeling between my legs. "Dream girl," I murmur, sleepily turning my head from side to side to search the room.

"They're gone," she whispers, lowering her head to kiss my bare abs. "Jevaun said we can leave the tables on the porch, and they'll retrieve them later."

My cock notices his favorite person's proximity and springs to life. Juliette flashes me a saucy smile as she lowers the sheet to fully expose my growing erection.

"Damn, baby," I groan when she licks a stripe up my length. Fisting my dick, she lifts it and proceeds to lick every single inch of me, stopping just short of the head. I fucking ache for her.

When her hair falls around her face and impedes the spectacular view of my dream girl treating my cock like her favorite popsicle, I gather the blonde locks in both hands and hold them against the back of her head. She must have had the same peppermint oil treatment I had because the strands are slick between my fingers.

Aqua eyes sparkle in the candlelight as she opens her mouth and takes the tip of me inside. She's warm and wet, and my eyelids flutter at the incredible sensation, but I manage to keep them open. I don't want to miss a second of this.

"You taste so good," she murmurs, drinking down the wetness dripping from me. "I'm going to suck this big cock until my jaw hurts."

"Fucking Christ, baby," I grate out. "You are the sexiest woman I've ever seen."

"Mmm," she hums, taking me deeper, the sound vibrating down my cock and into my balls. Her pink lips surround me, her tongue dancing along the underside of my shaft as she slides her mouth up and down in a slow, sensuous rhythm that threatens to unhinge me.

I fucking love some tongue action when a woman is going down on me, but most don't do it, instead sticking to the simple in and out motion. Which—don't get me wrong—feels damn good, but this is on another level. Juliette McNamara is a damn master at pleasing a man.

She continues like that, her pretty mouth lowering inch by inch with each bob of her head until her lips meet the fingers grasping the base of my cock. Then she swallows, her throat tightening around my crown.

"Yeah, just like that, honey. You suck cock like such a good girl."

She speeds up, her free hand coasting up and down my torso, tweaking my nipple and caressing my abs. Every touch sets my body on fire. My fingers tighten in her hair as I lift my hips from the table and force a gag from her. She pulls back for only a second before deep-throating me again. And again.

"Fuck yeah. You like gagging on my dick, don't you?"

Her lips stretch around my girth, but I can still make out the slight smile as she nods. Pulling out to the tip, she worships the head of my cock with that velvety tongue as she dips one hand between my legs to cup my balls. Rolling them expertly between soft fingers, she works her mouth back down my shaft.

My hands grow rough in her hair as my control slips. Juliette's saliva eases the glide of her mouth over my heated flesh, and I bite out a string of curse words that would make a sailor gasp.

I can make out the swell of her ass as she bends over me, giving me the best head of my life. With her hair bunched in my hands and her long lashes fluttering closed to rest against her cheeks, she is simply breathtaking. One tanned arm bunches and releases as she jacks me off while completely devouring my cock.

"So motherfucking perfect, Juliette. Tell me your cunt is dripping for me. Tell me you're so wet, my cock will slide right home in that perfect little pussy of yours."

Her eyes open, and she responds with a wink that makes my balls want to explode. I inhale, finding her scent over the others in the air and reveling in it.

"I can smell how turned on you are, baby. I'm going to fill you so full of my cock you'll never be able to feel another man without thinking of me. Without wishing it was *me* inside you."

Juliette whimpers and continues sliding her mouth up and down my length while also stroking me with her hand. And her fucking tongue never stops.

The scent of her arousal intensifies when I twist my hands in her hair and fuck up into her mouth with sharp snaps of my hips. I'm being rough with her, but she seems to like it as much as I do. Well, maybe not quite that much because I'm about to...

"Fuck. Stop, sweet girl. Please," I beg, my voice harsh with restraint.

She takes her time working her way back up to my tip before releasing me with a soft pop. "What's wrong?"

The playful glint in her eyes tells me she knows *exactly* what's wrong.

"I don't want to come yet. I want you to ride my cock like you're mad at it."

As Juliette sits up with a vixen-like grin, my hands release her hair and let it fall around her bare shoulders. She's completely naked and a million percent glorious, her golden skin glistening in the soft light.

"Next time, I want you to blow down my throat," she informs me, and I feel a muscle clenching in my jaw.

"Done. Now let me get up and wash my hands so I can find a condom and then touch you." I wiggle my fingers. "I've got peppermint oil all over me, and I don't think it's approved for pussies, but I need to get you ready."

She stretches one arm over to her massage table and triumphantly holds up a foil packet. "I got one from the bedroom after Jevaun and Birgitta left." Resting her hands on either side of my head, she presses her lips to mine. "And I don't want you to get me ready. I want you to watch me struggle to take every hard inch of your dick."

Fuck me. I almost spontaneously combust on the spot. Grabbing her hips, I adjust her until she's straddling my stomach. "Rub yourself on me, dream girl. Let me see how wet you are for me."

Juliette hesitates, so I gently urge her to move with my hands. "Ohhhh," she breathes, letting her teeth skid over her bottom lip, the flesh swollen and red from my carnal treatment of her mouth. "That feels... good."

She takes over, grinding her cunt forward and back on my abs, using the hard ridges to pleasure herself. I can tell when she's almost there because her hips take on an erratic rhythm and soft whimpers spill from her parted lips.

She begins to come, and I grip her tighter, steadying the movement of her hips. "Good girl, Juliette. Get yourself off."

With soft pants of my name, she comes all over me. When her eyes go drowsy and her lips turn up in satisfaction, I stare down at the wetness she left on my stomach before arching a stern look at her.

"Look at this mess, Juliette."

Her breathing is ragged as her eyes drop and then return unapologetically to mine. "Is that a complaint?" she asks sassily, rolling her lips inward to mask her smile.

"Lick it up," I command. "And then let me suck your cum from your tongue."

Her eyes widen, but she scoots back, purposely dragging her soaked cunt across my cock before bending to thoroughly lap her juices from my abs. Then she works her way back up my body with her tongue out.

I grasp the back of her head and suck her tongue into my mouth, my cock pulsing at her sweet, salty taste.

"Reno," she gasps into my mouth. "I need you. Now. Please."

Fuck me sideways up the ass if I don't need her just as much. "Condom. Hurry," I tell her, urgently pushing her up so she's sitting astride me. My penis is so swollen, I'm a little concerned I might not be able to hold back until we get that damn protection on. He's ready to plunge in head first.

Juliette unwraps the rubber and sheaths my shaft before positioning herself over me. She reaches for my dick, rubbing it through her wet center before angling the head against her opening.

"Take me, baby. Let me feel that pussy eat me up," I growl as she begins to lower herself.

I'm dying to give her clit the attention it deserves, but I'm afraid the peppermint oil on my fingers isn't safe for that most sensitive area. A trip to the hospital for some kind of vaginal burn is not how I want this evening to end.

So I grip her hip with one hand and cup her breast with the other, thumbing her nipple. It hardens beautifully for me. "Take your time and work your pussy down on me, Juliette. I want every inch of my cock buried in your sweetness."

"That's... a lot of inches," she pants, and I grin. Because what guy doesn't like hearing that? "Talk me through it. I love when you do that."

And I love speaking my filthy thoughts to her. "You can take it, dream girl. Roll those hips for me." With my guidance, she does, sinking further down onto my stiff rod. "That's it. Such a good girl with a perfect pussy. Made to take my cock. Made to be fucked."

Juliette whimpers and swivels her hips in tiny circles until she's worked herself all the way down on my erection. "So good," she tells me, her eyes turning into aquamarine jewels in the delicate light from the candles. "I like when it hurts a little bit."

I'm not the kind of guy who enjoys hurting women, but I can't deny the effect her words have on me. My cock swells, stretching her inner walls even more. I abandon her hip and cradle both her breasts in my hands. They are the perfect size, filling my palms like they were made to be there.

With my thumbs and forefingers, I pinch them hard, earning me a succulent cry from the woman on top of me. "Fuck me, baby. Show me what you've got," I rasp.

"Oh god, Reno," she breathes, her voice pitching up an octave as she lifts and lowers herself on my dick. The friction and heat threaten my tightly held control.

"Yeah, sweetheart. Say my name. Tell me whose cock you're riding. Who's going to get you off tonight, Juliette?"

She slides up and down again, her eyes rolling back and her lids shuttering closed. I miss those beautiful gems immediately, but when she tips her chin to the ceiling like she's in ecstasy, I decide I can deal with it. Because Juliette has entered full-fledged goddess mode.

"Reno. Fuck, Reno. You're so deep."

I slide one hand up to her beautiful face, tracing her lips with my thumb as she bounces up and down on my dick.

"You really are my dream girl," I tell her. "I could watch you ride me all night long." Dropping my hand, I cup her throat, and her eyelids drift open. "Is this okay?" I ask, watching for her reaction.

I can see the lusty film of desire in her gaze when she nods. "I like it." She rests her hands on my broad chest for leverage and works her pussy up and down my length, faster and faster. Her ass slaps against my pelvis as the sights and sounds and smells of sex fill the room.

I'm meeting her hips with my own, pounding so hard up into her, I'm afraid we may break the table. When I tighten my fingers and thumb around the sides of her neck, Juliette lets out a series of *ohhh* sounds, each longer than the last.

"That's it, baby. I can feel your hot little cunt tightening around me. Show me how a good girl comes."

Juliette's entire body shudders, and she throws back her head as a hell of an orgasm takes over. She's riding me with furious pumps of her hips, her hands sliding sensuously up her body to plunge into that mass of blonde hair. I've never seen anything quite so provocative as she loses herself in the act of orgasming.

Words stick in my throat as I simply watch her taking me, that beautiful body writhing and riding and coming so damn hard she's about to break my cock in half. I don't care what anyone says. This—*this right here*—is the greatest show on earth. With three more heaving breaths, Juliette collapses forward onto my chest, her face nestled in my neck.

"Wow," she pants. "That's about all I can manage right now."

"Wow indeed," I say with a chuckle, easing my hands down to her round ass. She's slowed her pumps, and I can still feel her pussy fluttering around my dick with the aftershocks of her climax.

"Sorry I went without you," she murmurs, breathing heavily against my now damp flesh.

"Hey," I admonish, urging her to look at me with a nudge of my chin. She lifts her head a little, those lovely eyes meeting mine with a sated fog clouding them. "Never apologize for giving me your pleasure. It's all I want."

Weirdly enough, it's true. My own pleasure has taken a backseat to my desire to satisfy this woman. Well, my greedy cock disagrees, but the rest of me is happy with the results.

Juliette cups my face and kisses me slowly, her tongue finding entrance into my mouth. Our mouths meld together, and we're totally lost in each other until she finally breaks away.

"I want to make you come now," she says against my lips, and my cock offers his willingness to volunteer for that particular activity with a sharp twitch inside her. When Juliette tries to sit up, I hold her against me.

"No, like this. I want to feel your body against mine."

We begin to move together, her tits pressed against my chest, her knees bracketing my hips. My fingers dig into her ass, urging her to grind her clit against me. Do I want to come so hard my brain explodes? Yes. Do I want to feel Juliette come around me again? Also yes. In fact, hell yes.

We start out slow, with hard, deep grinds of our pelvises, but after a few minutes, things grow more heated as our bodies reach for that ultimate peak.

"Kiss me," I demand, and her lips crush mine in a tangle of tongues as we go primal on each other.

It's not gentle, but it's so fucking intimate, bodies rocking and mouths fused together. I slide one hand up to clutch her hair and allow her to take over... and she does not disappoint. Keeping her chest against mine, she lifts and lowers her hips, fucking me to within an inch of my life with loud slaps of flesh on flesh.

Our joining is sticky and sweet, hot and supremely dirty. I feel it the instant she turns that corner from searching to finding, her next climax within reach.

"Reno," she moans into my mouth. "I'm..."

"I know, baby. I can feel it. Come with me this time." My hand fists roughly in her hair as I hold her head in place to accept my lust-fueled kiss once again. My release jets up the length of my dick at the same time Juliette's walls clamp around me.

I come so hard, I lose the majority of my senses. I can't see; I can't hear. All I can do is feel. And I'm currently feeling some very big feelings...

And they aren't entirely sexual.

"What is that thing?" I ask warily as Juliette unwraps a smallish disc in the bathroom.

She looks up at me in surprise. "A shower steamer. You haven't used any of yours yet?"

I shrug. "I saw them in the basket in my bathroom but didn't pay much attention to them. I figured it was girly soap or something."

She tosses the metallic wrapper in the trash and holds up the disc for me to sniff. It's slightly smaller than her palm and smells fresh and soft.

"This one is called Ocean Cottage, and it's my favorite so far. You just toss one on the floor of the shower and let the aroma mix with the steam."

She drops it at the edge of the enormous shower but not directly beneath the spray. A few seconds later, I catch a whiff of that fresh scent mixed with something minty.

The shower is a replica of mine, lined with intricate tiles of taupe and teal. And also like mine, it's huge. You could probably comfortably fit eight people in here.

But it's just *us* stepping in and closing the glass door. Juliette and me. Together. I try not to think about the time we have left, which is seeming all too short with each day that passes.

We hold each other. We kiss. I clean between her legs and wash her hair. She does the same for me. I whisper soft words of praise to her while my hands roam over her slick body. We kiss some more.

And I don't want this night to end. But there's that stupid *rule one* hanging over my head like a precariously perched boulder. So after we get out of the shower and dry off, I get dressed and fold up the massage tables before placing them on the front porch.

And then I go back to cottage five...

Wishing I was still in cottage four.

Chapter 18

Juliette

I would let that man disrespect me.

My fingers fly across the keyboard, but my brain is only halfway engaged. The rest of it is reserved for the man who is probably fast asleep in cottage five. I wish he was still here.

Rule one, Juli, I scold myself. *You both agreed on it.*

I'm halfway through my chapter when the ringing of my phone startles me. Picking it up, I see it's a FaceTime from Holly.

"Hey, you're up late," I announce when I answer. My sister-in-law is a game warden, so she generally gets up early in the mornings.

"Yeah, Aiden woke up and decided he was hung-y," she tells me, and I laugh at the cuteness of my nephew.

"Did you feed the little angel?"

"Your brother gave him a little snack. They're both back asleep now, but I—I couldn't sleep." A tear slips down her brown cheek, and I'm instantly alarmed. Holly never cries.

"What's wrong. Are you sick?"

She shakes her head and swipes at the tear, which is promptly replaced by another. "No, I had to rescue a turtle today. He got caught in a trotline on the river."

Awww, my poor friend. "Was he... Did he make it?" I ask cautiously.

Holly rolls her lips in and out a few times, her head bobbing in the affirmative. "Yeah, he's okay. I just..." She looks away from me, blinking up at the corner of the room.

Then it hit me. *Turtles.* "It made you think of Evie," I surmise in a gentle tone, and her face crumples.

"Y-yes. He was a Sabine map turtle, not a sea turtle like Evie loved. But I still couldn't stop thinking of her the entire time I was disentangling him."

"Oh, Holls. I'm so sorry. I've been thinking of her too."

She looks back at me, her head tilted to the side. "Because you're in a tropical location? Like where she went missing?"

My own tear escapes my eyelid and tracks down my face. "Yeah, Evie's always on my mind when I think of the ocean. She loves the beach so much." *Loves*, present tense. Not *loved*, past tense. Because even after seventeen years, I can't bear to think of my full-of-life friend not being out there. Somewhere.

Holly scrubs at her face. "What if I hadn't gone straight to bed that night? She said she was going to the ice machine. I should have walked with her. I didn't hear a struggle or anything. Why didn't I hear anything, Jules? How could she just disappear off the face of the motherfucking earth?" She was getting worked up, a mixture of grief and anger turning her skin ruddy.

My sister-in-law and I first met in college, and a group of six of us went on a Spring Break trip together, including Evie Bouvier. The hotel was unable to place all our rooms together, so while I was on the third floor, Evie and Holly's rooms were on the seventh.

"Holly," I say soothingly, "don't start spinning. It's not good for the baby."

She closes her eyes and nods, taking several deep breaths to calm herself. "You're right," she finally says, lifting her eyelids. Her hazel irises shine with the guilt I know she always carries with her since she was the last person to ever see our friend alive.

"It's not your fault," I say for about the millionth time since the disappearance. "When we're done talking, I want you to go get in bed and cuddle up with Bubba. And if you're not feeling better tomorrow, maybe you should call your therapist."

Holly sighs. "Okay. I'm sorry. I don't know why I'm like this."

My heart pinches in sympathy but I attempt to lighten the mood. "I hate to pull the pregnancy hormone card, but it does heighten your emotions. Remember the McDonald's ice cream incident when you were pregnant with Aiden?"

A scowl falls over her face, her mood instantly shifting. "Seriously though, is it too fucking much to ask to get a caramel sundae at midnight on a Thursday? It's absolutely ridiculous that their ice cream machine is always down. Is there some kind of ice cream machine repairman shortage that I'm unaware of?"

"It's completely absurd," I agree, stifling a laugh, but she notices anyway.

"Don't laugh at me, bitch. I'm fragile."

I can't hold back anymore and snort with laughter. "Oh yes. You're a delicate flower, Holls."

"Distract me," she demands with a wave of her hand. "Tell me what's going on with you and Sir Forearms."

Sinking back into my chair, I rake my teeth over my bottom lip. "Girl, he's so fucking hot. I've had more sex in the past few days than I've had in the past year."

"But is it *good* sex?" she asks with an arch of her dark eyebrows.

"Phe-nom-en-al," I sound out, syllable by syllable. "I would let that man disrespect me in any way he wanted to. Like, I'd give up every ounce of dignity I possess for five seconds of his rude-ass mouth."

"Ohh, I love when they get rude," Holly groans. "Your brother does this one thing where—"

"Ah, ah," I scold, holding up both hands and scrunching my nose. "Let me just stop the kinky train before you pull it into the station, sis."

She lets out one of her hearty laughs. "Right. You don't like it when I talk about your brother banging me like a barn door in a hurricane."

"And yet you continue to do so," I reply archly, tapping my fingertips against my lips before continuing. "Anyway, he's got this filthy mouth while we're engaged in our… activities. But when we're done, he's a total dreamboat. And not just the regular aftercare. He gets really sweet and praises me."

Holly's hand covers her heart. "Aww, I love that for you, honey. Now that we have a kid, we're usually exhausted by the time we're finished, so I'm happy to get a smack on the ass and a *good job, babe.*"

I giggle because that sounds exactly like something my gruff brother would do. Holly covers a yawn with her palm, and I bring my face closer to the screen. "Why don't you go get some husband cuddles and try to fall back asleep."

Her eyelids droop a little, and she nods. "Sounds good. Thank you for talking me through my breakdown. You're one of the only people who understands how it feels to have been there."

"I know, sweetie. And you can call me any time." I chew the inside of my cheek. "You know, one good thing came from Evie's disappearance."

Holly tilts her head in thought before a soft smile crosses her rosy lips. "I wouldn't have met your brother if he hadn't driven you to that TV interview we did after she went missing."

"Yeah," I say quietly. "And you know Evie would have totally taken credit for you two meeting and getting married."

Holly's smile turns sadly nostalgic. "She would be the best honorary aunt in the world." She yawns again.

"Go," I order. "Husband snuggles. Now."

"Maybe I can wake him up and get him to wear me out to the point of exhaustion," she suggests with an eyebrow wiggle.

"Go for it. Just don't tell me the deets."

"You loved hearing about my exploits when we were in college," she argues with a teasing frown.

"That's before your exploits included *my freaking brother*," I point out.

"He is a freak," she adds cheekily, and I groan.

"Go away, brother fucker."

"Bye, Sir Forearms fucker."

Once we disconnect, I stare at the blank screen of my phone, a sense of envy settling on my shoulders. Holly is probably curled up with her husband right now, taking comfort in not being alone.

And I'm here. By myself in my cottage.

Before I can think about it, my thumbs tap out a message to Reno.

Juliette: I miss you.

I immediately want to take it back. *Shit! Stupid, stupid, stupid.* That sounded so needy. My brain scrambles to remember how to unsend a message. My younger brother, Xander, showed me once. He's the tech-y one in the family.

My thumb presses against the dumbass message I'd just sent, and a menu pops up. I'm about to hit the *Undo Send* option when a knock sounds on the back door a few feet away. My head whips around.

"Who the hell?" I murmur, but then I know. *Or is that hope?*

Setting down my phone, I cross to the sliding door and pull back the vertical blinds to reveal one very large hockey player standing on my back porch. In his goddamn underwear.

Disengaging the safety bar and lock, I yank the door to the side. "Reno..."

But he doesn't give me time to say much more than that because he barges in like a bull, lifting me from the floor with his big arms before charging toward the bed.

"Fuck rule one," he snaps before tackling me to the soft mattress.

Happiness fills my soul as Reno begins to rip my pajamas from my body. *Oh hell yes.*

Fuck rule one, indeed.

Turns out the big bull is a cuddler. I awake at dawn on Saturday morning to the feel of a hard body plastered to my back, a tree trunk of a thigh draped over my hip, and a hand holding my left boob hostage.

At some point in the night—between rounds three and four, I think—Reno got up and closed the door, which he unceremoniously left open when he did the whole hot tackling thing. But he forgot to close the blinds, so the first gossamer strands of sunrise are now slinking into the dark room.

I wiggle a little, and that movement is met with a disapproving grunt from the man behind me. His arm bands more tightly around my middle.

"I have to go to the bathroom," I protest, and he grunts again but releases me.

As soon as I do my business and return, Reno yanks me back onto the bed, facing him this time, and tucks my head beneath his chin. "Five more minutes and then I have to do my workout."

"Stupid workouts," I murmur, quite content with my face buried in his neck. He smells like sex. Like, an ungodly amount of sex.

When I wake again to the sound of heavy breathing, I peer over the edge of the bed. Reno is a shirtless, sweaty mess, obviously just having come from a run, and he's on the floor banging out approximately five million push-ups. His spine is ramrod straight, and the muscles of his arms and shoulders bunch with every movement.

Then he has the audacity to roll over and begin doing sit ups while I watch with rapt appreciation. When he's done, he rolls back onto his shoulders and then shoves forward, landing on his feet like some kind of goddamn super-sized gymnast.

While I lie there with my mouth gaped open, he grabs a towel from the chair and rubs his head, leaving his hair a sexy-ass mess of damp raven locks. Then he turns around and notices me, flashing a half-cocked grin that hits me right in the vagina.

"Hey, babe."

"If my vajajay didn't need physical therapy from last night's marathon of debauchery, I would be all over you right now," I warn, lifting up on one elbow.

Reno chuckles and walks over to me, bending to place a soft kiss on the tit that just popped out to say hello. "Relax, dream girl. You have other holes." Then he sucks my nipple into his dirty mouth, and *oh my muffins,* my pussy decides maybe she's not so sore after all.

"Give me a minute to check my insurance co-pays, and maybe we can..."

He laughs around my boob before pulling off slowly in a long suck. "I'm kidding, Juliette. We can just hang out. We don't have to fuck like rabbits every time we're together."

"I think your cock begs to differ," I tell him when he straightens and I see the heavy rod suddenly standing at attention beneath those tight workout shorts of his.

And again with one of those adorable smiles... "Don't pay him any attention. He has no self-control when he sees you." He adjusts himself, and I try to figure out exactly how one is supposed to ignore something of that magnitude. "I'm going to take a quick shower, and then we can grab breakfast."

"I don't usually eat breakfast," I tell him, earning me a scowl.

"You have to eat something," Reno protests. "Even just some fruit or a protein bar."

"I'll eat a good lunch."

He strokes a hand through my messy hair. "I'll order you some fruit after my shower."

Stubborn-ass man.

"Do you need help with this in the shower?" I inquire sweetly, palming the bulge in his shorts.

Reno cocks an eyebrow. "I wouldn't turn that down, but *no sex*," he says firmly.

We stuck to the *no sex* rule. Well, kind of. I gave him a hand job and let him come all over my stomach, and then he dropped to his knees to slowly, gently eat my pussy with a single finger inside me to stroke my G-spot.

And now we're having some hammock time while I tap away on my computer. I don't generally like anyone watching me while I write, but Reno has actually been quite helpful.

"I like the way you worded that," he says about my last paragraph.

"There are so many things expected in a romance book, but I try to phrase them slightly differently or come up with something unique." I chew on my bottom lip. "Like every single female character wears smokey eye makeup and red lips, but I want this character to be different."

I feel Reno's eyes on my face. "What's that pink stuff you wear on your eyelids when we go to dinner?"

"Just a pink shimmer."

He nods, still inspecting me. "Yeah, go with that. It's pretty and soft." Lifting my chin with one finger, he kisses my mouth. "And lips don't have to be bright red to be sexy. That pink lip gloss you wear makes me have very unsavory thoughts."

Good lord, this man...

"Unsavory. I like that word," I tell him, going back to my writing before I jump him like a cat in heat.

When I finish the chapter, we read over it, and I nod. "I like it."

"Me too," he says, taking the laptop and placing it on the ground beside us. Then he removes my glasses from my face and sets them on top. "Now make out with me until it's time for lunch. Then we can hit the beach."

"Can we do the pool today instead? I'm feeling cocktails and a lounge chair."

"Perfect," he says. "Just like you."

CHAPTER 19

Juliette

Wetter than water

THE NEXT FIVE DAYS go much like that Saturday. Reno works out in the morning, we have breakfast, and then I write in the hammock while he watches and commentates. After lunch, we spend time together on the beach or at the pool.

And the nights? Yeah. The nights are the best. I don't know what kinds of vitamins Reno Swain takes, but they need to be marketed with a big photo of him and our sex stats on a cleverly designed graphic. Perhaps with some graphs and pie charts detailing stamina and orgasm counts.

By Thursday, I'm completely addicted to the man, and the thought of him leaving in three days makes my stomach clench.

"I think it's right up here," Reno says, gesturing to the left before maneuvering the open-air Jeep down the bumpy road. A few minutes later, the most beautiful waterfall I've ever seen comes into view. It's not super high, only about twelve feet, so the fall of water is gentle.

"Wow," I breathe, pulling out my phone to take some pictures for inspiration. I'm a visual learner—hence the cock folder on my computer—so these will come in handy when I'm writing later.

I stand and poke my head out the top of the vehicle, closing my eyes and inhaling the intoxicating scents. It smells earthy and sweet like flowers and grass after a fresh rain, with notes of salty water layered on top.

After opening my eyes and surveying the landscape, I tap some notes about the colors into my notes app. Deep purples and magentas. Bright yellows and oranges. Splashes of vibrant reds. It's absolutely breathtaking.

When I'm done, I glance over to see Reno standing patiently beside my door with his hands in his pockets, an affectionate smile on his face.

"You done, or do you need more time?" he asks, and I toss my phone onto the seat and shake my head.

"All done."

Without opening the door, he lifts me from the vehicle like I'm light as a feather and sets me on my feet.

I run my hands up his bare chest, letting my fingers slide through the dark hair there. "Can I petition someone so that you're required to walk around shirtless at all times? Is there some kind of organization like the International Association Of Hot Guys Who Should Go Nipples Out At All Times?"

"Ahhh, yes," he says, nodding sagely. "The IAOHGWSGNOAAT. A fine institution."

I giggle, loving how silly he can be with me. "They're truly doing the Lord's work over there."

His hands slip around me and untie my silver bikini top with little effort. "You know, the only way to enjoy a waterfall is naked."

"Is that so?" I tease.

"Uh-huh. It's Reno's Law, and it's been approved by the IAOHGWSGNOAAT," he says, his voice taking on a deep timbre as he goes to work on my denim shorts.

"I certainly wouldn't want to be in violation of the law."

"No, ma'am, you do not. The punishment is quite severe." My shorts hit the ground, leaving me only in my swim bottoms.

Hovering my lips over his, I whisper, "Are there spankings involved?"

Reno nips my bottom lip. "Violators will definitely experience RAS?" When I lift my brows in question, he explains. "Red ass syndrome."

"Aren't you full of acronyms today?" I ask, untying the drawstring at his waist. "Better get these trunks off before I'm forced to punish you. Give you your own dose of RAS."

He grins and helps me to get his shorts down before removing my bottoms, retrieving all our clothes, and then tossing it inside the Jeep while I grab the beach towels. Then we hold hands and walk to the edge of the turquoise pool that spans the length of the private area.

The pool is surprisingly warm as we step in and swim out to the center, where the water is slightly more teal. We flip onto our backs, link outstretched hands, and stare up at the azure sky.

After a few minutes, I note, "There aren't any interesting clouds today."

"Naw, they all look like cotton balls," Reno agrees and then sighs. "I miss Sexy Bunny."

I giggle, but the sound soon fades away as my mind turns to Reno leaving. *Three days.* I don't want him to go.

Turning my thoughts to safer topics, I say, "I'm trying to decide what the waterfall sounds like. For my book."

"Hmmm," he grumbles. "It's not a rush of water. Much softer than that."

"But it's more than a trickle," I add.

We both close our eyes and listen as we hold hands, our bodies floating in the buoyant warmth of the water.

"It's soothing and peaceful," Reno notes.

My brain sorts through all the words, rearranging them into something pretty. "A thousand peaceful trickles that combine into a soothing melody that surrounds us."

"Mmhmm, that's good shit," he says, and I giggle and turn my face toward him. He's even gorgeous in profile.

"You ever thought about becoming a writer? I think you could nail a romance book."

He smiles at the sky. "I'd rather nail you." Then he opens those pretty green eyes and looks at me. "So there's a waterfall scene in your book?"

"Yep, it's near the end. But first I need to infuse a little drama into the situation." I do an evil witch cackle, and Reno laughs.

"What's rolling around in that beautiful brain of yours?"

I love that he likes my brain. My chaotic, scattered brain that's sometimes difficult to keep under control. But Reno likes it. Appreciates it, and *dammit, I'm going to miss him.*

"Anna's ex is going to come into town and try to get her back."

"That twat, Bradford?" Reno mutters. "Tell me she's not going to entertain that bullshit."

"Of course not," I scoff. "Bradford is going to want to come to her place, but Anna insists on meeting somewhere public. Then Reid is going to see Bradford and Anna at the restaurant, and that's when he's going to realize he *can't* lose her."

"Because he loves her," Reno finishes.

"Exactamundo. So he shows up at her apartment later and..." I pause dramatically. "Claims her."

Reno's grin widens. "Ahh, the claiming fuck. Took him long enough."

"Well, he's a stubborn jock who refuses to get in touch with his feelings," I explain.

"He's stupid for not realizing Anna is exactly the kind of woman he needs." Reno's eyes search my face for a long moment, and then his eyelids shutter closed as he turns his face back to the sky.

The silence that follows is heavy, an oppressive thing that threatens to push me beneath the surface of the water and drown me. So I do the only thing I can.

I pinch Reno's ass, yell, "Got your goose!" and then dive beneath the water to swim away. Even with my head submerged, I hear his yelp of surprise, and then I can sense him behind me, giving chase.

The waterfall smacks against my back as I swim underneath it and surface on the other side. Seconds later, Reno pops up in front of me, a playful scowl on his forehead as he swipes the water away from his face with one big hand.

"Got your goose?" he asks, lifting one dark eyebrow.

I grin. "My friend Evie and I used to play that when we were little girls at summer camp."

"Sounds delightful," he says sarcastically before hauling me against him. His body is big and warm, the skin sleek beneath my fingers when I run them over his shoulders.

We're in a kind of cave thing behind the waterfall, and it's somehow quieter back here. Darker too, though scant streams of light penetrate the dimness and glint off the rocky surfaces. The water hits Reno up to his shoulders, and he holds me surely in his arms.

I wrap my legs around his waist, and his dick begins to harden. Fuck, he's so long and thick. My hips move of their own free will, rocking against his shaft. A groan echoes through the space, and I realize it came from me.

"You're so goddamn hot," Reno murmurs before latching his mouth onto the side of my neck. I let out more tiny noises of encouragement as his tongue begins to swirl against my flesh.

"You're making me wetter than this water," I tell him, when he wraps his hand around the ponytail braid fastened high on the crown of my head and tugs it to the side to give himself better access. He works his way up my neck and to my ear. He knows that's my trigger point, and he takes full advantage, nipping and sucking on my lobe.

"And you're making me harder than the stone around us," he mutters in my ear.

I roll my hips against his firm erection. "I can feel that."

Reno releases my hair and grasps my ass in both hands, lifting me a little. "Need to suck on these perfect tits." His lips surround one nipple, and he suckles, lapping at the peak with his plush tongue. He feasts on me, first one breast and then the other until my nipples could cut glass.

In this position, the head of his cock rests right at my entrance, and I swirl my lower body, rimming his dick with my pussy.

"Fuck, dream girl. You feel like heaven," he moans, urging my hips back and forth over the very end of him. "Can you get off like this?"

"I could get off from the sound of your voice," I inform him, holding onto his shoulders as he slides through my slit. "Need you to kiss me."

Reno cups the back of my head to pull me down toward him, and when he does, my body shifts. I'm so freaking slick between my legs, the head of his cock slides in easily.

We both freeze, our eyes meeting in the soft light. "Don't move," he orders, his voice going raspy as a shudder courses through his body. "Don't fucking move or..." He crashes his lips to mine, his mouth welcoming my tongue inside.

As we kiss, our bodies begin to move in tandem as we play *just the tip*. God I want to slide down the enormous cock between my legs, but we keep things shallow, even as our kiss deepens. I can feel myself dripping all over his head as it stimulates my opening.

When Reno rips his mouth from mine, his breathing is heavy and his eyes practically feral. "I've never fucked anyone raw, and I've never wanted to, but god help me, Juliette. I want to bury myself so deep in your hot cunt I'll need a map to find my way back out."

"I'm clean," I blurt out, my needy pussy apparently finding a direct line to my vocal cords and taking charge. I don't just want him inside me. It's a visceral *need*.

"I am too," he assures me.

"And I'm on birth control," I tell him, giving him the final permission he needs. And he takes it, bucking his hips upward until he's balls deep inside me. Bare.

It. Is. Indescribable.

"Goddammit," he grits out between clenched teeth. "This is the most incredible thing I've ever felt."

"Me too," I admit, my voice going breathy.

Reno cups the sides of my neck with both hands, his thumbs resting on my jaw. "Go. Slow. Please, baby. Or you'll pull my trigger way too soon."

I nod and give a tentative swivel of my hips, pulling a moan from both of us.

"You're so deep."

"I know, baby," he croons before closing his mouth over mine again. The kiss is exceptionally sweet, our tongues moving slowly in a rhythm that matches the slide of his erection in and out of me.

I'm so full of him, filled in a way I've never felt before. My tight walls grip him, attempting to hold his dick hostage when I pull out to the tip and then glide all the way back down without an ounce of hurry. I do it again and again, tilting my hips at the perfect angle to ride my G-spot against his crown.

As my orgasm approaches, I lose my breath and pull my mouth from his to gulp in a lungful of air. But his green eyes boring into mine is too damn much, too damn intimate, and I drop my face to his shoulder. Reno doesn't seem to mind, wrapping his arms around my back and binding our bodies together.

"I like having you close like this," he murmurs into my hair before burying his face in the side of my neck.

I like that too. Probably a little too much.

We hold each other, our bodies taking on a deep grinding movement as we both near our completion. There are no more words, only soft moans and heavy breaths.

And yet we both know when the time is right, our releases coming simultaneously. I bite into his shoulder at the intensity of the orgasm, and when I feel him pulsing and spilling himself inside me, I cry out, "I don't want you to leave on Sunday."

It's one of the most vulnerable things I could have said to him, but I couldn't help it. It was the bald, unfiltered truth.

I don't want him to leave because I'm falling for him.

Reno is quiet on the way back to the resort. Uncomfortably quiet.

Since I hate awkward silences, I decide I should babble about soundtracks. "The eighties and nineties had some movies with great music. *Breakfast Club. Beverly Hills Cop.*"

"Uh-huh," he mumbles, eyes locked on the dirt road ahead of him.

"Ooh, and *Purple Rain*. Anything by Prince is supreme. Don't you think?" I ask and receive the same response.

"What about *Willy Wonka*?" I ask, throwing out a red herring to see if he's listening.

"Yeah, good," he replies.

Dammit. My mind spins out of control as I lean back in the seat and stare out the windshield, though I can still see him in my peripheral vision.

Reno is lost in his own little world, and it worries me. *Is he regretting having unprotected sex with me?* God, that was stupid. There I was, rubbing myself all over his bare dick and telling him I was on birth control. *Shit, did he feel like I was pressuring him? What if he didn't believe me? What if he's sitting there worried I'm trying to baby trap him?*

Though it seemed like he wanted it too. The way he held me, the way he kissed me. Yeah, he was definitely into it.

Another thought hits me, something I've been trying to ignore since I blasted him with my truth bomb while I was coming.

I don't want you to leave on Sunday.

Uggggh! What the holy hell is wrong with me? Why did I feel it necessary to say that while I was coming, even if it was true?

Unable to contain myself for another second, I blurt out, "I really am on birth control, Reno."

That gets his attention and he finally glances at me, eyebrows pinched together. "Sorry, what?"

"I'm on birth control. I have the implant." I hold up my left arm. "You can't really see it, but you can kinda feel it."

"Okaaay?" he draws out. "Is it hurting or something? They have a medical staff at the resort. I can take you there."

"It's not hurting," I say, frustrated. "I just... you seem really quiet, and I thought maybe you were worried I lied about being on birth control."

His lips twitch, and he stops the Jeep in the middle of the road before putting it in park and swiveling to face me. He's smiling, which is... a good sign? Maybe?

Reno takes my hands and kisses the backs of each one. "I'm sorry I got quiet. I tend to do that when I'm trying to work something out. But no, I didn't think for a second you were lying to me."

I release a relieved breath. "Okay, I really do have the implant. You can feel it if you want." I attempt to lift my arm again, but he shakes his head.

"I know, baby. I've kissed every inch of your body, and I noticed it was there." Well. All right then.

"So you're not mad at me?"

He chuckles. "Not at all. I think you're the most genuine person I've ever met. If you told me the grass is purple, I'd believe you."

"Is it because I said I didn't want you to leave?" I ask quietly, not sure if I want to hear his response because *clingy much?*

"That's what I was thinking about," he confirms, and my stomach clenches. He glances out the windshield for a moment and then looks back at me. "What if I stay another week?"

The stomach clenching instantly turns into heart pounding, and it takes me a second to respond. "Do you want to stay?"

He nods, his face serious. "I do. I can check with the resort and see if my cottage is booked for those dates."

"I—wow, okay."

Reno slides one hand up my arm and drags his knuckles against my cheek. "I'd like more time with you."

"I want that too, but there's no need in paying for your room when you spend every night in mine anyway."

His grin steals my breath. "You want me to stay in your cottage?"

I feel like my face might split in two with my enormous grin. "Yes, please."

He leans forward and presses a kiss to my lips. "Dream girl, you've got yourself a roommate."

Chapter 20

Reno

Mine.

That was either the smartest or the dumbest thing I've ever done. The jury's still out. But I feel happier right now than I've felt in months. Maybe years.

Ten more days. That should be enough to get this obsession with Juliette McNamara out of my system, right?

My hand rests on her bare thigh as I navigate through the thicket of trees, my thumb drawing lazy circles on her smooth flesh. Juliette's wearing her silver bikini top and those hot little fringed shorts that had me biting my knuckle when she walked out of the cottage with them on this morning.

"What's your favorite animal?" she asks.

"Hmm, dogs are cool, I guess. What about you?"

"Goats," she replies without pause, and it makes me laugh. I've begun to expect the unexpected with Juliette.

"What do you like about goats?"

"Besides the fact that they're freaking adorable?" she asks, squeezing my forearm. "Well, they're nature's weed eaters. Just put a couple goats in your yard, and they take care of everything."

"Do you have any goats?" I ask.

"Oh, heavens no. My backyard is way too small. One day I'd like a big backyard where I can put a couple goats and sit on the back porch and watch them run and jump and play." She giggles, and *damn, she is so cute.* "I may or may not follow, like, ten different goat accounts on Instagram."

"I hope you—" I'm cut off when the vehicle begins to make a whining noise. "What the hell is that?"

Juliette scrunches her face. "Might be the starter." She leans over and looks at the display before tapping her finger on a lit up symbol. "Uh-oh."

"Battery light," I groan, pulling the car over again.

Popping the hood release switch, I hop out of the vehicle and lift it. I'm not a mechanic, but maybe I can see if there's anything obvious going on. Juliette appears beside me, peering in at the engine. A quick glance beneath the hood tells me I have no fucking clue what's wrong so I pull out my phone.

"I'll call the resort, and they'll send someone to get us." I tap on the screen and frown when I'm unable to get a signal. "I'm going to walk up on that rise and see if I can get my phone to work. Stay right here," I tell Juliette, giving her a reassuring kiss on the lips.

Turning to the right, I make my way up the hill, praying I can get in touch with someone. If not, we'll have to walk back. It would be faster if I just ran the last couple miles, but I'd feel uncomfortable leaving Juliette by herself. Nope. Not doing that.

Five minutes later, I trudge back down the hill, annoyed that I still couldn't get a signal. Probably because of all the damn trees. When I reach the road, my feet falter when I see Juliette with her head beneath the hood, and I break into a jog. What the hell is she doing? She's going to hurt herself.

"Hey," she says, shooting me a look over her shoulder when she hears me. "I found the problem. The alternator belt slipped off."

"I, uh, what?"

"Alternator belt," she repeats, turning her attention back to the engine. That's when I notice she's holding a socket wrench.

"Where did you get that?" I ask suspiciously.

"Toolbox in the back," she says all nonchalantly. "Can you turn on the light on your phone, pretty please?"

I should tell her not to mess with anything, but all I can do is hold my light up and stare dumbfounded while she loosens a bolt on what seems to be the alternator. Then she stuffs the wrench into the back pocket of her jean shorts and starts to work the dark-gray belt back over the pulleys. A faded red rag hangs out of the other pocket.

What in the fucking fuck is going on right now?

My eyes return to her backside. The bottoms of her cheeks are hanging out the bottom of her shorts, which is sexy enough in itself, but then I focus on the tool in her pocket. For some reason, this whole scene—Juliette bent over with her legs spread, working on the Jeep's engine with a socket wrench in those tiny shorts—makes my cock lengthen in my swim trunks.

It's so effing hot.

"Almost done," she updates, tilting her head a little to smile at me, and I notice a smudge of grease on her cheek. Apparently, my dick also finds this incredibly sexy because it hardens to full mast. Then she pulls the wrench from her pocket, flicks the lever to reverse the direction, and proceeds to tighten the bolt back in place.

Goddamn, I think I'm in love.

"How did you learn how to do this?" I ask, unable to keep my eyes off the curve of her back, the sway of her hips, the muscles bunching in her shoulder as she works.

"Dad's a mechanic," she replies, giving the most adorable grunt as she finishes tightening. "I used his office at his shop to do my homework after school because my younger siblings were kinda rowdy and distracted me. After I was done, he let me work with him. I picked up a few things."

"A few things," I repeat as she slams the hood down.

Juliette turns and looks up at my face, which I'm sure looks pretty stunned right now. "Yeah, and when I was a teenager, he gave me a part-time job to make spending cash, so I learned a little more. Plugging tires, oil changes, stuff like that. Why are you looking at me like that?"

"Because I'm so fucking turned on right now, I could put a dent in this vehicle with my cock," I growl.

Her eyebrows rise, and then a sly smile creeps across her lips. "Is it this?" she asks, lifting the socket wrench and stroking the handle of it in a very suggestive manner with one fist.

I chuckle. "It's all of it."

"You should see me with an impact wrench or a power drill," she shoots back sassily.

"Huh. Did I just hear you say you want to get drilled?" I ask, stepping closer and resting my hands on her bare waist.

Juliette giggles and runs her hands down my stomach, leaving streaks of grease in her path. "I do believe that's what I said." She cups my crotch. "Wow, that's quite a drill bit you're packing, sir."

Mother of god... this woman.

She completely matches my sexual energy and brings a playfulness to our interactions that I haven't experienced before. I lean down for a slow kiss.

"There's nothing sexier than a capable woman, Juliette."

Her eyebrows form a shadow over her pretty eyes. "Glad you think so. I've been told by men that it's not very feminine to work on cars."

"Fuck them and their insecure asses," I bite out, rubbing the frown lines between her eyes until they fade away. "I've never seen anything more feminine than you with a wrench in the pocket of those little shorts. Or with engine grease on your face."

"Oh crap." She reaches up to swipe at the smear, but I still her with my hand around her wrist.

"No. Leave it."

"So you're into capable femininity?" she asks skeptically, and I nod before placing my palm on the vehicle's hood behind her. The metal is hot to the touch.

"If the drill bit in my pants hasn't convinced you, I guess I'll have to show you how much it turns me on." I smack her ass, and she squeals in surprise. "Be right back. Lose the shorts."

Taking the wrench from her, I round the Jeep and put it back in the toolbox. Then I snag a few towels and leave my phone in the console. When I come back to the front, I see Juliette has followed my order, standing there naked from the waist down.

I lay out the towels on the hood before lifting her to sit on them. "Lie back and spread your legs," I command, and my cock surges when she complies, giving me a gorgeous view of her pink pussy.

"Beautiful," I murmur, bending my head to drag my tongue straight up her center. She tastes so damn good. There's a slight saltiness from our swim, but I can also taste myself in that little spot of paradise between her legs.

And that's something I've never experienced since I've never come inside a woman before. Not even Leia. Because I didn't trust her. At this point, I can't even remember why I'd been with her in the first place, much less why I'd almost married her.

It had never been like this with Leia, this overwhelming connection that made me want to lose myself in another human. Give her all my time and attention. Watch her fall apart on my mouth. Sure, I've always tried to be a generous lover, but with Juliette...

Fuck, I've been taken over by her. She's woven a spell around me that I find impossible to break. Not that I want to break it. No, I relish the fact that she fucking owns me.

I drive my tongue inside her sweet channel, and she cries out my name. I've never heard a more enthralling sound than my name on her perfect lips.

With her hands clenching my hair, I bury my face between Juliette's legs, tongue-fucking her slowly before sliding up to lap at her clit. The little button pulses to the same beat as my heart, and I ease two fingers inside her hot little cunt.

"Fuck, Reno. That's... that's so good."

"Eyes on me, dream girl. I want you to watch me devour this pussy while you come all over my goddamn face."

She moans and rises up on her elbows, locking eyes with me as I go back to the very important task of driving her to that peak of bliss. I lick. I suck. I fuck her with my fingers as her nostrils flare and her bare heels dig into my shoulders with her impending orgasm.

When I can tell she's right on the precipice, I wrap my lips around her clit and curl my fingers to press against that most sensitive area inside her, sending her over the edge.

A flock of birds takes flight from the trees when Juliette screams my name. Her eyelids droop, but she never breaks eye contact with me as she pants out the rest of her release.

The bottom of my face is soaked with her desire when I finally lift my head and give her a final soft kiss. Then I lift her, set her on her feet, and spin her around to face the Jeep.

"Bend over and spread your legs," I tell her gruffly. My dick is straining for her, and I lower my shorts to give myself a few rough pulls. Juliette's ass is presented beautifully for me, round and supple as she lays her chest against the towel-covered hood. "I'm going to fuck you raw again."

"Yes. Please," she whimpers, and I stroke a hand up and down her back while swirling the head of my dick through her wetness. Then I push in on one swift thrust, groaning at the heat and snugness of her.

"Goddamn, you're like silk around me," I grit out through clenched teeth. "And so fucking tight."

Juliette flashes a pretty smile over her shoulder. "Because your drill bit is enormous."

"Smartass," I tell her, smacking the globe of her ass, and she clenches around me. Hmmm. "You like when I spank you, baby?"

"Yes," she whimpers. "Be rough with me."

Fuck me.

Gripping her hips, I pull out to the tip and slam back in. She pushes back against me, and I swat her butt again. "You want me to treat you like a dirty little slut, dream girl?"

"Mmm, yes. I'm such a slut for you."

Another spank, another rough thrust. The sunbeams seeping through the canopy of trees highlight the gorgeous pink of her ass from my hand. "Only for me. Say it."

"Only for you," she agrees.

I trace each bump of her spine with my fingers until I reach her head and wrap my fist around her long blonde braid. "Put your hands behind your back," I order, and she does. With my free hand, I clasp both of her wrists and hold them against her lower back.

"God this is so hot," she pants, her cheek flush against one of the towels beneath her.

"Say my name while I fuck you like you've never been fucked before. Tell me who this pussy belongs to." I pull almost all the way out and pause, waiting for her response.

"Reno," she whines, "my pussy is yours. Only yours."

Those words turn my cock into a tool made for her pleasure. Holding her hair in one hand and her wrists with the other, I ride her hard and fast. My desire to make her mine morphs into its own entity, an unrelenting need.

"You. Are. Mine," I growl. And right there on a deserted island road, I claim her, fucking into her with so much force the Jeep rocks and creaks with each movement.

The aroma of hard sex blends with the sweet flora surrounding us and drives me further over the edge of obsession. "Mine, mine, mine," I chant as I rail her from behind, my hips making loud slaps against her perfect ass.

"Yes, yours. And you're mine," she demands right back, effectively topping me from the bottom.

"Damn straight," I agree, releasing her wrists and leaning over her back. Despite the crude roughness of the act, I need to be close to her. Need to feel the sweat of her skin mingling with my own.

Because even though the impending deadline of our time together grows closer with each passing moment, right now, we *do* belong to each other.

Juliette's fingers close around the towels as I put every muscle in my thick thighs and muscled ass into the pounding I'm giving her. I'm claiming her body, but I crave more. So I take her mouth in a searing kiss as we both near our completion.

And when we both fall into the sweet oblivion of our mutual orgasms, I whisper against her lips one more time...

"Mine."

Chapter 21

Juliette

Breaking rule two

HALLE-FREAKING-LUJAH. IT'S MONDAY AFTERNOON, and I've managed to finish this damn book ahead of schedule. Reno has made himself scarce while I do a final read through before sending to the beta team.

I pop a cherry Starburst into my mouth and chew absently as I frown at my laptop screen. Why the hell did I use the word *slacks* here? I hate that word. *Slacks*. It gives me the ick, so I quickly change it to dress pants.

Reno lets himself into our cottage without a word, refills my Dr Pepper, and sets a plate of cheese and fruit beside me before kissing the top of my head and leaving. Seriously. The man is a dreamboat.

I nibble on a piece of gouda and a juicy grape as I wrap up yet another chapter. Then my phone buzzes beside me. Checking the display, I see it's my younger brother, Xander. That's weird. He usually doesn't call much.

Swiping the screen, I drawl out, "Alien abduction line. If you've been probed, please press one. If you'd like to be probed, please press two."

"Yes, ma'am. What if I've been probed and want to do it again?"

"That depends. Will you be providing your own lube?"

"Of course. I'm a very self-respecting human."

"Okey doke. Then push five."

Xander snickers and cuts the act. "Sorry to bother you, sis. Is this a good time to call?"

"Of course, Xan. What's up?"

"I, uh, you know I'm studying for my MCAT?" he asks.

"Yes, it's in September, right?" My little bro is so smart. He plans to go to medical school when he graduates college in two years.

"Yeah, well my roommates are being loud."

"Go to my house to study," I say immediately, and I hear the relief in his sigh.

"You sure, Jules? I don't want to—"

"Xander," I say sternly, "you know you're always welcome at my place. Just go. You can even stay there until I get home on Sunday. There should be clean sheets on my bed."

"Okay," he agrees. "Thank you so much, sis. You're the best."

"I'll make sure to inform Bubba and Jordie," I tease, referring to our other two siblings. "Oh, and let Pops know because he's been checking on my house while I've been gone."

"I'll take care of everything and water your plants," he says eagerly. "And I'll run to the store so you'll have bread, milk, and eggs when you get home."

"That's sweet of you. There should be some cash in the cookie jar."

"All right. I'm going to pack a bag. Thanks again, J."

"No problem, sweetie. I'll see you on Sunday. Love you."

"Love you too," he replies before hanging up.

I adore that kid. Well, he's twenty-two, but he's still a kid in my eyes. Xander is absolutely the sweetest, and for the millionth time, I pray he finds his balance. He studies so hard, and I often have to gently remind him that he's still young and should be having fun. But while he's preparing to take one of the most important exams of his life in a few months, this isn't the time.

Putting thoughts of Xander out of my head, I take a drink of my soda and munch on the snacks Reno brought me while I finish reading through my completed manuscript. Two hours later, I smile as I send it to my team.

After rewarding myself with one more Starburst, I text Reno to let him know I'm done. He arrives ten minutes later with a bouquet of colorful flowers in his hand.

"Reno, what did you do?"

He shrugs a little shyly. "I'm just proud of you. I never realized how much goes into writing a book. I mean, I knew it was a lot of work, but watching you try to make every single word perfect..." He lifts and lowers his shoulder again. "You're pretty fucking amazing."

Tears sting my eyes at his sweet words. I rise from my chair and take the flowers before laying a long kiss on his lips. "Thank you. You have no idea how much that means to me."

After I put the flowers in the pretty vase he got me a couple weeks ago, we take a walk to the beach. It feels good to be outside in the fading sunshine.

"Do you want to eat in the formal dining room or the diner tonight?" Reno asks. We discovered the resort's casual diner this past weekend.

"Diner. I could use one of those big burgers with the slice of grilled pineapple."

Concern immediately weaves its way into his voice. "Are you hungry now?"

I chuckle. "Not a bit after all the fruit and cheese I ate. Thank you for that, by the way."

He squeezes my hand before we remove our shoes and leave them in one of the cabinets reserved for that purpose at the edge of the beach. "You're welcome."

We walk until our toes are in the surf, and Reno loops an arm around my shoulders and tucks me close to his body while we take in the sultry air and the sounds of the sea.

"Why are you always so obsessed with me eating?" I ask teasingly, but his reply is anything but teasing. It's as serious as a heart attack.

"I can't stand the thought of you going hungry."

I look up at the tight clench of his mouth as he stares out at the water. Something is bothering him, some distant memory, and a horrifying thought pops into my head. Stepping in front of him, I massage the muscles of his jaw until they relax a bit.

Then I leap directly over the line we'd sketched out for rule two—limit talking about our personal lives—and ask, "Did you not have enough food growing up?"

Reno closes his eyes so tightly, tiny wrinkles appear at the corners. "I never went hungry, but my mom did."

Oh. My. Heart.

"I'm sorry. You don't have to talk about it, but I'm here if you want to."

His green eyes open and stare down into mine for a long moment before he cups the back of my head and brings my cheek to his chest. Message received. It's too hard for him to look at me right now.

"My father was a piece of shit," he begins. "He used to hit my mother. Me too sometimes, but when he came home drunk, Ma would usually shove me out the door and tell me to go play with the neighbor kid. When she would call and tell me to come home, it was usually obvious he'd been hurting her. He didn't leave bruises where they were visible, but there were other signs. She moved more slowly, sometimes with a limp."

"God, I'm so sorry, Reno," I said, feeling the pinch of tears on the insides of my eyelids.

"When I was ten, I'd finally had enough. I was already pretty big for a kid that age, a little over five feet, but I was still a lot smaller than my father." Reno's hand drifts absently up and down my back, and I wrap my arms around his middle. "Anyway, when my mom sent me to the neighbors' house, I didn't go. I waited on the front porch, and when I heard what was going on inside, I went back into the house."

He's silent for a long while, and I give him a squeeze, trying to lend my strength to him.

"He didn't hear me come in," Reno says quietly. "They were in the kitchen, and the fucker was... he was standing over her. She was on the floor holding her stomach."

I feel the enormity of the moment as if I were standing there myself, seeing a scared ten-year-old boy watching his mother be abused.

"So I picked up a metal pot from the counter and hit him in the back of the head," Reno says, and I weirdly want to give him a high-fucking-five. "Knocked him out cold."

"Good," I say fiercely even as my tears leak onto his dark-green palm tree shirt. "What did your mom do?"

"She crawled over to me and hugged me, like I was the one who needed comforting," Reno says bitterly. "Then I laid down the law."

I smile against his shirt. "Of course you did."

"I told her I was tired of this shit and I wasn't going to put up with it anymore. She either called the cops and left him, or I was running away from home."

Jesus, what a brave little boy. One who's grown into an amazing man. "What did your mom do?"

Reno chuckles. "She told me not to say *shit*." He kisses the top of my head. "Then she apologized for staying so long and making me have to live like that. I could literally feel her backbone growing back. Maybe it was because no one had stood up for her for so long, and now that someone had, she drew on that."

"I'm proud of her. And you," I say, my voice muffled with emotion.

"She did call the police, and they came and arrested him. Of course, he was released the next day, but we were gone. Went to a shelter a few towns away. They gave us a room and helped her get a job in a diner."

The memory of Reno donating Leia's clothes to a women's shelter floods my system, and I bite back a sob. His childhood obviously still affects him, but he used that pain to do something good. I'd wager to bet he donates money to women's shelters too.

"And he stayed away?" I asked, praying it was so.

Reno nods. "Ma didn't have a cell phone back then so he couldn't track her or anything. There was also a lawyer at the shelter who helped her get a divorce." He kisses my head again. "After a month, we moved into a tiny apartment. It was run down, but we scrubbed it to within an inch of its life, so at least it was clean."

The surf eases up to wet our feet and then recedes. This goes on for a few cycles before Reno speaks again.

"Ma would bring me meals from the diner every night. Enough for dinner and then lunch the next day. When I tried to share with her, she said that food was for me and that she ate at work."

"But she didn't?"

I feel the long inhale and exhale of breath from Reno's lungs. "It became obvious after a few months, even to a kid. She was so damn skinny and her clothes hung off her like she was wearing a tent."

Swiveling my head until my face was pressed against his chest, I hold him tighter. "She was starving herself so her little boy wouldn't be hungry," I surmise, and he nods.

"Yeah. To backtrack a little, Ma was an only child, and both her parents were dead. I never knew my father's family because they'd had some kind of falling out before I was born." Reno's hand toys with my ponytail. "So when she was asleep one night, I found her little address book."

"What was in it?"

"I saw a phone number for a man named Arlo. She'd written *Leon's dad* beside it. Leon was my father, so this was obviously my grandfather I'd never met. So I memorized the number, and when Ma was at work the next day, I called him. Told him the whole story and that I was worried my mom wasn't getting enough to eat."

"Crap, did your mom freak out?"

Reno huffs out a laugh. "I didn't tell her, but that evening, Gramps showed up in a big black truck and knocked on the door of our apartment. Told my mom we were going to live with him and Grandma, and he wasn't hearing a single word against it."

"Good for him," I say, turning my head to press my cheek to Reno's chest again.

"We lived in their farmhouse for about a year while my mom went to school to finish her degree in social work. She'd been almost done when she met my father, and he somehow talked her into quitting school. She's a counselor for a shelter now."

I nuzzle against his shirt and smile. "Would it be weird if I said I have a girl crush on your mom?"

His lips curl against the top of my head. "Not weird. She's pretty fucking amazing."

I look up at him. "You are too, for having the balls to call a man you'd never met and ask for help because you were worried about your mother."

"I guess. I give all the credit to my grandparents. They took in their daughter-in-law who they hadn't seen in over a decade and a grandson they didn't know existed. I had a real family for the first time." He stares wistfully out at the horizon where the sun seems to be dipping into the water. "I had some anger issues, so Gramps got me involved in sports to help me work out my shit in a more healthy way."

"This is the grandfather that has dementia now?"

Reno nods. "Besides my mom, he's the most important person in my life. I'd do anything for him."

I'll be honest. I'm finding it very difficult not to fall head over heels for Reno Swain right now. Especially when he dips his head to press soft pecks against my lips. "Thank you for listening to me, dream girl. I know it's not a pretty story."

"Many stories aren't, but you were lucky to have a beautiful ending to it."

"Very lucky," he agrees. "So many women don't get that."

A fresh round of tears assaults my eyes as memories flood my mind. Ugly memories. So I bury my face in his chest and let them fall. It's a response I hate, but one I can't control, and my body begins to shake.

Reno's body stiffens, and he's silent while he strokes my back and hair with aching gentleness. My soft cries turn into full-blown sobs, and I don't even know why. I haven't cried over my asshole ex in over a year.

Maybe it's the tenderness with which Reno is rubbing me or the strong feel of him surrounding me and making me feel safe. Treasured.

He sinks to the ground with me straddling his thighs and holds me. I glance down to where the water is soaking his shorts.

"Your clothes are getting all wet," I hiccup.

"I have plenty of clothes I can change into," he replies, reminding me he'd used the resort's laundry service since he decided to stay an extra week with me. Then he cups my chin to lift my tear-stained face. "Did someone hurt you, Juliette?"

"It was a few years ago," I reply.

He shakes his head, the flame in his pretty green eyes a mixture of concern and barely disguised fury. "It doesn't matter. Stuff like that leaves a scar on your soul, and that can't be fully erased by time." His lips are so soft when they brush across my forehead, I wonder if I imagined it. "Tell me who hurt you."

"It was my ex."

"Name?" he asks curtly.

"Collin."

"Collin what?"

"It doesn't matter. He's gone now."

"Did someone kill him?" He asks that so apathetically—like he wouldn't give a shit if Collin was dead or not—it makes me smile just a little.

"He's not dead, but he would have been if my brother had gotten hold of him."

"I think I like your brother," he replies, one side of his lips hitching up before his face turns serious again. "What happened?"

I don't like talking about this, but after the painful story Reno had shared, I feel an almost irrepressible need to tell him. I blow out a raspberry before scooching closer to press my torso tightly against his. Burying my face in the side of his neck, I begin to talk.

"When I first met Collin, everything seemed to be fine." One of my shoulders makes a little shrug. "But I guess that's how all these situations begin. No one says, 'Hey, this guy is a total twat muffin. Maybe I should see if he wants to go out again.'"

"Twat muffin?" Reno asks, a hint of amusement in his voice.

"It's my name for him. Though Bubba always called him colon behind his back because he said Collin was full of shit." I sigh. "And I guess Bubba was right. Anyway, everything started out fine. There were tiny signs that I suppose I should have recognized as potential red flags, but they were few and far between."

"What kinds of signs?"

"Mostly eye rolling and long sighs when he'd get annoyed with me. He seemed to have a bit of a short fuse when I did something scatterbrained or had to be reminded of something. Nothing overt; he would just get bothered easily."

"Impatient twat muffin," Reno mutters.

"Fast forward a year, and we got engaged." I feel Reno stiffen before he relaxes his posture and strokes my ponytail. "Everything was still okay, but Collin's fuse got a little shorter, especially when..."

I pause, trying to phrase this properly so Reno wouldn't know who I was talking about. And he *would* know if I went into too much detail.

"He got transferred because of work," I explain. "He wanted me to move with him, but I was right in the middle of the summer reading program for kids at my library, so I said I would move in the fall."

The cool water brushes against my knees, and I roll my lips inward before going on to the next part of the story.

"I decided to go visit him one weekend, but my flight was delayed. Collin had made reservations at some fancy restaurant, so he was aggravated as hell when I finally arrived two hours late. He..." I swallow hard. "He yelled at me when we got in the car."

"Motherfucker," Reno bites out. "How the hell did he think that was your fault?"

"Because he's a twat muffin," I reply dryly. "So he already wasn't in the best mood, and when we were almost to his apartment, I realized

I'd forgotten to pack my phone charger. You know, because of the aforementioned scatterbrained-ness."

Reno nuzzles my temple. "I think every adult has forgotten their phone charger at least once. That's nothing to get upset about."

I nod against his neck. "That's when he called me fucking stupid."

The man I'm sitting on lets out a string of curses that would offend an entire ship of sailors. Then he eases me back and cups my face, his eyes warm on top of the anger he must be feeling.

"Juliette, you are not stupid," Reno says, enunciating each word. "No one should ever talk to you like that."

"I know." An errant tear treks down my cheek. "I made good grades in high school and in college. I know I'm not stupid, but it still hurts to be belittled."

Reno pulls my face to his and kisses my lips, gentle as a butterfly. "You are smart, Juliette McNamara. The way you can put words together to tell a story is such a rare talent." Then he presses his lips to my forehead. "What's in here is just as beautiful as the rest of you. I am in awe of you."

Well, a girl can't hear that enough. He pulls me close again, and my body melts against him, his warmth rivaling the heat of the setting sun.

"After we got to his apartment, he acted like nothing even happened. I finally told him he'd hurt my feelings by saying I was stupid, and he acted confused. Said he didn't even remember saying it."

"Did he apologize?"

"He did, and it seemed sincere, but a couple weeks later, he called me a dumb bitch." I feel Reno's body quake, but despite his obvious anger, I'm not afraid in the least that he might hurt me.

"I'm going to need this prick's full name and address. Now." His voice is an iceberg, cold and resting just beneath the surface.

"It's in the past. It was two years ago," I defer.

"What did your brother say about *the colon* talking to you like that?"

I pause. "I didn't tell him. I thought it would blow over."

"But it didn't?"

Shaking my head, I inhale the fresh scent of Reno's thick neck. "No. I was beginning to seriously rethink things because he seemed to be calling me names more and more often, like it just became habit for him. Never in front of anyone else though."

"What made you finally break it off?" Reno's hands are gentle as he caresses the back of my head and the length of my spine.

"I... I was FaceTiming with him one night. He was in his apartment, and I saw a naked woman walk across the room behind him."

"What the fuck?" Reno snaps.

"Those were my exact words," I say wryly. "I had finally reached my breaking point and called him a dumb, cowardly, cheating-ass, little bitch."

Reno's shoulders shake. "Sorry, I know this isn't funny, but that's the best damn thing I've ever heard."

I giggle too. "It felt good to say. As soon as I told him it was over, I felt fifty pounds lighter. Like my body was relieved my brain had finally gotten with the program."

Rolling my lips between my teeth, I pause before telling him the next part. "Collin caught a flight and showed up at my house the next morning. He was apologizing all over the place and begging me to forgive him. Then he started explaining how it was all my fault since I wouldn't move with him immediately."

"What an asshole," Reno mutters. "Is that when he got violent?"

Nodding, I say, "Yes. He grabbed my shoulders and shook me so hard my teeth rattled. I was scared, and at that point I knew I had two choices." I let out a breath. "I could either speak quietly and try to talk him down, or I could knee him in the balls."

"And what did you do?" His voice is strained like a guitar string someone tightened three turns too many.

"I went for the balls," I state and feel Reno's exhale against my neck, like that's the answer he wanted to hear. "The twat muffin twisted at the last minute, so I only grazed his crotch, but it was enough to make him double over."

Reno gently pushes me back and cradles my cheeks in his big hands. I'm finding it easier than expected to say this next part face to face. There's no pity in his eyes, only steadfastness, like he's sharing his energy with me.

Only a slight quiver mars my voice when I speak again. "I ran, but he caught me. Twisted my arm up behind my back. There was a horrible pop. I know he heard it because he let go immediately."

"Fuck, dream girl. Was it your shoulder?"

I nod. "Yes, it was dislocated. I fell onto the floor, and he stared at me like he couldn't quite figure out why I was lying there. I pulled my phone from my pocket, and Collin immediately began apologizing. Saying he didn't mean to. You know, all the bullshit abusers spew afterward."

Reno's lips flatten into a harsh line. "I'm aware."

"So I called my brother Bubba and told him Collin hurt me. He started yelling so loud even the twat muffin could hear him. And... he ran."

"Cowardly motherfucker," Reno spits out. "Hurting a woman and then hauling ass when he knows someone his own size is about to show up. Did Bubba ever catch him?"

I shake my head. "No. He and his wife took me to the hospital. The doctors took lots of pictures of my shoulder and the bruises Collin left on my arms when he shook me. For the police report."

Reno's eyes immediately drop to my thighs where a few fingerprint bruises have bloomed from where he held my legs apart last night. He looks horrified.

"Shit, Juliette. If I'd known, I wouldn't have been so rough with you. I'm..."

I cover his mouth with my palm. "Don't apologize," I say sternly. "It's *my* body, and *I* decide what kinds of bruises I want on it. These are marks left by passion, not anger." Uncovering his mouth, I kiss him there, hard and firm. "You left those on me while you were going down on me, making me feel good, and I wear them with pride."

His exhale is ragged as he nods. “Okay, but you have to promise to tell me if I ever get too rough with you.”

“I promise,” I tell him, though we both know our time together is limited.

Only three more days.

And that thought makes my heart hurt.

Chapter 22

Reno

My new guilty pleasure

While Juliette takes a call from her editor on Thursday, I stroll over to the gift shop to give her some privacy. Karissa greets me as soon as I walk in.

"Mr. Swain, hi! Did Juliette like the flowers?"

"Loved them. Thank you for your help again. Um, I have a special request."

A sly grin crosses her face. "What did you have in mind?"

Ten minutes later, I leave the shop with a satisfied smile on my face. Karissa said she'd have my package ready to pick up Saturday.

My phone rings, and it's a number I don't recognize. Frowning, I sit on a bench beneath a flowering tree and answer. "Hello?"

"Is this Reno Swain?"

I don't recognize the man's voice, but it doesn't sound like a spam call. "You got him."

"Hey, man. This is Baylor Ward. From the Dallas Brewers?"

Relaxing against the back of the bench, I smile. I know Baylor from hockey, and he's always seemed like a nice enough guy. A fucking beast on the ice, and we've knocked each other into the boards more than once, but that's the nature of the sport. He's a fair player and doesn't take cheap shots.

"Good to hear from you, Baylor. Though my hip isn't your biggest fan after that final game last year."

He laughs good-naturedly. "Sorry about that, bro. If it makes you feel any better, my shoulder still protests from when you smacked me into the glass in that same game."

"Old ass," I tease, though I think he's around the same age as me.

"And feeling older every day. Hey, I know it hasn't been announced yet, but a little birdy told me you're going to join us this season."

"That's what a little birdy told me too," I say, and I'm surprised I don't sound bitter about it.

"Fuck, man. I'm so excited. Defense was our weak spot last season. I think we could have gone to the playoffs if we'd had someone of your caliber on the Brewers. I respect the hell out of you."

"I feel the same about you, Ward. You're one of the best centers in the league."

"Good. Now that we've kissed each other's asses and we're practically engaged, let's get down to business."

I laugh out loud at that. "I'll be expecting a particularly large diamond ring. What can I help you with, Baylor?"

"Actually, I'm calling to help you. I know this is a huge change for you since you've been with Denver for so many years. It can't be easy to switch teams. I have no idea what that organization is thinking by letting you go, but I intend to take full advantage of their idiocy. So it's my goal to make your transition as smooth as possible."

"I appreciate that."

"I'd love for you to come to Texas soon. I can show you around and help you find housing or whatever else you need."

I think about my mother's request and ask, "Do you know of any nice areas to live that aren't right in the city? Maybe something with a bit of a slower pace?"

"Hell yes," he crows, sounding pumped. "I live in a small town on the outskirts of Dallas. It's a great community, and several of the Brewers live there. Sorry, but I don't know a lot about your personal life. Do you have a family?"

"Just my mom and grandfather. That's something else I could use advice on." Swiping a droplet of sweat from the side of my neck, I say, "They'll both be moving with me, but Gramps needs... special care. He has dementia."

Baylor's voice grows softer. "Sorry about that, man. That's a hard situation to deal with, but I've got you covered. We may be a small town, but we have a great retirement facility with a top-notch dementia ward. Funnily enough, the retirement home is called Shady Pines. You know, like from *The Golden Girls*?"

I smile at that. "Sounds like someone has a good sense of humor."

"It was actually my great-aunt who founded the dementia ward. Using our last name, it would have been called the Ward Ward, so instead she named it the Illumination Ward because she said she wanted it to be a place of light for those who live there."

A tightness in my gut relaxes at that. "I would love to take a look at it when I come down for a visit."

"I'll get that set up. Most of my family volunteers in one way or another at Shady Pines. My dad is an army veteran, and he goes up and visits with the old guys and gals who also served. They love the opportunity to shoot the shit with another vet."

"Gramps is a veteran too, so he would love that. I can't tell you how much I appreciate this, Baylor. Truly."

"Like I said, I'm thrilled you'll be joining us. And I know the other guys will be too once everything goes public. I have a realtor I can set you up with for housing. Does your mom live with you?"

"No, she'll have her own house. Nothing too big since it's just her. What's the apartment situation in your town? That's usually what I prefer so I don't have to worry about yard upkeep when I'm away on road games."

"Only two apartment buildings in town. One is definitely a no-go. Trust me." I can practically hear his eye roll. "The other is where I live, as well as some of our teammates. Most of the units have indoor plumbing, but for the ones that don't, the superintendent keeps the outhouses super clean."

Did he say outhouses? My face scrunches into a scowl. "I'm sorry... what?"

A bark of laughter reaches my ear, and I relax again. "I'm fucking with you, dude. Nah, this place is nice. What my wife calls small-town luxury. You're not gonna have gold plated bidets or anything, but they're spacious and have high-end appliances and fixtures. I'd be happy to set you up with a tour if you want."

"That sounds good."

We talk a few more minutes about what I'd like for Ma, and Baylor says he'll relay that to the realtor so she can start working on it. By the time we hang up, I'm actually getting excited about the move.

I walk back onto the path and see a familiar blonde up ahead. She's staring at the sign in front of her that leads back to our cottage, and I grin. Juliette has been here for almost three weeks and still consults the little signs to make sure she's going the correct way. Her lack of a sense of direction is adorably endearing.

Sneaking up behind her, I grab her cute ass and whisper, "Got your goose."

Juliette squeals, whirls, and throws whatever is in her right hand straight at my face. I easily catch the small bright yellow bag and laugh when she recognizes me.

"Reno, you ass!" She pats her chest. "I think you scared ten years off my life."

"Sorry," I tell her, putting on my best puppy dog eyes as I hand over what I now recognize as one of the gift shop bags. She's holding another one in her left hand.

Her face softens, but she still gives me a mock glare. "Just for that, maybe I won't give you the little prize I bought for you."

Gripping her hips, I back her against a palm tree and take her mouth in a long, sensual kiss. She tastes like cherry Starbursts.

"Please, dream girl," I murmur against her lips, smiling when I feel her melt like a Hershey bar in the sunshine. "I'd be more than happy to earn my reward."

Juliette giggles before pushing me back a couple steps and rummaging in one of the plastic sacks. "It's nothing big. I just wanted to get you a little treat for being such a good listener and for opening up to me yesterday. I know that wasn't easy to talk about." She produces a large bag of Cheetos and blushes when she holds it out.

"My guilty pleasure snack," I say, my heart on fire for this woman. She is so kind, so thoughtful. Sure, it's just a bag of chips, but she remembered that conversation we had weeks ago.

I pop open the bag and pull out one of the cheesy snacks, putting the end of it between my lips. I lean forward, and she grins, getting my drift. Then she wraps her perfect lips around the other end of the Cheeto, *a la Lady and the Tramp style*, until our mouths meet.

We both bite off our ends, and I give her a peck on the lips, tasting the salty, cheesy taste there. Someone passes behind us and lets out a little *woohoo*, and then we hear giggles as they continue on their way. Juliette and I smile at each other.

"Sorry I scared you and thank you for the Cheetos. That was really sweet of you." Her cheeks flush even deeper, and I'm reminded of the pinkening of her neck and face when she comes. My cock remembers too and makes an appearance against the soft fabric of my crotch.

"You're welcome," she whispers.

"What else do you have in those bags?"

"Nothing else we can use to act out romantic cartoon moments. Just some souvenirs for my family."

"What did you get for them?" I ask, guiding her down the correct path toward cottage four.

"I tried to get items without the resort's logo so my family doesn't suspect that I've been up to any hedonistic activities."

"Then you probably shouldn't tell them what I'm about to do with these Cheetos," I tease, walking up the steps to our temporary home and unlocking the door.

After setting down her purchases, her eyes narrow on me, and she props her hands on her hips. "If you think you're going to put a Cheeto in my pussy, you better think again, mister."

Huffing out a laugh, I shake my head. "I had something else in mind. Take off your clothes."

She eyes me skeptically but peels off her clothes and undergarments while I grab a towel from the bathroom. When I return, I drag my gaze up and down her form, over the swells of her breasts, the dip of her waist, the curve of her hip. She is so fucking hot.

I unfold the towel and lay it out on the marble countertop before lifting Juliette to sit on it. "Put your feet here," I direct, tapping two spots on the edge of the counter to indicate that I want her spread for me. Her teeth dent her bottom lip as she complies.

"You're such a good girl for me," I tell her, setting the bag of snacks beside her and stepping between her thighs. Then I touch her, my hands roving over every pretty inch of her tanned body. Except for the parts she wants me to touch the most.

When she's whimpering for me, I pull a Cheeto from the bag, and her eyebrows lift. "It's not what you think," I tell her, dragging the stick across her lips and then licking off the powdery residue.

"Oh," she breathes, catching onto my plan. I trace a line down her neck and chest before following it with my tongue. When I circle each nipple with the snack, her breathing hitches. I pause with my mouth an inch from her right breast, watching it peak before my eyes as I let the anticipation build. She parts her lips and whispers, "Please, Reno." It's quiet, but the plea is as loud as a bullhorn.

So I give her what she wants, my mouth around her rose-colored nipple. Juliette's head falls back with a thunk against the teakwood cabinet behind her, and she emits a satisfied moan. The sound of her pleasure is music to my dick. I give equal attention to the other perky tit before continuing to make trails down her body with the Cheeto. And I lap up every trace of seasoning left there.

As promised, I don't put anything inside her. I wouldn't want to cause any kind of fake-cheese-related health issues to her perfect cunt. But I do take two of the snacks and roll them up and down the insides of her thighs, coating her with the faint orange powder.

Then I kneel and very thoroughly clean her up with my mouth before finally getting to the promised land at the apex of her thighs. Her arousal is dripping onto the towel beneath her, and the smell of her has me feral.

I lock eyes with her before diving in and claiming my new guilty pleasure snack.

Chapter 23

Reno

The sex hammock

"Juliette!" a brunette calls, waving her hand in the air as soon as we enter the diner. "You guys come sit with us."

She's with a group of people sitting at a large table along one wall, and the two men rise to scoot another table over to make space for us.

"Is this okay?" Juliette whispers to me as we make our way across the pink and black tiled floor.

"Sure," I tell her, though I'd rather be alone with her. It's Thursday evening, meaning we only have two more full days together.

We take our seats, and Juliette apparently knows everyone at the table because she introduces them all to me by name. There are three couples: Erin and Jason, Brittany and Melissa, and Gaston and Jane, as well as three of the Unicorn Unit ladies, Wendy, Donna, and Stephanie. Wendy is the dark-haired one who summoned us when we walked in.

A waitress in an old-fashioned hot-pink diner uniform approaches and takes everyone's orders. I relax as the conversation flows easily around the table. A couple of the women pepper Juliette for hints regarding her upcoming release, and she happily gives them a few tidbits to whet their appetites.

As our food is served, Juliette motions to the blonde across the table. "Jane, is your daughter feeling better? Her name's Marley, right?"

"She's much better. Thank you," the woman replies. "It was just a mild allergy to my sister's cat."

"That's good. You and Gaston haven't been on vacation in a few years, so I'm glad you didn't have to cut it short."

How the hell does she know all this?

I watch in fascination as Juliette chats with everyone at the table, asking about their job at the fire station or their dad's gout flareup. Meanwhile, I'm over here wishing everyone was required to wear name tags because I'm finding it difficult just to keep up with them all.

My girl is so fucking beautiful my eyeballs go dry from staring at her. I wish I could stow away in her suitcase and go home with her on Sunday.

The conversation turns to some big party that's taking place on Saturday night, but I'm only vaguely listening. I'm too busy watching Juliette eat her burger and fries like it's the most interesting thing I've ever seen. Though my ears perk up when one of the women—*is that Stephanie or Donna?*—squeals, "Juli, you and Reno *have to* come."

"Oh, I love karaoke," Juliette gushes.

Ugh. I fucking hate karaoke.

"And the best part is that it's costume karaoke," Brittany chimes in. *Great. Even better.* "We were here for it last year, and it was a blast."

"It was," her wife, Melissa, agrees. "The drunker we got, the braver we got with our singing. I mean, we were terrible, but that's what made it so much fun." Everyone laughs at the memories.

Juliette's pretty aqua eyes dart toward me, and she puts on a smile I can tell is fake. "Oh, I'm not sure—"

"We'd love to come," I interrupt, my stomach flipping over when her smile turns up to full wattage. If my dream girl loves karaoke, I guess we're going to fucking karaoke.

"Really?" she asks me.

I brush a tendril of hair behind her ear and lie. "It sounds fun."

The look of pure happiness on her face would be worth every second of torture I'd have to endure. But under no circumstances would I be singing.

“I picked out the most amazing costumes for us,” Juliette gushes as the sea breeze sways our shared hammock behind cottage four on Saturday afternoon. “The resort has a little rental shop for guests.”

“What are the costumes?” I ask, trying not to let the trepidation seep out through my tone.

“It’s a surprise,” she sings, kissing my bare chest before resting her head there. “Can I ask you a question?”

“Anything.”

Juliette traces her fingers over my chest. “Why don’t you have any tattoos? Not that I’m complaining. You just seem like a guy who would have some ink.”

“I don’t know. I guess I’ve never found anything important enough to want on my body permanently. It would have to mean something.”

“I get that,” she says, smiling up at me.

I trace the script E over a small purple flower tattoo I’d noticed on Juliette’s wrist. “What’s this about?”

Her smile turns wistful. “That’s for my friend Evie. Lilacs were her favorite flower. She disappeared about seventeen years ago during Spring Break.”

Something niggles at the back of my mind before making its way to the front. “Wait. Are you talking about Evie Bouvier, the fashion heiress who went missing in Mexico?” Juliette nods. “She was your friend?”

“My best friend. We were from totally different worlds, but when we met at summer camp as little girls, it’s like... our souls connected.” She smiles. “I know that sounds weird, but that’s the best way I can explain it. We became pen pals. Then when we were old enough to have phones, Evie and I talked or texted almost every day. We went back to that camp in Arkansas each summer and decided we would go to the same college and be roommates one day."

"I remember when she went missing. It was national news." I roll until I'm facing Juliette so I can trace her face with my fingertips. A tear meanders down her cheek, and I swipe it away. "I'm so sorry, baby. I can't imagine how hard that would be."

She nods and sniffles. "It was awful. I was the one who called her dad and told him we couldn't find her."

The truth hits me hard and fast. I've always thought nausea was reserved for the stomach and digestive tract, but suddenly, it's like every cell in my body is nauseated at the realization. *It could have been Juliette.*

"You were there? On that trip?" I rasp.

"Yes, there were six of us in total. The local police weren't very helpful. They kept telling us she was surely around somewhere, probably in a guy's room." Juliette's nose scrunches, leaving little wrinkles above her mouth. "But I knew Evie wasn't the type to have random hookups, so I called Paul Bouvier. With his money and influence, he was able to get the authorities to get off their asses and take the situation seriously." Anger flushes her cheeks.

"But by then, it was too late," I surmise before kissing the tip of her nose. "From what I remember, there wasn't much to go on."

Juliette shakes her head sadly. "Not a trace. She simply disappeared. The FBI got involved and the assumption was that Evie was taken, probably by human traffickers."

"God, that's so sad. And I can't imagine what her poor family has gone through for all these years. Have you stayed in touch with them?"

"I have." She snuggles closer to me. "In the beginning, we talked daily, sometimes multiple times a day. Now it's a few times a year. I mostly deal with Auburn, Evie's older brother."

Something akin to jealousy spears through my abdomen. Auburn Bouvier is now the billionaire CEO of the Bouvier fashion empire, and he's objectively a very good looking dude. *Did they ever...* But that jealousy is quelled almost immediately with Juliette's next words.

"I actually went to his wedding when he married Gianna. She's a complete doll, and the big grump is head over heels for her." Her smile is all fondness and affection for the couple.

"There was a younger brother too, right?"

"Yes, Monty. He went through a lot of stuff around the same time Evie went missing, and he moved to Florida and became a police detective."

Flashes of a burly man at a podium pop into my head. "He solved that serial killer case in south Florida a couple years back."

"He did," Juliette affirms. "Now he's back in New York, working for his family's company. He got married to his high school sweetheart, and they're expecting a baby this summer. I went to their wedding too." She lets out a soft laugh. "I guess I'm kind of an honorary member of their family."

"I love that. I mean, the situation with Evie is horrific, but I'm happy you've stayed in touch with the family."

Juliette's lips graze the underside of my jaw. "I think I'm done talking about this now. Can we move on to a more pleasant topic?"

My cock automatically joins the party and hardens. "If by pleasant topic, you mean you want me to fuck you on this hammock, then yes." I trace my hand up her bare thigh. Juliette is wearing a short sundress the color of pink cotton candy, the color setting off her golden tan.

"We haven't done it on the hammock before," she purrs. "I think we should turn it into a sex hammock."

My finger pulls aside the slip of satin covering her pussy and slides through her slit. Within a minute, she's dripping.

"Mmm, wet and swollen. Just the way I like you," I growl, slanting my mouth over hers as I finger fuck her with slow, measured thrusts.

"You on top," she pants, pulling at my shoulders until I roll on top of her... and keep rolling.

"Fuck," I bark as the hammock flips. It happens in a second and yet in slow motion at the same time. I twist my body to make sure I hit the ground first and land on my back with Juliette on top of me.

"Ooof," she grunts when we make impact with the grassy floor beneath us.

"Are you okay?" I wheeze out, vaguely aware of a pain I can't quite pinpoint yet.

Juliette scrambles to her feet before reaching down to give me her hand and help me up. "I'm fine. How about you?"

"You're bleeding," I snap more harshly than I intended. "Shit, baby. You're..." I grab her arm and inspect the scrape on her elbow. It's about the size of a quarter and barely dripping red, but it might as well be the size of an asteroid crater. "We need to get you to the infirmary."

She twists her arm to try and get a look at the wound. "It's not that bad." Then her eyes flit to my left hand and widen. "Reno! Your finger!"

At my insistence, Larry, the resort's nurse practitioner, tends to Juliette's scrape before taking X-rays of my left hand. She's sporting a pineapple-shaped Band-Aid when he delivers the news.

"Your pinky finger is broken, Reno, but luckily, I don't think it's going to need surgery. You can follow up with an orthopedic doc when you get back to the States, but for now, I'll splint it." He pulls out some supplies from a neatly arranged cabinet. "That will make sure it heals nice and straight."

Ten minutes later, we leave the exam room to find Kat, the resort manager, pacing the shiny wood floor of the waiting room. "Oh my goodness," she breathes, rushing to us when we emerge. "Are you two okay?"

"We're okay. Juliette has a scrape on her elbow, and my finger is broken, but we should both heal fine."

Kat grabs my hand and tsks. "Oh dear. I am so sorry about this. At the Pineapple Island Resort, we strive to provide a safe environment for all our guests. How did this happen?"

Juliette immediately flushes the color of a ripe tomato and flails her hands around. "You see... there was a hammock, and then all of a sudden, it was a sex hammock. Well, not quite a sex hammock yet, but it was about to be. Reno's hand was—"

Shutting her up with a tight arm around her waist and a squeeze of her hip before she can launch into a babbling play-by-play, I say, "It was my fault, Kat. I shifted too suddenly, and we flipped. Not the fault of the resort at all."

The manager's lips twitch, but she maintains a professional demeanor. "Very well, but I'd love to offer you another couple's massage." She taps on a tablet. "I have an opening tonight."

"That's very nice, but we're going to the karaoke party. Juliette has already picked out our costumes," I reply.

Kat lifts her chin. "All right, but please do let me know if you need *anything* before you leave."

"Will do."

As we walk back to our cottage, Juliette loops an arm around my waist. It feels so natural there, like we're a real couple on vacation. But we're not, and after tomorrow...

"Thank you for saving me from myself. I can't believe I was going on about the sex hammock." She groans and leans her head against my chest. "Poor Kat. She probably thinks I'm some kind of maniac."

"Luckily I'm the only one who knows what kind of maniac you truly are, dream girl." I kiss the top of her awkward little head. "A sex maniac."

She looks up at me with those beguiling aqua eyes. "Is your finger okay? We can skip tonight if you want to."

“I’m fine,” I assure her. “And we can’t back out now because I’m too curious to see what our costumes are.”

Chapter 24

Reno

I want to keep her.

An angel.

You may be thinking, *Oh, Juliette would make a gorgeous angel with all that blonde hair and that pretty little face.* But no. It's me. I'm the fucking angel. I chuckle at the mere thought of it.

The costume consists of white pants, vest, and tie, along with a matching sleeveless shirt, leaving my arms bare. My gold halo sits slightly crooked atop my dark hair, and a small pair of white feathery wings are strapped to my back.

"If only ESPN could see you now," a man says from beside me at the bar. I recognize him as the guy who recognized me on the beach that day. He has a cheeky smile on his face, and I return it with a chagrined one of my own.

"I didn't pick it out."

He laughs loudly. "I'm assuming that's Juliette's work."

"You assume correctly," I say, signaling the bartender for another scotch on the rocks.

The resort's nightclub, The Upside Down Club, is vibing with pounding dance music. The decor is dark blue, making it easy to spot the servers, who are dressed in skimpy bright yellow outfits. I'm doing my best to keep my gaze above the equator because the yellow hot pants on the males leave absolutely nothing to the imagination, and dong gazing is not my cup of tea.

"I'm sorry I forgot to introduce myself before. I was a little excited to meet my favorite hockey player. I'm Ryan." He reaches out a hand, and I shake it as I take in his attire.

"Nice to meet you, Ryan. Or should I call you Batman?"

He laughs, a deep, rich sound, hinting at his good-naturedness. "My partner, Carlos, picked it out. He's the one dressed as Robin." Ryan nods toward the dance floor where a man dressed as Batman's sidekick is dirty dancing with two women.

"Is Carlos bisexual?" I ask before wincing. "Sorry, that was invasive."

Ryan elbows me. "Not a problem. We're much more open here than we are back at home in Wyoming. Yes, he's bi, and I'm gay." He takes a sip of his drink. "Though I'm not attracted sexually to women, I'm attracted to them in every other way. I have a deep appreciation for the female form and think they are the most beautiful creatures ever to grace this earth."

"I couldn't agree more," I say, my mind going to a certain blonde. *Who should have been here by now*, I think, glancing toward the door.

Ryan smiles over the rim of his cocktail glass. "I have a bit of a voyeurism kink and enjoy watching Carlos with a woman." He takes a sip. "It's not something we do often. We come here once or twice a year to scratch the itch."

"It's nice that you have a place where you feel safe to explore what you like," I say, clinking glasses with him. "To be honest, I ended up at this resort accidentally and was a little apprehensive at first, but it's actually pretty freeing to be here."

"Agreed. We call this place our *kinda secret Caribbean gem*," he says with a chuckle. "By the way, where's Juliette?"

"Getting ready with some of the other ladies. She told me she would meet me here."

My attention is drawn to the door of the club, where a group of ladies is entering. They're dressed as *Wizard of Oz* characters, their outfits short and sexy. I recognize Wendy as Dorothy, and my brow creases. She's one of the women Juliette was getting dressed with. So where is she?

Then, like the parting of the Red Sea, the costumed ladies fan out to the side, leaving a statuesque blonde woman standing in the center.

And dear god in Heaven...

My mouth gapes open, and my grip tightens on the glass in my hand with so much force, I'm surprised it doesn't shatter. Juliette is standing there looking fierce as fuck with her blonde hair down and full around her face. Her makeup is dark and dramatic, with lips the color of blood.

And her outfit? *Mother of all fuckers.* My cock thickens in my pants at the sight of her. She's wearing a strapless, one-piece, leotard thing that's made of shiny leather in a deep red color. The top of it is cut to resemble flames against her chest. Fishnet hose crisscross down her mile-long legs, ending with tall red rhinestone boots that sparkle in the flashing lights.

I can see black-and-red feathered wings peeking over her shoulders, and illuminated red devil horns sit atop her mass of blonde hair. She is sinfully stunning.

"Damn," Ryan cackles. "Looks like you're going to have your hands full tonight, buddy." He slaps me on the shoulder and wanders off. At least I think he does because all I can see is *her*. My she-devil.

Juliette's eyes meet mine, and her top teeth sink into her plump, glossy bottom lip. My feet move without me telling them to, and I hear titters from the other women as I pass them, my eyes taking in every sexy inch of my dream girl.

When I reach her, she dips her chin coyly and turns those bright eyes up to me, sooty lashes framing her gaze. My hands automatically find her slim waist, the slick leather softer than I expected.

"You look very... pure," she purrs, running her hands up and down my bare arms.

"I'm feeling anything but," I growl, pressing my hips forward so she can feel every inch of my impure-ness. "You look positively wicked, dream girl."

"Maybe I'll take wicked advantage of you later," she says airily, her eyes sparkling with mischief.

"That's what I'm counting on."

And I'm damn well going to let her.

The karaoke party is in full swing, the drinks are flowing, and Juliette and I are happily tipsy. Actually, everyone in the bar is feeling pretty fine at this point.

Most of the singers are not great, but I think that's the point. Juliette has been on stage three times already with various groups of women, the last one a very loud rendition of "It's Raining Men."

We're standing near the backlit bar while Jane and Gaston sing "Islands in the Stream." They're dressed as Dolly Parton and Kenny Rogers.

I cop a feel of Juliette's ass. No one gives a fuck here. Everyone is all over each other. My eyes dart to a dark corner booth where a woman is straddling a man's lap, and I lean down to whisper in Juliette's ear. "Who is Marilyn Monroe with over there?"

She squints and then pops her eyes open wide. "Austin Powers, and I'm pretty sure they're fucking."

Sure enough, their rhythmic movements suggest some very naughty things are happening beneath Marilyn's iconic white dress.

"Is that Victoria?" I ask, and Juliette nods.

"Yes, and Austin Powers is Chris, Inge's husband. According to what Victoria told me yesterday, they're swapping tonight. I saw Inge and Elvis kissing in the corridor when I went to the bathroom earlier."

"I'm assuming Elvis is the one dressed as Elvis?" I ask sardonically, remembering the guy in a sparkly jumpsuit I'd seen on the dance floor earlier.

"That's him," Juliette giggles before leaning over the bar to get the bartender's attention. Of course he runs right over. And stares at her fucking chest while asking what she wants. Not that I can blame him;

her tits look amazing in this outfit. "Another shot of Fireball, please," my girl—*mine*—requests.

I step up behind her, plastering myself possessively against her back while cradling her curvy hips with my hands. "These boots are hot. I want you to wear them while I fuck your mouth later," I whisper in a low, commanding voice in her ear.

She turns to face me, her eyes glinting with mischief. "The angel wants the she-devil to suck his big, hard cock?"

The cock in question swells against her belly. "More than I want to breathe," I say, the words not much more than grunts because all the blood reserved for making my mouth work has migrated much farther south.

The bartender sets the shot glass on the bar behind Juliette, and I take it, holding it in front of her. Her glossy red lips part, and I press the glass to her lower one, tipping it up and pouring the contents into her mouth.

She winces only slightly before smacking her lips in satisfaction. "Thanks. I need some liquid courage. I'm about to go solo."

"What are you singing?" I ask, still staring at the cherries of her lips, imagining all sorts of devilish thoughts.

"You'll see," she sings, flashing me a cheeky wink.

I'm vaguely aware of someone approaching, and then I hear Kat's accented voice. "Okay, hot stuff. You're up next."

Hot stuff, indeed. This bombshell is fire personified.

"Be right there," Juliette answers. Once Kat departs, the hot-as-fuck devil woman drops her hand to my crotch and gives me a soft squeeze that almost makes me come in my fucking angel pants. Then, without another word, she saunters toward the round stage, her luscious ass swaying, while I'm left drooling like an infant with a new tooth.

That fucking woman...

She gives Jane and Gaston a high five as she takes their place on the stage, shimmying her shoulders as if to pump herself up for the song. I migrate to the front of the crowd and laugh when I hear the unmistakable sounds of a fiddle.

Juliette's eyes meet mine, and she grins before launching into "The Devil Went Down to Georgia." She's not a great singer, but she's surprisingly adept at hitting every single word with precision, despite her mildly drunken state.

I watch in fascination as the she-devil commands the stage, strutting from one side to the other, tossing out winks and pointing at people in the crowd while she sings. Everyone is eating it up.

As she nears the end of the song, Juliette plants herself in the center of the stage and cocks her hip, stomping one booted foot in time with the music. Everyone—including me—claps along and then cheers when she finishes with a flourishing, upraised arm.

My legs eat up the small space in front of the stage, and by the time she's handed off the microphone to the karaoke guy, I'm there. I lift her off the low stage by her waist and settle her on her feet.

"That was so fucking fantastic," I praise. "You could be an international superstar, dream girl. You were like Taylor Swift up there."

"If only I could sing like her," she says with a self-deprecating eye roll.

"There is that," I tease. "But you were still amazing."

"It was exhilarating. It made me..." She glances around before taking my hand and tugging me through the crowd toward the back of the nightclub.

"Made you what?" I ask, dutifully following along.

But she doesn't answer right away, instead opening a door across from the ladies' room and dragging me inside. Though the room is bathed in darkness, I can tell it's an office with a large desk and filing cabinets against the back wall.

"Wendy told me about this place," Juliette finally says, flicking on a small dark-green desk lamp and turning to face me with a look of determination. "Lock the door, Reno."

Holy hell. Four more beautiful words have never been spoken, and I fumble behind me to click the lock on the knob.

The woman with an angel's face and the body of the devil sashays toward me, one foot crossing over the other in a walk of pure seduction. Placing her hands on my waist for balance, she sinks to her knees on the gray carpeted floor.

"Dear god," I breathe as she makes quick work of my white trousers, unfastening them to reveal white boxer briefs. I lean back against the door as she pulls my cock from its confines and smirks up at me.

"All that singing made me hungry," she coos, finishing her previous statement as she stares at my erection like it's her favorite food.

Her hand is warm around my root, but not as warm as her tongue when she meticulously laps up every bit of pre-ejaculate leaking from my tip. Then she takes me into her mouth, twirling her tongue around the crown and setting my entire body on fire.

"This is going to be embarrassingly fast," I lament. "You've had me so goddamn turned on all night, Juliette."

She hums and takes me deeper, cradling my balls with one hand. Her lips are full and red around my shaft, and I have to close my eyes and count to ten to try and control the orgasm that's already building in my core.

Then she proceeds to suck my soul out through my dick, bobbing her head with the beat of the music from the club. I bury my hands in her hair, which is stiffer than usual, probably from hairspray.

"Fuck, baby," I push out through gritted teeth, my eyes roaming over every inch of her. The full tits pushed up high on her chest. The leather clad curves. Those provocative red boots with high stiletto heels that could pierce a man's heart.

And that's when I realize, that's exactly what she's done. Juliette McNamara has poked a hole in my heart and wormed her way inside, resting in a spot that seems to have been made just for her.

I'm falling for her.

And we're leaving tomorrow.

And there's rule fucking three to contend with.

I brush away thoughts of the *no contact once we get home* rule and focus on what's happening in this office right now. Namely, the stunning woman who's on her knees for me, sucking my cock like she has vacuum cleaner DNA in her cells.

She pulls off and looks up at me, her lipstick a complete mess, but she's never been more beautiful. "Fuck my mouth, Reno."

That immediately supersedes *Lock the door, Reno* as the top four-word phrase I've ever heard. It's a command, one I happily comply with, arching my hips forward to push my cock back into her warm, willing mouth.

I let out a loud growl of male satisfaction at the feel of my tip hitting the back of her throat. "That's it, my dirty little girl," I praise. "You'll take me deep and drink my cum like Kool-Aid."

She makes an erotic noise of agreement, and I tug roughly on her hair as I use her mouth for my pleasure. In and out. In and out. My ass slaps the door on every back thrust, and I don't give a ripe fuck if anyone hears. I'm lost in the thrill of pleasure, too close to that ultimate peak where my body is made for only one thing. Climaxing.

And I do. With an unholy roar, I push deep and release myself in the tight warmth of Juliette's throat. When I try to pull back a bit, she reaches around me and grasps my ass, holding me in place while her throat works to swallow every drop of what I'm giving her.

My spine loosens, and a full-body shiver wrings me into nothing more than a gelatinous lump of flesh. I'm pretty sure even my bones have ceased to exist as I slump back against the door.

"That was... life-changing," I pant, and Juliette slides her mouth off me and smiles up with pure feminine satisfaction for a job well done.

With her smeared makeup, mussed hair, and swollen lips, she's absolutely the picture of perfection.

And I want to keep her.

Juliette wouldn't allow me to return the favor in the office, instead retreating to the restroom to fix her face and hair while I wandered like a satiated zombie back to the main room.

And now we're slow dancing, our arms around each other while the couple on stage belts out "Everything Has Changed" by Taylor Swift and Ed Sheeran. I kiss the woman I've become obsessed with, tasting my salt on her tongue.

When we finally break the kiss, I notice Kat gesturing for my attention, and I glance over to see her mouth, "It's time."

I turn back to Juliette. "We're up next, dream girl."

Confusion clouds her face for a second before it brightens. "You're singing with me?"

"Against my better judgment, yes," I reply wryly, twirling us toward the stairs at the side of the stage.

"What song?"

I counter with her own words from earlier as the previous song ends. "You'll see."

We take the stage, Juliette brimming with excitement, and she grins like she won the lottery when I sing the first lyrics of "I've Had the Time of My Life." Oohs and ahhs fill the room, but I only have eyes for my pretty girl.

Is this the cheesiest duet I could find on the list a few minutes ago? Yes. But is it also the most fitting for how I'm feeling? Also yes.

As we sing the poignant lyrics, our bodies turn to face each other, and I wrap one hand around her back to hold her close. And a desire loops itself around my heart and tightens its grasp.

A desire to make my dream girl truly mine.

Chapter 25

Juliette

Well bless her heart.

THIS DAMN OUTFIT... *GRUNT*... is so fucking tight...

As I struggle to get undressed in our cottage, I feel warm hands on the sides of my half-exposed torso. "Need some help with that, sweetheart?"

"Please," I squeak, my voice sounding slightly strangled. Because this leather monstrosity has turned into the equivalent of a boa constrictor.

"Allow me."

A few seconds later, all of my clothing, including the flaming she-devil leotard, is on the floor, and I can breathe semi-normally again. "You're very good at undressing women," I tease, and Reno's face turns into a storm cloud of displeasure.

"I only want to undress *you*, Juliette," he says fervently, pressing a firm, demanding kiss against my lips. "Only you."

"O-okay," I stammer, a little surprised at his insistent tone.

He sweeps me off my feet—literally—and carries me to the bed we've been sharing, pulling the sheer drapes closed to cocoon us in our own little world. He's already deliciously naked, and I run my hands all over his taut, muscular body. Reno Swain is absolutely the most perfect specimen of man ever created.

Sliding down beside me, he pulls the covers over us and holds me close. This is different. We're usually not beneath the covers during sex. They always end up in a tangled heap at the foot of the bed from our vigorous... activities.

The light from the lamp is muted by the gauzy white material enclosing the bed, lending a softness to those gorgeous green eyes I've become addicted to. Reno leans up on one elbow, looping his leg over one of mine and pulling it wide as his fingers trace every inch of my face.

He seems to be mesmerized, and the feeling is a hundred percent mutual. A team of stormtroopers could bust through the door right now, and I wouldn't be able to look away from this beautiful man hovering over me.

We're in our own little bubble together, one charged with emotions I can't quite define. He finally breaks the silence.

"Juliette..." He closes his eyes, and for that brief moment, I feel like crying at the loss of contact. But then he opens them again, and they're swimming with affection. "I want to make love to you, baby."

Make love. Not fuck or screw. He said he wants to *make love* to me. That's some very un-Reno-ish talk, and something sparkly fires off inside my chest. I'm unable to form complex words around the lump rising in my throat, so I nod and whisper, "Yes."

Reno covers my body with his own and nestles his hips between my thighs, his erection already evident. He nudges my entrance, rocking his hips to coat himself with my slickness as his lips pepper sweet kisses all over my face.

Resting on his forearms, he latches his gaze onto my face and presses forward, entering me slowly until his pelvis is flush with mine. His shaky breath flurries across my lips as he rests his forehead against mine.

"Nothing's ever felt better than this," he says, his voice sounding a bit ragged.

"Same for me," I croak, feeling my heart opening up for this man. When he pulls back and enters me again with another measured thrust, it's like he's plunging into my soul at the same time.

And Reno does make love to me. His movements are raw but not rough, his words fervent but not dirty.

"You are so beautiful, Juliette. So sweet." He kisses down the side of my neck and then back up to whisper more heart-bending words into my ear in his deep, sultry voice. "I've never met anyone who makes me feel the way you make me feel."

Tears leak from the corners of my eyes and drip down my temples. Reno notices and sips them away with soft sucks.

"Don't cry, pretty girl," he gently scolds.

"I can't help it. You make me feel so full." My lips curve into a small smile, and I lift my hips from the bed, driving him even deeper. "And I don't mean down *there*. I mean in here." I tap my chest.

Reno's eyes soften at the corners, and then he lowers his mouth to mine, kissing me with a tenderness that has me aching for more from him. More kisses. More time. More *everything.*

Our bodies move together, rocking like a boat on a gentle sea while our tongues tangle. The bedsprings creak with our rhythm, but there's no headboard banging. No, our lovemaking is sweet and poignant, an unhurried joining of two people who feel an innate connection.

It's so much better than any sex I've ever had. It's almost like our goal is not to reach for orgasms; it's to revel in this night together. *Our last night.*

A hiccuping sob escapes from my mouth to his, and he breaks the kiss, pulling back a couple inches to study my face. "Are you okay, dream girl? Am I hurting you?"

Only my heart.

But I answer with a soft *no*, and he nods in understanding, as if he feels the same pull that I feel.

"Stretch your arms over your head," he requests, and I do. Reno drags his hands slowly up my arms until his fingers link with mine, pressing the backs of my hands into the mattress.

We have full-body contact in this position, and it only heightens the emotional impact of our lovemaking. He's warm, slightly damp, and the dark hair on his torso lightly abrades my soft skin as he moves over me.

His eyes are so intent on mine, I couldn't look away if I wanted to. And I *don't* want to. The intimacy between us is almost palpable, and I revel in it.

"I wish we had more time together," I whisper, giving him my vulnerability. I wrap my legs around him and use my heels against the backs of his thighs as leverage to lift my hips. He goes impossibly deeper, binding our bodies together until we are no longer two separate people but a single entity.

"I do too," he tells me softly before kissing me again. Our quiet moans echo and then combine in our mouths, and we finally come together. It's a slow, drawn-out orgasm, one that leaves me trembling beneath him for what seems like forever.

But we don't have forever. We only have tonight, and I suppress the urge to sob into his shoulder and beg him for more.

Reno releases my hands and wraps his muscular arms beneath me, holding me tight as he nuzzles his face into the side of my neck. "You really are my dream girl, Juliette," he says in a slightly muffled voice, though I can hear him clear as day. "Whenever I think of the perfect woman for me, it will always be your face I see."

Crushing my eyes closed, I loop my arms around his neck and cling to him, letting the tears escape like a leaky faucet. I no longer care about my *I don't date hockey players* rule. Or that we live so far away from each other.

I don't care about any of that because...

I'm completely in love with Reno Swain.

"I can't believe you wouldn't let me take a shower," I mumble as the flamingo-pink van glides through the gates of the small Pineapple Island airport.

It's barely past dawn, the sun peeping through the trunks of the palm trees lining the road. Because of the early hour, there are only four passengers in the van—me, Reno, and a couple I don't know.

"I told you why." he retorts in a low voice, a smirk teasing the corners of his lips.

"Because you want me to have the crusty crotch?" I shoot back with a mock glare, giving him an easy elbow to the ribs.

Reno pulls me closer with the arm wrapped around my back and kisses my ear. "Because I want my cum between your legs for as long as possible."

"So that's a yes to the crusty crotch," I declare.

He laughs. "I didn't shower this morning either because I want you on me as well. And besides, we showered at one point in the middle of the night, so we're not completely gross."

"Ahhh, yes. I believe that was after round two," I muse.

His smile relaxes into fondness at the memory. "That was a good one."

"They were all good," I say wistfully, thinking of the marathon sex we'd had all night long.

Twice I woke with Reno's face between my legs because he declared it unfair that he didn't get to taste me before bed. Then he made love to me again and again with only cat naps between sessions. He was insatiable... not that I'm complaining. I was just as rabid for him. As the night stretched into morning, the lovemaking took on an almost frantic air of need, our bodies clinging to each other in desperation.

Somewhere in the night, I made up my mind. I'm going to talk to Reno about trying for something more. Now that I'm aware of my true feelings for him, there's no way I can let him go. And I'm pretty sure he reciprocates those feelings, or at least he's on his way to loving me. The way he was with me all night... the loving looks... the sweet words... the gentle touches... Yeah, he's definitely feeling more than a casual fling.

My resolve strengthens.

Long-distance relationship? Bah! We can overcome that.

Hockey player? Screw it! They're not all the same.

We can do this. It won't be easy, but when you find the one you're supposed to be with, you do what it takes.

And Reno Swain is *the one*. I've never been more sure of anything in my life.

"Let's go, dream girl."

I'm snapped out of my love-fueled reverie to find that the van is in front of the terminal and Reno is standing with his hand outstretched for me. I smile as I take it and allow him to lead me out onto the sidewalk where Frank has our luggage unloaded.

Reno takes his suitcase and one of mine, leaving me to follow with my small one. "I can get both of mine. They have wheels," I protest, earning me a *not gonna happen* scowl over his wide shoulder. "And you really didn't have to upgrade my ticket to first class."

"I need the extra leg room," he replies, approaching one of the baggage kiosks. "And there's not a chance in hell I'm not sitting with you on the plane to Miami."

I close my mouth and allow him to scan our codes and print the luggage tags.

"You seem to have overpacked," he teases. "Not that I'm complaining, but your island clothes are pretty small."

"I always overpack," I explain. "Like if I'm going for a week, I bring twelve pairs of underwear, so for three weeks, I brought thirty-six pairs. Just to be safe."

Reno's hands over our bags to the attendant, his forehead crinkling in confusion. "Safe from... what?"

I widen my eyes. "What if I pee in my pants?"

He leads me to a small bar near the security area, and we wait in front of the hostess stand for the woman to finish seating another couple. "You do that often? Are you a secret pants-pee-er, Juliette?"

"No, but what if I'm out having an adventure and have to pop a squat in the woods?"

With a shake of his head, he says, "I don't understand."

I take his hand and pat it in mock patience. "You see, girls and boys have different anatomy, Reno."

His lips twitch at the corners. "You don't say."

"I thought I taught you a thing or two these past weeks, but maybe you weren't paying good enough attention."

He loops an arm around my waist and hauls me close, whispering in my ear. "Juliette, I know your anatomy better than my own balls at this point." A shiver runs through me, and he squeezes my hip. "I'm going to need a more thorough explanation of the peeing situation though."

The hostess returns and seats us at a booth in the corner. The tabletop is a sunny yellow, and we both squeeze into the same side of the booth. Reno uses the tabletop device to order us both a mimosa.

"Okay," I begin. "Guys can just whip out their equipment and let 'er rip, but girls have to squat. Depending on positioning and the fullness of the bladder, sometimes a little pee gets where it shouldn't. That's why I bring extra socks and shoes too."

His lips press together, fighting a smile, and he nods. "Okay, I see your point."

"And it's not just the pee situation. I also bring extras because if I take a swim in the afternoon, I'm not putting on the same panties I had on that morning because... gross."

"Reno?"

We look up to find a woman standing beside our table, her brunette hair cut into a classy, asymmetrical bob. It's before seven in the morning, but she has on a full face of what looks like professionally done makeup.

"Leia?" Reno asks, his body stiffening.

Oh shit. Leia? As in his former fiancée, Leia?

Her mouth morphs into a smile worthy of a toothpaste commercial. "What are you doing here, darling?"

His lips tighten at the pet name. "I've been staying on the island the past three weeks."

Her smile falters a little. "At the Pineapple Island Resort?" I'm sure she's trying to figure out what exactly he did there.

"Yep," he replies curtly.

"Oh." Her blue eyes flick to me and then back to her ex, her over-fluffed lips pursing into something resembling disapproval. "I thought you weren't into sharing."

She's been here for all of thirty seconds, and I'm already done with her shit.

"Oh my goodness," I drawl, inching so close to Reno, I might as well be in his lap. But I'm feeling a little possessive. "I would never share *my man* with anyone." I gaze lovingly up at him and see the hint of a pleased smirk on his lips. "I knew once I found someone as perfect as Reno, there's no way I could let anyone else touch him. I'm Juliette, by the way. And you are?"

I hold out my hand and Leia hesitates before giving it a limp, one-pump shake.

"Leia," she replies shortly. "I'm sure you've heard about me."

Oh no this heifer didn't.

Tapping my chin with my forefinger, I tilt my head and pretend to think about it. "No, I don't believe Reno's mentioned you. Are you a cousin or something?"

Leia appears to have sucked on a rotten persimmon, her gorgeous face revealing her insult at the thought of Reno not going on and on about her.

"No, we were engaged," she informs me with a curl of her lip.

I grace her with my sweetest smile and deliver the quintessential southern barb wrapped in sugar. "Awww. Well, bless your heart for letting this one get away." Translation: *You're not very smart, are you?*

As I curl my arms around Reno's bicep and squeeze, he covers his snicker with a cough before piping up with, "So where's Jeffrey?"

Leia's blue eyes dart to the wall beside Reno, her discomfort obvious. "We're, uh, not together anymore," she mumbles before inching her chin haughtily. "Apparently, I'm high-maintenance."

"Shocking," Reno says flatly. "So sorry about that."

His sarcasm seems to go right over her perfectly coiffed head because she flashes that toothpaste commercial smile again and touches his arm. I resist the urge to smack it away. Barely.

"I decided I deserved some fun, so Daddy sent me on this little vacay." Leia bats her eyelashes. "Are you arriving or leaving?"

"Juliette and I are leaving," he replies, resting his hand on my thigh.

"Oh." Her smile fades a bit before going full-wattage again, her voice turning into a catlike purr. "You could stay, Reno...."

I note that she didn't include me in the invitation, and my nerves sizzle with trepidation. Here she is looking like a freshly picked rose in an elegant ivory dress, and I'm in a tank top and shorts with a haphazard braid and no makeup. And I was just discussing peeing on my own shoes. I'm not exactly feeling like the winner in this situation.

But Reno's sitting beside *me* and his hand is on *my* leg, so that reassures me a bit. Still...

"I don't think so, Leia," he replies, further soothing my nerves.

"Hmm," she says, unimpressed. "Well, if you change your mind, you can stay in my cottage."

Bitch.

A man in an orange-and-white striped uniform that resembles the outfits worn by inmates at our county jail approaches with our drinks.

Reno speaks with semi-politeness. "It was nice to see you again, Leia, but our breakfast is here." He turns away and takes a casual sip of his mimosa, effectively dismissing his ex.

"It was great to meet you," I pipe up sweetly. "Make sure to try the hammocks while you're at the resort."

Reno snorts, and some of the bubbly drink goes up his nose, tossing him into a coughing spell. He reaches for a couple napkins to control the dribbling as I pound him on the back. By the time he's recovered, Leia is gone.

Good riddance. I hope she has raging diarrhea in that ivory dress.

"Did you really bless her heart and then suggest she try one of the hammocks of death?" he asks in a cough-rasped voice, though he's grinning.

I pick up my glass and smile smugly over the rim. "I did. She needed some heart blessing."

Reno falls asleep on the plane as soon as the wheels leave the ground. Poor man must be worn out from all our extracurricular activities last night.

I suppress a giggle and stare at him like a lovesick puppy. He is one gorgeous man. His eyelashes are completely unfair. How the hell does a man have such perfectly thick eyelashes that rest on the cheeks of that perfectly proportioned face?

Though I was up all night as well, I can't seem to find sleep. I'm too busy planning what I'm going to say to him once we reach Miami. We both have layovers before we fly to our respective cities, so we'll have at least two hours to hash out a plan.

The flight attendant brings me another mimosa, and I whisper a thank you to her from my window seat. Reno continues his deep slumber while I sleep stalk him.

After almost an hour of me gawking, I notice his brow crease into a frown, his hands tightening on the armrests. He releases a noise from the back of his throat, and I'm about to wake him when he utters a name.

A few seconds later, he murmurs, "I pucking love you."

My blood turns into ice in my veins, and I can't quite feel my fingers and toes. As I watch, his mouth curves into a brilliant smile, and my previously soaring spirit crashes into a fiery heap.

Because the name he said wasn't mine. It was...

Leia.

Chapter 26

Reno

Fuck the rules.

Jack Black—yes, the famous actor—flashes his trademark cheesy smile at the camera. He's wearing a hot-pink three-piece suit with a combination of pineapples and hockey sticks scattered over the too-shiny surface.

Weird as fuck wardrobe selection, but you do you, Jack.

"Aaaaand, we're back with our pucking bachelor, hockey superstar, Reno Swain, also known as Reno Swoon," he says in a loud, bombastic voice, his hand smacking me between the shoulder blades. "I'm pretty sure every woman in America is lamenting the fact that Reno has found the woman he pucking loves, amirite, ladies?"

He pops a dorky wink, and the studio audience cheers. I can't see their faces, but they mostly sound like women.

Jack continues. "We're down to the final two contestants. Kevin, can you bring out the lucky ladies?" Then he cackles and pops an eyebrow at the camera. "Well, I guess only one of them will feel lucky in a couple minutes."

The crowd hoots and hollers as comedian Kevin Hart—dressed the same as Jack—leads two women onto the stage. My eyes go immediately to the tall blonde in a yellow satin formal gown. Yellow really shouldn't look good on her with her hair coloring, but it does. Juliette looks like a ray of pure sunshine. And the way that fabric clings to her every curve...

I bite my knuckle, and the audience laughs, which startles me. Shit, I'd forgotten they were there.

And why am I even here? My brow creases, and I glance around. A huge neon sign hangs on the curtains at the back of the stage. It reads: I Pucking Love You.

I'm apparently on some kind of dating show. Must be some shit my agent signed me up for. At least I got to meet Juliette though. My eyes go back to her, and she smiles a bit apprehensively. Dear god, she is beautiful... and entirely crazy if she thinks I'm not picking her. I'm not even sure who the other woman is.

Glancing over, I see that it's Leia. Nope. Not interested. Not even a little bit. I immediately turn my attention back to Juliette, who is looking up at the ceiling. Only, there's no ceiling, just open sky above us.

What kind of bizarre-o setup is this? Soft fluffy clouds dot the sky, and I spot Sexy Bunny. He waves at me and gives me a thumbs up. I didn't even know rabbits had thumbs, but I wave back before I'm interrupted by Jack Black's voice.

"Reno, are you ready for the final pucking selection?"

My gaze returns to Juliette, and I take a deep breath. It's her. She's the one for me. That's why Sexy Bunny grew a thumb... so he could tell me I'm on the right path.

"I'm ready, Jack," I say confidently.

"Fantastic. Angie, can you bring out the final two pucks, please?"

I try not to frown when Angela Lansbury pushes a small rolling cart onto the stage. Wait... what? I thought she was dead.

The actress is dressed in the same pineapple and hockey stick fabric as Jack and Kevin's suits, only she's wearing a long skirt and sensible black shoes like my grandmother used to wear. She leaves the cart, kisses Jack Black on the mouth, and strolls off the stage to much applause.

At this point, I've given up trying to figure out what the fuck's going on here. I'm just ready to get this show on the road so I can be with my dream girl.

Dream... That word sparks something in my head but before I can define it, Jack lays a hand on my shoulder.

"Reno, you're on your way to your pucking happily ever after." The audience claps as Jack turns somber. "But before that, you have the difficult task of sending one of these ladies home."

I want to tell him it's not really that difficult, but I figure that will make me look like an asshole, so I simply nod stoically. Jack gestures toward the tray the apparently-now-alive Angela Lansbury left, and I see a sleek rectangular plate with two hockey pucks. One is round like a normal puck, but it has a bright red X printed on it. The other is shaped like a heart.

He doesn't have to direct me. I know what to do. I pick up the X-puck and walk toward the women.

"Leia," I say, holding out the X-puck to her.

Her mouth drops open in an expression of shock before that emotion turns to outrage. She snatches the puck from my hand, whirls around, and stomps across the stage, her black dress billowing behind her before I can say anything else. Then there's a curse from offstage and a loud thunk before someone yells, "Watch where you're throwing that thing, lady."

A bunch of oohs sound from the studio audience, but I ignore everything except Juliette McNamara, who is beaming up at me, looking like everything I've ever wanted in my life.

I'm in such a love haze, I forget I'm on some kind of TV show until Jack presses the heart-shaped hockey puck into my hand and whisper-hisses, "Don't forget to say the line, buddy. It's in your contract."

Taking a step closer to Juliette, I catch a whiff of her sweet pomegranate scent, and my cock takes notice.

Dude, not now. We're on national TV, and it is definitely not boner time.

My penis droops a little at my scolding, thank god, and I can get back to making Juliette mine. Holding out the puck, I say the dumb line I'm contractually required to say. "I pucking love you."

I have so many more words for her, but just as I cradle the side of her face in my palm, I hear a voice and feel a gentle hand shaking my shoulder.

"So sorry to bother you, sir, but can you please bring your seat back into its upright position?"

Jerking my eyelids open, I swivel my head from side to side, confused at my surroundings. I'm not on a television show. There's no Jack or Kevin or resurrected-Angela. No audience or lights or hockey pucks. I'm on a plane, and the flight attendant is smiling patiently down at me.

It was a dream.

"Oh, yes. Sorry," I mutter, straightening my seat as requested while trying to shake off the ludicrous dream I'd been dropped into. This happened once before when I drank champagne. I'd had a bizarre dream about Kelly Clarkson sitting on the roof of my car, singing Christmas songs while I drove.

No more champagne for this guy.

I twist my head to look at Juliette in the seat beside me. She has her chin in her hand, and her temple is tilted against the window. We're above the cloud line, and when I lean closer, I can see lots of fluff beneath us.

"See any interesting clouds?" I ask.

She shakes her head and continues staring out the window.

I try again. "It's probably cool to cloud gaze from above, huh?"

Juliette still doesn't look at me. "It's different."

I stroke her long braid with my hand. "Everything okay?"

She finally turns her face toward me, and I'm surprised at the dullness clouding her normally bright eyes. "Just tired. Some sex-crazed fiend kept me up all night."

"That bastard," I denounce. "Do you want to watch baby goat videos on my phone?"

That earns me a tiny smile, and she nods. I tug her toward me, nestling her in the crook of my arm while I log on to the plane's Wi-Fi. I barely watch the screen, instead keeping my eyes on Juliette. She smiles at the antics of the little animals, but she's definitely not her bubbly self. Maybe she's just tired. Or hungry. I'll feed her when we get to Miami.

Lifting Juliette's hand, I kiss the back of it. "Is something wrong with your breakfast burrito? You've only taken a couple bites."

She rolls her lips between her teeth and shrugs. "Not all that hungry, I guess."

I study her face, getting the feeling something is off with her. She's been quiet, and she sat across the booth from me instead of on the same side.

"Is everything okay?" I ask, studying her face.

She doesn't quite meet my eyes. "Of course. Just got a lot to do when I get home."

"For the children's summer reading program at the library?"

Juliette's face turns a bit mushy at the mention. From our talks, I know it's one of her favorite parts of her job.

"Yes, I need to email all the guests I have scheduled and make sure everything is still on track. Plus, I'm anxious to see the renovations the crew has been working on. They haven't messaged me about any problems, but it's important they have everything done before we have a bunch of kids there."

That must be what's bothering her. She's got a full plate running the library and with her writing career. So I step out on a limb.

"I'd love to come to one of the events, if you'll tell me where your library is located. The guy with all the animals sounds cool."

She startles, her eyes widening. "I, uh, think that would break rule two. And three."

Rule two is no talking about our personal lives, and rule three is no contact once we return to our respective homes.

"Sweetheart," I say with a chuckle, "I think we obliterated rule two a long time ago, and to be honest, I'm not a big fan of rule three."

Instead of commenting, she shifts in her seat and roots around in her backpack before pulling out a few bills and tossing them onto the table. "I'd better get to my terminal so I don't miss my flight."

Her change in attitude staggers me. Last night was so perfect. So meaningful. To me anyway. When we made love, it felt like we had this soul-deep connection I've never experienced with another person.

The eye contact. The kisses. The whispered words that verged on some very serious declarations. All of it combined into something... special, for lack of a better word.

But now she's standing and pulling her backpack onto her shoulders. I quickly rise and snag the money she left on the table—because yeah, that ain't happening—replacing it with my own before handing hers back to her.

Juliette lets out an exasperated breath. "I can pay for my own food."

"I'm certain you can but not when you're with me."

With a roll of her eyes, she puts the money back into her bag before lifting her face to look at me. "Thank you. For everything. It was really nice to meet you, Reno."

It was really nice to meet me? What the fuck?

Gritting my teeth, I take her hand because she looks like she's ready to make an escape. "Come with me," I demand, and she makes a hmph noise but follows me anyway. My eyes dart around, looking for a quiet place where we can talk. Not the easiest task in the busy Miami International Airport, but I remember a kind of quiet zone from when I had a long layover here a couple years ago. I think it was in this terminal.

Spotting a familiar corridor, I turn right and see couches lined up against the walls. A few people are resting on them, most wearing noise-canceling headphones.

"Reno, my flight," Juliette whisper yells.

"You have an hour and a half," I tell her quietly, walking past the couches and finding a relatively secluded area. Then I swivel to face her and rest my hands on her hips. "Juliette, I want to see you again."

"But rule three..."

"Fuck the rules," I snap. "We made the rules; we can change them." Softening my tone, I step into her warmth. "I don't want this to end, Juliette."

Her beautiful face morphs into something resembling pain. "I can't, Reno."

"You can't or you don't want to?" I question.

"Both," she replies, dipping her gaze to my chest like I have a puzzle printed on my black V-neck shirt. The lack of eye contact tells me she's not being completely honest, which is unlike her. Juliette is the most guileless person I've ever met.

"Can we still be friends?" That's the furthest goddamn thing from what I need, but it would be better than nothing. And perhaps we could build on that. If I get my foot in the door she's trying to slam, I know I could win her heart.

Her aqua eyes are filled with tears when she lifts them to mine. "I-I think a clean break would be best."

A stiletto of agony cramps my stomach, and I pull in a long breath through my nose before releasing it slowly through my mouth. It doesn't soothe me in the least because she looks as broken as I feel.

"But why?" I sound like a needy little bitch, but I don't care. I am needy when it comes to Juliette McNamara. In a few short weeks, she's become my addiction. Her smile. Her endless chatter about soundtracks and goats. Her softness mixed effortlessly with her strength. I don't know how I'm supposed to live without her.

She swallows. "Because it's what I need."

What about my needs? I want to ask, but I love her so fucking much, her needs trump my own.

Cupping her exquisite face with both hands, I ask, "Can I kiss you goodbye?"

A tear slips down her face, and she nods. I close my mouth over hers, doing my best to show her how well we fit. How perfect we are together. The kiss is poignant and sweet, filled with an emotion that threatens to undo me in the middle of an airport.

Her arms wind around my neck, and our tongues tangle into a mass of passion and want—on both our parts. I can taste the saltiness of her tears, and I kiss her harder, pouring myself into her with a desperation I can't remember ever feeling.

When we break, her lips tremble when she swipes a tear from my cheek. I didn't realize it had fallen, but I'm not ashamed in the least. She's worth all my tears. She's worth everything.

"Goodbye, Reno," she whispers.

And then she's suddenly striding down the corridor away from me, but I don't miss the hitch of her shoulders that tells me she's sobbing. Why is she shutting me out if she's this upset?

My fingers brush against the tingling sensation on my lips. Would that be the last kiss we ever shared?

I bend at the waist against the raw ache inside me, placing my hands on my knees as I watch the love of my life leave me.

Then she turns the corner without looking back and...

She's gone. Dragging my shattered heart behind her.

Chapter 27

Juliette

Down the drain

After a quick sobbing trip to the restroom in the Miami airport, I manage to hold myself together during the three hour flight to Dallas. And then for the thankfully traffic-less drive home to Pine Tree Falls.

By the time I reach my adorable little house, I'm ready to collapse into a heap of sorrow and regret. But...

"Hey, baby girl!" Pops greets me at the door, his arms open wide.

I fall into them, managing to only let a couple tears slip past my tightly held facade. He smells like Calvin Klein Obsession cologne, the only one he's worn since I was a little girl. And home. He smells like home.

"Hi, Pops," I breathe into his neck.

He pulls back and studies my face, his smile dimming into concern. "What's all this?" he asks softly, swiping at my tears with both thumbs.

Forcing a smile I don't feel, I respond, "Oh, just a bit of vacation hangover, I guess."

"I understand that," he says in his kind, sonorous voice. "You made lots of friends?" When I merely nod, his face creases with amusement. "Of course you did. My Juli could make friends with a brick wall."

That brings a genuine chuckle rolling up my throat. "There was some great cloud gazing on the island. You would have loved it."

Pops pats my cheek affectionately. "You'll have to tell me all about it later, but for now I'm going to get out of your hair and let you unwind. I just wanted to be here to hug you when you got home."

Though I'm happy to see his handsome face, I'm a little relieved he's going to give me some time to myself so I can finally let my emotions run loose. I've been holding them in for hours since I left... *him.*

No. Nope. Not thinking of that right now.

After another hug, Pops leaves, and I look around the room. Since leaving that corridor in Miami, I feel like I've gone partially color blind. Or maybe someone has hit the edit button on my brain and turned down the saturation setting.

Even the normally bright pops of color in my living room seem duller. My raspberry couch appears more of a sluggish magenta, and the vibrant art on my walls has been reduced to nothing more than splashes of blah.

Will the loss of Reno Swain always mute my perception, or will I one day wake up and be able to accurately see colors again?

Perhaps I'm mistakenly attributing this weird visual phenomenon to Reno when I've actually had a mini-stroke or something. If I go to a neurologist and explain that I'm either suffering from a neurological defect or my system is misfiring due to walking away from the man I'm pretty sure is the love of my life, would they be able to figure it out? Is there even a diagnosis code for loss of color vision secondary to a broken heart?

I sigh and walk back outside to get my luggage from my vintage Volkswagen. As I'm pulling out the second one, I hear, "Hold up. I got that."

Turning, I see Xander loping across the postage-stamp-sized yard. I put on a smile for my little brother, though little isn't an accurate term for him physically. He's as tall as Bubba but not nearly as stocky, sporting a leaner build.

After giving me a quick squeeze, he hands me a bottle of hazelnut coffee creamer, explaining, "I used all yours this morning, so I ran to the store." Then he grabs the handles of my suitcases and wheels them up the sidewalk with me trailing behind.

"Thanks, Xan. You didn't have to do that."

"No prob. I just appreciate you letting me stay here. I managed to keep your ferns and azaleas alive."

"I see that," I tell him, smiling at the hanging ferns and the flowering bushes on either side of my front porch. "Did you get a lot of studying done?"

"Yup," he says, opening the door and taking my suitcases inside. "I'm about finished with the psych shit portion of my study guide."

"Psych shit? Is there actually a section called that?"

He laughs. "I think it's something like Psychological, Social, and Biological Foundations of Behavior."

I shake my head and gesture for him to follow me to the kitchen. "That's too complicated. They should definitely change the name to Psych Shit."

"I'll pass on your recommendation," he says, leaning his butt against the counter and crossing his arms while I put away the creamer. "You look tan. Was the resort nice?"

"It was top-notch," I reply. *Especially my neighbor,* I think, though I keep that part to myself.

"Cool. Maybe I'll *swing* on down there for a vacation some time." The emphasis on that one word has me narrowing my eyes in suspicion until Xander bursts into laughter and admits, "Holly told me."

"Oooh, that big mouth," I fume, but I'm not really all that mad. "I told her not to tell."

Xander raises one finger. "You told her not to tell *Bubba*."

"Ole loophole Holly," I say, rolling my eyes and then cringing at my next thought. "Did she tell the dads?"

"Nope. Just me and Jordie. Oh, and that red-headed cashier down at the Piggly Wiggly."

"Nora?" I shriek. "She's the biggest blabbermouth in Pine Tree Falls."

Xander chortles and tugs at my braid. "Kidding. You know Holly wouldn't tell Nora shit because she, and I quote, *has the lusty eyes for Bubba*."

I nod. "It's true. Bubba danced with her once in seventh grade and she's been in love with him ever since."

My brother pushes off the counter and pulls open the refrigerator to pull out a bottle of water. "So, did you meet any cute unicorns you could introduce me to?"

Propping my hands on my hips, I ask, "How did you know about unicorns?"

Xander shrugs. "The internet. I follow a cool couple called The Impulsive Duo on Insta. They're all about providing proper education on the lifestyle. They even have an app called Unicorn Landing, which is a safe place for women in the lifestyle to get more information and resources."

I nod thoughtfully. "Is that something you're interested in, Xan?"

He tilts his head from side to side a few times and swigs his water. "I dunno. Maybe. Depends on if my future wife or husband would be into it."

I smile at that. My younger brother is very open-minded about sex. He does gravitate toward women most of the time, but he's had a couple boyfriends.

"I met a lot of really nice people at the resort. I understand there are places that are a bit wilder if you're into that, but... I don't know... Pineapple Island seemed like one big family. Even though I'm not in the lifestyle, they never made me feel like an outsider." I steal Xander's water and take a sip. "And they didn't pressure me to get involved just because it's something *they* like. It was a pretty chill atmosphere."

Xan bobs his head up and down. "That sounds cool. Maybe I'll go when I'm no longer a broke-ass college student. I could be a bull."

My eyebrows knit together. "Do I even want to know what a bull is?"

He grins, and there's a bit of wickedness in it. "It's a man who plays with a couple. He's usually very well-endowed, and I do have a really big—"

I cover his mouth with my hand and point to the front of the house. "Out. Now."

He responds by sticking out his tongue and licking my palm. With a noise of annoyance, I pull my hand away and wipe it on his shirt.

"You asked," he points out, still smirking at me.

"I did not ask about your penis size, Xander James," I scold, pulling out the middle name for effect. "I'm open to most any discussion with you, but talking about your manhood is off-limits. Boundaries, bro." Then I quickly add, "Unless you have an STD or erectile dysfunction and need me to take you to the doctor. You can always come to me about health issues, okay?"

That makes him laugh, and he pulls me forward with his long arms. "God I adore you. You really are the best big sister."

I hug him. "I totally am. Now scoot on out of here. I need to unpack and take a shower."

He pulls back, his face serious now. "I mean it, Jules. You're always there for me, and I appreciate it. Having you was better than having a mom."

Then his sweet moment is gone, and he pokes me in the side with his index finger, eliciting a yelp from me. "You need a good spanking, Xander James," I call at his retreating back.

I'm met with a chuckle. "Don't threaten me with a good time, Jules. Lock the door behind me."

Shaking my head, I lock up when I hear his truck roar to life outside and replay his comment about *better than having a mom*. It makes me sad and proud at the same time. Sad that my siblings grew up without a mother but proud that they grew up so well adjusted despite that.

As a teenager, I'd attempted to step into the mother role for the little ones because I thought that's what they needed. Until my fathers sat me down and informed me that being Xander and Jordie's mom was not my job. Then they went with me to Dr. Hough's office, and she explained about parentification and how it's not a good situation for anyone involved.

Dad and Pops assured me they could handle parent duties and I should focus on being a good big sister and a female role model for the younger ones. And that's what I've always tried to do. Even when I was asked to babysit as a teenager, I was paid just like Pops or Dad would have paid anyone else. I realize now how important and valued that made me feel.

With a sigh, I decide to tackle my suitcases, opening the small one and sorting my dirty clothes. When I unzip the larger one, I freeze at the sight of a white box with a pretty bow on top. *I didn't put that there.*

My fingers tremble when I pull out a card nestled beneath the bow and flip it over. I know who it's from before I even see his handwriting.

> *Think of me when you use these. I hope we can use one together one day.*
>
> *Love,*
>
> *Reno*

A beach ball seems to swell in my throat as I open the box and find three rows of shower steamers wrapped in blue foil paper. I wedge my fingers into the box and pull one out, a sob wrenching from my chest when I see the label reads, *Ocean Cottage,* my favorite scent from the resort.

Cradling it in both hands like it's a delicate baby bird, I abandon my unpacking efforts and walk to my bathroom. Tears obscure my vision as I turn on the shower, unwrap the disc, and carefully place it on the floor of the shower. A minute later, I'm naked and standing beneath the hot spray as the familiar scent rises up around me.

And that's when I let myself go. It's the very definition of an ugly cry, complete with disgraceful noises and snot bubbles.

Reno's dream-induced words come back to me.

Leia.

I pucking love you.

It's not his fault he still has feelings for his ex, ones that must have resurfaced after he saw her for the first time in a while. So I don't blame Reno, and I'm not mad at him. At all.

I am heartbroken though. I had it built up in my head that we could make things work. We could overcome distance and limited time together. But the one thing we can't overcome is if one of us is still in love with someone else.

I tilt my face up toward the shower head to wash away my tears, but they're immediately replaced by more.

Finally, I drop to my knees and watch as the shower steamer melts away and the residue washes down the drain. I'm sure there's some kind of metaphor I can draw about that, but I just don't have the fucking energy right now.

All I know is a bone-deep sadness that I'm not sure will ever go away.

Chapter 28

Reno

Still thinking of her

Four days after I return from Pineapple Island, I step into the aisle of yet another plane with a Dallas Brewers duffle bag in my hand. I heft it and smile at the additional weight. With Juliette on my mind, I'd packed almost my entire underwear drawer for my three day trip to Dallas.

What if I pee my pants?

Her funny words and wide, sincere eyes flash through my brain as the petite flight attendant rushes to me.

"Mr. Swain, I hope I made your flight enjoyable," she breathes, pressing a slip of paper into my hand. It's no doubt her phone number because she's been flirting shamelessly with me since I stepped onto the plane.

"It was fine," I say in the most non-encouraging way possible as I turn my shoulders to edge past her and out the door. I cram the note into my shorts pocket to throw away later.

When I reach the baggage claim area, I spot my own name... on a Raptors jersey worn by a little kid who looks to be about five or six. Stepping up behind him and the man I assume is his father, I tap him on the shoulder.

"Hey, kid," I say, and when he looks up, the expression on his little face is priceless.

"Y-you're.... You're..."

I squat and hold out my hand. "I'm Reno Swain." He shakes it respectfully but his eyes are still taking in my face with wonder.

"I knooooow. I got your jersey on." He spins to show me SWAIN printed across the shoulders. Then he does an excited one-eighty jump back to the front. "But I want a new one cuz you're coming to the Brewers. We gotta wait till Dad's next paycheck though," he babbles, obviously parroting something he's heard the adults say.

Glancing up to his father, I see him shake his head and blush slightly. "We just heard the news yesterday, but I, umm, we'll get him a new jersey soon."

"You guys live in the area?" I ask.

"We do, though you're Rocco's favorite player," the dad answers. "He's been beside himself with excitement since the announcement was made that you're coming to Dallas."

Because I remember how it felt to want the newest sports jerseys when I was a kid—and not being able to afford them—I make up some shit on the fly.

"Since I'm going to be a Brewer now, the organization has asked me to hand out some jerseys to fans. They want people wearing number ninety-six to generate excitement. Would you do me a favor and wear my jersey around?"

The little boy nods with enthusiasm, and his father gently scolds, "Use your words, Rocco. He can't hear your head rattle." That makes me smile because Ma used to say the same thing to me.

"Yes, please," the boy says dutifully, and his brown eyes flick down to my bag.

"I don't have them yet, because they've got to get some new ones made. If it's okay with your dad, I'll get one in the mail to you."

He glances up at his father with a pleading gaze, and the man rubs a hand across his dark hair. "That would be really nice. What do you say to Mr. Swain?"

"Thank you, Mr. Swain," Rocco gushes, throwing his arms around my neck.

"You're welcome, kiddo," I tell him, patting his back. He smells like a combination of sugar and little boy sweat. "And just call me Reno because we're buds now, right?" I release him and hold out my fist for a bump. Rocco obliges with a happy, snaggle-toothed grin.

"Best buds," he clarifies.

"For sure," I agree affably before standing and addressing his father. "Do you mind giving me your address and Rocco's size so I can send you the jersey?"

He smiles and digs through his wallet to find an old receipt before pulling a pen from the pocket of his work shirt, which has the name of a sanitation company embroidered on the chest. He scrawls down the info and hands it to me, and I put it in the pocket of my shorts.

"I can't tell you how grateful I am to you for this." He lowers his voice. "Rocco's mom has been sick..." The man looks away and blinks rapidly before lifting his chin and continuing. "Anyway, it's been hard on him. On all of us. So thank you for taking the time to talk to him."

"Hey, man," I say with a chuckle, "I'm just glad to have at least one fan in this city." My tone turns serious. "And I'm sorry about your wife. I hope everything will be okay."

"She's doing much better now, but it's been a long road."

"Do you have other children as well?" I ask, an idea coming to me.

"No, just our Rocco," he says, running his hand through the messy curls on his son's head. "We're here to pick up my wife's mom. She's coming to help out while I'm at work."

I glance back at the kid, who's beaming up at me, and my heart melts a little. "Well, good luck with everything, and I'll get a package sent out as soon as possible."

"Thank you again," the man says, his eyes abnormally damp. "We're glad to have you in Dallas."

We say our goodbyes, and I watch as they stride toward a woman in a floral dress who just entered the baggage area.

"Got a fan already?" I hear and turn to see Baylor Ward standing a couple feet from me. He's a Black man with a goatee and shoulders the size of a semitruck.

"Hey, man," I greet with a genuine smile. I've always liked Baylor, though he's a force to reckon with on the ice. "That's one fan in my column. Only a few million left to go."

We do the whole bro-hug thing and he gestures toward my bag and attire. I'm wearing a hat and shirt with the Brewers' red, white, and blue branding on it. "I see you got the stuff I sent."

"Gotta represent," I say with a laugh.

"Damn straight," he replies firmly. "You got any checked bags?"

"Nope, just this," I tell him, jiggling the duffle. "You care if I make a phone call to take care of the stuff for the kid right quick?"

"Nah, go ahead. I'm parked illegally, but the security guy out there is a fan, so he won't let me get towed."

I reach into my pocket and pull out a piece of paper, confused when I see the note that's obviously not from Rocco's dad. Unless the man wants to do borderline illegal stuff to my cock.

"Shit," I mutter, digging in my pocket to find the correct paper.

"What's wrong?" Baylor asks.

"Note from a flight attendant." He peers at it and his dark eyebrows shoot up.

"Goddamn. I don't think that's legal in Texas."

I bark out a laugh and toss the note into the trash can. "Dude, I don't think that's legal anywhere."

Baylor clocks the move. "Not your type?"

To be honest, I don't even remember what the woman looked like. I shake my head. "Not interested. I've got a girl."

Okay, the more correct statement would be that I'm obsessed with a girl that's not technically mine, but potato, po-tah-to or whatever. I take a picture of the info Rocco's father jotted down and shoot it off to my agent before giving her a call.

"Reno, my favorite client," Carly Hanson answers merrily. "What did you just send me? Is this Rocco someone I need to put a hit out on?"

I laugh at her nonsense, though Carly's a badass broad and could probably make that happen if I requested it. She's a beast for her clients.

"It's a kid I met in the airport. Family's going through a hard time, but he's a fan."

"Say no more. I'll send a jersey, hat, and full swag package. Maybe a hoodie too. Kids like hoodies." I can hear her clicking away on her computer.

"Thanks, Carls. You're my favorite agent."

"Of course I am. Anything else?"

"Yeah, I'm not sure how Dallas handles their ticketing requests for players, but... hold on." Baylor is nudging me with his elbow.

"Tell her to talk to Marjorie in Community Relations," he says in a low voice.

"Baylor said to talk to Marjorie in Community Relations."

"On it. I know Marj. I'll get tickets to the season opener for the family. How many?"

"The mom is sick, so I don't know if she's well enough to attend, but there's also a grandmother."

"I'll send six to be safe. The kid can bring some friends." Then her voice turns shrewd. "Baylor Ward, I'm assuming?"

"Uh, yes."

"Hmmm," she muses. "I hear his agent is retiring this year. Put in a good word for me."

I laugh. "Always a shark, aren't you? I'll talk to him."

"Good man. If there's any other way I can serve your every need, just call." Her tone is sarcastic, but that doesn't make it less true. Carly is so much more than an agent. She runs her own firm with a slew of employees that serve as personal assistants for her clients, making sure even the oddest requests are taken care of.

"That's a nice thing you're doing," Baylor says once I disconnect the call. "By the way, what happened to your pinky finger?" He gestures to my still splinted digit.

Before I can think of a better excuse, I say, "Sex hammock incident."

He chuckles. "I think we're going to get along really well, Reno."

Baylor wasn't wrong. He and I are becoming fast friends. He gave me a private tour of the arena, and then we had a catered lunch at the swanky private dining room there with the entire team and coaching staff. Even the owner of the team made an appearance to welcome me. The Brewers did everything short of rolling out the red carpet, and this sense of *belonging* begins to settle into my bones.

Now we're back in Baylor's big charcoal-gray truck, headed east as he gives me a rundown of the owner and his family. "Mr. Carmichael bought the team about eight years ago and changed the name to the Brewers. He and his family are in the beer business."

"That explains the name change," I comment. "And the outstanding bar."

"They open that up on weekends, even when we don't have games. A lot of the players go there to socialize, and management keeps the crowd small and low-key so we can relax. It's like our own private lounge."

"That sounds nice."

"It is. They usually let in some puck bunnies for the single guys, but they know to leave us married players alone. I can put the word out that you have a girlfriend so they know not to hit on you."

"Thanks. I appreciate that," I reply.

The last damn thing I'm interested in is any woman but Juliette. I'm pretty sure if she doesn't somehow change her mind, I'll be celibate for the rest of my life.

"Anyway, Mr. Carmichael financed a whole-ass new arena for us. Our previous one was old and shitty."

"I remember," I say with a small laugh. "The new one is fucking beautiful though. Thanks for showing me all the behind-the-scenes stuff today."

"No prob, man. I'm taking you to the town where I live. It's about a thirty minute drive east of the city, but the drive really isn't too bad."

"What's the name of the town?"

"Pine Tree Falls."

"That sounds nice," I say.

"It is. Like I told you, it's small but a great community. The public schools are excellent. There is a private school too if that's something you want for your future kids, but to be honest, their sports teams suck."

Future kids. That hits me hard in the chest. It's not something I've contemplated a lot, but I would have a baby with Juliette in a heartbeat. My mind goes back to Rocco and his hug in the airport. *Will I ever have that? A son or daughter who wraps their tiny arms around my neck. A kid I can take to the park and get ready for bedtime?*

I picture myself tucking a little blonde girl with a pretty braid into her pink bed with Juliette leaning against the doorframe. She would watch me with that sweet smile on her lips as I read our daughter a bedtime story. And when the little one is asleep, I'd take my wife to bed and try to put another baby in her. Yes. Lots and lots of babies.

Snapping out of the reverie, I realize Baylor is still talking, and I tune in mid-sentence. "...nice park and a great library. The grocery store is small, but there's a Whole Foods in the next town over that my wife likes to shop at."

"You said a lot of our teammates live in..." I forgot the name of the town.

"Pine Tree Falls," he fills in. "And yes. Our goalie lives here. You played in college with Gibby, right?"

I laugh. Bryce Gibson is a damn good goalie and quite a character off the ice. "I did. I'm surprised they haven't run him out of town."

Baylor grins and puts on his blinker. "He's calmed down a lot since he got engaged." He exits and turns right. A few minutes later, I see two gas stations flanking the road before we take a side street into the town square.

The courthouse sits in the center, rising above the other buildings in a mass of tan brick. Everything is so green, from the manicured lawns to the lush oak trees that appear to be at least a half century old. Most of the buildings are two-story and boast wrought iron balconies reminiscent of old New Orleans architecture.

I feel myself relaxing because I'm hit again with that sense of belonging, like this little town could be a real home.

"Not a ton to see," Baylor chuckles, pointing at various buildings. "That's our diner there. Couple boutiques, mostly women's clothes. We don't have a Starbucks or other chain coffee shop, but Caffy's is excellent and has the best damn homemade pastries you've ever had." His finger waggles toward a neat wooden storefront on the corner.

"The kind that makes you have to put in extra hours at the gym?" I ask with a sardonic smile.

"Exactly." He turns beside a sign that reads *Oak Street* and nods at a stunning brick building. "That's our library. The whole town is really proud of it. It's one of the only Carnegie libraries still in existence that functions as an actual library."

I stare at the imposing structure with its wide stone steps and zone out again, wondering how Juliette's summer program is going. Are there lots of kids there? Does she want kids of her own?

"But they're done with that now," Baylor is saying, and I mentally force myself back to real life because I have no idea what he just said. "This is the nursing facility I was telling you about." He slows down in front of Shady Pines, which is a sprawling design that takes up an entire city block. Pine and oak trees surround it, and a few elderly people sit on the wide front porch sipping what looks like lemonade. Several nurses are seated with them, also enjoying a cool drink on this warm Texas day.

"This is beautiful," I say.

"It really is. And very well-run. We'll come back to it in a bit so you can check it out. I want to get you settled in your room first. The team arranged for you to stay at one of the bed and breakfasts."

After another turn down a shaded street, Baylor pulls up in front of a three-story Victorian home painted in a pale lavender. A few minutes later, I've been greeted warmly by the owners, Gayla and Sam, and placed in one of the second-story rooms.

Back downstairs, Sam slaps my shoulder. "I make a mean breakfast, Reno, so make sure you come down in the morning before ten." The man is probably in his sixties and sports a beard that wouldn't look out of place on a ZZ Top album. He leads me into a living area with antique-looking furniture and a sturdy mahogany bar along one wall. "You can help yourself to the spirits if you want to unwind in the evenings. I'm a retired bartender, so I keep it well-stocked for our guests."

"Thanks, Sam," I reply, taking the keyring he offers.

"The gold one will get you in the front door, and the silver one is for your room. Come and go as you like, but just lock up when you come in." He has a deep Southern drawl and an affable smile hiding behind all that facial hair.

His wife is a kind, stout lady who's constantly fussing with a curtain or a lampshade, making sure everything is perfect in their bed and breakfast. "We live on the third floor," she remarks, swiping non-existent dust from a spindle-legged end table, "so you let us know if you need anything."

"I will, and thank you. Your home is beautiful."

She offers me a beaming smile that tells me that was the exact right thing to say.

With their arms around each other, the couple stands on the porch and waves at me and Baylor as we walk down the pristine sidewalk. They look like they should be on a postcard. Hell, the entire town is postcard-worthy, and I think Ma is going to love it here.

“We can just walk to Shady Pines,” Baylor says as I dash away a rivulet of sweat from my forehead. “And you’ll get used to the heat.”

Two hours later, I know Shady Pines is the place for Gramps. The staff is friendly and almost annoyingly energetic, but you can tell they have a deep affection for their guests. No, they don’t call the people who stay there *patients* or *residents*. They refer to them as *guests* because they want them to feel pampered and cared for.

The rooms aren’t luxurious, but they are very spacious and clean. I took Gramps out of a place in Colorado because the room he shared with another man was barely big enough to turn around in. He was constantly agitated and uncomfortable, so I found another facility where he could have his own space, and his demeanor almost instantly improved.

I meet with a team of nurses and doctors with impressive resumes and caring attitudes. They also introduce me to Crystal, their social activities director, a lovely lady in her forties with an easy smile and soft voice. I gawk at the calendar printout she gives me detailing the various activities and events at the facility. Almost every box is filled.

“I understand your grandfather is a veteran?” Crystal asks, and I nod.

“Yes, ma’am. He was in the army.”

“Excellent! Our local VA provides military flags for those who want one in their room. They also come here to honor our guests for their service on Memorial Day and Veterans Day. It’s a nice ceremony, and we welcome families to attend.”

I’ve heard that phrase more times than I can count since I’ve been here. *We welcome families.* That sets my mind at ease more than anything. In Gramps’s current facility, I have to make an appointment to visit him. The care he gets there is fantastic, but if I want to see my grandfather, I damn well want to see my grandfather without going through some gatekeeper. I completely understand the need for me to check in with security, but I’d like to be able to pop in and not have to make an appointment like I’m going to the fucking dentist.

I step outside into a pretty courtyard and give my mother a call, telling her everything I've seen, and she agrees that it sounds like the place for Gramps. She may be his daughter-in-law and not an actual blood relative, but she loves him like he's her own father, making her opinion just as important as mine.

So I go back inside and sign the paperwork.

"Will your grandfather require medical transport from Colorado?" the admissions clerk asks, tapping the thick stack of papers on her desk to straighten them.

"No, my mother and I will drive him. His current doctor approved it already. Gramps does pretty well on car trips, but we'll make it a two-day trip so he's not stuck in a vehicle for so long." I smile, remembering our trip to California last year. "He loves stopping at every cheesy sightseeing spot we can find, so it might actually take us three days."

The lady laughs. "My mother is the same way. I can't even tell you how many giant balls of twine or fake dinosaur statues we've had to have our picture taken with. And there was a fifty-foot Budweiser can in Arkansas that she was obsessed with when I took her to the Ozarks." She shakes her head fondly. "All those beautiful mountains and caves, and my mom's favorite place was a big beer can."

"Sounds like she would get along well with Gramps. I think it's good for them to get out and travel a bit while they still can."

"I agree, and we encourage that. You're welcome to come and get Arlo any time you want. We do require that you check him out due to security reasons. And if there are any medical reasons that would preclude a trip, we'll let you know."

"Of course." Glancing at the nameplate on her desk, I say, "Thanks for all your help, Flora."

She places the paperwork in a blue folder and smiles at me. "No problem. I'll contact his current facility and get his records transferred here. Just let me know your expected departure date so I can fill in all the blanks."

I walk out of the facility feeling about a million times better. Finding a safe and welcoming place for Gramps was my number one priority. Now to locate housing for Ma and me...

"Everything good?" Baylor asks when I step onto the front porch of Shady Pines. He's sitting in a rocking chair with a glass of lemonade among some of the guests and nurses who are wearing scrubs in a soothing sky-blue color.

"All set up. Thank you for recommending this place. It's perfect."

"No problem. Anything I can do. We'll look at real estate tomorrow."

That evening, I recline back on the bed in my room and stare at the whirling ceiling fan. I like Pine Tree Falls a lot. Maybe it's because I can literally picture Juliette here in this town. It just seems like... *her.* The grassy spot beneath a tree in the town square where she can lay back with a book. The unassuming coffee shop. The beautiful library.

Yeah, my dream girl would fit right in here.

Chapter 29

Reno

I'm moving to Pine Tree Falls.

The next day in Pine Tree Falls goes as well as the first. The apartment building where some of my teammates live is more luxurious than I would have expected.

The complex sits on the edge of town, and the units are enormous and tastefully furnished with marble countertops, hardwood floors, and top-of-the-line appliances. I sign a year-long lease before Baylor and I meet the real estate agent, Keri, who I learn is also the town's mayor.

The first house she shows us is a Tudor style that's just way too much house for Ma. The second is the perfect size but is a bit of a fixer-upper. With hockey season approaching, I nix that one since I won't be around much to help.

"I think this next one has a lot of potential," Keri tells us, driving onto a pretty street with old-fashioned iron lamp posts.

"It's a good neighborhood," Baylor adds. "My sister—the one I was telling you about yesterday—lives around the corner."

I don't remember him mentioning a sister yesterday. Must have been one of the times I zoned out, and I make a mental note to do better.

As soon as Keri pulls up in front of the house, I have a good feeling about it. It's single-story, which is nice since Ma occasionally suffers from bursitis in her left knee. But more than that, it simply looks homey. The outside is red brick, and there's a sweet white porch with a wooden swing on one end. The landscaping appears to be well-tended. Ma enjoys gardening on the weekends, so she will appreciate that.

"It's a relatively new construction," Keri says as she opens the burgundy front door. "Only eight years old, so it's in great shape. The couple that lived here moved due to a job opportunity in Brazil for the wife. They are selling it furnished."

She shows us around, and I kick the metaphorical tires, making sure I don't see any noticeable leaks or structural issues. I snap some photos of the interior and exterior and send them to Ma.

There are two bedrooms, two baths, and a cozy study, and the furniture is modern and clean. Overall, I think it's pretty perfect, not too big and not too small.

"How much?" I ask bluntly, and the price Keri spits out almost has me dropping my teeth. "Not that I'm complaining, but why is the price so low?"

"The couple is anxious to sell, but I think you'll find the cost of living is much more reasonable here. If this same house was in Dallas, it would be three times as much."

Pausing for a moment, I tell her, "Pending an inspection, I'm interested."

Sensing the blood in the water, Keri grins and hands me a report from the leather folio she's carrying. "Already done. I'll give you some time to look over it."

I scan through the pages and don't see any red flags, but I decide to get my real estate guy in Colorado to look over it since I'm no expert. My phone rings, and I smile when I see it's my mother calling.

"Reno, it's lovely," she gushes. "I've been looking up the town on the internet, and I adore it too. How much is the house?"

She gets even more worked up when I tell her the price, and her excitement bleeds through the phone and directly into me. "I'll get Carlos to look at the inspection report, and if he says everything looks good, I'll have the agent here email you the paperwork."

"Thank you for handling all this," she says.

"Of course, Ma. You're handling Gramps. Have you spoken with him today?"

I hear the tut in her voice. "I had lunch with him earlier. He thought I was his sister who's been dead for thirty years."

So obviously not one of his good days.

We talk for a couple more minutes, and then I go back into the house. "Ma likes the house," I tell Keri. "If you could email me the inspection paperwork, I'd like to have my friend take a look."

"Of course."

So I guess it's official. I'm moving to Pine Tree Falls.

After dinner with Baylor, I receive a call from Carlos, who advises me to snap up the house as soon as possible. I message Keri, who sends my mom the paperwork.

I go downstairs to the living area of the bed and breakfast and pour myself two fingers of a nice scotch. Taking it up to my room, I sit on the edge of the cream-colored bed, down the contents of the glass, and run a hand through my hair.

Everything in my life is coming together. My career, this move... everything except for the woman I love. I restrain my twitching fingers from picking up my phone to call Juliette. She said she wanted a clean break. I know she felt something for me too, but for some reason, she doesn't want to pursue a real life with me.

I stand and dig out a blue pajama top from my bag, holding it to my nose and inhaling the sweetness. It's both soothing and heartbreaking.

When I moved into Juliette's cottage for that final week on the island and began putting away my clothes, I found these fancy little sachets that she had tucked beneath her clothes. They smelled like bramble-berry—whatever the fuck a brambleberry is. When I got home and unpacked, I found this top, which is infused with the subtle floral scent, in my suitcase. I don't know if it ended up in there accidentally or if Juliette put it in there, but it's been my lifeline.

Stripping down to my underwear, I turn off the lights and crawl beneath the covers, holding the shirt to my face like a kid with a security blanket.

And I drift off to sleep, dreaming of the most beautiful face I've ever seen.

The face I'll probably never see again.

CHAPTER 30

Juliette

Oh. My. God.

"THIS IS JUST FUCKING adorable," Keri says as we stand at the back of the activity room in the Pine Tree Falls Library.

"I know. I reached out to the author to see if she'd come speak to the kids and maybe read her book, but she said she had something even better."

Around thirty kids are scattered over the multicolored carpet, laughing and cheering as puppets act out a popular children's book.

"I wonder how one becomes a puppeteer," Keri muses, and I roll my eyes.

"Don't even think about it. You have enough irons in the fire."

Besides being my cousin, Keri is also a real estate agent, a mom, and the mayor of Pine Tree Falls.

"I'm just curious," she huffs. "I mean, we had a career fair every year in high school, but never once was playing with dolls presented as a career option."

"That's true."

Keri suddenly snaps her fingers and hisses, "Kyle!" Her five-year-old son, who's sitting near the back, looks over his shoulder with faux innocence, even though his hand is a mere inch from a little girl's head. "Don't you dare pull Sarah's hair," his mother mouths, and the little stinker flashes Keri a mischievous smile. But he returns his hand to his lap and resumes watching the puppet show.

"You're such a meanie," I tease, and my cousin surreptitiously scratches her nose with her middle finger.

A couple minutes later, she reaches into her pocket and pulls out her cell phone, checking the screen. “Yes,” she says quietly with a fist pump.

“Sold another house?” I ask, and she nods happily.

“That red brick one in your neighborhood. A lady bought it, though her son is the one I dealt with.” She fans her face. “Swear to god, that man is hotter than a firecracker. If I were a single woman, I would have thrown my panties at him. Want me to introduce you?”

“Nope,” I say immediately, “but you can help me hand out these books.” I’m not in the mood for any fixups.

The show ends, and the author is taking the small stage to introduce the puppeteers and then talk about her story. She brought enough books for every kid in attendance to go home with a free one.

Keri and I pass them out, and my heart swells at their excitement. I love seeing kids develop a passion for books and reading. As the author, a middle-aged former teacher named Lilah, talks animatedly to the children, I check my phone and see an email from my beta reader, Eden.

> *Hey, I know this is out of the blue, but can we have an online chat when you get home from work?*

A little thrill works down my spine. Before she became a beta reader, Eden Osbourne was one of my ARC readers since the beginning of my writing career over a decade ago, but I’ve never seen her face. That’s not completely unusual in the online book community though, especially if the person reads spicy romance and doesn't want someone from their real life to recognize them.

I send her back a message, and we arrange for a time. Then I go back to work.

I sit at my computer at home wearing one of Reno's T-shirts. He'd slipped it over my head before we went to sit out on the porch one night, and I loved how soft and comfy it was, so he let me keep it. He'd been wearing it before we... well, you know... and his strong, masculine scent clung to the fabric.

I dip my chin down to take a whiff and can barely detect him anymore, which makes me sad. That's when I put my fingers to my keyboard. My writing has been fueled by sadness and grief since I got home from the island. This story is so much different from what I usually write, filled with the pain of true love lost.

At some point, I'm going to have to turn the story around and find my character a happily ever after, but at this point, I simply can't fathom how to do that. My emotional capacity does not extend to anything other than the ache inside me. So I use it.

By the time my alarm sounds to let me know it's almost time to meet with Eden, my eyes hurt from crying so much. Going into the bathroom, I splash some cool water on my face and dab a bit of concealer over the dark circles beneath my eyes.

"That'll have to do," I sigh at my unsmiling reflection. It's hard to remember the last time I put on anything but a facade of happiness. I know when it was, but it seems like a decade ago instead of almost a week.

I miss him so much.

Before I can start crying again, I paste on the mask of a smile that barely conceals the torrent of emotions I feel on the inside and return to my computer. Clicking on the link for the online meeting, I take a deep breath.

For some reason, I'm nervous about this. There's no reason to be, but I can't stop the fluttering inside my belly.

The screen changes, and a woman appears. She's pretty, with stylishly short dark hair like Lori Petty in *Point Break.*

But her eyes... I know those eyes even though I haven't seen them in seventeen years. It takes me a long second for the pieces to snap into place.

Oh.

My.

God.

My jaw is hanging open because I'm staring at the face of my missing best friend, Evie Bouvier.

"Eeeee!" I squeak out, unable to form her entire name, so I try again. "Eeeevie!"

Her lips press together and she nods. "It's me."

Those two words solidify what I already know because *that's her voice! That's my bestie's voice!*

And I burst into tears, a tragic geyser of emotion that erupts like Old Faithful from my eyeballs.

I smash my knuckles against my lips so hard I taste blood, but not even that can contain my sobs. Evie's beautiful heart-shaped face—aged slightly from time—crumples into a mixture of joy and sadness, and she's crying too.

We simply stare at each other and bawl our faces off for a long while, neither of us uttering a word.

Finally, I pull my fist from my lips, inhale deeply, and say, "Well, I see you haven't lost your flair for the dramatic."

That instantly transforms the mood, and our tears turn into laughter. Like the crazy, out-of-control laughter we used to share as kids and teenagers. Evie has the kind of laugh that can only be described as infectious, but it's the kind of virus you want to catch because it's loud and lively and fun.

With my hand against my pounding chest, I heave out the last few guffaws before asking the questions I've carried in my heart for years. "What happened to you, Evie? Where have you been?"

Her smile turns sad, and she swivels her eyes upward, staring at the ceiling for a few seconds before turning those cerulean orbs back on me.

"I was kidnapped." I gasp, but she continues. "By human traffickers. That guy I danced with at the beach bonfire that last night, Felipe, he was one of them."

I didn't think my heart could hurt any worse than it had for the past six days, but I was wrong. The pain radiates outward until my bones hurt. "Evie, noooo," I cry, the damn tears back now.

My friend nods. "But I'm okay, Juli. I promise. Some dickhead bought me, but before I could be delivered to him, an angel rescued me." Her gaze darts from the screen, and a faint smile appears on her lips. I get the feeling she's looking at someone else in the room. "A very dark angel, but he was the only one who could save me."

"I don't... I don't know what that means," I tell her.

She returns her eyes to me and puffs out a raspberry. "It's a long-ass story, but here's the quick version. I lost my phone at the bonfire, and when I went back down there to look for it, Felipe and his asshole friend snatched me." Evie's bottom teeth saw back and forth over her top lip for a second. "They put me on a boat, and I was eventually transported to New Orleans."

"Did they... hurt you?" I rasp out, needing to know but also not sure if I can handle the truth.

Evie leans forward so her face takes up the entire screen. "I was not sexually assaulted, Juli." Relief floods through me, and I cover both eyes with my hands, feeling the hot sting of tears against my palms.

"O-okay," I stammer, sliding my hands down my cheeks and attempting to find some damn backbone for my friend.

"I'm not saying they were very nice to me, but at least they didn't touch me like that." She blows out a long exhale through her nose.

"Anyway, they told me I had been purchased by someone, and he'd be there to pick me up."

"What kind of asshole," I mutter through gritted teeth.

"The worst kind you can imagine," Evie says with a humorless laugh. "This next part, I need it to stay between us, okay? Not everything we did after that was entirely legal."

I cross my fingers and tap them against my heart. "I swear, Evie. I would help you bury a body and then take the secret to my grave." That earns me a small smile, and then something she said hits me. "Who's *we?*"

"Dane Osbourne, my husband."

"You're married?" I shriek, though I shouldn't be surprised. She's in her thirties like me.

"Yes, to the man who showed up and rescued me."

"Your dark angel," I repeat, and she nods.

"Yes, he... *took care* of Felipe and the other guy." Her eyes widen significantly, and she doesn't have to spell out what she meant by *took care* of them.

"Good," I grunt out. "I hope it was painful."

Evie just smiles. "The guy who purchased me like I was a fucking cow is—*was*—a very dangerous man. The kind who doesn't tolerate being crossed. The kind who would target my family and friends if he ever found out I was still alive."

Her chin quivers, but she carries on with her heartbreaking story. She is so amazingly strong. "Dane and I had to assume different identities and go into hiding. We made the man think we were dead so he wasn't actively looking for us. That's why I couldn't contact you or my family. Jules, I am so, so sorry for that. I know you... you... were... so... worried."

Evie's breathing hitches between each word, and I shake my head. "Are you crazy? Don't apologize to me for keeping yourself safe, Evie Bouvier. Don't you dare!" My demand is delivered with a vehemence I feel to my soul.

She presses her fingers over her mouth and nods, whispering, "I know." A man's torso suddenly appears behind her, and large hands rest on her shoulders.

"Who is that?" I ask, snappier than I mean to, and Evie lets out a short laugh.

"This is my husband, Dane." She looks up adoringly, and the man bends to kiss her softly on the lips. He's freaking huge, with long black hair and a full beard. When he rests his chin on Evie's shoulder and looks at me, his eyes are dark and dangerous. I suppress a shiver.

This is her husband? Holy hell, the man looks like he could eat someone and then pick his teeth with their bones.

"Hi, Juliette. I've heard so much about you."

"I... hi," I say, a little flustered at the intensity of Evie's husband.

She reaches back and pats his cheek. "Honey, stop looking like you're about to do something felonious."

"Sorry, Wildcat." He kisses the side of her neck. "I'll let you two talk."

"Would you go get Paulie, please?"

"Who's Paulie?" I ask when Dane disappears.

Evie's lips widen into a grin. "He's our baby boy."

My hand goes to my throat and my voice turns raspy. "You have a baby?"

She nods happily. "He's nine months old, and just the most beautiful little boy." Glancing offscreen, her face visibly brightens. "There he is. Come to Mommy."

Dane sets a little angel on her lap. The child has black hair like his father and blue eyes like his mom. He wears a mint-green onesie and flaps his arms happily.

"Well, hello, Paulie," I coo, and he pokes his little pink tongue in and out of his mouth. "God, Evie, he is precious."

Dane kneels beside Evie's chair, his eyes affectionately on his little one. When Paulie grasps his dad's finger and pulls it to his mouth, Dane's smile mellows the harsh edges around his eyes, and he doesn't look quite as intimidating. He looks more like a big, slightly scary teddy bear.

I croon and twiddle my fingers at Paulie, and he bounces and babbles. He loves attention and obviously gets plenty of it from his parents, who hang on his every movement and smile.

Something pools in my belly, a vivid longing I can't quite explain.

When the baby tires and lets out a little whimper, he's gone from Evie's lap in an instant, and I hear what sounds like a lullaby in a deep, melodious voice.

"Is he singing to the baby?" I ask, barely managing not to squeal. Because sa-woon!

My best friend looks to the side as the singing drifts away, and then she returns her gaze to me, doing a little shoulder wiggle now that we're alone.

"He always does that," she gushes. "If Paulie shows even the slightest bit of displeasure, Dane has him on his shoulder, singing Italian lullabies. He's going to spoil him to pieces." Her sappy smile tells me she's not all that worried about it though.

"He seems like a good dad." I pause. "Is he a good husband?"

Evie crushes her eyelids closed, as if remembering something unpleasant. "He's the absolute best, Jules." She opens her eyes, which are now swimming with tears. "I had a bit of PTSD after... everything. A lot of triggers. I was afraid of the dark and of closed spaces."

"Oh, honey," I sob, my tears returning at the thought of what she'd gone through to give her those fears.

"I'm okay now, thanks to Dane. He was beside me, getting me through every nightmare and freak out." A fat tear drops down her cheek. "He saved me in so many ways."

"I guess your family knows you're okay now?"

A smile peeks through my friend's sorrow. "Yes, we're back in New York. We've been living in the Florida Keys. The... situation changed, and we finally felt safe to come home."

"If I were there, I'd give you the biggest hug in the world," I tell her, wiping beneath my eyes with my forefingers.

Evie leans forward and rests her chin on her hand, a smug grin creeping over her lips. "That's what I wanted to talk to you about."

CHAPTER 31

Juliette

I need more wine.

I'M THRUMMING WITH EXCITEMENT when the car pulls up in front of the large stone apartment building in New York. The Bouviers sent a car for me so we didn't make a big reunion scene at the airport since news of Evie's return hasn't hit the media yet.

The driver—I'm ashamed to admit I don't even remember his name—comes around to open the door, but I'm already out of the car and sprinting inside. If I weren't so geared up, I would probably notice the elegant marble floors and extravagant furnishings in the lobby.

"Can I help you, madam?" the uniformed concierge asks in a formal tone as I skid to a stop in front of him.

Before I can do some banshee screech to inform the man that I'm here to see my best friend and he needs to take me to her NOW before I skewer his liver with the nearest sharp object—because perhaps I'm feeling a bit emotional and dramatic today—a deep voice rings out through the space.

"I've got this, James. She's with me."

Whirling, I find Auburn Bouvier, billionaire extraordinaire, CEO of Bouvier Fashions, and Evie's older brother, striding across the floor. I'm vaguely aware that the concierge is practically curtsying in the man's presence, but Auburn owns the whole damn building, so I guess it's to be expected.

I launch myself at poor Auburn, and he laughs, returning my embrace amid the *of course, sir, very good, sir* mumblings from James behind me.

"She's just as excited to see you," Auburn murmurs into the top of my hair. "Let's go."

Backing up, I'm horrified to see my makeup streaking his perfectly pressed yellow shirt. I didn't even realize I was crying. Again. I've been a big bucket of happy tears since finding out Evie's alive and well.

"Shit, I'm sorry," I say, swiping at the mess, and he stills my hands with a chuckle before wrapping a comforting arm around my shoulders.

"No problem, Juliette," he says, leading me toward the elevators. "I have plenty of shirts." His grin is cheeky because of course the man has approximately a million shirts. He owns a high-end fashion company.

The elevator arrives instantly, as if it knows the owner is summoning it, and we step inside.

"She's really okay?" I ask when my stomach flips at the speed of the car as we jet up toward the penthouse.

"She is, and she's happy."

"And alive," I say, swiping at my face.

"Yeah, she's alive." His voice is quiet and filled with so much weary emotion. I can't even imagine what this family has been through. Of course it's been hard on everyone who knew and loved Evie Bouvier, but to have your sister disappear has to be devastating.

"Thank you for always taking my calls," I tell him. "I know you're a busy man."

Auburn scoffs. "Of course I took your calls. You are Evie's best friend."

I have to fight back another round of tears at those words. He didn't say "you *were* Evie's best friend." He said "you *are* Evie's best friend."

Because nothing... not time... not distance... could ever break our bond.

The elevator doors slide open, and I see the grand door in front of me. I take two steps forward and freeze. For some reason, I'm inordinately nervous. My best friend is behind that two inches of wood, and after seventeen years, I'm finally going to see her in person.

Auburn skirts around my still form and swings open the door. And she's there, the biggest grin on her gorgeous face. With a squeal, she's on me, jumping up and wrapping her arms and legs around me like a spider monkey. I almost fall over but am braced from behind by Auburn's hands on my shoulders.

There are tears and laughter in equal measure as Evie and I squeeze each other so hard I'm surprised I don't hear bones cracking.

"You're here!" she shrieks.

"You're here!" I yell back, twisting our bodies from side to side. "And you're still short."

"Oh, shut up," she giggles, squirming until I set her down. We stand less than a foot apart, studying each other. Evie is no longer the almost nineteen-year-old I'd last known, but she's still undeniably her. Bright blue eyes, brilliant smile. Her hair is shorter and a little darker, but it's cute and stylish, framing her pretty face with its familiar delicate features.

"I still can't believe you're really here," I breathe.

"I know." She grabs my hand and drags me into the living room. "Come on. Gianna's dying to see you again."

A freaking goddess walks in from what I assume is the kitchen. She has long, dark hair, an adorable baby bump, and a radiant smile. "Hey, nice to see you again," she says in a darling drawl. "I only got to talk to you for a minute at our wedding."

Auburn's wife is younger than him, but she walks with the confidence of a woman who bagged the most eligible billionaire bachelor in New York City. She grips both my hands and leans in for a cheek kiss.

"Thank you for having me. Are you sure I don't need to get a hotel room?" I ask.

She rolls her green eyes. "Bitch, please. We could house an army in this apartment."

I love her. She's real, unlike so many of the women Auburn had been with prior to meeting Gianna.

Auburn follows us into his palatial penthouse apartment, nudges us toward the oversized red couch, and takes his wife's hand. "You two catch up. I'll help Gianna in the kitchen, and then we'll make ourselves scarce."

I watch them go before turning wide eyes back to Evie.

"Don't say it," she warns, like she can read my mind, even after all these years.

"I have to."

"Don't."

Ignoring the warning, I wobble my eyebrows at her. "Your brother gives off some serious BDE, Evie. And I say that respectfully."

My best friend claps her hands over her ears. "Don't want to hear about my brother's big dick energy. Don't. Want. To. Hear. It."

"That's not the BDE I was talking about. I meant..." I pause dramatically and coo, "Big *Daddy* Energy."

"Honey, you have no idea," Gianna chirps, striding into the room with a square black plate of chocolate chip cookies, and my face turns the approximate color of a ripe tomato.

"I, uhhhh. Shit, sorry."

She sets down the tray and waves a dismissive hand. "Pssshht. Don't worry about it. You think I don't know I'm married to a total Zaddy?"

"Someone call my name?" Auburn asks with a smug smile as he brings out a tray of hot appetizers and sets it on the coffee table. It looks like it's been assembled by a Michelin star chef.

"Are y'all hiding Gordon Ramsey in your kitchen?" I ask, pretending to peer around them.

Gianna rests her hands on her belly. "Some women nest when they're pregnant. I cook."

"She cooks like a queen," Auburn says, grasping his wife's chin and lifting her face to his for a soft kiss. I feel like an intruder viewing a very intimate moment. He's looking at her as if she's his entire world, and it reminds me of that last night on the island. With the man I've been trying to forget.

Evie groans. "Don't you two get started. We have company."

Gianna steps back, a self-satisfied smirk on her lips as she brushes her red lipstick from her husband's mouth. "Go get the fruit board, Zaddy, and then we can leave."

"Oh my gosh, this is too much already," I say, wiggling my fingers at the vast amount of food.

"We just want you two to have a nice visit and not be bothered by having to worry about food and stuff. Juliette, I didn't know if you drank red or white wine, so we have both." She gestures to the bottles on the coffee table. "Evie knows where the wine fridge is, so help yourselves if you need more."

Auburn returns with a black ceramic tray overflowing with enough fruit to feed the population of Rhode Island. Then he pulls a plump purple grape from the stem and licks it before popping it in his mouth and rolling it around. He lets out a low hum of approval, and the entire time, his heated blue eyes never leave his wife's. Gianna's face flushes a pretty pink, and Evie and I slowly turn our heads toward each other, eyebrows raised in question.

A knock on the door interrupts the moment, and Auburn gives Gianna a wink before literally strutting across the living room.

"What was all that with the grape?" Evie hisses to her sister-in-law.

"Trust me, you don't want to know," she says, biting her bottom lip as she watches her husband's ass.

"You're probably right," my best friend mutters with a wince.

Auburn returns with my two suitcases. "Juliette, I'll put your bags in your room."

"You can leave the smaller one here," I tell him. "It's for Evie."

"What did you do?" she asks suspiciously.

"You'll see," I tell her slyly, reaching for a toast point topped with smoked salmon, a thin slice of cucumber, and a fat cherry tomato.

After Auburn and Gianna leave, Evie pours us both a glass of crisp, white wine.

"Well, those two are hot as hell," I comment.

"They are disgustingly steamy," my friend adds. "And wait till you see Monty and Kassie again." She leans closer and lowers her voice. "I think my little brother is a Dom."

I fan my face and take a swig of my wine. Images flash through my mind of strong fingers digging into my hips, of that spanking, of the hand necklace.

Stop it, Juli. We're not thinking about... *him*.

For the next two hours, my best friend and I talk a lot, cry a little, and laugh like maniacs. She fills in some more of the details of her disappearance as we drink enough wine to get deliciously tipsy. It's the best reunion I could have imagined, like we'd never been apart. But we had.

"Okay, don't think I'm weird, but..." I stand and grab the small floral suitcase Auburn left behind.

"Too late," Evie shoots back with a grin. God, how I've missed her smile.

"I bought you a present every year on your birthday," I admit, unzipping the suitcase.

"Juliiiiiii," she whines. "You're gonna make me cry."

"Meh, don't get all sappy on me. Most of them are kinda cheesy," I tell her. "Well, this one is special." I turn over my arm and show her my tattoo.

Her soft hand grips my wrist, and she rubs her thumb over the lilac. "You got a tattoo for me?"

"The other girls did too. On the first anniversary of your disappearance, which was right before your nineteenth birthday, so we got our ink right before your twentieth."

Evie pulls me into a hard hug. We hold each other for a long while, and the tears return in full force. Then I pull back and give her a tremulous smile. "Okay, enough of that. On to birthday number twenty-one. This one will make you laugh."

We go through the gifts, year by year. Most of them aren't really profound, just stuff like a cute pair of earrings, a turtle-printed pajama set, or quirky little things I knew she'd like.

"I still can't believe you got me a cheese-flavored condom," she says, falling over onto the couch in a fit of giggles with the foil packet held to her chest.

"It made me laugh when I saw it, and my first thought was that I wanted to call and tell you about it. So that was your gift for your twenty-third birthday." I shrug. "That was over a decade ago, so I wouldn't suggest using it."

"Yeah, probably wouldn't taste very fresh." She holds it between two fingers and wiggles it. "But I'm gonna think about this every time I eat a bag of Cheetos."

And I'll think about *him* every time I do. Damn, the things Reno Swain can do with a Cheeto.

Brushing away the thought, I pull out the final gift. "Here's the last one. I had an artist draw it up for me earlier this year," I tell her, handing over the flat package in lavender wrapping paper.

Evie tears open the paper like a kid on Christmas morning. Then her eyes fill with tears, and her voice cracks. "Juli, it's us."

The framed artwork shows two women from the back, one with long caramel hair and the other with long blonde hair. Arms around waists. Heads tilted slightly toward each other

"Sorry, your hair is different now," I apologize.

"No, it's us back then, and I love it." She reads the calligraphed words aloud. "I may not always be there with you, but I will always be there for you."

"I don't know how, but I knew you were still alive. Those words hit me hard, and all I wanted was for you to feel my support and love, no matter where you were." I reach over and grasp her hand. "And unknown to me, you were the one supporting *me* almost the whole time by being on my ARC team."

"I told you in Cancún when I read those few chapters of your first book that I wanted to buy the first copy when you published it. This was as close to doing that as I could get." She squeezes my hand. "And I bought lots of copies of all your books, one for me, one to donate to our local library, and the rest as gifts."

"Shit, I need more wine," I croak, grabbing the bottle of red as tears threaten again. I drink straight from the bottle before handing it over to my best friend.

"Well, aren't we a couple of winos," she comments before taking a long swig. "I've missed the hell out of you, Juliette."

I slump down and tilt my head over onto her shoulder. "I missed you too, Evie."

We sit wordlessly for a long time, passing the bottle back and forth and simply being together. Evie picks up the artwork again and angles her head. "Our asses look really good in this pic."

Snorting, I shake my head. "Do you really think I'd pay someone to do artwork for me and then tell her to give us barn asses?"

We dissolve in gales of laughter again before Evie nudges me with her shoulder. "Tell me about your writing retreat. It was obviously successful because that turned out to be one bomb-ass book, but I want to know if you had time for some fun." She does a drunken bump and grind while still seated on the couch. "Of the bow-chicka-wow-wow variety."

I haven't told anyone about Reno, aside from a brief, nameless mention of him to Holly. But this is Evie, my best friend since I was a little girl.

"There was a guy..."

"Eeeeek!" Evie smacks my arm. "I fucking knew it! Your sex scenes were so detailed and raw. I just knew you had some carnal inspiration."

"Oh, it was carnal all right," I muse, covering my eyes in embarrassment. "I kinda sorta accidentally booked my writing retreat at... a swingers' resort."

You could hear a pin drop in the room, and I peep through two of my fingers to find Evie staring slack-jawed at me.

"You went to a swingers' resort?" she finally asks, and I nod before receiving a smack to the left tit. "You kinky bitch!"

"Oww," I complain, rubbing my boob. "I didn't go there on purpose. At first I didn't even know it was that kind of place."

Evie throws back her head and laughs from deep in her belly. "Oh my freaking god. Only you, Juli."

My eyes roll to the coffered ceiling. "That's the same thing Holly said."

"I still can't believe she's married to your brother," she says before shaking her head. "We'll come back to Holly later. Did you hook up with a couple? Oooh, or participate in group activities?"

"No," I protest. "It was just one guy. He found himself there accidentally as well. Someone else booked his getaway, and when he got there, he instantly realized from all the upside down pineapples that it was a swingers' resort."

"And you didn't?" she asks incredulously.

I give her a flat look. "No. Unfortunately, I was not aware of the meaning of inverted fruit."

Evie snickers. "I love how you can write the raunchiest shit ever in your books, and yet you still have this certain naivety about you." She turns to face me, sitting cross-legged. "So tell me about the guy. I'm assuming he's not into the lifestyle?"

"He's not." Slipping off my shoes, I mirror her position. "His name is Reno Swain." I pause to see if she recognizes the name, and by the rounding of her eyes, she does.

"Shut the front door. The hockey player? Reno Swoon?"

"That would be him."

She flops dramatically back onto the seat of the couch. "Holy hell, woman! Reno's a total stud muffin. He looks like he could do some damage."

"Oh, he did some damage all right," I mutter, and Evie snaps back to sitting with narrowed eyes.

"Did he hurt you? Because I will ram a hockey stick so far up his ass, he could use it as a toothpick."

This is why she's my best friend. Evie is both hilarious and brutally loyal. I pat her knee and shake my head.

"No, he didn't hurt me. We decided at the beginning of our fling that we would just be together while we were at the resort. He agreed to help inspire my writing."

"He did a damn good job of it. That book is fuck-hot, and I think you should keep him on retainer." I try to smile at that, but it's halfhearted at best. Evie notices and takes my hand. "Juli, did you catch feelings?"

I press my lips together and nod, staring down at our hands. A heavy tear falls onto my ankle. "It's stupid, really. It was only a few weeks."

"Oh honey, that doesn't matter. Is there any way you can contact him?"

"I have his number," I admit, looking up at her.

"Then call him," she insists gently. "I'm sure he's smitten with you too. I mean, he'd have to be stupid not to be. You're so gorgeous and talented."

"And a complete nitwit who doesn't know about upside down pineapples," I add with a shaky laugh to lighten the mood.

"You're the most lovable dingbat I know," Evie says. "Will you think about calling him?"

"I can't. We agreed to have an island fling, hot and uncomplicated. I don't want to be that girl who calls weeks later and says, 'Hey, guess what? I fell for you.' No guy wants that, especially not someone who literally has women bowing at his feet."

"What if he feels the same about you?"

I'm pretty sure he does if his face when I walked away from him in the Miami airport was any indication. Instead of saying that, I shake my head.

"A few fun weeks on vacation is fine, but I can't let it go any farther than that. I'll just... get over it, I guess."

But the sharp constriction of my chest tells me that getting over Reno Swain will be easier said than done.

Chapter 32

Reno

Should I?

THE MOVE TO TEXAS went well. Gramps was lucid and in the moment the entire time, though the trip took four days because he wanted to stop at practically every convenience store on the eight-hundred mile trip to "see what kind of beef jerky they have."

I didn't give a damn how long it took. It was just nice to see him having fun. We even took a short detour into Oklahoma to visit one of the casinos. I lost my ass at blackjack, but Gramps racked up almost a thousand dollars beside me, and Ma won fifty bucks on a penny slot.

My grandfather is now in his new home at Shady Pines, and he's happier than a pig in shit. A couple old-timers from the local VA came by to visit with him the second day he was there, and he hasn't stopped talking about it.

Ma adores her house and has been exploring the town. I'm pretty much a hermit, only coming out of my apartment to work out at the arena with Baylor and some of the other guys during the day. In the evenings, I have dinner with Ma or Gramps, sometimes both.

Tonight I'm sitting on my black leather couch in my shorts with Juliette's shirt draped across my chest so I can smell the brambleberry that's barely discernible now. Opening the Amazon app, I search for sachets for a few minutes before something on the television catches my attention.

Tossing my phone aside, I lean forward with my elbows on my knees and turn up the volume. My mouth drops open in utter shock at the newscaster's report.

"Fashion heiress Evie Bouvier has returned home to New York after being missing for over seventeen years. The FBI held a press conference with the Bouvier family today to inform the public about Ms. Bouvier's harrowing ordeal."

The scene switches to a clip of the press conference where an agent lays out the story. "I'll be damned," I mutter when he wraps up by asking for privacy for the family.

My thoughts immediately turn to Juliette since Evie was her best friend and because she was fucking *there at the resort* where Evie was taken. I shudder to think that it could have happened to her.

I'm overcome with the need to call Juliette so I can check on her and see how she's doing with all this. Picking up my phone, I pull up her contact info and hover my thumb over the call button.

Should I?

Her words that day in the airport come back to me.

I think a clean break would be best.

Because it's what I need.

With a curse, I drop the phone onto the couch and lean back, digging the heels of my hands into my eye sockets. "Why is this so fucking hard?"

After sleeping on it for a night, I compromise. Instead of calling Juliette, I decide to text her. But what should I say? Congratulations doesn't seem quite right. I mull it over and finally tap out a message.

> ***Reno: I know you said we shouldn't contact each other, but I saw the news about Evie. I just wanted you to know I'm thinking of you.***

I almost piss myself with excitement when she responds a minute later.

Juliette: That's so sweet of you. I went to see her last weekend. We're planning a getaway with all six of the women who were there.

Reno: Are you going to Pineapple Island for this getaway?

Juliette: Haha, no. We're going to Evie's house in Florida.

I type "I miss you" and erase it six times before finally sending another text.

Reno: Please be safe.

Juliette: Aww, are you worried I'll get lost?

Reno: It's not outside the realm of possibility.

Juliette: Luckily, I had a big stud to keep me from getting lost on my last vacation.

Fuck, she's flirting with me. I think about how to reply and grin when I put my thumbs to the screen.

Reno: Name the time and place, and your own personal stud service will be there for you.

Juliette: That's a very generous offer. I'll let you know if your services are needed.

Reno: I take pride in providing top-notch service, dream girl.

Juliette: I can't argue with that. Thanks for checking on me, but I have to get to bed. Work in the morning.

My cock, which has been pretty much stagnant for the past couple weeks, is now making a resurgence. The thought of Juliette underneath me while I "service" her has me hard as stone, and I reach down and palm myself.

My girl is getting in bed now. Will she be having the same kinds of raunchy thoughts that are currently flooding my mind? Will she touch herself and think of me?

Rising from the couch, I head to the bathroom in my new apartment and turn on the shower jets before stripping down. Stepping inside the amber-and-cream tiled shower, I allow the water to beat down on my back while I beat something a little lower with my fist.

It doesn't take long, and when I crawl into bed ten minutes later, I fall into the most satisfying sleep I've had since I left Pineapple Island.

Chapter 33

Juliette

Sperm talk

"That's the third time you've checked your phone, Jules," Xander says from across the table at Primo's Pizza. "You expecting a call or something?"

"Her book just went out to ARC readers yesterday. She always gets obsessive," Holly answers for me, though that's not at all why I was sneaking a peek at my screen.

Since Reno's initial text a couple weeks ago, he sends me daily messages. They're usually of a cool cloud he's spotted or a funny meme, but occasionally I get one of the flirty ones. And those are the ones that have me reaching for Mr. Lemon or one of my other toys. God, I miss the real thing.

"Eighty-two of them have downloaded it, and several have messaged that they finished already," I say excitedly, bringing myself fully back into the conversation with my siblings.

"It's definitely one of those all-nighter books," Holly replies with a wink. She and Bubba are seated with Xander across from me, and Jordie is in the chair to my right.

"I can't wait to read it," my younger sister says, wiggling in her seat. "And I think it's so cool that your friend Evie has actually been that Eden person this whole time. Did y'all enjoy your trip to Florida with her?"

Holly and I, along with the other three members of our original college Spring Break group, stayed in Evie and Dane's Florida home last week. Bubba came too, and he and Dane stayed at a friend's house a couple doors down to keep Paulie and Aiden busy while the ladies caught up with Evie.

We regale them with stories from our time there. The Papadopoulos twins still constantly snipe at one another, so that made for some prime entertainment.

"Aiden was obsessed with Paulie's cute little nose," Holly says with a giggle. "He kept trying to put his finger in the baby's nostrils."

"I want one," I blurt out, and everyone's eyes turn to me. "I want a baby."

Bubba grins over the rim of his beer glass. "You know you're welcome to borrow our little nose miner any time you want."

I fidget with the napkin in my lap. "I know that, and I adore Aiden, but I want a baby of my own." Bubba's mouth gapes in astonishment, but I continue. "I'll be thirty-seven this year, and I feel like Marisa Tomei, stomping my boot and worrying about my biological clock. And... I just want to have a family."

Jordie reaches for my hand on the table, and Holly beams. "I think you should do it."

"Are you even dating anyone?" Bubba asks, setting his beer down with a thunk.

"She doesn't need a man," his wife argues.

My brother lifts both his eyebrows at her. "She literally does, babe."

Holly waggles a finger at him. "No, she needs *sperm*."

"Which comes from *a man*," he insists.

My sister-in-law rolls her eyes. "But said man does not need to be present in order to accomplish the goal." She shrugs. "Women have options. Juli could go to a sperm bank."

I nod my thanks. "That's what I was thinking. I mean, I have a job and house."

"And a good support system," Jordie adds, squeezing my hand.

Xander takes a sip of his pale ale and shrugs. "If it's what you want, I say go for it."

Bubba's eyes bore into me, assessing, and he finally smiles. "I agree, sis, if that will make you happy. You've seemed a little down lately. Though I still think the old-fashioned way is the most fun." He places a proprietary arm around the back of Holly's chair.

"Thanks, Bubs," I tell him. "Being around the babies in Florida and all the kids at the library this summer has made me think long and hard about what I want going forward." I hold up my palm to my brother because I fucking know his crazy ass mind. "And I don't need to hear any long and hard jokes."

"I actually tried to donate sperm last week," he says matter-of-factly, and every head at the table turns slowly toward him. His wife gives him some serious side eye. "And now I'm not allowed in Goodwill anymore."

It takes a second for the joke to sink in, and then everyone bursts into laughter. Holly swats him on the back of the head.

Xander pipes up with, "I've been thinking of donating to make some spending cash. I've got *loads* to offer." Holly swats him too as we all continue to chuckle.

"I've heard guys can make money hand over fist donating sperm," Jordie adds dryly, which only makes us laugh harder. It's totally unlike her to make a dirty joke.

"Good one," I mutter, bumping her shoulder with my own. I'm pretty sure Jordie is still a virgin. I've offered to go with her to get on birth control, but she always informs me that it's not necessary.

Holly draws our attention with a wave of her hand. "I decided to donate plasma for money in college. I show up at the donation site and realize there's only men in the waiting room. So I ask the guy beside me, and he tells me I'm in the wrong place. The plasma donation place is next door, and all these guys are there to donate sperm."

"Oh how embarrassing," Jordie says, her cheeks flushing.

"We start comparing numbers, and I tell him I would get twenty dollars per plasma donation. And he told me he gets a hundred and fifty per whack for sperm! Can you believe that?" she asks indignantly.

"Well, it is a *handmade* donation," Bubba quips, causing the rest of us to snicker.

Holly shoots him a withering look before continuing. "So the next week, I come back to the same office. Run into the same guy. He kinda laughs and tells me I'm in the wrong place again. I put my hands on my hips and inform him that..." Holly closes her lips and points at her puffed out cheeks. "Mmmph mmph mmmm mmmph."

Our entire table erupts. I'm cackling so hard tears stream down my face. "Holly, y-you're a nut," I gasp out, holding my stomach.

She gives me a regal swirl of her hand. "I'm just here to entertain."

When the server brings three pizzas and sets them on the center of the table, Holly asks Jordie to switch seats since she and Bubba usually share, both liking disgusting anchovies on their pizza. They make pregnant Holly sick to her stomach.

My sister and sister-in-law swap places, and Holly settles in beside me. We both reach for a slice of pepperoni and extra cheese, our favorite since our college days.

"I'm proud of you," she says, giving me a gentle smile. "And we'll be here to help you in any way we can."

I look around at my beautiful, crazy siblings, and an undeniable warmth spreads through me. "Yep, I'm a lucky girl."

If only I had someone to share my life with.

Chapter 34

Reno

I'd never sleep with a teammate's sister.

Training camp is going well. The Brewers hold theirs a little earlier than most of the league because they always play an exhibition game for charity in August.

This year the charity is actually Lorna's Home, a local shelter for women and children who are victims of domestic abuse. Ma works there now as a counselor, and I'm so damn proud of her.

At the end of practice on a Thursday, Coach Albertson calls me into his office at the practice facility. My intestines knot up, remembering the last time I was called into a coach's office.

"Coach Al," I greet, using the nickname most of the team uses.

"Have a seat, Swain."

Déjà fucking vu.

I sit, and the man runs a hand over his balding head. He has one of those monk-like hairdos with a half-ring running along the back of his head.

"I had high hopes for you when we made this trade," he begins, and I swallow hard. This sounds ominous. Hell, I thought I'd been killing it out on the ice the past couple weeks.

"I hope I haven't disappointed you, sir," I say politely.

He lets out a chuckle. "Disappointed me? Hell, son, I'm goddamn thrilled. You're playing the best hockey of your life right now, and you're making me and Mr. Carmichael look like fucking geniuses for this trade. I just wanted to make sure you're happy here. I know moving to a new place with a new team can be difficult."

"Oh. Well." I shrug, a bit surprised at the turn this conversation has taken. "Everything's good, Coach. Baylor has been a great resource for pretty much everything, and the team and staff have made me feel very welcome."

"Good. That's good, Swain, because we want to keep you. And Ward is a good lad. Nice family too. Have you met them?"

"Just his little boy. Baylor brought him to skate with us one day. Cute kid."

Coach chuckles. "Training them young. I like it. Just stay away from his sisters. He's very protective of them."

I hold up my fingers in a Boy Scout salute. "Don't worry about me, Coach. I'd never sleep with a teammate's sister. I'm aware that's a big no-no."

"Alrighty. Just thought I'd warn you. I also wanted you to know I have you in the first defense pairing for the exhibition game and for the foreseeable future. As long as you continue to put forth the effort I've seen from you in this camp, you're our top defenseman."

"I'm... thanks, Coach. I'm honored."

Yeah, I know I'm a great hockey player, but I'd kind of assumed he wouldn't give me a starting position the first game since I'm new to the team.

"Well earned," he says gruffly. "Now don't get the big head and start slacking off now. Keep that fire."

"I will," I promise, rising from my seat and shaking Coach Al's hand.

As I walk down the hallway of the practice facility to get geared up for the afternoon practice, I wish I could call Juliette and tell her my news. Then I laugh to myself. She probably doesn't know the first thing about hockey.

CHAPTER 35

Juliette

Wait just a damn minute.

I FUCKING LOVE HOCKEY.

Standing in the first row at Brewers Arena, I inhale the scent of the ice mixed with popcorn and sweat. I'm wearing a dark-blue jersey with red-and-white trim and the number twenty-seven emblazoned on the front and back. Along with my brother's last name.

"We have got to find some open ice hits tonight," I say to Holly, who gives me an amused grin. "And the Brewers need to use their superior speed and agility because that's how they're going to beat these guys. Have you seen number five for Oklahoma? He's slow as fuck, and he can barely skate backward without falling down."

"I always love your commentary," she tells me. "Just try to keep the cussing to a minimum since I brought Aiden."

I frown in concern. "I'll try, but you know I get riled up, Holls."

She sighs. "I know, crazy. I brought some noise-canceling headphones for him in case it's too loud. But maybe they can also serve as a curse blocking device since his Auntie Juliette has a potty mouth when it comes to hockey," she teases.

With a dismissive sniff, I roll my eyes. "I'll do my best to control myself. For Aiden."

"Are you excited to see your daddy play hockey for the first time in person?" Pops asks the little one. He's sitting on the other side of Holly. Dad, Xander, and Jordie are in the row behind us.

At the mention of his daddy, Aiden swivels his head from side to side and calls, "Dada!"

Pops tickles his grandson beneath his chubby chin. "You'll see Dada really soon."

"Tooooon," my nephew tries to parrot, making us laugh.

When the crowd amps up, we all stand, our attention pulled to the ice. The players are coming out for pre-game warm-ups, and I watch Aiden to make sure the noise isn't bothering him. He seems fine, so I find Bubba with the practiced eye of a sister who has been to a million games since we were kids.

"There's Dada," I coo at Aiden, pointing at number twenty-seven. My brother finds us immediately and skates our way before placing his hand on the glass. Holly leans forward and lets Aiden put his tiny hand over his dad's big one, and I tear up, yanking my phone from my pocket to snap a quick pic of the special moment.

Then Bubba's eyes go to Holly and they lock into an intimate stare, despite the crowd of fifteen-thousand crazy fans around them. "Love you," he mouths through the glass, and his wife returns the words. These two are seriously fucking cute, and I take a picture of their exchange as well before Bubba skates off to join his team.

After sending both photos to Holly's number, I put my phone away and reach for my adorable nephew. "Let me hold him and give your back a break."

She kisses his forehead, calls him her *little chunky butt*, and hands him over. "Thanks, Jules. I'm going to run to the bathroom *again* before the game starts."

Once Aiden's in my arms, I whisper in his ear, "We need to come to an agreement, buddy. Don't repeat any of the bad words Auntie Juli says tonight, 'kay?"

"Chewy!" he yells, and I squeeze him against me, hoping that one day I'll have a son or daughter of my own.

I'd called my OB/GYN a few days ago to make an appointment to get my birth control implant removed and discuss my options. The receptionist informed me that Dr. Fergus is visiting her family in Scotland for a couple weeks, so she can't see me until early October. They offered to get me in with one of her associates, but I told them I'd rather wait for Dr. Fergus since I already have a good rapport with her.

"I'm excited about the defense this year," Pops says, snapping me out of my baby daydream. That's weird because defense was our main weakness last year. He adds, "With the new guy and all."

New guy? Who did we acquire in the off-season?

My eyes catalog the defensemen: Hornick, Lundquist, Isakov, Swai n… Hold up. Wait just a damn minute.

With my heart racing and my gaze super-glued to the newcomer's back, I nudge Pops. "Uhh, who's the guy doing the handshake with Gibby? Number ninety-six."

I don't know why I ask that. It's completely ridiculous because I can clearly read the name right there on the back of his jersey. *SWAIN.*

Pops chuckles. "I'm aware you don't watch hockey news, honey, but I know you've seen enough games to know Reno Swain."

Hearing his name is a lightning bolt to my system, but the jolt of electricity intensifies when Reno turns around and his green eyes fall directly on me. They darken in confusion before rounding in realization. He seems to be as shocked as I am.

And then his mouth forms the words I've wanted to hear for two months.

My dream girl.

Chapter 36

Reno

Total shit show

Even though this is just an exhibition game, the Brewers locker room is in complete hyped-up mode.

"You ready for this?" Baylor Ward asks me, tossing an arm across my shoulders.

"I was born ready," I tell him with a cocky smirk.

He laughs and smacks me on the back. "Hey, you're still coming to dinner with us after the game tonight, right?"

"With you and your family?"

"Well, me and my wife and older sister. My younger siblings are at the game, but they have college shit to do afterward, and my father is taking Aiden home." Then he sweetens the deal. "The steakhouse has an amazing chef."

"Yeah, that sounds good. I need to check with my mom and make sure she doesn't need help getting Gramps home, but it should be fine."

"Nice wine list too, though..." He lowers his voice conspiratorially. "I probably won't drink since Holly can't have any. We haven't really shared this with anyone beside our immediate families, but she's pregnant. It's early, still in the first trimester." His wide grin lights up his face.

"Congrats, man," I tell him, genuinely happy for my friend.

"Let's go out for warm-ups," Coach hollers from the door, and we all head that way.

Ten minutes later, I take the ice for the first time as a Brewers player. It's exhilarating, the atmosphere electric in the arena.

"Gotta go say hi to my wife and baby," Baylor says. "They're over there in the front row." He gestures with a thumb over his shoulder.

Before I can look, Gibby slides up beside me and screams, "Swaaaain! Let's do our thing, chicken wing." The guy is a fucking maniac, but I love the hell out of him.

The goalie and I resurrect the handshake routine we used to do in our college days. It's complicated, involving hand slaps, a chest thump, and some utterly ridiculous footwork where Gibby pretends to fall and I "save" him.

The crowd is laughing by the time we're done. I spin around, noticing Baylor headed my way with a goofy smile on his face. Guess seeing his wife and kid is what gets him going before a game.

I look to the front row. I still haven't met Baylor's wife, though I did meet Aiden that one day. I spot the little guy, and I'm about to wave at him when my eyes fall on the woman holding him.

She has golden hair plaited into two long braids beneath a navy-blue Brewers beanie. The jersey she wears has Baylor's number on it and fits loosely on her slim frame. I take in all that a split second before I meet her eyes.

Aqua ones that I recognize instantly.

Because I'd stared adoringly into those gorgeous orbs while I made love to her during our last night together two months ago.

My dream girl.

My lips whisper the words as a thrill runs down my spine. But the thrill is short-lived and replaced by cold dread when I realize...

I fucked Baylor's wife. *Oh my fucking god. I fucked my teammate and friend's wife!*

"Swain! Why you standing there like you've got a hockey stick up your ass?" Coach's rebuke has me jerking around, away from the woman I could spend all night staring at.

No! She's not yours, Reno. She never was.

I join my team for warm-ups, though internally, I'm freaking the fuck out. Especially when I remember what Baylor told me in the locker room a few minutes ago.

Juliette is pregnant. In her first trimester. It's August now, so that lines up with when we were on the island together. Is the baby mine? Fucking hell, this is a nightmare.

Could she have lied about being on birth control? Maybe they were having trouble conceiving, and she decided to sleep with some sucker she met on vacation to get knocked up. But...

My mind is a tornado, swirling around uncontrollably. Why did she choose me? I'm white. Juliette is white. Baylor is Black, though I suspect he's mixed because he's not extremely dark-skinned. Why wouldn't she have found someone who looked more like her husband so the baby might have a chance of looking like him?

Jesus, Juliette. What the hell were you...

Wait. Wait, wait, wait. Baylor said his wife is named... Molly? No, that's not it. Holly! Not Juliette.

Fuck me, maybe she lied about that too.

No, she wouldn't do that. I know her. I spent three weeks with her. She's good and honest and sweet. She's my dream girl.

She's not yours, the annoying little voice in my head reminds me. But even though this is a total shit show, even though it's wrong, I still wish she were.

I somehow manage to make it through pre-game, though mostly through pure muscle memory. I forced my eyes away from the stands every time I was tempted to look at her—which was about every two seconds because she looked as beautiful as I remember.

Stop. It. Asshole.

A body plops down on the bench beside me, and I know who it is without even looking. Guilt threatens to eat me alive.

"Dude, why the fuck were you staring at Juliette?" Baylor's voice is harsh, and I do my best not to cringe. This is so fucked up, and I still have no idea who the woman I'm in love with actually is.

"Ju-Juli-what?" I stammer, attempting to play dumb.

I'm staring at the wall behind him, but his glare is so compelling, my eyes finally turn to face his fierce ones. Yeah, he's pissed.

"Juliette," he repeats. "The blonde that was holding Aiden."

Unable to come up with a viable excuse, I'm saved when Gibby sits on the other side of me and laughs raucously. "Dude, never mess with Baylor's sister. He'll fuck you up."

His... *sister*?

My spine feels like it's melting, and I almost slump to the floor in relief when it hits me. Though sleeping with a teammate's sister is a very bad idea, it's not as bad as sleeping with his wife, for fuck's sake.

"Sorry," I tell him. "I didn't know that was your sister."

Baylor's face relaxes a little, and he points at his face. "What? You don't see the family resemblance?"

I'm finally able to huff out a laugh. "You're not exactly twins."

"Nah, we're half siblings. We share a mother."

Juliette's story about her family comes back to me, and the pieces begin to make sense. Her mom and biological father married and had her. Then her mom married another man and had a child—who's apparently Baylor. When she came back years later, she married Juliette's bio dad again and had two more children. That also accounts for Baylor and Juliette's differing last names.

"I apologize again for staring. I saw her holding your son, and I was trying to figure out who she was. Didn't mean any disrespect."

Though I disrespected the shit out of your sister when she was on her knees for me and I was attempting to fuck her esophagus.

And have mercy on my soul because I want to do it again.

We beat Oklahoma handily, and though it was an exhibition game and wouldn't count toward our season, it still felt really good. Next year, we'll play on their home ice for a charity of their choice.

Knowing Juliette was in the stands, I played my heart out. The other team didn't even score a goal on us.

As soon as I step out of the locker room, I spot Ma and Gramps standing against the wall. My grandfather reaches me first and pulls me into a hug, resting his hand on the back of my shower-damp head.

"My boy. I'm so proud of you."

I close my eyes and hug him back, amazed as always at how strong he still is. Physically anyway. That's what makes his disease so difficult to understand. He's a big, hardy man on the outside, but his mental status is slowly fading away.

"I'm so glad you were able to come, Gramps."

"I told everyone around us you were my grandson." He wiggles his gray eyebrows. "They were mighty impressed. I got two phone numbers."

My mother swats his arm playfully. "Oh, Arlo, hush. You did not."

The old man chuckles wickedly, and I love seeing him joke around. "Well, I could have. I bet Reno would make a good... what's it called? A bird man?"

It takes me second to figure out what he's trying to say. "I think you mean wingman."

He snaps his fingers and points. "Yeah, that's the ticket. Wingman. Even though you're a rookie, I'll bet the ladies still love you."

Ma and I catch each other's eyes, and she winces slightly at his blunder.

"Gramps," I say gently, "I'm not a rookie anymore, remember? I've been in the league for a while." *More than a decade.*

"Ohhh, yeah. I just forgot for a second." He puts on a good front and nods slowly, but I can see the confusion starting to set in.

"Need me to take him?" I whisper to my mother when we embrace.

"No, honey. Arlo and I will be fine. Home is only about thirty minutes away, and traffic should have cleared out by now."

"All right. I'll have my phone on me if you need anything. I'm just having dinner with a teammate." And his sister, who I happen to be in love with.

When I walk with Ma and Gramps to the exit so I can make sure they get safely to their car, one of the security guards, Barney, stops us.

"Mr. Swain, there are a couple hundred people outside this door, waiting for players to come out. You'll probably want to go out the players' exit in the back."

I rub my forehead in frustration. "This is my mother and grandfather. Her car is in lot two, and I need to make sure they get there okay."

"Allow me," the burly man says, shooing me away. "Unless you want to be here all night."

I do not, in fact, want to be here all night. I generally love greeting fans, but I've got a shit-ton on my mind tonight, namely figuring out how the hell I've ended up in the same town as the woman I've been thinking about constantly.

When he senses my hesitation, Barney pats my arm. "We do this all the time, sir. I'll personally see that they get to their car safely."

"We'll be fine, Reno," Ma assures.

Barney adds, "If you go to transportation services next week, they can give you a special pass so your family can park in the players' lot. As you know, it's gated and under constant guard."

I thank the man and then hug Ma and Gramps one more time before heading back to the locker room area of the arena.

And back to Juliette.

CHAPTER 37

Reno

Man nipples and blue balls

"SWAIN, GET OVER HERE and meet my family," Baylor calls, waving me over with one beefy hand. I see him standing with a group of people outside the players' lounge, but Juliette is like a beacon, drawing me nearer with each glance.

Baylor introduces me to his wife, who is not, in fact, Juliette McNamara. Holly has dark skin, short curly hair, and lively hazel eyes. Then I meet his fathers, Isaac and Emmett.

"It's a long story," he says with a chuckle. "I'll tell you later."

I nod like I don't already know the story of why he has two dads, my eyes constantly flitting to Juliette without being obvious. She seems to be doing the same, looking at me and then jerking her eyes away. But when our eyes do meet, I can read the warning in her gaze. *Don't tell.*

Isaac Ward, Baylor's biological dad, has skin about two shades darker than his son, and his brown eyes look out from round, wire-rimmed frames. He looks every bit the wise professor of English Literature he is.

Emmett McNamara, on the other hand, is lighter complected, though he has the tan of a man who works outdoors a lot. His hands are rough when we shake, and I remember that Juliette told me he's a mechanic.

Both fathers are proudly wearing their Baylor Ward jerseys. The entire family is, in fact. The two youngest siblings, both college-aged, step forward and accept my handshakes.

Xander gushes for a minute about the improvement of the defense as compared to last season, and I like the kid. He's got dark-brown hair and eyes that are slightly bluer than Juliette's aqua ones.

Jordan, or Jordie as her family calls her, is almost the exact replica of the woman I'm trying not to gawk at constantly. Though of course Jordie's only twenty, sixteen years younger than her sister, so she has a bit more of a baby face.

"And this is Juliette, the old lady of the family," Baylor tells me, hooking an arm around Juliette's neck and rubbing his knuckles across the top of her head in the age-old display of brotherly assholeness. But I can tell it's done with the utmost of affection. As is her soft elbow to his gut.

"Get off me, butthead," she scolds, and my knees almost buckle at the sound of her voice. Dammit to hell, I've missed hearing her talk. And smile. And sing stupid karaoke songs. And writhe beneath me while I fuck her into the mattress.

Great. Now I'm popping a boner at the most inopportune fucking time ever.

She's removed the beanie, and tiny strands of loose, fuzzy hair shine in the overhead light of the hallway as she attempts to smooth it down. Though I prefer her looking a little messy. It reminds me of her post-coital appearance, ruffled and flushed after I handled her roughly from behind, one of my hands fisted in those golden locks.

Update: The erection situation has not improved.

Clearing my throat, I hold out a hand and attempt to rein in my rogue body parts. Hell, even my man nipples are hard in Juliette's presence.

"It's nice to meet you, Juliette." I'm impressed that my voice sounds even and smooth when I feel the exact opposite. *She's here. She's really standing right in front of me. My dream girl come to life.*

She reaches out to shake my hand, and as soon as our skin makes contact, I have to brace myself from the jolt I feel.

"Nice to meet you too, Mr. Swain."

Mr. Swain? Well that's not fucking helping. My goddamn nipples are so firm they hurt, and my balls are turning bluer by the second.

"Please, call me Reno." *In fact, why don't you scream it for me, baby.* "Did you enjoy the game?"

Juliette's pretty eyes widen. "It was freaking awesome. I think the Brewers really have a chance this year with you on the team. I mean, you forced four turnovers, and the way you neutralized their forward was textbook."

Color me impressed. The woman knows her hockey. More importantly, she kept up with *my* stats during the game. It's hot.

When I realize I'm still holding her small hand in front of all these people, I ease back, allowing my middle finger to drag suggestively against her palm. The pinkening of her cheeks has my insides doing a happy dance. *She's still affected by me.*

"Why don't we head to the restaurant?" Baylor interrupts. "I could eat an entire cow right now."

He and Holly kiss their son and hand him off to Isaac before everyone exchanges hugs. They're a close family, and there's obviously a lot of love between the siblings and the two fathers.

Emmett slaps my arm with a strong hand. "Reno, you should come to our family's Labor Day cookout. Bubba can give you the details." I've finally figured out that Baylor's family refers to him as Bubba, the same Bubba Juliette referred to when we were on the island.

"I don't want to intrude," I lie because I want to intrude like a motherfucker if Juliette is going to be there, which I'm assuming she is since Emmett said it was a *family* cookout.

"Nonsense," Bubba Baylor says. "Everyone's welcome. Bring your mom and Gramps too."

He was with me one day when I stopped by to take Gramps a new book I ordered online, so he got to meet my grandfather. Then Baylor suggested the local library if I wanted to borrow books instead of buying them.

Fuck, if I'd only taken that advice, I most likely would have run into Juliette weeks ago since it's the only library in town. I'm flabbergasted at my next thought.

She's been right under my nose almost this entire time.

Rather than the formal atmosphere I expected, the steakhouse is decorated in a rustic theme, so we're not out of place in our casual clothing. The ladies are still wearing their jerseys and jeans. For the record, I'm not exactly happy to see another man's number on Juliette's body, brother or no.

Baylor and I are in our *leave the arena* uniforms, consisting of a Brewers polo and nicely pressed navy shorts. We have to wear a suit upon arriving, but after the games, Coach lets us dress down. I'm a fan of this system because no one wants to put on a stuffy suit after spending a few hours in our heavy gear. Especially not in the Texas heat.

A portly host greets us at the door and finds our reservation before leading us down a side hallway and through a door marked *Private.*

Baylor and Holly walk in front of us, so I rest my hand on the small of Juliette's back. I'm pleased when she slightly bows her back for more of my touch.

We're shown to a quiet table in a private room, which is apparently reserved for celebrities and sports stars. Matthew McConaughey sits at a corner table with a woman I assume is his wife. I think I read somewhere he's from Texas, though I'd forgotten until now. There's also an actress from a soap opera, but I can't remember her name.

A couple of our teammates are here, as well as a famous baseball player from Dallas. I like this setup. It allows privacy for well-known people who just want to have dinner without autograph and photo hounds all over them.

Baylor pulls out Holly's chair and then starts to round the table to do the same for his sister, but I've already got it handled. He frowns a little but returns to his seat beside his wife. I sit to Juliette's right and slyly place my hand on her knee over the denim of her jeans. She doesn't protest, though I see her eyebrows pop up once in surprise.

Energy thrums through my body at her proximity as I scan the one-page menu. "Hmmm, how's the prime rib?" I ask Baylor, rubbing my thumb over Juliette's denim-clad knee. Does she remember that's what we both ate at our first dinner together?

She bounces her leg once, and I bite my bottom lip to keep from grinning like a fool. She remembers.

"It's excellent," my teammate says.

"Good. I'll have that." I swivel my head to Juliette and ask casually, "Do you like meat, Juliette?"

Her face is deliciously comical, but she coughs lightly and nods. "Love it. I think I'll have the same."

The waiter comes by and takes our orders, but before he can leave, I stop him. "Make sure to bring horseradish with both of the prime ribs."

I realize my mistake instantly when Baylor's brow furrows. "How did you know Jules likes horseradish?" *Fuck.*

Feigning a touch of confusion, I shrug. "I thought that was how everyone ate prime rib."

He nods grudgingly until he's interrupted by a deep voice. "Well they just let anyone in this joint." We all look up to see a grinning Axel Broxton standing next to our table with a beautiful redhead. Ax is a veteran tight end for the Fort Worth Wranglers and is touted by many as the best in the nation. I have to agree. The man is a beast on the football field.

Baylor laughs and stands, pulling Axel into a back-slapping hug. "You crazy sonofabitch. How are you?"

"Good. Just busy, you know? You remember my wife, Blaire." He gestures to the redhead.

"Of course," Baylor replies. "Holly and I have met her. She scoped my shoulder a couple years ago." He turns to us and explains. "Dr. Broxton is the best orthopedic surgeon in the state."

She nods humbly, and Baylor introduces Holly to Axel before gesturing across the table. "And this is my sister, Juliette McNamara."

Axel's eyes dart back and forth between the siblings, obviously clocking the lack of resemblance before telling Juliette, "You apparently got all the good looks in the family."

We all laugh as Baylor rolls his eyes and nods at me. "And have you met Reno Swain?"

"Met him?" Ax asks. "We did a sports drink commercial together a couple years ago."

I stand and give him one of those handshake-hug combos. "That was a fun one. How are the triplets by the way?" He brought his sons to the shoot, and they were so cute, the director gave them a small part in the commercial.

Blaire sighs with the kind of weariness that can only be achieved by the mother of three rowdy boys. "They are prepubescent and completely feral. Danica, our youngest, is the exact opposite. She's nine, always with her nose in a book."

"And your oldest?" Baylor inquires, and Axel beams.

"Carrie graduated high school and is about to start college at SMU. She was going on a basketball scholarship, but she got invited to try out for the women's football team. Really impressed the coaches, so now she's decided to try her hand on the gridiron."

Juliette bounces in her seat. "Our little sister plays for SMU. Jordie McNamara."

Axel's blue eyes widen. "Jordie is your sister?" Baylor and Juliette nod. "Wow, she's a freaking fantastic tight end."

"I'll tell her you said so," Baylor says with a chuckle. "You're her favorite player, so that will make her entire year."

"She's one of the top draft prospects for the new women's professional league they're starting," Ax muses. "I hope I get to work with her one day."

I lean forward and ask quietly, "Are you thinking about hanging up your cleats and going into coaching?"

The footballer's lips curve into a sly smirk. "I didn't say that. But I didn't *not* say that either."

Blaire shakes her head. "My husband, Mr. Mysterious." She loops her arm through his. "Ax is forty now, and his old bones aren't what they used to be."

"I thought you liked my bo—"

His wife shuts him up with a hand over his mouth before tossing us an apologetic look. "I'll get him out of your hair, so you can enjoy your dinners without bone innuendos."

After a round of laughter and goodbyes, the Broxtons find their table near the window.

I'm about to ask Juliette when her book is releasing, but I catch myself. How would I explain that I know she's an author?

"So, Juliette," I say instead. "You're a librarian?"

She nods, and Holly pipes up. "She's also an amazing romance author."

I'm grateful for her input because now I can ask about Juliette's upcoming book. "That's really cool. Do you have anything new in the works?"

"My latest releases in two days," she replies.

"That's why I wanted her to have dinner with us tonight. To celebrate," Baylor says, pride for his sister etched in his smile.

"I'll have to pick one up," I say. "I've recently developed a taste for reading spicy romance books."

Juliette chokes on her sip of water and nudges my knee beneath the table as I stifle a smile. "I can get you a copy," she remarks, her voice a little husky. "I look forward to hearing what you think about it."

"Make sure to sign it," I request.

Her eyes meet mine, and I read the questions in her eyes. "How will I get it to you?"

"Reno moved in on the fourth floor of our building," Holly supplies, and Juliette makes a little squeaking noise.

"You live in Pine Tree Falls?"

"Moved here in late June."

She blinks rapidly. "I'm surprised we haven't run into each other since The Falls is such a small town."

Her brother snickers. "And yet you still have to use your GPS to get to the grocery store."

"Pfff," she scoffs. "I do not."

I try not to laugh, remembering that my sweet dream girl is directionally challenged.

The server brings our plates, and we all dig in. When I'm not cutting my meat, my left hand is on Juliette's thigh. *High* on her thigh. So high, she occasionally lets out little moans but manages to disguise them as enjoying her food.

While we wait for our dessert course, I slide my fingers up until they rest against her pussy. Even through her jeans, I can feel her heat. She picks up her glass of water and downs a gulping swig.

"Jules, you look flushed," Holly comments with concern. "Are you feeling okay?"

I massage her with tiny circles, and she rolls her lips between her teeth. "Fine. Just warm in here." With her finger and thumb, she plucks at her jersey and fans it against her chest.

Baylor rests an arm over the back of Holly's chair. "Reno, why didn't your girlfriend come to the game?"

Juliette stiffens and tries to close her legs, but I press my fingers more tightly against her cunt. "I don't have a girlfriend."

He tilts his head. "Oh, huh. I thought you said you did."

With my middle finger stroking up and down over Juliette's clit, I say, "There was a woman, but she left me brokenhearted in an airport."

Juliette inhales sharply, her eyes flashing to mine before darting away.

"Yikes," her brother says with a wince, oblivious to what I'm doing to his sister beneath the table. "That's harsh, man."

When the server drops off our desserts, I eat the delicious blueberry and lemon cake with one hand. My other one is busy reminding Juliette who owns her pussy. Because make no mistake, it belongs to me, and I'm going to reclaim it as soon as possible.

I know her orgasm is close, and I caress her clit with two fingers over her jeans, just the way she likes it. She lets out a shaky moan, and I feel the rush of heat and wetness as she whimpers, "Soooo good."

Fuck me, she's coming. With her brother and sister-in-law directly across the table.

"The cake?" I ask innocently.

She quickly stuffs a bite into her mouth and nods as she subtly lifts her hips from the chair, riding out her sneaky little climax.

"Yes," she mumbles around the bite. "I haven't had cake in sooo long."

When she's done quietly getting off, I pull my hand from between her legs and pretend to scratch my nose. Her smell is as intoxicating as I remember, and my cock is absolutely about to explode in my pants.

"Neither have I," I say, watching from the corner of my eye as she clutches the edge of the table and works to control her breathing. "And I've missed it so much."

CHAPTER 38

Juliette

Pucking love

I STILL CAN'T GET over the shock of seeing Reno at the arena tonight. And then that little stunt he pulled beneath the table at the restaurant?

But hell, I can't even make myself be mad about it because that orgasm was phenomenal, better than any I've self-administered the past couple months.

Sitting in the backseat of Bubba's truck, I stare at my phone, unable to pull my eyes from a photo of Reno and me from Pineapple Island. In the pic, I'm holding the phone at a high angle and grinning up at it. But Reno? His face is turned to the side, looking at me like I invented bacon.

God I've missed him so much, the way he touched me... the way we laughed together... the way he treated me like I was the only thing that mattered. And when I blathered on about everything from goats to clouds to movie soundtracks, he joined in on the conversations, unlike my asshole ex. I can't even count the number of eye rolls I'd endured from Collin, usually accompanied by ugly words about my "stupid babbling."

But now Reno's here in my town, and I'm not sure what to do with that. Did he get back with Leia or is he still suppressing his latent feelings for her? I refuse to play second fiddle to anyone. I may be sweet, but I do have more pride than that. Collin broke my confidence, and it took me a long while to get it back, but as I built myself up, I vowed never again.

A text notification pops up on my screen, and I swallow hard before checking it. It's short and to the point.

Reno: Give me your address.

Jesus, help me. The thrill that demand sends down my body and to my core should be embarrassing. What should I do? I put my thumbs to my screen and respond.

Juliette: I'm not sure that's a good idea.

Mere seconds pass before I get another message.

Reno: Now, Juliette, or I will knock on every goddamn door in town until I find you.

Sometimes a person's tone is disguised in a text message, but yeesh! Reno's is crystal clear. He's not fucking around. Exhaling, I tap out two texts.

Juliette: 45 Maple Court

Juliette: Park in the garage. I'll leave it open.

By doing that, am I also leaving my heart open and vulnerable for him to work his way back in? I inwardly laugh at myself.

Like he's ever been truly gone.

I pace my small kitchen, my bare feet slapping against the linoleum as I cross the floor so many times I'm probably wearing grooves in the surface.

I pick up my phone and send Evie a text. She's the only one who knows the identity of the man I was sleeping with in paradise.

Juliette: Freaking the fuck out, Eve-ster!

Evie: What's wrong? Do I need to send Dane to handle something?

I blow out a laugh. My best friend's ability to make me smile hasn't been erased by time and distance. And I have no doubt Dane would do anything she asked if she batted her pretty blue eyes at him and cooed, "Honey, someone hurt Juli. Would you pretty please rip their eyeballs out? For me?"

And he'd no doubt reply with a gruff, "Of course, Wildcat. Should I use a knife or my bare hands?"

But I don't need anyone snuffed out. I need advice.

Juliette: Reno got traded to the Brewers.

Evie: Holy shit, are you serious? I haven't watched any sports news in a while. I was too busy, you know, coming back to life and shit.

I shake my head at her ability to joke about even the most serious of subjects before typing again.

Juliette: He lives in Pine Tree Falls!!! Literally a few blocks from me.

Evie: Everything in PTF is literally a few blocks from you.

Juliette: Not helpful.

Evie: So let me get this straight. You didn't want a long-distance relationship, and now the fling you have feelings for lives in your town. Thereby alleviating the whole long-distance thing. That about sum it up?

Juliette: Pretty much.

Evie: I'm not seeing the problem here.

Juliette: You forgot the part where he's my brother's teammate. Sisters are off-limits. Especially with Bubba.

Evie: Uhh, your brother married one of your best friends. Double standard much?

Juliette: It totally is, but it's a whole thing with hockey players. I've seen teams blow up over shit like this.

Evie: Hmmm.

I can picture her drumming her fingertips over her lips as she thinks, so I wait.

Evie: I think you have two options. Number one, you can bang Reno to your heart's content and tell your brother to put on his big boy panties and deal with it.

Juliette: That option is very tempting, but what if things go sideways with me and Reno? I don't want to be responsible for discord among teammates.

Evie: That brings us to option two. You bang your boy toy in the privacy of your own home and see how things progress. If it's good, you both sit Bubba down and tell him the truth. That will circle back to option one and the whole big boy panties thing.

Juliette: So both options involve me banging Reno Swain?

Evie: Exactly. You're welcome!

Juliette: He's on his way to my house right now. I know we need to talk because I think he's still hung up on his ex.

Evie: Where is she?

I frown at my phone screen in confusion.

Juliette: I have no idea.

Evie: I'm assuming she's not at your house?

Juliette: Uh, no.

Evie: But you are, and that's where he's headed. To YOU, not her.

She makes a good point.

My body freezes when I hear a vehicle slow on Maple Court and then turn into my driveway. *It's him. He's here. Holy shit.* I send Evie a quick goodbye and thank you text before setting my phone on the dark-green countertop.

I twist my fingers into knots at my waist as I hear a car door open. Peeking out the door, I see a large, dark figure rounding a silver SUV, and I make a mental note to change the overhead light in the garage. It's been out for a couple weeks, but I need to borrow a ladder from someone.

I press the button to close the bay door, and my eyes follow the big man mounting the two steps from the garage to my kitchen.

Before I can even say hi, I'm being lifted into strong arms, the door is kicked closed, and my legs are around his waist. Lips and tongues meet in a desperate greeting as he slams my back against the door.

Dear god, this man can kiss.

"Do you know how long I've been wanting to do this? Kiss you and hold you like this?" he mutters into my mouth.

"Me too," I admit.

He pulls back an inch and goes to work on my earlobe, nipping and sucking the soft flesh as our bodies meld together.

"I had to drive home one-handed, dream girl, because I couldn't stop smelling my fingers."

My body heats at the dirty implication, and I drop my head back against the wood as Reno licks down my neck before biting the spot where it meets my shoulder. Dammit, he's distracting me with that mouth of his.

"Reno, we need... to... talk," I pant.

"Later," he grunts, trying to kiss me again, but I turn my head, knowing I need to get this off my chest. He lifts his gaze to mine, eyebrows pinched together. "What's wrong, baby?"

"What about Leia?" I ask.

The space between his eyebrows narrows even more, forming a dark unibrow. "What about her?"

I suck in a fortifying breath. "I think you still have feelings for her."

Reno's nose scrunches like he smelled a rotten egg. "Bullshit. The only feelings I have for my ex are apathy and annoyance."

"Y-you said her name when you were asleep. On the plane to Miami, you said 'Leia' and then a minute later, you said 'I pucking love you.'" It hurts to even repeat the words that broke me, and I blink to stave off the tears.

But the response I expect from Reno is not the one I get. After about a thousand confused blinks in the span of five seconds, he laughs. Fucking laughs!

"Put me down," I insist, getting angry and shoving at his chest, but Reno suddenly turns serious. Grasping my wrists in his big hands, he holds my arms over my head while he pins me to the door with his massive body.

"No, you're going to listen to me, woman," he growls, his eyes turning into round green flames. "It's not what you think."

With his compelling gaze holding me as captive as his body is holding mine, he tells me the story of his dream. It's crazy, too bizarre to be made up with Jack Black, Kevin Hart, and...

"I thought Angela Lansbury was dead," I blurt, and Reno cracks a grin.

"She is, but she was in my weird-ass dream. That doesn't mean old Angie is my dream girl though. You are, Juliette. No one else."

"Oh," I whimper, finally understanding the whole scope of what I did as tears spring to my eyes. "I didn't... I mean... I was so hurt when I heard you say you love Leia."

"And now you know that didn't happen. I was talking about *you*."

I'm finding it hard to breathe, and I tug my arms until he lets them go. Wrapping them around his neck, I bury my face in his shoulder, and let the tears fall onto his shirt. "I'm so sorry, Reno. Can you ever forgive me?"

He strokes my hair and kisses the side of my head. "I'm not going to say I'm happy we were apart for two months, but I understand. You were hurt, sweetheart. Run-ins with the exes are always awkward, and I should have realized why you were acting so distant afterward."

I shake my head and lift it to look at him, my hand against his scruffy cheek. And dammit if the man can't rock some scruff. "It wasn't you. This was all my fault. I should have told you what I heard, but I couldn't get the words to come. I felt too raw inside."

"We were both dealing with a lot of emotions." He twists a finger around a strand of my hair. "When everything blew up with Leia last year, I was hurt. My ego, for sure, and it made me feel insecure, which I didn't like at all." His brow creases. "But looking back, I realize I didn't feel that utter pain in my heart like I felt when I saw you walk away from me."

"It was the hardest thing I've ever done," I admit, my heart thumping against my chest at the memory of it.

"I hope we never see my ex again, but if we do, I want you to remember that she is nothing to me. She's a tiny candle flame that blew out a long time ago. But you're my wildfire, Juliette."

More tears sting the backs of my eyelids, and a couple make their way down my cheek. "That's the most beautiful thing I've ever heard."

His lips brush softly against mine. "Just to make myself perfectly clear, you're the one I love. You, Juliette McNamara."

His words are a lightning rod stuck directly in my heart, and I crash my mouth against his, pouring myself into the kiss with everything I have.

"I love you too," I murmur as Reno grunts and turns our bodies, moving across the floor to my breakfast nook. With our mouths still attached, he sets me on the round table and begins tugging at the button and zipper of my jeans.

"Now. Need you now," I moan into his mouth, pulling the hem of his shirt from his shorts. My hands go beneath the polo, and I caress his hard body with my fingers.

"Fuck yes," he bites out, pulling back so he can work my jeans off. Then he yanks my jersey over my head and waves it in front of my face. "I don't like seeing you in another man's jersey."

"It's my brother," I protest and then add, "and I don't think we need to tell him about us right now. Not with the season about to begin."

Reno eyes me speculatively for a long moment and then nods on a long exhale. "You're probably right, but I'm going to get you some of my gear. You can wear a T-shirt under Baylor's jersey so it's *my* name and *my* number against your body."

It's possessive and sweet in a kind of dirty way, so I nod my agreement. "Okay."

His gaze burns my skin when it rakes down my almost naked body. "So many nights, I took my cock in my hand while I thought about this body." He raises his eyes to mine. "And this face. But my memories didn't do you justice. You are absolutely beautiful, baby."

"Reno," I breathe, working my thumbs into my panties to pull them off. As soon as I toss them aside, he's on his knees in front of me, and I clamp my thighs together. "No! I haven't waxed since I've been home."

A wicked grin crawls across his lips. "Sweetheart, I once ate a sucker that had fallen on the dirty carpet of a cheap motel room." He parts my legs and brushes his fingers through my light pubic hair. "So if you think these pretty little curls are going to keep me from devouring your pussy, you better think again."

Then his mouth is on me, licking and sucking with a voracious hunger that has my eyes rolling back in my head. He wasn't joking about devouring me. The noises he makes are like something out of a National Geographic documentary about a predator eating their prey. Though unlike some gazelle or deer, I'm the most willing prey in the world.

He gets me there quickly, and I push against his shoulders with my feet before I can come. "Reno, please stop."

With a frown, he lifts his head. He is so fucking hot with my arousal glossing the bottom of his face. "What's wrong, baby?"

I lift up onto my elbows. "The first time I come for you, I want it to be around your big, hot cock."

The smugness is evident on his face when he stands and undoes his shorts before pulling them and his underwear down below his hips. "I'm happy to fulfill that request."

He pushes my chest until I'm once again lying flat and rests one palm on the table beside my head. After a couple long pulls on his dick, he lines up with me and eases the head in.

"I'm not sure I can be gentle with you tonight, Juliette," he warns.

"I'll be disappointed if you are," I shoot back a second before he practically splits me in two with his first thrust. Holy fucking shit. He's big. And so hard he could bust diamonds with that erection.

He wasn't kidding about not being gentle because Reno Swain pushes me to my absolute limits, bucking into me with a desperation I've never felt before. Though he's really letting me have it below the waist, his words and kisses are ragged and vulnerable.

"Thought I lost you forever. Never leave me again, baby. Please."

"I won't," I promise, spreading my knees wider and taking every inch of his thick, pounding cock.

"God, you feel so fucking good, Juliette. I'm not sure how much longer I can last."

"I'm close," I whimper, sliding my hands beneath his shirt and digging my fingernails into his back. The pain only serves to spur him on, and he yanks one of my legs over his shoulder and places one hand beneath my ass to shift the angle. It's exactly what I need, and I writhe beneath him as the orgasm possesses my body.

With an unholy grunt, Reno starts to come inside me. I hear a loud cracking sound and wonder if he snapped my damn spine.

"Fuck!" he yells, yanking me up as the table disappears beneath me.

He stands upright holding me, my leg still over his shoulder, as our climax continues. When I finally catch my breath, I look down at my table, the top splintered down the center and lying on either side of the wooden base.

"Damn, I'm good," he alleges. "That table's at least an inch and a half thick."

I can't help but laugh. "Sex with you is getting dangerous, Swain. First the sex hammock, and now the sex table."

He carries me down the hallway, and I direct him to my bedroom. "Let's see if we can find some more shit to break. I'm going to turn every surface in this house into a sex platform."

A few minutes later, we're both blissfully naked and on my bed. The lamp casts a soothing glow around us, and we take our time relearning each other with gentle roaming hands.

My eyes follow the trail of my fingers down his muscular chest and freeze. I lean up on one elbow and squint. "Reno, what is this?"

"Oh. That. Ummm, I decided to finally get some ink."

I tilt my head as the image begins to look familiar. "Is that... Sexy Bunny?"

Reno puts on a faux shocked face. "Of course not. That would be ridiculous."

With my index finger, I trace the outline, the lumpy body and the soft ears. "I don't kno-ow." I sing. "It looks a lot like Sexy Bunny."

"Fine," he snaps but there's no heat behind it. "It was the first cloud we looked at together, so I... got fucking Sexy Bunny tattooed over my heart. Are you happy now?"

I roll on top of him and grin. "Mr. Swain, I'm about to show you just how happy I am."

CHAPTER 39

Reno

Betty and the blow job

MY LIFE IS FUCKING fantastic. I have a new hockey team that treats me like family. Ma is happy with her new job. Gramps has more good days than bad.

But the best part of it? I have my girl back.

For the remainder of August, I spend every night at her cute little house. It doesn't have the luxuries of my apartment, but I don't give a damn. Being with Juliette is my luxury.

I tell her every single day that I love her, and when she says the words back, I feel like the luckiest bastard in the world.

I spend my days at practice, and we have dinner together when I'm not with Gramps or Ma. Sometimes she cooks and sometimes we order in from the only delivery place in town. Yeah, small-town life is taking some adjustment on my part, but I'm falling in love with Pine Tree Falls.

I bring Juliette snacks while she's writing, and she rubs down my sore muscles after dinner each night, which usually leads to other, much more fun activities. Yeah, life is perfect except for one thing...

I'm keeping a huge secret from Baylor Ward. He's quickly become one of my best friends and not telling him about my relationship with his sister weighs heavily on my shoulders. Every time he tells me a story I've already heard from Juliette, I have to bite my tongue not to blurt it out.

But she's insistent that we keep things under wraps. She knows her brother better than I do, so I follow her lead.

Today is going to be hard though. I'm going to the Ward/McNamara Labor Day cookout at Isaac's house, and I'll have to pretend I don't spend my nights in Juliette's bed... and that I'm not madly in love with her.

"This looks nice," Ma says, dipping her head to look at the white Craftsman home when I park on the street out front.

I hop out and round the vehicle to help my mother exit. She adjusts the foil covering the pie she baked and beams a sweet smile up at me.

Ma is loving small-town life. Her job is going well, though she has a short commute to the next town over each day. And she joined the Garden Club and the Study Club—whatever the hell that is. People are starting to greet her by name when I accompany her to the grocery store or the diner, and it makes me happy to see her thriving.

I turn to help Gramps out of the backseat, but he's already standing there appraising the house with his hands on his hips. "Hope they got ribs," he comments, and I laugh and drape an arm over his shoulders.

"Baylor told me they will have ribs, sausage, and brisket," I inform him.

"And potato salad?"

"He didn't say, but I'm sure they will," I chuckle.

"Good deal. Let's slap on the old feed bag." Gramps straightens his shoulders like a soldier and marches up the concrete walkway with Ma and I in his wake.

Holly answers the door before we can knock and ushers us into a small foyer. "Great to see y'all," she says. "Everyone's out back."

My grandfather stares at her with lowered eyebrows, finally saying, "Do I know you, young lady?"

She pats his arm. "You do. I met you at Shady Pines when I came to talk about the animals."

Realization dawns on his weathered face, and he grins. "Right, you're the, uhhh... is it park ranger?"

"I'm a game warden and wildlife biologist," she corrects gently, holding out her hand. "Holly Ward."

"Arlo Swain," he announces, shaking her hand heartily. "This is my daughter, Elizabeth, and my grandson, Reno."

I smile at that. Even before dementia took root in his brain, he always called my mom his daughter, not his daughter-in-law.

Holly's tone is kind. "I've met them already. Reno and Baylor play hockey together."

Gramps's eyebrows lift excitedly. "That's right. You're Baylor Ward's wife. I remember now. I bet the boys are going to have a great season."

Ma and I exchange a significant look. The doctors started Gramps on a new medication last month, and we've seen several small improvements as of late. Nothing will ever fully cure him, but the new meds are definitely promising.

"I'm sure they will," Holly says, hooking her arm into Gramps's elbow as we walk toward the back yard. "Hey, Arlo. Do you like ribs?"

I stand beneath the covered back porch and survey the scene. We've been here for an hour, and the party is in full swing. Juliette's sister, Jordie, is chasing Aiden around the yard, pretending to nab the small Nerf football he has tucked under his arm like he's a professional running back.

She scoops him up a second before he almost bowls into Isaac's sister, who, upon meeting me, ordered me to call her Aunt Nedra. She's a heavyset older woman who kisses everyone on the cheek and calls them *sugar britches.* I have to say, that's a new one for me.

Gramps and Emmett are beneath a shady tent with the Brewers logo on it. They were sharing old war stories the last time I checked on them.

Ma is in the corner of the yard where a cornhole game has been set up while Isaac patiently shows her how to play. She makes a shot, and the two high-five. My mother giggles and fidgets with the collar of her red blouse, and my eyebrows shoot to the top of my forehead. *Is she flirting?*

"Those two seem kinda cozy."

I look down to see Juliette standing beside me with a platter of cookies. She's fucking beautiful in a bright blue off-the-shoulder dress that shows off her tanned shoulders.

My eyes dart back to Ma, who is swatting Isaac playfully on the arm. "I'm not sure how to feel about that," I say. "I don't think I've ever seen my mother flirt before."

"Pops is a good man," Juliette tells me. "The most gentle man I've ever known."

I hadn't realized I was scrunching my shoulders until they relaxed at her words. "I've always hoped she could find someone who would be good to her, but she's never seemed interested."

We watch as Ma and Isaac's hands touch. Only for a brief second, but they both smile like goofy teenagers with a crush. "She seems a bit interested now," Juliette remarks with a giggle. "I think it's cute."

Isaac and Ma return to their game, and I nod. "I think so too."

"You want a cookie?" Juliette asks with a teasing lilt in her voice.

I take one, letting my finger brush across her thumb on the clear platter. "What do you call them?"

"These are three-O cookies."

I'd actually been with her when she was baking them this morning. As soon as she put them in the oven, I bent her over the counter to see how many orgasms I could give her before the timer went off, hence the name.

"You ever make four-O cookies?" I ask, and she shrugs, blinking innocently up at me.

"Not yet."

My lips twitch as I slyly swat her on the ass. "You will."

Someone calls her name, and she takes two steps before looking over her shoulder at me. "Promises, promises," she mouths. Then she sashays off with a little extra swing in her hips that I know is for my benefit.

Goddamn, I love that woman.

Two ladies approach the table beside me and begin arguing over whose potato salad is best. I've tried both, but I don't tell them it's the one in the chipped yellow bowl because I know better than to get in the middle of that particular war. Hockey fights ain't got nothing on two southern women battling over potato salad.

I take a bite of the chocolate chip cookie and look around the yard again. Ma and Juliette are now under one of the tents, sitting on the bench of a wooden picnic table. Ma is eating one of the cookies, and I chuckle at the thought of Juliette telling her the name we made up for them.

Xander is in a lawn chair, sitting in the shadow of a weeping willow tree as he reads what looks like a textbook. Juliette told me he's been studying for his med school entrance exam. Jordie is wrestling in the grass with Aiden, who is giggling like a maniac.

I locate Gramps, who's playing horseshoes with a group of men in the other corner of the yard, and he seems to be having the time of his life.

My eyes find Emmett and Isaac beside the grill, but they're not currently watching the meat. No, they're watching all the beautiful chaos around them, both with looks of pride on their faces. This is their family, as unorthodox as it is, and they love them.

I admire those two. There could have been so much bad blood and jealousy between them since they'd both married the same woman, but they didn't let that stop them from doing what was best for the kids. It's truly what family is all about.

And as the two paternal figures clink their beers together, I hope one day, I'm a part of it.

When I pull into Juliette's garage later that night, she's standing beside her VW bus. The damn thing is the color of Barney the dinosaur. Only my girl could pull off that particular shade of purple. It's a vintage number from the sixties, and she told me she and her dad had completely rebuilt it together when she was younger.

"Hey," she says, wrapping her arms around my neck as soon as I get out of my SUV. "Did you have fun at the party?"

I encircle her waist with my arms. "I did. Gramps and Ma did too. The only way it could have been better was if I could have kissed my girlfriend in front of everyone." I dip my lips to hers as a demonstration.

"Sneaking around is kinda fun though, right?"

My right eyebrow hitches up. "Except when your brother almost caught me here last week when he came to take a look at your toilet."

She winces. "I know. I almost freaked the hell out when he said he forgot a wrench and wanted to grab one from my garage."

"Where my vehicle was parked," I add dryly. "And while I was hiding naked in your closet. We should just tell him. I want to be with you out in the open."

"I do too, but he's your teammate, and I know how something like this could screw up your team vibe. After hockey season is over, we can tell everyone," she promises.

It's frustrating for me, but she's probably right. "Why are you waiting in the garage? You need me to fix something else?" I glance up at the light I replaced for her as soon as I noticed it was out, but it's working fine.

Juliette's coquettish smile tells me I'm going to like the reason she was waiting out here for me. I know that look, and it always ends with sexy times.

"I've never had sex in Betty before." She bumps her hip against her vehicle and arches an eyebrow.

Yep. I knew it.

"Say less," I tell her with what I'm sure is the goofiest grin ever as I strip off my shirt.

Juliette laughs and walks around to the side of the van... bus... whatever... and opens the large door, revealing quite a little setup in the back. There's a large fluffy animal-print blanket, along with pink pillows from her couch. Actually, I've been informed more than once that said pillows are *raspberry*, not pink. Whatever.

"There's something else I want to try," she tells me. "It's for a book and I need feedback on whether or not it's as good as it's described online."

"Whatever it is, I'll make it good for you, baby," I swear, crawling into the back and leaning on my side in a Sexy Bunny pose that makes her laugh. I pat the spot on the blanket beside me. "Tell me what you need."

Her pretty teeth scrape over her bottom lip. "Actually, sweetie, I'm going to make it good for *you*."

Five minutes later, my entire world view changes. "Jesus fucking Christ, Juliette. Oh god...."

My vision has gone black around the edges, and I can no longer feel any of my extremities. And I might be bleeding from the ears from the effort of holding back this orgasm.

Juliette is between my legs with my cock in her mouth. And yes, that's usually enough to blow my mind, but mother of all that's good and holy... This is on another level.

She rests the Altoid mint on her tongue and slides it up and down the bottom side of my dick as she bobs her head.

"I'm coming," I groan. "Again."

Yes, I fucking came already, and now I'm about to bust another nut in her sweet mouth. Don't fucking judge me until you've experienced it because the cool tingles the mint produces combined with the heat of her mouth? It will be eternally etched on my soul.

She's not even taking me particularly deeply, but it doesn't matter. I spill into her mouth for a second time, and my vision goes all the way black. I think she killed me, but what a way to go.

I open my eyes and find Juliette kneeling beside me, her hand stroking my hair. "How long was I out?" I rasp.

"Only about ten seconds. Are you okay?" I nod, and she asks, "How was it?"

"How was it?" I repeat, trying to raise my head to look at her incredulously, but it flops back down to the pillow. I stare at the ceiling and chuckle. "It was phenomenal, dream girl. Like, the best head ever."

"Hmmm." She grabs her sparkly pink notebook and seems to be speaking to herself as she takes notes. "Lost consciousness for approximately ten seconds. Skin of the face is pale and clammy. Two consecutive orgasms." Then she looks at me and taps the matching pen against her lips. "What specifically did it feel like on your penis?"

"Baby, I can barely talk right now. I feel like I have a concussion. Can we do this little exit interview after some of my bodily fluids have been replenished?"

Her eyes round. "Oh shit. I'm so sorry. That was thoughtless of me. I brought a Gatorade." She reaches into a small cooler and produces a bottle before cracking the lid open and holding it to my lips, supporting the back of my head with her other hand.

After a few long swallows, I determine that I'm probably not paralyzed for life and give her a smile. "Better, but do you have any more of those Altoids?"

Juliette eyes me suspiciously but produces the tin, rattling the tiny white mints inside. "You want to go again?"

I laugh. "Fuck no. Not tonight anyway. I want you to put one on my tongue and then sit on my fucking face. We're about to see if this little trick has the same effect on you."

Spoiler alert: It did.

CHAPTER 40

Juliette

Bunny ears

EXCITEMENT THRUMS THROUGH ME as I sit in the front row of the Brewers' arena. Tonight is the season home opener for the team, and the atmosphere is electric in here. All the hardcore fans saw the exhibition game, and they can sense that something is different this year. Namely, the defense.

My man...

The entrance music, "Boom! Shake the Room" by DJ Jazzy Jeff & The Fresh Prince, begins, and everyone jumps to their feet. It's an old-school tune, but it gets the crowd hyped as hell.

Since our families are acquainted now, Reno arranged for his mom and grandfather to sit in our section. Gramps is directly to my right, and he and I do a little hip bump dance as we watch the entrance.

And the guys take the ice. I always love this part, but seeing Reno skating across the rink gives me an extra thrill. Especially when he finds me immediately in the crowd like I have a tracking device on me.

He tosses up two fingers in front of his chest, which looks like a simple peace sign, but I know it's meant for me. He said he wanted a secret signal to show me he loves me, so he decided to do bunny ears. It's truly the most fucking adorable thing ever... and it makes me feel special.

I make the sign back to him and then casually lift the front of my brother's jersey to flash the red tank top underneath. The one with Reno's name and number on it. That makes him grin.

I wish with all my heart I could wear his jersey with pride, but I know it would look suspicious. Next season everything will be different. We'll tell Bubba about our relationship, and he'll have time during the off-season to come to terms with it. And everyone will live happily ever after.

As long as my brother doesn't kill us. *Good times.*

Reno skates to a section near us and approaches a little boy with dark hair. I watch on the Jumbotron as he hands the kid a puck and then receives a big, happy hug from the boy.

When they pose for a picture and Reno kisses the top of the kid's head, my ovaries stage some kind of coup where they wrestle all the rest of my internal organs into submission and take over my entire body. I'm just one big, needy reproductive organ at this point.

I smile sadly as I think about what I have to do at my doctor's appointment tomorrow.

The game isn't going as well as expected. Our defense and goaltending are great, but our offense is struggling to score. Seattle is doing a good job of keeping our center and wingers contained, and we're tied at one goal apiece near the end of the third period.

Reno is covered with sweat, his face an intense picture of determination as he skates backward and angles to control the play. He looks so fucking hot, I'm surprised he hasn't melted the ice.

Seattle's center is heading toward the net, trying to score, and I yell, "Come on, Gibby!" at our goalie. Gibby reaches to the right to save it, but instead of taking the shot, the center suddenly passes to the right winger, and the entire crowd gasps. Dammit, he's going to score.

Then Reno comes out of freaking nowhere and steals the puck before making a crisp pass to Bubba. He's got wide open ice in front of him, and the crowd absolutely loses their minds as my brother puts on a burst of speed toward the other goal. And just as the final horn sounds, he sneaks the puck past Seattle's goalie to put the Brewers on top.

The crowd erupts and the other players swarm my brother. I'm crying the happiest of tears when Reno picks up Bubba with both arms, and the camera zooms in to show the pure joy on their faces, projecting it on the large overhead screen for everyone to see. Then they headbutt each other like the idiot hockey players they are.

When they're done with their celebration, Reno's green eyes find mine, and I flash him bunny ears. He laughs and does the same, his smile doing very naughty things to my vagina. Yeah, my man deserves a treat.

I might have to break out the Altoids again when we get home.

Strong arms surround me as I push through the fog of sleep the next morning. This is how I wake up every morning, Reno kissing the back of my neck and holding my boob like it's his own personal security blanket.

"You're gonna be late for work," he murmurs. "Not that I'm complaining about morning snuggles with my girl."

I roll over in his arms and stick my nose in the hollow of his throat. He smells like soap and sleepy man. "I'm actually off today because I have a doctor's appointment. It's in the afternoon, but I took the entire day anyway."

"Good, baby. You deserve a day off." Then he pauses. "Are you feeling bad or something?"

"No, it's my annual exam with my gynecologist, but I was..." I exhale a breath and decide to tell him the truth. "I was going to have my birth control implant removed."

"Hmm, how often do you have to replace it?"

"Every three years. I think it's about that time, but I was actually planning on having it removed. Not replaced."

There's a beat of silence before he pulls his head back to look down at me. "Why would you do that?"

"Because I was planning to have a baby." His eyebrows almost shoot off the top of his head, and I rush to add. "It was during the time after our vacation but before I knew you moved here."

"That... doesn't make me feel any better, Juliette." His nostrils flare. "Who exactly were you planning to have this baby with?"

"A donor," I say, and Reno's face goes through several expressions in rapid succession. Shock, anger, confusion, and something else I can't name.

"You want to have a baby so you were going to use a sperm donor?"

"That was the plan, but like I said, it was before you came back into my life. I know it's too early in our relationship to talk about families and babies, so I'll just have Dr. Fergus put in a new implant." I say it in an easy-breezy tone I don't quite feel.

I feel the ice seep in around us as Reno's jaw hardens. "And you weren't even going to tell me about this plan?"

Apprehension makes my stomach hurt. He's angry. "What do you mean? I just told you I'm getting the implant. I'm not trying to baby trap you or anything, Reno."

He snorts out a humorless laugh. "I didn't say you were. What I'm hearing is that you'd rather have a baby with some fucking stranger than with me."

I'm stunned and perplexed by his attitude. "I don't understand what you're so mad about."

Reno lets out a frustrated sound and rolls onto his back, rubbing at one of his eyes with the heel of his hand. He stares at the ceiling for a long time, like he's trying to gather his strength, before turning back onto his side.

"Do you still want a baby, Juliette?" he asks point blank.

"I..."

"The truth," he demands, and I crush my eyes closed and nod. "But you don't want one with me. Is it because you're afraid I'll be like my father?"

My eyes fly open. If I'd thought I was stunned before, now I'm completely flabbergasted.

"Of course not, Reno. You're nothing like your father." Resting my hand on his cheek, I say, "You're the exact opposite, and that's why I fell in love with you so fast and so hard. I think you'd be an amazing dad."

In his eyes, I can see the vulnerable little boy who didn't understand why Daddy hurt them when he softly asks, "Then why don't you want me to be your child's father?"

Oh. God. I get it now. He's not upset about me wanting a baby that he's not ready for. He's hurt because he thinks I don't want a baby *with him*. But that couldn't be farther from the truth.

Cupping his handsome face with both my hands, I kiss him with the kind of tenderness I hope he can feel in his heart.

"I do want that, Reno. More than anything in the world. When I picture having a child, he always has dark curls and green eyes. He's sweet and laughs at my silly jokes when he grows up, and he never rolls his eyes when I ramble." My voice trembles with significance on the next part. "Because I picture a little version of you."

Reno's lips roll in and out a few times as he attempts to get his emotions under control. His hand drops to my bare stomach beneath the covers, and his voice goes husky.

"I don't want you to get the implant replaced," he says with confidence before quickly adding, "It's your body, Juliette, and I would never, ever try to tell you what to do with it, but if it were up to me, I'd cover your body every night until I put all the babies you wanted into your belly. Because I want them too. With you."

"You do? We've only been a couple for less than two months, Reno."

His green eyes search my face. "Are you afraid we're not going to last? Because if you're even the tiniest bit unsure, you should get the implant today, and we can table this discussion for a later time."

Tears drip down my face at the empathy and understanding this big, strong man is showing me. "You're my forever, Reno Swain. I know that in my heart, and I have complete faith in your love for me."

That draws a smile from him.

"It's still your choice. I know it seems fast, but if you're ready to have a child, I'm your man. Not some random *jack-off-in-a-cup* guy." He kisses my forehead with firm lips. "Take your time and think about it. You can always postpone your trip to the doctor. Whatever you decide, I'll support you."

I'm unsure on exactly which direction I should go, but it's those last three words—*I'll support you*—that tell me no matter what decision I make, Reno will be by my side.

CHAPTER 41

Juliette

Surprise!

"HOW WAS YOUR TRIP?" I ask Dr. Fergus when she comes into the exam room.

"Bloody fantastic except for my sister," she replies with the hint of a Scottish accent. "She's a lot to deal with. How are you doing?"

"Great, just busy."

"Ah, yes. Hockey season has started, hasn't it? I'll have to try to make a game." She pulls up something on her laptop and peruses it before humming. "Well, I see you're here to get your implant out and to discuss intrauterine insemination."

"Right, about that," I start. "That was the plan when I made the appointment, but I've recently started seeing someone."

Her smile is genuine. "That's wonderful, Juliette. So you want to just replace your current implant? I think it's about time for that. Let me just check here..." She consults her laptop before I can reply. "Oh."

"Oh what?" I ask, sitting up straighter and tugging at the silly pink gown to try and keep it in place.

Her blue eyes lift to mine. "You're actually overdue for a replacement. It should have been done in August." Her brow furrows. "The receptionist should have scheduled you with one of my associates since I was out of the country."

"She offered," I say quickly, not wanting to get the sweet woman in trouble. "I decided to wait till you got back."

Dr. Fergus waves a casual hand. "I'm sure it's fine. Those implants generally have a bit of an overlap period. We'll just do a pregnancy test to make sure."

An hour later, I leave the doctor's office like a zombie. I feel like I've been shell shocked. With a white bag of vitamins in one hand and a black-and-white photo in the other, I make my way to my car.

Reno's at practice, so the house is empty when I return. I don't even remember getting inside and sitting on my raspberry-colored couch, but I must have because when he returns—however many hours later—I'm still sitting there, staring at the sonogram picture.

I'm not sure how the human mind works at its basest level, but somehow I'm frantic and completely calm at the same time. Freaked out and content... that's me.

"Hey, babe!" he calls, and I hear the thunk of his bag being tossed down beside the kitchen door. He always parks inside the garage to hide his SUV from view. I'd even given him my spare garage door opener.

I feel his presence as soon as he enters the living room. Then a kiss on the top of my head. "How was your day? Did everything go—"

His words halt, and I know he sees what I'm holding in my hands. I wordlessly hand it to him over the back of the couch, my eyes focused on the black TV screen on the far wall.

Did he mean everything he said this morning? Is he really ready for this, or were they simply words? Because this... this is a lot.

I feel him sit beside me, and the scent of the ice rink still clings to his clothes, mixed with the clean smell of his soap. It's a comforting aroma to me, one I've known for years. I had my driver's license two years before Bubba, so I drove him to practices and sat in the stands while he perfected his skills, even after he was old enough to drive. It was our tradition, our brother-sister time, and the smell always evokes a sense of calm in me.

Bubba… we're definitely going to have to tell him now.

"Juliette?" The question of my name on Reno's lips almost startles me, and I slowly turn my head to look at him. He's staring at the picture, and I'm unable to read the expression on his face.

"I'm pregnant," I say quietly, and I see his cheeks hollow for a second before he blows out a breath. "I was going to have the implant removed, but Dr. Fergus wanted to do a pregnancy test first because…"

He finally looks at me, his eyes the softest green I've ever seen. "Because what?"

My lips are numb, like your foot gets when you sit with your legs crossed for too long, but I force them to work. "I didn't do this on purpose. My doctor was out of town, so I decided to wait for her to get back for my appointment instead of seeing one of the other docs. I was apparently supposed to have the implant replaced in August. I-I didn't realize it was time already," I stammer, desperate for him to understand.

His tender kiss on my forehead almost breaks me. "I know you didn't do it on purpose, sweet girl." His trust in me has tears slipping over the rims of my eyelids and down my face. "How do you feel about it?"

"Excited. A little freaked out." I pause before repeating his question. "How do *you* feel about it?"

His brilliant smile answers before his words have the chance to, but it still warms me to hear them. "I'm fucking over the moon, dream girl." His eyes flit between me and the sonogram pic. "We're having a baby."

Time for the next surprise. Not sure he's going to handle this one quite as well as the first.

I hold up two fingers, unable to say the words aloud. Reno mistakes the gesture for our bunny ears love signal and grins, holding up two fingers of his own. "I love you too, Juliette."

"I meant two babies, Reno," I explain, still holding my two fingers up. "We're having twins."

He stares at my fingers, then at the sonogram picture, then back to my fingers. He looks like a cartoon character, and I fight the urge to laugh.

His bulging green eyes finally rest on my aqua ones, and his voice drops to a whisper. "That's fucking awesome."

The words are so heartfelt and said with so much wonder, I can't help but burst into giggles. "You're happy?"

Reno sets down the picture and hauls me into his lap until I'm straddling him. His big hands cup my cheeks.

"A minute ago, I told you I was over the moon, and now I'm... double over the moon." His smile is broad and infectious. "That probably doesn't make a lick of sense, but it's how I feel."

"I love you," I tell him, my voice thick with emotion as I cover his hands on my face.

He kisses me then, long and sweet, before wrapping his arms around me and flipping our bodies until I'm lying on the couch with him on top. "I love you too, dream girl. And I'm going to take care of you and our little bunnies. I promise."

It's like a dream. Every woman should feel this loved, this supported, when she tells a man she's pregnant. There is no apprehension in his eyes, only devotion.

"And I'll take care of you," I tell him.

He lifts his eyebrows. "Will you take care of me if I'm in the hospital after we tell your brother?"

I laugh. "I'll handle Bubba."

Reno brushes a strand of hair from my cheek. "I want to be there when you tell him. Promise me you won't do it without me."

"I promise."

"I want to look him in the eye, man to man, and tell him I'm crazy in love with his sister. I want him to know how dedicated I'll be to you and our little family. I'll make sure he knows I plan to wife you up as soon as you'll have me."

"Wife me up?" I ask with a giggle as the word *wife* sends a delicious shiver up my spine.

Reno dips his head and speaks against my lips. "Be ready, Juliette McNamara, because I'm going to wife you up so damn hard."

And then he seals the promise with a kiss.

Chapter 42

Juliette

Beavers and basting

I'm at Primo's Pizza with my siblings again, but this time our dads have joined us. They do that sometimes, though they usually let us "kids" have our fun bonding time. Aiden is with us too, and I can't help but stare at his precious little face as he gnaws on a breadstick, thinking that in a few months, I'll have a baby too.

Babies, plural, I remind myself, and a smile unwittingly steals my lips.

"Season looks like it's going to be a good one this year," Dad says, beaming at Bubba with pride.

It's been around two weeks since I found out I was pregnant, and the Brewers have won three more games, making them undefeated so far. One was an away game, which I missed, but I was front and center for the other two.

Reno has updated our little two-finger signal. Now when he takes the ice, he holds up both hands with his index and middle fingers lifted into a V. He told me one is because he loves me and the other is because he loves our two "little bunnies" growing in my belly.

Though fans don't know he's directing this salute toward me, and they certainly don't know the meaning behind it, they've picked up on it. Someone started making Swain T-shirts and hats with what they think is a peace sign on them, and it's become a bit of a craze.

I love it, seeing our secret love signal spread across arenas. *Secret* being the key word. We decided to wait until the pregnancy reaches twelve weeks before we tell everyone. Well, I decided. Reno wants to shout it from the rooftops, but he's respecting my wishes.

I'm currently at ten weeks, which probably means I got pregnant right after the exhibition game in August. Right after Reno and I found each other again.

My man has gone completely bonkers. Seriously, it's like he's been smacked in the head by some deranged baby fairy. He's obsessed with online shopping, sending me at least twelve links a day to get my opinion on which crib or twin stroller I prefer.

And then he buys them. The few times I've snuck into his apartment to see him, I found myself barely able to move around because of all the boxes. He's also car shopping, determined to find the safest vehicles in existence to drive our precious cargo that will be arriving next May.

Despite my protests, Reno has a new SUV on order for me, a custom-made Porsche Macan with all the bells and whistles. The custom part? Yeah, he's having the damn thing bullet- and bomb-proofed, like someone is going to be shooting RPGs at me and our babies in the middle of Pine Tree Falls.

He's completely ridiculous but also incredibly cute, and I love that crazy, baby-obsessed daddy with all my heart.

I tune back into the hockey talk around the table as the server begins bringing pizzas. My lips turn up at the corners when I look across the table at Aiden, who claps happily when he sees his cheese pizza.

"Just a second, you little monster," Holly says, picking up a piece of it and blowing on it. "Let me cool it off first."

Bubba, who's sitting beside me tonight, distracts his son with goofy faces.

"And the last one," the server says, placing a pizza in front of Bubba and Jordie. "Supreme with anchovies."

The pungent scent of the tiny fish turns my stomach, and I slap my hand over my mouth. "Sorry, stinks," I mumble, leaping up from the table and dashing to the restroom in the back. I barely make it before I lose my guts in the toilet.

"Shit," I breathe, spitting one last time into the bowl before blindly reaching for the toilet paper.

"Jules, you okay?" the sweet voice of my sister asks from outside the stall.

"Yeah," I croak out before wiping my mouth and flushing the toilet. When I open the door, I see Jordie leaning against the sink. "I'm fine. I'm not sure what happened there." I add a chuckle that I hope doesn't sound as nervous as it feels. Because I do know what happened. In a word: pregnancy.

My sister wets a paper towel and dabs at my sweaty forehead. "I have some mouthwash in my purse." She produces a travel-sized bottle, and I take a mouthful, swishing it around before spitting. "Better?" she asks.

"Much. Thank you. You didn't have to follow me in here."

She gives me a careful hug. "I don't mind. Do you need me to drive you home?"

I return her embrace and shake my head. "I'll be fine. Let's go back out there."

When we arrive at the table, I find that my family has rearranged themselves, leaving an open seat at the opposite end of the table from the offending pizza.

I take my seat beside Holly, and smile through wobbly lips. "Sorry, everyone. Not sure what happened."

My friend bobs her eyebrows up and down. "Oh, I think I know." I zip a glare at her, warning her not to say it, but she does anyway. Gleefully. "You're pregnant."

It's like *The Exorcist* at our table with heads spinning in my direction, six sets of eyes asking me for confirmation. All except Aiden because he's blissfully munching on his cheese pizza, bless his cute little heart. My thoughts whir around in my brain, looking for a foothold but finding none.

Except for the truth. I can't exactly tell my family I'm not pregnant, and then when the designated time comes, yell, "Surprise! I was a big fat liar two weeks ago!" Even with a bright smile and jazz hands, that wouldn't go over well.

So I paste on a smile and admit, "I am."

There's only a beat of processing time before chaos ensues. Someone knocks a drink over, someone else claps, and everyone is talking at once.

"Congratulations, sis."

"That was fast."

"When are you due?"

"You're going to rock this."

"I didn't even know you were dating anyone, honey."

That last one was from Dad, and I wince. My siblings know about my plan to have a child, but I hadn't told my fathers yet, so me being pregnant is kind of out of left field for them.

Plus, I promised Reno I wouldn't divulge our relationship without him present, but what choice do I have? Maybe this would be better. There's no way Bubba would flip the table in a rage in the middle of a busy restaurant.

Probably.

But before I can answer Dad's inquiry, Holly covers my hand protectively. "Juliette decided a while back that she wants to have a baby, and we're all going to support her, right?" She glares around the table until everyone nods. "She's a grown woman who can make her own reproductive choices, and if she wants to go to a sperm bank, that's perfectly fine. Women do it every day."

Well. Shit.

While I appreciate the sentiment behind her rah-rah-ree speech, she's now given everyone the impression that I used an anonymous donor.

This is a clusterfuck of epic proportions.

I open my mouth to set the record straight, but all of a sudden, everyone is on their feet, taking turns hugging me and whispering supportive words in my ear as happy tears begin to flow from my eyes.

Pops presses a paper napkin into my hand and kisses my forehead. "Another baby in the family. I'm so happy, sweetheart."

"I... thank you," I say, dabbing at my eyes before taking my seat.

Okay, maybe this way wouldn't be so bad. I could let this little misconception ride until I can talk to Reno. If he wants to have a private conversation with Bubba before we explain the misunderstanding, since they're such good friends, that will be fine. It will all be fine.

Everyone sits back down, and Dad motions for the server to bring a towel for the spilled drink. Holly bumps me with her shoulder. "I'm so excited we'll have kids about the same age. They'll be cousins and best friends."

"Or they'll fight like cats and dogs like Xander and Jordie did when they were little," Pops says with a chuckle.

As if to prove his point, Xander pulls Jordie's blonde ponytail, and she punches him in the arm.

Meanwhile, Holly has both her index fingers in the air and is doing a wiggle dance while singing, "Preggy, preggy, preggy. Juliette is preggy."

Aiden points at me and yells, "Peggy!"

I scowl at Holly. "Thanks a lot. Now my nephew thinks my name is Peggy."

She laughs and kisses my cheek while everyone resumes eating. "How did you do the procedure? At the clinic or did you do it at home?"

I bite my lip to restrain the giggle about to escape. "The procedure? I, uh, did it at home." Many, *many* times.

"You should have told me so I could help you. I took animal husbandry classes in college."

The bite of pizza I'd just taken falls out of my mouth and into my lap. "Help me?" My voice is higher than that last key on a piano.

"You know." She mimes sticking an object into an... orifice. "Help you get the baby juice where it needs to go."

Bubba stares at his wife in disbelief while Dad glugs down the rest of his beer in one go. I'm speechless, but unfortunately, Holly is not.

"I inseminated a beaver once," she says conversationally. "Used a tiny little thing similar to a turkey baster." She pretends to pinch a small dropper, and poor Pops goes into a coughing fit. Jordie pounds him on the back, her eyes almost bulging from their sockets.

Bubba lowers Holly's still pinching fingers to the table. "Honey, thank you for sharing that *with the entire family*," he says pointedly, but she doesn't get the hint.

"Of course, I would have used a large one for Jules since her—"

"Holly!" I snap before we get into a whole conversation about my apparently super-sized vagina, and she shrugs.

"Whaaat? It's science."

Swear to god, this entire dinner is trying to kill me.

"Welp," I call out, marching into Reno's apartment and dropping my purse on the table. "The cat's out of the bag. One of them anyway. I feel like we have an entire litter of cats in our secret bag."

Reno is on the couch, looking at his phone, and he doesn't seem to have heard me because he replies with, "Babe, do you think the babies need watches?"

Oh for the love of...

"What are you talking about, Reno?"

"I was just reading where this guy had a kid-sized Rolex commissioned for his daughter. You think they can do that for babies too?" He looks up questioningly at me, holding up his phone, which shows a small platinum watch with diamonds around the face. His smile is boyish and sweet, and *why the hell is he so damn adorable?*

"No, honey. The babies do not need watches," I say, trying to garner some patience at his ridiculousness. "Number one, it would be a choking hazard. And number two... *Babies. Can't. Tell. Time.*"

His lips twist in disappointment, and he looks longingly at the absurd watch. "Huh. Guess you're right."

I stomp my foot in frustration. "Reno, can you stop baby shopping for two seconds? We need to talk." At least he seems to have put all the boxes away, probably in one of the three spare bedrooms.

He looks up again, concern creasing his forehead. "What's wrong, sweetie?"

I drop the truth bomb on him. "My family knows I'm pregnant."

He jumps off the couch, his head whipping back and forth like my family is secretly hiding behind the entertainment center to ambush us. "What? How did they find out?"

"Because I puked at the restaurant."

Reno is on me in a second, his hand to my forehead, checking for a fever. "Are you okay? Do we need to go to the hospital? Did you take anything?" He spits the questions in rapid-fire succession, and I can't help but feel touched at his doting.

"I'm fine. I smelled the anchovies on a pizza, and blech." I make a puke face.

He doesn't look convinced and releases me to pick up the pregnancy book he's read about four-hundred times. There are colorful tabs sticking out everywhere, and he calls it his Baby Bible.

"I read something in here... Let's see... Green tabs for nausea and vomiting..." Flipping through the pages, he finds what he's looking for. "Ha! Ginger tea. Sit down, and I'll bring you some."

He points at his plush French-blue couch, and I inhale a deep breath for patience. "Reno, focus," I tell him, snapping my fingers in front of his face. "Family, pregnancy, remember?"

When he sees I'm not going to sit, he takes my hand and leads me to the kitchen before lifting me to sit on the blue agate countertop near the stove.

"What happened after you barfed?" he asks as he digs through an overhead cabinet, ostensibly looking for tea bags.

"Well, Holly gets nauseated when she smells anchovies too. A lot of pregnant women have that problem with strong odors. Who the hell came up with anchovies on pizza anyway? Like someone was sitting around and thought, 'Hey, let's take the most delicious food ever invented and throw some stinky-ass fish on it?'"

"True. Make sure to stay away from Caesar salad dressing too. It has anchovy paste and some of them are prepared with raw eggs, so that's not safe for you while you're pregnant."

"How did you know that?"

"Baby Bible," he says, flashing me a smug look before reading the back of a small box. "So they guessed it because you got sick?"

"Yes. Well, Holly did and then blurted it out to everyone."

He presses his lips together and nods resignedly as he puts the water on to boil. "Okay, I'll go talk to Baylor as soon as I'm done making your tea. How mad was he?"

"He doesn't know about you and me yet. You said you wanted to be there when I told him."

"Right. In two weeks." His eyebrows inch together as he walks toward me and wedges his hips between my thighs. "So who do they think the father is?"

I close my eyes and breathe deeply in and out. "A sperm donor."

Reno's mouth pops open. "You lied to them?"

"Not technically," I hedge, shaking my head. "I'd mentioned the whole sperm bank thing to my siblings and Holly once before, so they automatically assumed that was how I got knocked up. So I... didn't correct them," I finish with a shrug.

Soft lips brush across my temple as Reno pulls me close. "Were they as excited as I am?"

I chuckle and rub my hands up and down his back. "I don't think anyone anywhere has ever been as excited as you. But they were all thrilled and very supportive."

"Good," he says, leaving the cradle of my legs to work on the tea. "Because I want you to have all the support you need with the twins while I'm on the road."

"Shit!" I say, realizing something I'd forgotten. "I didn't even get the chance to tell them I'm carrying twins."

Reno looks at me oddly as he steeps the tea. "How did that not come up?"

I blow out a sigh. "Because Holly's crazy ass started talking about inseminating beavers and turkey basters and..." I look down at the spot between my legs. "Do you think my vagina is normal? You know, like a standard size and everything?"

He snorts, and the tea bag slips from his fingers and plops onto the floor. I can see his shoulders shaking as he bends to pick it up. When he stands, he's schooled his face, though a muscle beside his lip is twitching.

"A standard-sized vagina? What does that even mean?"

I huff. "Well, Holly said she'd use a large turkey baster to inseminate me. I mean, I know I don't have a beaver-sized hole," I tell him, holding up my pinky finger, "but now I'm wondering if I'm normal. Down there."

Reno hands me the cup and then places his elbows on the countertop beside me, burying his head in his hands. His shoulders are shaking again.

I take a sip of the tea—it's actually pretty good—and wait for him to finish. When he does, not even bothering to conceal his wide grin this time, he stands between my legs again.

"Let me assure you, dream girl, you have an absolutely perfect pussy, but I wouldn't call it standard. It's extraordinary."

My lips tug up on one side. "You think my pussy is extraordinary?"

Reno presses a kiss to my lips. "Baby, it is absolutely exceptional." *Kiss.* "Pink." *Kiss.* "Tight as fuck." *Kiss.* "And delicious."

"So in the grand scheme of things, you'd describe it as not too shabby?"

My man drops to his knees and reaches for the waistband of my leggings. "Lie back and relax, Juliette, and I'll remind you exactly how much I love it."

Later that night, I'm sitting up in Reno's bed. The covers are black and gray, but he let me add a few red throw pillows to give it some pizzazz. One of those pillows is on my thighs, boosting my laptop so I can comfortably type.

"Whatcha writing?" Reno asks as he comes into the room.

"About a woman who's worried her vagina isn't standard," I say airily. "But her man reassures her it's..." I pretend to check my notes and then look at him over my red-framed glasses. "Extraordinary."

"Hmmm, sounds vaguely familiar," he quips. "I forgot to tell you, I stopped by your house while you were at dinner and picked up your mail."

He hands me a small stack, and I flip through. It's all junk mail and sales papers until I get to a hot-pink envelope.

"Awww, this is from my author friend, AK Landow. She must have sent me a card," I say sliding my finger beneath the flap. "I told her about the babies, but she promised to keep it on the down low until we make it public."

I pull the card out. It feels thick. Maybe it's one of those that plays music. Or makes fart noises. You never know with her.

When I open it, I let out a shriek as something shiny shoots into the air and then rains down all around me. Like... confetti?

"What the fuck?" Reno shouts, rushing over and climbing onto the bed in a panic. He swipes at my shoulders and hair before picking up one of the tiny metallic scraps. He studies it for a long moment. "Is this a dick?"

I scoop up a handful and see that they are indeed tiny penis cutouts, and I burst out laughing. I'm going to be picking cocks out of my hair for weeks.

After almost an hour of sweeping and vacuuming confetti—as well as cursing AK—we finally crawl back into bed. Reno wraps himself around me from behind and places a hand on my belly.

I speak into the darkness, nuzzling my butt back against him. "I think since my family already knows about the pregnancy, there's really no need in waiting until I'm twelve weeks to tell them we're together."

"Agreed," Reno says against the back of my neck. "Maybe we can talk to them after the game this week? Ma and Gramps too."

"Sounds like a plan," I say.

But you know what they say about the best laid plans...

Chapter 43

Reno

Goober and gator food

"Good to see you, man," Marcus says, smacking me on the back as we bro-hug.

"You too," I say before giving the same attention to Lane.

The Brewers are playing my old team tomorrow, and my two favorite buddies from the Raptors came to Pine Tree Falls a day early so we could catch up. We take seats at a table in the local bar and grill, The Tipsy Bulldog. It's named after the local high school mascot, which seems to be a thing here. There's also Bulldog Hotel, Bulldog Cleaners, and The Big Dawg Diner.

"So what's going on with you?" Lane asks. "You seem smilier than usual." He circles a finger at my face. He's not wrong. I smile like a loon all the time now. I have my dream girl, and in a few months, we'll have the twins.

Leaning forward, I lower my voice. "You remember the woman from the resort, Juliette?"

"The one that busted your balls?" Marcus asks with a way-too-pleased smirk.

"That's the one." I pause for maximum dramatic effect. "She lives here in Pine Tree Falls."

Lane lets out a whoop. "Fuck yes! This is just like one of those romance books."

I can't help but laugh. "You're closer than you could even imagine, buddy. But you can't tell anyone because her brother is... Baylor Ward."

Two mouths drop open across the table from me, and Marcus shakes his head. "Dude, you're playing with fire. Ward's your teammate. He is going to snap your neck in two when he finds out you're banging his sister."

Anger boils up in me, but I do my best to put a lid on it. My friends have no idea of the depth of my feelings for Juliette. "It's a lot more than that. We're in love." I cross my arms over my chest. Maybe I'm pouting, just a little. "And you're acting like I can't take care of myself against Ward."

"Naw, man. You know you're a bad motherfucker, but what's that saying about a brother scorned?" He arches one eyebrow.

"A woman scorned," I correct dryly.

He swishes his hand through the air. "Same concept. I'm happy for you, but dating a teammate's sister is practically taboo."

I pop my chin up an inch. "Well, he'll have to get the fuck over it because I'm going to marry Juliette. In fact..." I reach into my pocket and pull out a ring box. When I pop it open, I'm pleased at their sharp inhales.

"Dayum, boy," Lane crows. "That's gorgeous."

"And it's totally her," I say, looking down at the most feminine ring I could find. When I saw it, I knew it was perfect. An elegant three-carat marquise cut diamond is surrounded by smaller pink diamonds, and the band is etched with a pretty filigree design. I could have gone bigger on the center diamond, but the ones I looked at with gigantic rocks didn't have the soft femininity I was searching for. They wouldn't be right for my dream girl.

"Congrats, man," Marcus says. "I hope you two will be really happy together." Then he mumbles something under his breath that sounds like *if you live long enough.*

I put the ring back in my pocket, and the server comes by to take our orders. We all get sparkling water since we're pretty fastidious about not drinking during the season. I'll have an occasional beer, but certainly not the night before a game. We do decide to split some greasy appetizers though.

"So, you're happy here in this little town?" Lane asks, looking around the small bar, not with snarky derision, just a curiosity about how I'm adjusting from living in a metro area to a rural one.

"Yeah, it's actually pretty perfect. You get the small-town feel, and yet the DFW area is only a short drive away. Best of both worlds."

Marcus leans his elbow on the table and drums his chin with his fingers. "Do they even have a ride share service here?"

A smirk toys with my lips. They're going to love this. "No, but there is a guy named Goober who will give you a ride in his twelve-year old Ford F-150 if you get too drunk to drive home. If you look like you're going to hurl, he'll make you ride in the bed of the truck. He's very particular about his upholstery."

"Goober?" they ask together.

"Yep, he even got a sticker made for the back of his truck that reads Guber with a U." Marcus and Lane fall into each other in a fit of laughter.

"Oh fuck. That's priceless."

"According to local legend, Uber tried to sue him, but they lost because he doesn't charge anything for his service," I add.

"Wait, Goober the Guber driver does it for free?" Lane gasps, and I nod in confirmation.

"Apparently, he was arrested fifteen years ago for drunk driving, and as part of his probation, the judge ordered him to give inebriated people free rides home on the weekends. I guess to show him what it's like to deal with drunks. He enjoyed it so much, he continued even after his probation period was over."

"Shit, this is one of my favorite stories ever," Marcus adds, grabbing a napkin from the dispenser and blotting his eyes.

"Another fun fact, Goober is married to the judge's sister."

My friends stare at me in disbelief for two beats, and then the hilarity starts all over again.

The locker room is filled with the sounds of rustling clothes, tape being torn, and small talk as we get ready for our home game against Denver. I'm sitting on the bench shirtless while I tape my stick.

"What is that on your back?" Baylor asks, and I crane my neck around to try and see.

"I don't see anything."

Baylor plucks something from the center of my spine and holds it up for inspection. "Dude, you have a dick on your back."

"I feel like there's a joke in there somewhere," Gibby comments, "but I can't think of it right now."

I'm fucking panicking, looking at the hot-pink piece of penis confetti on Baylor's finger and trying to come up with a reasonable explanation for why it was there.

I swear on my life, I'm going to send Juliette's friend a fifty-five gallon drum of cock confetti.

"That's, uh, a practical joke some guys from Denver sent me. I think it's called a confetti bomb. I've been finding the shit all over my house since last night." The second part is true anyway. Dick confetti is surprisingly tenacious.

It sounds pretty believable, and Baylor seems to buy the explanation because he laughs. "Just further motivation to kick their asses on the ice tonight."

And kick their asses we do. I'm having a game that will have me featured on multiple highlight reels tomorrow. I even scored a goal in the second period.

I'm feeling and playing like a beast, giving a metaphorical *fuck you* to Roland Priestner, the owner of the Raptors and the man who fired me.

Though I'm glad he did because it brought me to Juliette. Still, it feels good to be having a banner game in front of the man.

With only a minute left in the game, someone slams Baylor into the boards, and when he bounces off, he goes down hard.

And doesn't get up.

My teammate has regained consciousness by the time I get to the medical room. They already have his gear and uniform off, but I'm still fully dressed in mine except for my skates. I tore my laces in my haste to get them off.

"Hey, man," I say, pushing a smile I don't feel onto my lips.

Baylor looks at me blankly for a second before asking, "Are you my daddy?"

My eyes widen in alarm... until I see his little smirk, and I laugh with relief. At least that fall didn't knock his sense of humor away.

"You asshole. You'll do anything for a little attention, won't you?" I tease, nearing his bed on the side where there are the fewest medical personnel. He smiles, but it's replaced by a flinch when someone shines a pen light in his eyes.

We're joking and insulting like guys do when they don't want to admit they're scared. I loop our thumbs and press our palms together, almost like we're shaking hands, but I place my other hand on the outside of his, sandwiching his between mine.

We stay silent like that while the medical team tosses around info about pupils and trauma and neurologists.

"You all right?" I finally ask quietly, and his eyes meet mine, telling me he's not sure. I can tell his pupils are dilated from the blow.

"I'm dizzy," he admits. "Will you make sure Holly and Jules get to the hospital okay? They rode to the game together. Aiden is with Aunt Nedra because he had the sniffles today."

"I've got them," I promise, impressed that he's worried about his family even while he's lying here with an injured brain. I hope I can be half the husband and father he is. I want to tell him that, but this isn't the time for that discussion.

There's a commotion outside the room, and I hear my dream girl's insistent voice.

"I swear, Barney, if you don't let us in, I'm gonna... I'm gonna be really mad at you."

Then comes Holly's unmistakable voice, ramping up the threat from about a ten to a hundred.

"Open the door right now, Barney, or I will rip off your balls and feed them to a snapping turtle."

The door opens without pause, and the two women rush in, flanking Baylor's bed, cooing and petting at him until the doc finally makes them step aside.

"We're taking him to Presbyterian Hospital," he informs them before looking at me. "Mr. Swain, you have time to shower and change while we get him loaded into the ambulance."

I nod, though that's the least of my worries. I wrap a sweaty arm around each woman's shoulders. They don't seem to mind. Everyone's attention is on Baylor, who they're now wheeling out the door. He gives us a thumbs up on his way out.

After the quickest, and admittedly not the most thorough, shower of my life, I'm in my silver SUV with Juliette beside me and Holly sitting quietly in the back, her head tilted against the window. My hand snakes over the console, and I press my bunny ears fingers against Juliette's thigh. Her soft smile of appreciation warms my heart, and then she makes the sign back before grasping my hand.

And I drive. As fast and as safely as I possibly can to the hospital.

Two damn hours after arriving, we're led to a small private room. They said family only, but I planted my ass in there like I belonged and dared the nurse with a glare to try and make me leave. Holly and Juliette asked me to stay, so I'm fucking staying.

"It's a concussion, like we suspected," the neurologist declares. "He took a pretty good knock to the head, but he will make a full recovery."

The occupants of the room breathe a collective sigh of relief. Emmett and Isaac are slumped in chairs, their elbows on their knees, both of them with mirrored looks of worry on their faces. Holly and Jules are tucked beneath my arms as we stand. Xander and Jordie weren't at the game tonight, but Holly has been in constant contact with the younger siblings.

"But..." the doctor continues, sucking our attention to him with a single word. "He has to follow directions and not be stubborn."

Everyone glances at Holly with a *good luck with that* look. But by the hard set of her jaw, our stubborn-as-fuck patient has probably met his match.

The neurologist goes through the concussion protocol and instructs Holly to keep things quiet and dark in their home. And under no circumstances can he do any physical activity other than walking around the apartment.

"I'll take Aiden for a few days," Juliette offers. "He can go to the library with me, and I'll bring him by around nap time when he's quiet and sleepy so he can see his daddy. They can rest together."

Holly nods and reaches for her sister-in-law's hand. I love the bond between these two women, despite the whole weird beaver insemination deal. I still haven't gotten the full story on that.

"They said they're going to keep him overnight, so I'm going to stay here," Holly says, hitching her purse onto her shoulder.

"I'll arrange for someone to bring your car here from the arena so you can take him home tomorrow," I assure her, and she gives me a grateful and exhausted smile.

Without thinking, I link my fingers with Juliette's. It's something I do at least a dozen times a day… just not in front of anyone else. Holly's eyes drop to our joining, and then she looks back and forth between us.

After a long moment, she says, "The doctors said Bubba needs zero stress in his life right now." Her eyes narrow and fix on me. "And if you do stress out my husband with all…this…." She waves a floppy hand toward us. "Just remember three things. I know where all the swamplands in East Texas are. I have a truck to haul *things*. And alligators leave virtually no trace of a body."

Message received: Do not, under any circumstances, tell my teammate about my secret relationship with his sister.

Or I'll end up as gator food.

Chapter 44

Reno

The book fair

I WAVE TO THE guys at the security desk at Shady Pines as I pass and make my way to the Illumination Ward. When I reach his room, I find it empty.

That's not unusual. The staff here encourages the guests to get out of their rooms and socialize. It's one of the biggest differences I've noticed from his last home. When I went to visit him in Denver, he was in his room ninety percent of the time.

I backtrack to the nurse's desk, finding Shirley, one of Gramps's favorites. She's a short Latina woman with an easy smile for everyone.

"Hey, Reno. Looking for Arlo?" she asks as soon as she spots me.

"I am. Is he in the puzzle room?" They have lots of different rooms here, including one with board games, one with a pottery wheel and clay, and yet another with various crafts. But Gramps has recently been drawn to the space filled with jigsaw puzzles. He's been working on a huge one of downtown London for the past couple weeks.

One of the nurses explained to me that keeping their minds busy makes them forget to forget, and I like that philosophy. Even if it doesn't work, it improves their quality of life.

"No, he's in the gathering room for Juliette's book fair," Shirley explains. "You remember where that is?" She points a finger down the hallway to the right.

Book fair?

"Thanks, Shirley. I remember where it is from my tour."

The gathering room is a huge space with tons of windows, making it sunny and cheerful. It's in the main part of Shady Pines, so I head out of the Illumination Ward and round the corner.

The room is buzzing with activity, but I spot her first. Juliette is wearing a black pencil skirt and a red chiffon button-down blouse. Her black heels are chunky and not too high, but they still make her legs look a mile long. And her hair?

Whew! My girl in full-blown librarian mode is a thing of beauty. She's wearing her red Guess glasses and a prim bun on top of her head. Sexy doesn't even begin to describe her look.

I missed seeing her getting ready this morning because I had morning skate, but I'm damn sure seeing her now. I wind my way through the tables piled with books of every genre. It's set up exactly like the old book fairs I remember from elementary school.

People, most of them elderly, are milling about, all with smiles on their faces. My girl is making people happy through books.

I approach but hang back because Juliette is speaking to a tiny woman wearing a pink floral dress and pulling an oxygen tank behind her. She appears to be in her late fifties or early sixties.

"I remember reading these when I was a teenager," the lady says, tapping on a stack of Harlequin Romance novels. "I used to sneak them out of my mother's bedside table and read the good parts. You know which parts I mean, don't you, honey?" The woman cackles and pumps her eyebrows up and down.

Juliette's responding laugh is happy and genuine. "I know exactly which parts you're talking about, Ms. Wharton."

"Hmmm, I think I'll take these five here," Ms. Wharton replies. "For nostalgia's sake."

"Good choices. The one with the cowboy on the cover is fantastic." Juliette gathers the books and looks around, smiling brilliantly when she spots me before motioning to someone behind me. A teen boy jogs up and stops in front of her. "Gary, can you take Ms. Wharton to check out? Her total is five dollars. And get her one of the Fabio posters."

"Yes ma'am," the skinny kid says eagerly, sounding like he'd cut off his foot if Juliette asked him to.

Gary carries the books and leads the woman to a small register set up in the corner. Juliette turns her attention to me, her smile playful. "Mr. Swain, anything I can help you with? Perhaps a nice Harlequin?"

"You can tell me how you got all this set up and why you didn't ask for my help."

She rolls her damn eyes at me. "Because you had to be at the arena this morning. And because I have plenty of help. I've recruited the student council from PTF High School, and they get community service hours for it." Her lips quirk. "They set up the shelves and tables, so I didn't do *any heavy lifting.*"

She emphasizes those last three words, knowing what I was getting at without me even having to say it. God, I want to touch her, pull her against me and kiss that pretty pink mouth. Maybe give that fine ass a spank or two.

Before I lose my damn mind and do just that, a quiet voice beside us says, "Hi, Juliette."

My woman turns and hugs the newcomer with enthusiasm. "Annalise! How are you today?"

"Good. You got any Baby-Sitters Club books?" Annalise seems a little shy and shows the features of a young woman—probably in her twenties—with Down syndrome.

"Of course I do. I always bring some for my favorite customer." Juliette guides the now giggling girl to a table filled with a younger genre of books. I follow along. "I think you were on this one last time, right?" she asks, pointing at one in the middle of the row.

Annalise nods. "I want two."

"Awesome. I hope you enjoy them. I'll see you next time, okay?" Once again, Juliette motions for one of the teenagers, a girl this time, and tells her, "Make sure to get Annalise lots of stickers. She likes to decorate her notebooks."

"Yes, ma'am, Ms. McNamara. Two dollars for the books, right?"

"Yep, thank you, Kris."

They leave, and I brush an inconspicuous hand down Juliette's arm. "How are you able to sell these books for only a dollar? They're brand new."

She shrugs. "Most of them are donated, though I buy some of them. I originally planned to give them away for free, but after talking to the activities director, we decided I should charge a small fee. That way it's more like a real book fair than just another library. Plus, these people like to feel like they're..." She searches for the words. "Real customers out in the real world. They like to know they bought something, and it's theirs. Every day, they get their food brought to them. They get their meds brought to them. Their families buy their clothes. But this is something they can control, a purchase they *choose* to make."

The affection I feel for this woman grows with every single day, and I make a mental note to make a large donation to the library.

Juliette continues. "I use the money to buy the bookmarks, posters, and stickers that we give away." She lowers her voice. "And if we check their account and they don't have money on it, I give them the books anyway."

Of course she does. Before I do something stupid like dip her back over my arm and kiss the ever living hell out of her, I change the subject. "Have you seen Gramps?"

Juliette touches my arm, setting my skin afire. "He's over in the spy and military fiction section. He was trying to decide on which Tom Clancy book to get." She tilts her head. "Over this way."

I spot him. One of his nurses is hovering nearby, giving him some independence while also making sure he doesn't wander out the door. I give her a friendly nod before laying a hand on my grandfather's shoulder. He turns, his face lighting up.

"Reno!"

I love that I'm the one person he always seems to recognize. I know it won't always be that way, but I try not to think about that day. Live in the moment, and all that jazz.

"What are we looking at here?" I ask.

"Trying to remember if I've read this one." He reads the back of *The Hunt for Red October*, his forehead wrinkling in concentration. I can feel his frustration.

"You have," I remind him gently, "But it's classic Clancy, and you might want a copy for your bookshelf."

He looks up at me, and his green eyes seem to clear a bit. "We watched the movie too, remember? You were about ten, and we did a whole Jack Ryan marathon." He laughs. "You 'bout drove your Ma crazy talking like Sean Connery for a month."

"A great day, comrades. We sail into history," I quote in my best impression of the Scottish actor.

Gramps looks over at Juliette. "Terrible, right?"

She tuts and shakes her head. "I see why his mother was annoyed."

I give them fake outrage. "Hey! Why are you two ganging up on me?"

My grandfather laughs like he's having the best time of his life. He tips the top of his head toward Juliette. "I like this one, Reno. You should ask her out."

A grin steals across my face as I meet her eyes. "She's the prettiest woman I've ever seen, so maybe I'll just marry her, Gramps."

He looks back at Juliette. "At least I taught him something. His flirting game is much better than his Sean Connery."

"Agreed," she says with a smirk. "And if he proposes, maybe I'll say yes."

For the next five minutes, Juliette helps my grandfather select two more books from an indie author who also writes international espionage. "Make sure to let me know what you think about these, Arlo. I think you'll really enjoy them."

"I sure will. They sound like they'll be right up my alley."

We walk to the corner, and Juliette goes behind the small counter set up there, digging through a box of rolled up posters. I can't help but stare at her ass in that skirt.

"Ah, here we go." She holds up one of them triumphantly. "It's the movie poster for *The Hunt for Red October.* I thought it might be a good memory to hang on your wall since you watched it with Reno when he was a kid."

Gramps looks pleased as punch with his new treasures, and I walk him back to his room. When he starts nodding off, I urge him to take a nap before heading back to the book fair, determined to help Juliette pack up when she's done.

I watch as she flits around the room like a butterfly, smiling at everyone she meets. She points out the inspirational and religious section to a lady and then directs an old-timer to a stack of Louis L'Amour westerns. I crack up when a woman who has to be at least ninety asks where the reverse harem romance books are located. But Juliette doesn't bat an eye.

She's absolutely in her element. Sidling up to her, I tilt my head down and whisper, "What do I have to do to get you to wear this outfit at home tonight?"

Juliette eyes me up and down appraisingly. "I think a foot rub would do the trick."

I give her a mischievous smile. "Dream girl, I'll rub more than your feet."

Chapter 45

Reno

Modern day Starsky and Hutch

It's been four weeks since Baylor Ward's concussion. His doctors haven't released him to play yet, which sucks for us because we've lost three games in the meantime. However, they have released him to come to tonight's game.

We're playing Boston, and we really need this win. I think it will help to have Baylor sitting on the bench with us. He's a captain and a positive force for the team.

"All right, guys," Coach Al says during his pre-game pep talk. "I need you all to up your game tonight. Shively is back for Boston after his accident." His lip curls. "Just... remember who you are and play a clean game, okay?"

Shively used to play for Dallas but then was traded to Boston. After a car wreck, he's spent the past two years in hospitals and rehabilitation. I guess that's why the coach was reminding us to play clean. Maybe some of the guys had bad blood with Shively?

I mean, I've never cared for the guy. He never misses an opportunity to take a cheap shot on another player.

Baylor makes a snort of derision, and I think I'm right about the bad blood thing. My friend doesn't mind mixing it up if things get chippy on the ice, but he never plays dirty, and he doesn't tolerate anyone who does.

We take the ice. It's a hard-fought battle, and halfway through the second period, we find ourselves up by one point. Coach changes the line, and I collapse onto the bench beside Baylor.

"I think we can win this," I say, breathing heavily as one of the trainers hands me a squirt bottle of water. I spray some into my mouth and swipe the bottom of my face with the back of my hand.

Baylor's eyes are locked on the game, his lip curled up on one side. "God, I wish I was out there. I'd like to teach that motherfucker a lesson."

"Who?" I ask, trying to track his line of vision, but the players are moving too quickly.

"Collin fucking Shively," he sneers. "The goddamn colon hurt my sister—"

I don't even hear the rest of what he says because the pieces suddenly click into place. Collin Shively is Juliette's ex. The one who made her feel stupid. The one who put his hands on her.

The one I'm about to fucking kill.

I'm on the ice in an instant, ignoring the shouts from my coaches and teammates because I'm still supposed to be on the bench. My body is a bullet train, headed straight for Shively as my skates rake hard across the ice.

"Hey, what the fuck?" the prick asks as I barrel into him and take him to the ground.

I haven't felt this kind of anger since I was ten and saw my dad hurting my mom, the night I hit him with a pot. But I don't need a weapon now. I'm a grown-ass man, and I *am* the weapon.

Ripping off his helmet, I pummel his face. Over and over. I feel hands tugging at me, but I'm relentless. All I can think of is my beautiful, kind-hearted Juliette cowering on the floor, holding her dislocated shoulder.

That's what Collin Shively, the abusive coward, deserves too, so I flip him over and twist his arm up behind his back. But before I get the satisfaction of hearing the sound of his shoulder popping out of its socket, I'm suddenly yanked away.

It takes three of my teammates, but I'm being carried kicking and screaming away from the bloody man on the ice. "You fucking twat muffin," I yell, using Juliette's name for him. "I'm not done with you yet, motherfucker."

I'm ejected from the game, but I don't give a single shit about that. My blood is still boiling inside my veins. Coach shoves me in the chest.

"Out of my sight, Swain. I'll deal with you later. Locker room. Now," he barks before turning to Baylor. "Ward, go with him and see if you can't do something with his crazy ass. I've got to deal with..." He waves a frustrated hand toward the rink. "All this shit."

Gibby is locked up with Boston's right winger, and they're throwing punches left and right. The rest of both teams are on the ice, yelling curses and bowing up to one another.

Five minutes later, Baylor and I are alone in the locker room. He pushes me roughly onto one of the wide wooden benches where we usually sit to put on our skates and tape our equipment. The look of fury on his face matches my own, and he levels me with a glare that keeps me seated, despite my urge to go finish the job.

He paces back and forth in front of me about twenty times, hands on hips and eyes averted from mine. I can see the wheels turning in his brain, so I remain silent.

Finally turning toward me, his voice is deceptively low. "Why did you call him a twat muffin?"

I'm confused. Out of everything that just happened, he's worried that I called Shively a...

Wait. Fuck. That's what Juliette calls Collin. And there's no way I could know that unless she told me. And why would she tell me? Baylor is apparently asking himself that same question.

There's no denying it. He knows. So I remain silent.

He walks closer, hovering over me as his fists clench at his sides. I brace myself for the blow, but it doesn't come. Instead, he asks, "Are you fucking my sister?"

I don't like the question. Do I fuck her? Yes. Do I talk dirty to her and tell her I'm going to fuck her until she screams? Also yes. But the way

Baylor says it, like it's some dirty, horrible thing, pisses me right the fuck off.

"I'm in a *relationship* with Juliette," I clarify, my voice hard as stone.

"A relationship?" he yells, the sound reverberating off the dark-blue lockers. Baylor paces away, kicking a hamper and sending dirty towels flying all over the place before whirling back. "Why?"

"Because I love her," I say simply.

He gapes at me incredulously. "How can you love her? You've known each other for about five goddamn minutes."

"I actually met her on vacation early this past summer. I didn't know who she was then."

Baylor's jaw clenches. "So you thought you'd have a little fun and get a sweet piece of—"

He's cut off when I jump to my feet and push him back against the lockers. Not hard enough to reinjure his head because as mad as I am right now, I'm not that much of an asshole.

Placing my forearm against his throat, I snarl. "I suggest you don't finish that sentence, Baylor Ward. Not about the woman I love."

Something passes through his eyes—respect maybe?—before he places his hands on my chest and pushes me back a few steps. It's a shove but not a particularly hard one, merely giving us a little space to breathe.

"Why? Why didn't you tell me, Reno? I thought we were friends." The pain is evident in his voice, and it cuts into me.

"We are friends, but Juliette comes first. She will always come first."

That takes some of the wind out of his sails, and his shoulders deflate. "You could have come to me and talked man to man. It kills me that you snuck around behind my back."

I drag a hand through my wet hair and answer. "She asked me not to. She wanted to wait until after the season so she didn't cause 'discord' on the team." I do little quotes around *discord* and realize my knuckles hurt from all the punches I landed on Shively.

Baylor snorts and waves his arms around. "Yeah, I'd say this is discord all right."

"I'm sorry. Not for falling in love with your sister, but for hiding it from you. I wish I could have been honest, but have you ever tried to tell your sister no when she turns those eyes on you?"

He lets out a short laugh. "I know what you mean. She looks like that goddamn big-eyed cat in *Shrek*." Baylor puts his hands in front of his chest like little paws and widens his eyes. Seeing his big ass like that makes me laugh, and for the first time since this debacle started, I think we might be okay.

Then something dawns in his eyes, and he looks stricken. "There's... there's no sperm donor is there? You knocked up my sister."

Well, fuck. We're back to square one.

Holding up my hands placatingly, I say, "Give me a minute." Then I begin undressing.

"This is absolutely not helping your case, Swain," he mutters.

I toss my jersey aside and work on removing my black shoulder pads. "I've never had a tattoo before because I'd never found anything worth having on my body permanently." When I stand bare-chested in front of Baylor, I point at the ink over my heart. "I got this done the day after Juliette left me standing in the Miami airport. I knew I loved her already, but she was scared."

Baylor tilts his head to the side. "I've always wondered what the fuck that was on your chest. It looks like a cloud with ears. I figured you'd lost a bet or something."

"It is a cloud. It's the first cloud Juliette and I ever analyzed together," I explain. "We call him Sexy Bunny."

He barks out a laugh. "That's the most ridiculous thing I've ever heard in my life. Why didn't you just get her name tattooed on you?"

My hand rubs over the ink. "I thought about it, but this seemed more significant because it was something we shared together." I look down at the floor before lifting my gaze. "Watching her watch the clouds, I knew she was special. I think I started falling for her that very first day."

I neglect to mention that I was already enamored during the whole jacking off on the back porch thing because I'm pretty sure that would *not* make things better.

Baylor nods slowly, still with the hint of a smile on his face. "Okay, man. I guess that's... cool."

I lift one finger. "But wait, there's more."

"Swear to god, if you take off your pants to show me a dandelion tattoo on your dick or some such shit because you and Jules saw one in a meadow, I'm going to punch your lights out," he warns.

"No more tats," I promise, striding to my locker and opening it. I dig into the side pocket of my bag with my good hand until I find what I'm looking for. Turning back, I place the ring box into Baylor's hands.

He hesitates with his eyes on mine before finally dragging them to his hand and opening the box. He stares at the ring for a long while and then mumbles something under his breath that sounds like, "It's perfect for her." Handing it back to me, he smirks. "While I appreciate the offer, Swain, I won't marry any man who doesn't get down on one knee."

My future brother-in-law's got jokes.

I place the ring carefully back into its hiding place, and when I turn around, Baylor is digging through the first aid cabinet on the wall. "Sit down," he says gruffly, and I do. "Hand." I put out my hand.

He tears open an alcohol pad and begins dabbing at the cuts on my knuckles. It hurts like a motherfucker, but I don't flinch. We're both silent until Baylor breaks it.

"I never liked Collin Shively, not as a teammate and not as a man. I was happy when he got traded to Boston." He tosses the blood-stained pad into the trash bin and opens another. "And I certainly didn't like him as a partner for my sister. As professional athletes, we all have a bit of cockiness, but Shively's went beyond that. He had a *me first* attitude instead of thinking *team first.* He was the same with their relationship."

Baylor continues swiping at the cuts on my fingers while I listen. "Juliette has the kindest heart of anyone I know. She would give anyone the shirt off her back. When we were little, there was this kid at school who everyone knew came from a poor family. Skinny little boy who didn't look like he got proper meals regularly. He didn't smell great, and a lot of kids avoided him, but Juliette would sit by him at lunch every day and give him half her sandwich and chips. That's just how she is. She's a giver."

I finally speak. "I know. That's one of the things I love about her." Baylor's eyes jerk up to mine, and I clarify. "Not because I want anything from her but because she makes me feel like taking care of her. Letting her be the recipient for a change."

He nods and returns to his task. "I told our fathers what she was doing, and they started making two sandwiches and putting two bags of chips in her lunch every day. I don't think they ever said anything to her about it; they just did it."

"They're good men," I comment, and one corner of his lips quirks up.

"They are. Anyway, when she called me the day that asshole put his hands on her, I literally had to force myself to remember that my sister needed me more than I needed to teach Shively a lesson. I put her first like she always did for everyone else and stayed with her at the hospital. I guess she told you the prick took off when he found out I was on my way?"

"Yeah, she told me."

Baylor opens a small tube of antibacterial ointment and begins dabbing it onto my wounds with a square of gauze. "While we were in the emergency room, we heard a commotion out in the hallway. My wife, being the nosy ass she is, peeked out the door to see what was going on." His eyes leave his task for a moment, looking into mine. "It was Shively. The fucking coward had left Juli's house and went straight for the airport to get away from the ass kicking he knew was coming to him. Other drivers say he was driving erratically and way too fast."

My mouth falls open when it hits me. "That was when he had his car accident? The one that put him down for two years?"

He nods slowly. "It was like God had taken care of the punishment for me. I know that's not how it works, but that's how I viewed it." Baylor throws away the gauze and opens a bunch of bandages. "I never went after him, though I thought about it every day. I guess I was indirectly responsible for his accident because he was running from me when it happened, so that gives me a little comfort."

Baylor begins covering my cuts with bandages as he speaks. "That's the reason I'm so protective over my sister. It's the reason I don't like her dating hockey players." His jaw hardens. "I had bad vibes from Shively, but Jules was a grown-ass woman, so I kept my mouth shut." A tear slides down his brown cheek and he angrily swipes it away with his shoulder.

"You blame yourself." It's not a question but a statement of understanding.

His nostrils flare as he adds the last bandage to my pinky finger. "It was my fault she got hurt. Yes, she's an adult and can make her own decisions, but Juliette can be naive. That's not a bad thing, but she needs a man who sees that and doesn't take advantage of her sweetness."

I swallow hard. "I want to be that someone for her. I would never, ever hurt her in any way. I literally couldn't." Jerking my chin, I gesture for Baylor to sit beside me. After he disposes of all the packages, he flops down beside me on the bench, both of us facing a line of lockers on the wall.

My chest hurts, but he opened up to me, and I know I need to do the same. "My father was an asshole. He was like Shively. When I was ten, I caught him hurting Ma, so I hit him upside the head with a metal pot."

Baylor chortles. "Ballsy kid."

Then I take him through the rest of the story, us leaving, Ma struggling, and me calling a grandfather I'd never met for help.

"Gramps recognized that I had a lot of pent-up anger from the things I'd seen, so he introduced me to hockey. Most of the kids had been playing since they were toddlers, so I was kinda behind initially, but I caught on quickly. Worked my ass off. By the time I was thirteen, I was stronger and more skilled than anyone else on the team."

"You're not too terrible now either," Baylor teases and I laugh before dropping my head to my hands, my elbows digging into the pads covering my thighs.

"What if I'm a shitty dad?" My breaths heave in and out of my lungs as I spill my most vulnerable fear. "I know I'd never hurt my wife or child, but what if I suck at being a father? Mine was never around for me, so how the fuck do I know what to do, Baylor?"

He mirrors my position, elbows on legs. "You just told me your grandfather took you in, no questions asked. He recognized that you needed an outlet and got you involved in the game that would become your career. He was there for you from the time you were ten, and he's still proud of you today." He pats me hard on the shoulder. "So think about it, Swain. Do you really think you don't know what a real father looks like? Because I think you do."

His words are like a shot to my heart, and I drop my head down and let go. He's right. He's so fucking right. I watch the droplets of tears fall, forming little amoeba-like splatters on the dark-blue floor for a long time, and Baylor's hand is a force of strength against my shoulder. Finally, I slide my hands down the back of my neck and lift my head. I feel refreshed somehow.

"I can do this," I say to no one in particular before repeating it. "I can do this."

"I know you can," Baylor says quietly. "Just a warning though. The feelings of parental inadequacy never go away. For everyone, I'm sure, but especially for pro athletes. We have a job that demands a lot of time, and sometimes you're going to have to miss shit. You're going to feel bad if you get home late, and you don't get to say goodnight to your kid because they're already in bed. You'll have to schedule birthday parties around practices and games. It takes effort but it's worth it."

"We're having twins," I blurt out.

Baylor closes his eyes and tilts his face to the ceiling, blowing out a long breath. "Wow, okay."

"Yeah, it's going to be a lot, but we're both excited."

He nods and nudges my knee with his. "You can do it. The best advice I can give is to make sure your wife always feels supported, no matter what. During the pregnancy and when the babies get here."

"I will. I've been trying, but I think I'm going about it wrong."

"What do you mean?" Baylor asks suspiciously.

My lips twist wryly to the side. "I've been trying to be as prepared as possible before the twins get here. I know with my schedule a lot of it's going to fall on Juliette, so I just want to make everything as easy as possible for her. I want her to have everything she needs and not have to worry about buying anything. I'm afraid she'll refuse to ask me if she needs something, so I've been... shopping." *And that's an understatement.*

I can hear the amusement in Baylor's voice. "How much did you spend?"

"Not including the two new vehicles I bought, somewhere around twenty-two thousand dollars."

My future brother-in-law collapses against the bench in laughter. "Goddamn, man. You're worse than I was when Holly was pregnant with Aiden."

I groan. "Tell me something stupid you bought so I don't feel like such an idiot."

Baylor sits up, the remnants of a chuckle still on his lips. "Let's see. I bought a five-thousand dollar stroller that the kid hated to sit in. He preferred traveling in one of those body carrier things so he could be close to us."

My forehead furrows. "I haven't bought one of those yet. Can you send me the link?"

He laughs and bumps me with his shoulder. "Sure thing. Just remember that babies don't need much when they're little. Just diapers, food, and love."

"I purchased enough diapers to get the twins through age twelve," I mutter, feeling a little silly.

"Hopefully, you'll have them potty-trained by then," he remarks dryly. "I'm sure Juliette has some of the same fears as you since we grew up without a mom. How much did she tell you about that?"

"She told me Delphine left for a long time when you were little, and your fathers shared custody. Then your mother came back and had the younger kids with Emmett." I remember Juliette changing the subject then. "The story kind of ended there."

Baylor's lips tighten into a thin line. "But it didn't. Our *mother*," he kind of spits the title, "left again when Jordie was a baby."

I shake my head in disgust. "How can anyone leave their baby?"

Baylor lifts his voice a couple octaves into what I assume approximates his birth mother's. "Oh you know, places to go, people to see." He snorts, and his voice returns to normal. "Jordie was an infant and didn't know the difference, but Xander cried a lot over her, especially when she'd send little presents from wherever she was. Like a constant reminder that his mom wasn't there."

My stomach aches for them. "I'm sorry, man. I know that had to be hard."

"I was fine, but it pissed me off for the other kids."

I wasn't sure about him being fine if the tight clench of his jaw told the story. "Did she ever come back?"

Baylor shakes his head. "She called one day and said she was coming home, for good this time, but Jules and I didn't believe her. We talked about it and then sat our fathers down and told them we didn't want her to come back. In fact, we didn't want anything from her because feeling abandoned every time she caught a whim was worse than not having a mother at all. We didn't want postcards or birthday gifts because each one represented the fact that she'd rather be somewhere else than with us."

"What did they say?"

"They said they would handle it. Dad filed for divorce immediately because, while I think he'll always love Delphine in some way, he loved his kids more. The presents and cards stopped, and we never heard from her again. I don't know if she actually stopped sending them or if our fathers just returned to sender."

"I'm glad they listened to you and supported you."

He nods. "Me too. The point of all that was to remind you Juliette didn't grow up with a mother in her life. Do you think that means she doesn't know how to be a mom?" His eyes are piercing, and I meet his gaze.

"She's going to be an amazing mother," I say quietly. "Point taken. Our past doesn't have to determine our future."

"Couldn't have said it better myself." He stands and pulls me to my feet, keeping my hand in his like we're sharing a handshake. "We covered a fucking lot there. We good?"

"Except for one more thing," I say, and Baylor looks at me curiously. "Will you be my best man at the wedding?"

A myriad of emotions pass over his face, finally landing on a happy smile. "Fuck yeah, I will. Bring it in, bro."

He pulls me in, and we hug. Until the door to the locker room bursts open. Baylor and I turn to see Holly and Juliette rocket into the room like they're executing a raid. Holly jumps into a defensive stance with karate hands and yells, "Hi-yahhhh!"

Juliette enters with a can of sparkly pepper spray held out in front of her. "Break it up," she barks in an authoritative tone that leaves no room for disagreement. "Right n—"

They both freeze when they see Baylor and I standing shoulder to shoulder. Their heads turn slowly toward each other, back to us, and then back to each other.

"There's no blood," Holly says from the side of her mouth.

"And no one is throwing hands," Juliette returns in the same manner. She lowers the pepper spray to her side and addresses us. "You're not fighting."

Baylor clears his throat, obviously attempting to swallow his amusement at these two nuts who came to save us from killing each other. "No, we used our big boy words and talked it out."

Holly drops her karate hands, still appearing skeptical as she focuses on me. "Does he know *everything?*" she asks pointedly.

I loop an arm over Baylor's shoulders. "He knows I'm madly in love with his sister and that I'm the father of her babies."

"Oh." Holly looks to Juliette for direction, but my girl simply shrugs. "Well, carry on then."

The girls scurry out, and I can hear Holly asking, "Babies? Plural?"

Baylor looks over at me, his tone dry. "Are you *sure* you want to be a part of this family?"

I laugh. "With those two playing Starsky and Hutch? I've never been more sure of anything in my life."

CHAPTER 46

Juliette

Dream home for dream girl

"ARE YOU SURE YOU don't want to have a big extravagant wedding, babe? We can always do it after the babies come."

Reno is driving my 1967 VW bus, Betty, down a country road. I have no idea where we're going because it's apparently a surprise.

Smiling over at him, I turn my voice into a tease. "Are you trying to get out of marrying me tomorrow, Mr. Swain?"

He rolls his eyes. "Psssht, you know I'm not. I just don't want you to regret it."

"For the millionth time, I don't need ice sculptures and shoes that cost more than Betty to get married. I just need a groom. A *willing* one."

"I'm more than willing, dream girl. I wanted to make sure I'm not rushing you, but I'll shut up about it now." He slows to take a curve and protectively crosses my body with his thick forearm—even though I'm wearing a seat belt—before dropping his hand to my belly.

It's really sticking out there now. I'm almost four months along, and I've had to start wearing maternity clothes to contain my baby bump. Reno can't keep his hands off it. Or off *me*. I'd worried the changes in my body would make him see me differently, but he's as voracious as always.

"It was nice to see the Pineapple Island crew at lunch today," I say. "Thank you for inviting them to surprise me." Fourteen of our vacation friends arrived today to witness our nuptials, including Kat and her husband, Jevaun.

Reno slides his hand up and strokes the side of my face. "I thought it would be nice since they were like our own personal cheerleaders when we were there."

Strong oak trees line the packed dirt road, and sunlight dapples through them, forming patterns on the dusty surface. It's an unseasonably warm day in early December, and tomorrow is going to be just as beautiful.

A perfect day for a wedding.

Reno proposed at a Brewers' home hockey game... after he served his two game suspension for beating the crap out of my ex.

The twat muffin had threatened to press charges, but Reno's agent, Carly, put a stop to that right quick. She told him if he insisted on pressing assault charges, then she'd be happy to inform the world that Collin Shively enjoyed long walks on the beach and domestic violence.

He quickly declined that generous offer and shut the fuck up.

Carly is scary as hell, and I'm glad she's on our side.

Reno turns the vehicle onto a concrete driveway that swoops up toward a house on a grassy hill. It's a beautiful log structure that's too large to call a cabin, with a wraparound porch that makes me want to drink lemonade and listen to windchimes. A huge stone fireplace rises to the sky on the right side.

"Reno, what is this?"

He drives slowly so I can take it all in. "It's our new home, if you want it."

"For real?" I squeal. I'm already halfway in love with it.

"For real. It sits on fifteen acres, about half of it wooded, so the kids will have plenty of room to play."

He stops the van in front of the house, turns it off, and comes around to help me out. "Let's go inside and look around."

The home is laid out in an open floor plan. We enter into a spacious living room that stretches all the way to the right wall with a kitchen straight ahead. On the left side, there's a formal dining room and a hallway leading to the back.

Reno taps the hardwood floor with the toe of his loafer. The wood is a gorgeous honey color that's rich and warm.

"This is quarter sawn oak flooring that's newly installed. There's porcelain tile in the bathrooms. I've talked to a contractor, and he said his crew can make any changes like cabinets or countertops within a month if there's anything you don't like."

I wander into the living room, my eyes falling on the gray stone fireplace. I can picture our little family sitting on the hearth for Christmas photos beside a ten-foot tree decorated with strands of popcorn and homemade ornaments.

By the time we finish touring the four bedrooms upstairs, I know it's destined to be our home.

"What's down that hallway?" I ask when we come back down the stairs.

Reno leads me through the dining room and down the hall. "Ah, the pièce de résistance," he says in a French accent that's almost as bad as his Scottish one.

He opens the large mahogany paneled door to reveal... a library.

"Wow," I breathe, taking in the natural light coming through the transom windows at the back. The other walls are lined with floor to ceiling bookshelves. There's even one of those rolling ladders that makes my librarian heart go pitter patter. I skip over and step up onto it.

"Babe, be careful," Reno frets, behind me in an instant with his hands on my waist.

"I'm only on the first step." I wiggle my butt. "Give me a ride."

"I'll give you a ride all right," he mutters, but he grabs the sides of the ladder and runs the length of the room with me giggling between his arms.

When we get to the end, I turn around to face him, cupping his jaw with my hands. We're eye to eye with me standing on the rung. "I love this house almost as much as I love you."

"I'll make an offer next week." He kisses me softly before sinking to his knees. "And since the house is almost technically ours..."

He lifts my dress and whispers to my belly. "Cover your ears, little ones. Mommy and Daddy are about to christen our new house."

"Reno, I'm not sure we should—ohhh." I don't finish my sentence because he already has my panties pulled to the side, and his tongue is going to town on my clit.

Looking up at me, he grins wickedly. "I want my bride's taste on my tongue when I go to sleep the night before I wife her up."

I groan as he laps me slowly. "Only if you promise to fuck me over that desk. I want to walk down the aisle with my husband's cum inside me."

"Mmm, that's a promise I'm happy to keep."

Thirty minutes later, we both have satisfied smiles on our faces when we go outside to look at the back yard. I look to the right and gasp when I see the fenced-in enclosure about twenty yards away.

My feet are already moving, and I hear Reno chuckle as he follows.

Unlatching the gate, he swings it open and we walk through. Two pygmy goats run up to greet us. One of them is small and quite young, though not a baby. The other is a little bigger.

"Oh my god," I squeal excitedly, bending to pet their heads. "What are their names?"

Reno pats the smaller one's side. "This pretty girl is Jean, and the bigger one is Billy."

Jean lets out an adorable bleating noise and prances in a circle. A pink tulle skirt encircles her waist. I laugh and ask, "Why is she wearing a tutu?"

My future hubby grins like the cat that ate the canary. "You know how we don't have a flower girl for the wedding?" I nod, confused, and Reno sweeps a hand toward the female goat. "Meet Jean, our flower goat."

I cover my mouth and squeal in delight. "That's the cutest thing I've ever heard."

"Baylor and I rigged up a small container with a fan in it that Jean can wear on her back. It will blow the rose petals as she walks down the aisle."

"That's adorable. And what is Billy wearing to the wedding?"

Reno's expression flattens. "Billy is not allowed at the nuptials because of his attitude and disrespect."

He looks so serious I have to work hard not to laugh. "Okay, if you say so."

"Anyway, I wanted you to see Jean's skirt, but I need to get it off her so it doesn't get dirty before tomorrow." He bends and begins to try and get the tutu off the little goat, but she's not having it. She wiggles and turns as Reno attempts to gently wrestle the poofy garment from her body.

It's hilarious to watch, but also incredibly endearing because in my mind, I'm picturing my husband trying to wrangle a wiggly toddler out of their clothing for bathtime. He's going to be such a good daddy.

Hmmm, Daddy Reno. I might have to call him that later tonight. It always gets him going.

Suddenly, he yelps when Billy bites him right on the ass and then takes off across the enclosure, a grin on his goaty little face.

"Billy! Stop biting my ass. I still have a bruise from yesterday when I was trying to put your bow tie on." The goat merely bleats happily. I don't speak goat, but it sounds a lot like a taunt. Reno finally extricates the tutu from Jean and stands, shaking the garment at her brother. "And that, mister, is why I've rescinded your invitation to the wedding."

Yeah, these two rambunctious goats are certainly giving off major twin energy.

"Good use of your dad voice," I tell him, covering my mouth to hide my smile.

"Thanks. I'll have a talk with him."

My big, burly man strides across the grass and squats in front of Billy. He speaks to him for a minute and then kisses his head. My heart flutters with love for this man who buys me ass-biting goats and finds the perfect house just because he loves me.

As we walk around the house to the driveway, Reno tucks me beneath his big arm and holds me close to his side.

"Are you happy, dream girl?"

"I'm ecstatic."

He chuckles knowingly. "Because of the goats or the library?"

"Neither, though both are great bonuses. I'm happy because..." I stop and turn to face him, kissing him softly on the lips. "Tomorrow I'm marrying my dream man."

Epilogue
Juliette - Wedding Day!

"YOU'RE REMARKABLY CALM," HOLLY says, bending to buckle my shoes.

"I've never been more sure of anything in my life," I say. "

"The dress fits you perfectly," Evie says, adjusting one of the off-the-shoulder sleeves. "I knew this would be the one."

"And yet you sent twelve Bouvier dresses for me to try on," I say, tossing her a wry wink.

She shrugs unapologetically. "My bestie was planning a wedding in one month, and my family owns a fashion company. What did you expect?"

"I love it," Jordie adds. "Your baby bump is barely noticeable." She pats my belly beneath the empire waistline.

"You three look gorgeous," I tell them. "Thank you for the bridesmaid dresses too, Evie." My friend had also provided three floor-length dresses in a gorgeous crimson color for her, Holly, and Jordie.

Holly puts her hands on her back and stretches. She's due in less than a month, and her pregnant belly protrudes adorably. "I'm just glad you had a tent in a matching color."

"Oh hush," Evie admonishes. "You're glowing."

"I'm sweating," Holly retorts. "And I have to pee again."

Jordie raises her hand. "Me too."

"We should all go before the ceremony," Evie suggests.

I wave my hand. "You three go. I already went before I put my dress on."

As soon as they depart, I look at myself in the oval standing mirror. Despite what Jordie said, my belly is quite obvious, but I've never felt more beautiful. The sleek material of this creamy gown is pure luxury. I don't even want to know how much it cost.

My phone chimes, and I pick it up from the side table to see a message from Reno.

Reno: How is my wife feeling?

I grin and type back.

Juliette: I'm not your wife yet. You haven't said "I do."

Reno: I do, I do, I do. Now, how is my wife feeling?

Juliette: Excited to husband you up.

Reno: That doesn't have quite the same ring to it, but I'll let it slide. I love you.

Juliette: I love you too.

A knock interrupts us, and I go to the door of the bridal suite in the pretty venue that luckily had an opening for today. I open it to find Elizabeth, Reno's mom.

"Hi, sweetheart. I hope I'm not disturbing you, but I brought you a little snack." She holds out a plate of fruit.

"Heck yes," I cheer, letting her inside. "Besides your son, you're my favorite person right now."

Elizabeth laughs and hands me a large linen napkin, which I tuck into the top of my dress like a bib. "Well, I had to feed my daughter-in-law and my precious grandbabies."

We take a seat on the pretty pink settee, and I dig in. "Thank you for this," I say before spearing a bite of juicy pineapple on the fork and smiling internally at the fruit. *Pineapple Island... where it all began.*

Elizabeth and I chat while I eat, and when I lean back into the small sofa, my future mother-in-law shifts and pulls something from the pocket of her green velvet dress. "I wanted to talk to you, but here. You might need these."

I take the small packet of tissues, already feeling the tears welling up. "I have waterproof mascara, so let me have it," I tell her, and she laughs softly.

"I just wanted to welcome you to our family, Juliette, and let you know how happy I am to be a part of yours." Then she takes my hand. "I've always worried about Reno. I know he's shared some of his childhood with you, so you know what I'm talking about."

Nodding, I say, "I understand."

Elizabeth averts her eyes and blinks at the wall. "I was worried I'd messed him up by not getting out sooner than I did, but I felt so... trapped."

I squeeze her hand. "Oh Elizabeth, you were doing the best you could, and Reno turned out to be a wonderful man, and that's all because of you and his grandparents."

She plucks one of the tissues from the packet and catches a tear of her own before it falls. "I'm proud of my son and everything he's accomplished." Her green eyes meet mine, so much like her son's. "But I've never been more proud of him than when he asked you to marry him."

Oh hell. That does it.

A sob escapes, and I blot at my eyes with the tissue, taking a moment to fan my face until I can speak without turning into a complete basket case. Because what better words could a bride ask for from her groom's mother?

"That means more to me than you'll ever know," I say, my voice raspy.

"And if you'd like to, I'd love it if you called me Ma." She quickly adds, "But don't feel obligated."

Dabbing away more tears, I nod. "I would love that... Ma." We share a long moment of silence, just two women who are now bonded together by our love for the same man. Placing my hand over my belly, I say, "And thank you for being so understanding about the unexpected pregnancy. I know it's—"

Elizabeth cuts me off. "It's perfect," she fills in, "because they will be arriving to two parents who love them. And an entire family of people who adore them."

"That's the truth. I'm so lucky to have all of you and a husband who is so supportive."

She sighs and rolls her eyes to the ceiling. "I'm just happy Reno turned out relatively normal. At least I didn't completely fuck up the whole parenting thing."

Now I add a side of snort-laughing to my tears because *Elizabeth Swain just said fuck.* I can't wait to tell Reno.

"You did a great job, though he does have a bit of a shopping obsession for baby things. I put my foot down last week and threatened to take his phone away, and he seems to have gotten better. Not as many packages have arrived this week."

She lifts her dark eyebrows. "Or... he's having them shipped to another address."

"He didn't!" I gasp, and Elizabeth grins.

"A box arrived at my house this morning with two baby bottles shaped like beer bottles."

I burst into laughter. "Okay, that's actually kind of funny. But keep me updated if he gets too crazy."

"I will. We Swain women have to stick together." Elizabeth pulls me into a hug and pats my back. "He's yours now, Juliette, and I don't accept returns."

That makes me smile. "Good because I plan to keep him forever."

Elizabeth stays with me and helps me fit the ivory veil beneath my hair. Reno likes when I wear a bun, but I wanted something a little fancier today, so I had the hairdresser fashion a curly updo that shows off my shoulders in this dress.

I'm so touched that Elizabeth asked me to call her Ma. I haven't called anyone by any kind of maternal moniker in ages, and... it feels nice. Like my new mother-in-law could be the mother I never had.

Evie pokes her head in the door. "Hey, someone wanted to say hi," she tells me, stepping back to let my author friend, AK Landow into the room.

"Oh my god," I squeal, rushing over to give her a hug. She looks stunning in a royal-blue dress and stilettos I'm instantly jealous of. "I'm so glad you could make it. Come meet my mother-in-law."

I introduce the two women, and AK hands me a beautifully decorated pink box with a white bow. "I wanted to give this to you personally."

"Awww, you're so sweet. Thank you." I unwrap it and open the box, pulling out a single item as my eyes go wide. "Is this a..."

"A bridal butt plug," my insane friend says proudly. "Isn't it pretty?"

"I'm just going to give you two a few minutes alone," Elizabeth, *my freaking almost-mother-in-law,* says, scurrying from the room with a bright red face.

"Oh my gawd!" I hiss, poking AK in the chest with the offending device. "I can't believe you gave this to me in front of her."

"Pffft, she's a grown-ass woman. She knows you and her son are going to get freaky on your honeymoon."

I can't help but laugh, but another knock sounds at the door, before I can reply. I find Bubba on the other side. "Hey, sis. You look beautiful." He kisses my cheek, and I stroke a hand down his tie.

"You look pretty handsome yourself, Bubs. You're not coming to tell me my groom escaped, are you?"

He laughs. "I don't think a team of wild horses could drag that man away. No, AK's car is blocking one of the caterers." He looks to my friend. "I was wondering if I could borrow your key so I can move it."

"Sure," she says, her face registering confusion as she digs into her clutch and produces a car key.

"Thanks," my brother says, taking the key. "I'll bring it back in a few minutes." He glances at the item in my hand and chokes on his own spit before dashing from the room, muttering something under his breath.

Great. Now my brother and my mother-in-law have seen my new sex toy. Family dinners should be fun from now on.

I run my fingers over the surface of the plug. It looks like it's covered with lace, but it's smooth to the touch. I smile at AK. "Thank you, crazy lady. It really is pretty."

"Use it in good health, babe."

The ceremony was absolutely beautiful. It was put together in a rush because I wanted to get married before my stomach got too big, but my entire family had come together to help. And Reno had insisted on being in charge of the flowers. The entire room had been filled with blooms of every color. It was more than I could have hoped for.

The cake has been cut, I've danced with both my dads, and the bouquet and garter have been thrown. Now I'm in Reno's arms on the dance floor.

"Hi, husband," I say, grinning up at him.

He returns my smile and presses a soft kiss to my lips. "Hi, wife."

We've said those words every chance we could get since we arrived in the reception room. Yeah, we're kind of sickening, and I give zero fucks about it. I'm in blissful love with Reno Swain.

And now I'm *Mrs. Swain.*

"Today was perfect," I tell him, laying my cheek against his chest as he holds me tighter.

"Mmhmm," he hums, his face pressed into my hair. "You've made my life complete."

"You're really living up to your nickname, Reno Swoon," I tell him.

"I thought I was Sir Forearms," he teases.

"Well, maybe Sir Swoony Forearms would like to take his wife to get another drink."

He leads me to a chair and orders me to sit while he heads to the bar, returning a couple minutes later with a sparkling water for me and a glass of champagne for himself. "Are you sure you don't mind me drinking this in front of you?"

I pat his ass, which looks amazing in his black suit pants. "Of course not. You're not driving since we're taking a Guber to the bed and breakfast."

Reno groans and sinks into the chair beside me. "I still can't believe I let you talk me into taking my bride to our honeymoon suite in a truck driven by a guy named Goober."

"It's all part of the Pine Tree Falls experience," I tell him airily. I glance over to the bar where Goober is sipping on a bottle of water. He salutes me with a tip of his chauffeur's hat. *When the hell did he start wearing that?*

Reno swivels my chair to the side and pulls my feet into his lap before removing my shoes. I wiggle my toes in relief. The heels aren't extremely high, but it feels good to get them off. My new hubby rubs my feet while we sip and watch our guests.

"Your cousin Keri and her husband are looking pretty cozy over there with Wendy."

I shift my eyes to the corner and see the three of them leaning close across a table. "Maybe they're looking to spice things up a bit. By the way, I've been meaning to ask you something."

"No, I'm not sharing you," he says firmly.

Laughing, I shake my head. "That's not it. You know you said we would take an extended honeymoon once the kids are big enough?"

We plan to stay at the local bed and breakfast tonight, and then we're taking a short honeymoon trip to the hill country in south Texas, since we're still in hockey season.

"Yeah," he says, his tone wary.

"I was thinking I'd like to go back to Pineapple Island."

Reno's smile is sweet, his eyes soft. "Back to cottage four where we first fell in love?"

I nod. "Exactly."

"I'll make it happen once we feel comfortable leaving them. We certainly won't be lacking for babysitters." He chuckles. "We're going to have the luckiest little babies in the world."

AK Landow approaches and bends to give us each a hug. "I'm going to get out of here, but I just wanted to stop and tell you both congratulations. I have a pickleball tournament tomorrow, so I'm driving to Houston tonight."

I grasp her hand and squeeze it. "Okay, be safe, and thank you for the gift."

She winks one pretty blue eye. "Your hubby will be the one thanking me later."

When she leaves, Reno gives me a questioning look. "What was the gift?"

I bob my eyebrows up and down. "A bridal butt plug. Which she gave me in front of your mother."

He snorts. "Bet Ma turned all shades of red."

A giggle escapes me. "She did and then high-tailed it out of the room like her butt was on fire." I nudge him with my toe. "Also, your mom said fuck earlier. I almost died trying not to laugh."

My hottie husband leans forward and presses a kiss to my lips, which quickly turns more heated than is appropriate in front of half the town. But after a minute, we're interrupted by a throat clearing.

We break apart and look up to see AK standing in front of us, her dress dotted with... *Are those dicks? Yes, definitely dicks.*

She aims two fingers at her eyes and then jabs her index finger at my husband. "It's on, Reno Swain. Watch your back because it is *on*." Then she storms out, dripping tiny metallic penises in her wake.

I turn my head slowly toward my husband, who is grinning without an ounce of concern. "What was that all about? And was that penis confetti all over her?"

His chuckle is equal parts dark and amused. "Yep. When Bubba borrowed her keys, we dumped five trash bags of cock confetti into her car."

I can't help but laugh. "Remind me not to ever piss you off."

He wraps an arm around me and scoops me onto his lap sideways. "I can assure you, if you do, your punishment will be a lot more enjoyable, wife."

"Maybe you can show me tonight, husband," I purr.

"I hope you packed that pretty lingerie set Holly bought for you."

Stroking my hand down his face, I smile. "I did. And I packed something else too."

"Fifty pairs of underwear for a three-day trip?" He's such a smartass.

I lean forward and whisper into his ear, slowly so he doesn't miss a word. "An entire box of Altoids."

Before I know what's happening, I'm tossed over my husband's shoulder, and he's marching us toward the exit.

"Goober!" he barks. "Bring the truck around."

Everyone cheers, and I wave from my awkward upside down position. But I have the biggest smile on my face because this is better than any ending I could have written.

Today is the first day of our happily ever after.

***

I hope you enjoyed Reno and Juliette's story! For a look into their future, you can check out the Bonus Epilogue from Juliette's younger sister, Jordie.

Do you want a glimpse of Reno with his and Juliette's twin toddlers?

Would you like to know how the first ever draft for the new Women's National Football League turns out?

Are you wondering if Billy the goat still likes to bite Reno on his fine ass?

You'll get it all in this bonus epilogue! Just type this into your browser: https://dl.bookfunnel.com/qq02g8vmgk

***

Also, Juliette's bestie, Evie Bouvier has her own book, Love Without Control. It's Book Four in the Bouvier Family Saga. Book One is Love Without Numbers, featuring Gianna and Zaddy Auburn, so that's a good place to start. But be prepared to binge... you will fall in love with this family!

***

If you enjoyed the antics of AK Landow in this book, you're in luck! She's actually a real person. In fact, she's my best author friend in the world, and you should totally check out her books. Some of the texts and scenes with her are based on real-life events—yes, we really are that crazy. AK (The Queen of Raunch-Com) is the funniest person I know, and if you liked this book, you will love hers too.

Also by Jade

Bouvier Family Saga

Love Without Numbers Auburn and Gianna
Love Without Influence Monty and Kassie
Love Without Demands Cruz and Lehra
Love Without Control Evie and Damiano (Series Complete!)

The Fierce Protectors Series

Features six super-hot, possessive, growly former Navy SEALs who live to love and protect their women. They're all available on Amazon.

Dauntless Protector- Grumpy/Sunshine, Nanny Romance
Devoted Protector – Love After Loss
Deadly Protector – Second Chance Romance
Disgruntled Protector – Enemies to Lovers, Fake Marriage
Determined Protector – Single Parents
Damaged Protector – Age-Gap Forbidden Romance

You can also check out **Young Protector** – Deadly Protector Prequel Novella

Standalones

The (Kinda) Secret Pineapple Island Swingers' Resort *If you love laugh-out-loud rom-coms, vacation flings gone rogue, and a hero who definitely knows how to handle his (hockey) stick, The "Kinda" Secret Pineapple Island Swingers' Resort is your next must-read.*

Rating the Book Boyfriend – Hilarious Holiday Rom-Com

Delay of Game – Angsty, funny sports romance

I Dream of Johnny – Genie Rom-Com

Highway to Hale Series
Coming in 2025

Follow the Hale Family, owners of Hale Cosmetics, in their amusing and dramatic search for love.

Book 1: Hale Yes

Book 2: Hale No

Book 3: Hale Damage

Book 4: All Hale the Queen

(Titles and order of books subject to change.)

Make sure to follow me on my social media accounts below or visit my semi-neglected website at www.jadedollston.com

f
facebook.com/profile.php?id=100081302873689

instagram.com/author.jade.dollston/

tiktok.com/@author.jade.dollston?lang=en

The best way you can help indie authors is to leave an Amazon review, so if you'd be so kind, please hop over there and leave me a rating and a few words.

Acknowledgements

FIRST OF ALL, THANK you so much to my **readers**. It means so much that you took a chance on an indie author, and I appreciate the time you took to read **"The Pineapple Book."** I love when readers reach out to me while they're reading, so feel free to do so on my social media platforms that are listed on the "Also by Jade" page.

If you enjoyed the book, please leave me a review on Amazon. That's the best way to ensure an author's books get seen. You can also review on Goodreads and Bookbub.

To the beautiful TL Swan: I wouldn't be where I am today without your support and guidance. Thank you for being an amazing human being.

To The Impulsive Duo: I adore you two! Thank you for agreeing to advise me on this book. If anyone out these is interested in the swinging lifestyle, check out this couple on Instagram. They are full of resources and information, with a strong focus on safety and communication.

To Brittany and Mindy of Nerdy Girls PA Services: I don't even have words to explain how wonderful you two are. Thank you for being my support system and for answering all my crazy questions. I love you!

About the Author

JADE DOLLSTON IS A Texas author who loves reading, Doritos, and rum. She is married to her high school sweetheart, and they have one amazing daughter.

Her love of reading all things smutty has turned into a love of writing all things smutty. She enjoys a diverse selection of romance, and this is reflected in her writing style. Be prepared to laugh, cry, cringe, and fan your face, possibly all in a single chapter.

Jade is so excited to share her work with the world and hopes that you enjoy reading the words from her heart.

www.ingramcontent.com/pod-product-compliance
Lightning Source LLC
Chambersburg PA
CBHW020651110726
47901CB00001B/135
9798992052121